To Own Two Suns

Fran Tabor

Published by F. E. Tabor, 2022.

This is a work of fiction. Similarities to real people, places, or events are entirely coincidental.

TO OWN TWO SUNS

First edition. July 20, 2022.

Copyright © 2022 Fran Tabor.

ISBN: 979-8201463731

Written by Fran Tabor.

Also by Fran Tabor

The Mopsters
To Own Two Suns
Shhhh! it's a Secret. How to Compete Against Walmart and the Internet.

Watch for more at https://books2read.com/ap/8GkDdM/Fran-Tabor.

Dedicated to

My parents, who lived boldly.

A special dedication to an unknown group of cartoonists.

Before I could read, I watched a cartoon show of a trip to the moon. The next morning, I stared up at the moon's cloud-white circle in the blue sky. For the first time, I saw a <u>world</u>. I learned the sky is full of worlds without number.

How do you thank people who open your eyes to so much wonder?

"The most compelling science fiction I have read in years"

Monica Daniels, Real Estate Management Web Designer.

"THE MOST IMAGINATIVE alien encounter story I've read. I made my brother read this, and he thanked me."

Christian von Delius, Hang-gliding instructor and aeronautical design engineer.

"TO OWN TWO SUNS IS so intriguing, I'm sharing it with my fellow rocket enthusiasts!"

Curt von Delius, multiple altitude record holder for TRA certified single stage J,K,M Classes.

To Own Two Suns

A first-contact science fiction novel

By Fran Tabor

Edited by Monica Daniels

Copyright March, 2018 by Frances Elaine Tabor

ALL RIGHTS RESERVED for any and all mediums. Written permission from Frances Elaine Tabor is required to reproduce any section of this work by any and all means. The one exception: If you wish to give a review you may quote up to 2000 words as long as the title is correct, you give the author full credit and you tell your reader how to buy or rent their own copy of To Own Two Suns.

Fran can be emailed at franelainetabor@gmail.com.

This novel is fiction. Any resemblance to any person living, dead or yet to be born is completely coincidental.

Dedicated to
My parents, who lived boldly.

A special dedication to an unknown group of cartoonists. BEFORE I COULD READ, I watched a cartoon show of a trip to the moon. The next morning, I stared up at the moon's cloud-white circle in the blue sky. For the first time, I saw a <u>world</u>. I learned the sky is full of worlds without number.

How do you thank people who open your eyes to so much wonder?

Table of Contents

Chapter 1
Chapter 2
Chapter 3
Chapter 4
Chapter 5
Chapter 6
Chapter 7
Chapter 8
Chapter 9
Chapter 10
Chapter 11
Chapter 12
Chapter 13
Chapter 14
Chapter 15
Chapter 16
Chapter 17
Chapter 18
Chapter 19
Chapter 20
Epilogue
About the Author

TO OWN TWO SUNS

Some of our greatest heroes, to remain heroes, must forever be invisible to history. Earth Fact
"Divine Chance rules the Universe." Morgi Belief
"Only against Great Odds can Greatness be revealed." Morgi knowledge

Roster of The SMS, Solar Mission Ship, renamed by its crew "The Spaghetti and Meatball Special"

Commanders:
Capt. Jeremiah J. Jerrison, "Jerry," USA, Minnesota
Shirley Devlin, "Shirl," USA California
Ship Surgeon
Daniel Johnson, "Doc", USA, New York
Astro-specialists
Simon Artigeo, USA Wyoming
Ann Frankfort, "Frankie", Brazil
Communication
Ann Larson, British
Yan Ling, Chinese
Councilor
Yoko Williams, Japan
Ship Maintenance
Alan Peebles, Argentina-USA, Texas
Bartholomew Schmidt, Brazil
Hydro Farm Specialists
Samantha Smith, USA, Wisconsin
Melinda Davidson, Canada, Alberta

Chapter 1

On Board the first deep space Solar Missions Ship
The SMS, year 2112

Capt. Jerry Jerrison floated in comfortable weightlessness, scanning the Milky Way through his antique binoculars. Tiny Pluto and tinier Charon drifted into view.

Jerrison remembered his eighth birthday. His Great Grandfather gave him those binoculars, along with stories about how as a teenager he had used them exploring uncharted mountains in Alaska. That evening Jerry used his 'new' binoculars to look at the half-moon. The deep lunar shadows made the moon's mountains leap out. From that moment on, nothing excited Jerry more than the idea of exploring the universe the way his great grandfather had explored earth.

Jerrison reminisced the many nights spent lying on summer-warm grass in his front yard, staring at the night sky; the same pair of family-heirloom binoculars resting on his chest. Jerry pretended the weight of his binoculars to be the pressure of acceleration. He convinced himself he could feel the earth charging through the galaxy. His hands clenched the thick grass, holding tight as his Rocket Ship Earth charged through the galaxy!

Jerrison loved that sky. He knew within its depths existed time and space enough for *anything*. Somewhere in those stars, something, with eyes not human, stared back. He and it hurtled towards one another. In a thousand years they would meet. Thanks to Einstein's relativity he would still be eight. He and the alien would explore the stars together. Jerry's mind racing faster than mere light, every summer night he wove stories and stared at stars.

Now he lived in a real spaceship and studied computer-enhanced photographs, but Jerrison preferred his childhood binoculars and quiet times of free-range dreaming.

Years earlier NASA learned robotic probes give an economical first look, but for the best answers you need on-site, question-asking people. The discovery of an inbound cluster of alien asteroids motivated penny-pinching NASA to finally authorize a manned trip to Pluto and beyond. Jerrison had worked aggressively to earn the only NASA slot he desired: to be one of the twelve lucky people selected for the first manned mission to our solar system's outer fringes.

New Year's Eve 2100, the SMS coasted past Mars. Back then Jerrison envied Yan, the only Chinese Nationalist member of their crew. China as a point of cultural pride used only their revived calendar. The Chinese press never pestered Yan with inane requests to don New Year's Eve party hats.

The rest of the crew were not so lucky. For a full week reporters usurped their communication time with brain-numbing, time-robbing public relations efforts forcing participation in the International New Year's Celebrations. Now, twelve years later, Jerrison looked back on that week with laughter. The press no longer called. NASA rarely sent messages. Even personal calls came on condensed weekly signal bursts. He missed real-time exchanges, but at this distance just waiting for a return "Hi!" took hours. When Jerrison had left earth, his youngest daughter was a college freshman; when he returned, she could easily be a grandmother.

NASA bureaucrats claimed the new Mars-orbit telescopes made SMS information redundant. For the last six years, paid staff looked at SMS data only a money-saving once a week.

As Jerrison watched Charon dance around Pluto, he focused his binoculars on Charon's reddest patch. A star directly above twinkled; that fit his reverie.

Shocked wakefulness bolted through his system.

Jerrison slammed the palm of his hand on his communicator. "Shirl, turn all sensors to the area directly above Charon! We've a new dark object!" Adrenalin rushed through him. *Most likely an uncharted comet, but it could be an alien rock swept up from interstellar space.*

"'Tis done, commander." Co-commander Shirley Devlin, "Shirl," replied.

Jerrison 'swam' weightless through the connecting tubes to the Astronomical Surveillance Module, or ASM. The ship, constructed in weightless earth orbit, was a spherical linkage of twenty-one 50 foot to 200 foot spheres. Three to five connecting tubes left each sphere. This made life more interesting on board the SMS. It just happened, like every construction decision, to be the cheapest way to build the ship—-like the decision to replace the original nuclear power system with inefficient chemicals and 'scrap-yard' solar cells. Each module could provide safe, if Spartan, passage home.

As Jerrison propelled himself through the complicated path needed to reach the ASM, he wondered again if the ship had been designed by a man with spaghetti and meatball nightmares. He 'dived' into the large ASM sphere. "Shirl, we beat the hardware again! This is our second find and zero, zilch, nada for the automatic surveyor! What do you have so far?"

Laughing, Shirl set the console to show the latest data. "Assuming the few thousand spotted by the auto-scanners were all uninteresting and hence don't count, you're right. Machines, zero; humans, two. I have an occlusion picked up by the auto scanner, your object blanked out a galaxy just above and to the left of Pluto."

"Damn! That means the hardware spotted it before I did!"

She said, "No, I focused some of it in that direction as soon as I heard your call." Shirl paused, looked twice at the data. "It's traveling the wrong direction." Most objects in the solar system, even the confirmed 'hitchhikers'—-the asteroids from a different star system—-went around the sun in the same direction. This new object orbited the wrong way. Her voice lowered. "Jerry, I have its velocity." It had been years since she had used his first name. Whispering, she pointed to the screen. "It's on a fast hyperbolic orbit—"

Her eyes grew wide. At the same moment Capt. Jerrison activated all ship-wide alarms. For the first time since their testing over a decade earlier, each on board siren screamed throughout every tube and module in the whole Spaghetti Special Jumble.

The object decelerated from its hyperbolic orbit so rapidly it experienced thousands of G's.

It was an alien spacecraft.

Jerrison hoped live beings were within it; but that amount of deceleration stress made it seem unlikely. Could it be an unmanned—-un-aliened?—-probe from another penny-pinching government? "Computer, condense all information we receive every five minutes and burst it to earth, said information pattern to be continued until we state otherwise."

Shirl shouted over the alarm clarion, "That will take a lot of energy."

Jerrison shouted back, "We are Neanderthals. That thing is from beyond our future."

Twelve years of not much happening made the crew lackadaisical. It took a half hour for everyone to arrive. Dr. Schmidt, a Brazilian, arrived last. Still rubbing sleep from his eyes, his deep baritone rumbled out, "Turn off that—" his voice softened as the clarion silenced. "Oh, much nicer." Slowly coming to full wakefulness, he looked around. "What happened?"

Ann Frankfort, 'Frankie', his fellow Brazilian, said, "That's what we all want to know. Jerrison and Shirl insist on being secretive until everyone," She glared at Schmidt. "Arrived."

Frankie was a complete antithesis to her fellow countryman. Dr. Schmidt looked like he should be singing arias on an operatic stage; she seemed the quintessential new-rocker.

Jerrison turned to Shirl, "Your show, you've collected the data."

Shirl said, "Computer, scene one." Its large screen showed a wide-angle view of Pluto and tiny Charon. Using a laser pointer, she said, "Note this 'star' here, it's really a galaxy, and here, and here. Computer, start sequence." They all watched as the first point occluded, a few seconds later the second, and then the third. The screen clicked off.

Dr. Schmidt spoke, "Ah, I see! A very good reason for that infernal racket!"

Shirl continued, "The details." A graph showing the object's deceleration history appeared.

Dr. Schmidt, his voice filled with awed wonder, asked what all surmised. "It is artificial?"

They all understood the story the graph told. The object came from the wrong direction, was not gravitationally bound to the solar system; it then decelerated into a stable orbit. A barrage of questions erupted from the crew. "What does infrared show?" "Are we receiving signals from it?" "How big is it?" "Assuming it maintains that orbit, can we go to it?"

Capt. Jerrison cut in: "Yes." From the moment he realized it was an alien craft, Jerry asked himself the same question. "It's only a light minute beyond Pluto." For the first time since they had left earth orbit, he assumed the bearing of a commander. "We can, and we will."

All exchanged knowing looks. Each and every one of them sacrificed twenty five years of normal life because each valued exploration far more than anything home could offer.

They had grown up on stories of E.T.'s. In those stories, not all extraterrestrials were nice.

Schmidt's deep voice broke the silence. "Can earth get all our information?" Jerrison described the automated transmittal system. Schmidt nodded. "Might I suggest that every other broadcast be a summarization of all the others before it?"

Frankie grinned. "Then we better get data worth sending. That's our job, isn't it?"

An immediate chorus of "That's right!" and "Doing our job." rose from the others.

Dr. Schmidt growled, "Have you all gone mad? Have you never heard 'Let sleeping dogs lie?' That thing could be a rabid wolf, and you want to tweak its nose? Maybe it will ignore us and leave." He looked at each of them. "If we annoy it, it could swat us like the gnat we are."

Frankie laughed. "Artificial radio signals have been leaving earth for over two hundred years; we won't be a surprise. Besides, since we can't outrun it, we should go boldly forth."

Maintenance chief Alan Peebles spoke up, "I agree with Jerrison and Frankie. Let's go."

Schmidt stared at his fellow crewmen. "We're acting like a light minute is nothing. For that ship, it's a short hop. A light minute is over eleven million miles. That is a long, long way. Jerry, have you 'guesstimated' how long it will take us?"

Jerrison nodded. "About four days. If we had been going away from Pluto instead of approaching, it wouldn't even be possible." Jerrison kicked against the wall, propelling himself above the others. "Earth did their weekly review a few hours ago. We have at most seven days before the bureaucrats who run NASA know about *The Ship*. If we wait too long, those timid chair-sitter types are sure to order us to avoid contact at all costs. Let's go. Now."

Dr. Schmidt stared in horror as the rest enthused agreement.

Four days later, Jerrison and Shirl floated near an ASM viewport, staring at *The Ship*. Jerrison gazed through his ancient binoculars. "I thought we'd never finish the reprogramming."

Shirl nodded. "Me too. To be so close, and yet still too far..."

The Spaghetti Special was designed to maneuver gently into gravity-determined orbits. Making the severe course corrections required to approach the alien behemoth taxed everyone's ability. It also required all their fuel. They were down to solar-cell-powered batteries. At Pluto's distance, those solar cells received little sunlight. The SMS life supports barely functioned.

Shirl blinked. Her eyelids scratched like sandpaper. "I don't think I've slept since we've spotted that thing." Like most of the crew, when not working she stared at the silent, unblemished, blimp-shaped craft until exhaustion overwhelmed her.

Still looking through his binoculars, Jerrison nodded. "I've wanted to see real live aliens my whole life. I can't believe I'm this lucky."

"Lucky? Jerry, when we voted to use up our fuel getting here, we all knew that left our ship too underpowered to get us home. Unless that thing helps us, we've doomed ourselves to drifting forever out of the solar system, dying of old age so far away our sun is just another dim star. That thing could be dead or alive. Friend or foe. Lucky or—" Shirl paused, whispered, "Unlucky."

Jerry said, "We were scheduled to be out here another year before turning back. A lot worse could happen in a year." The cold of space seemed to seep into their ship. Seeking human warmth, they wrapped their arms around each other and floated together.

Jerrison whispered in her ear. "Did you really agree with my argument for sacrificing our trip home to come here?"

"Yes." Shirl remembered Jerry's final justification to Schmidt. She repeated those words to him. "The chance of sudden, meaningless death is a constant. The rare chance for a death that means something—that is worth living for." She nuzzled into his shoulder; she felt safer.

His body felt hers relax. Responding to deep instinct, his arms protectively held Shirl closer; she slipped into sleep. His binoculars, their strap still around his neck, floated behind them as he stared at the city-size alien spaceship.

Hours later, Schmidt and Frankie entered the ASM, arguing, as usual. Neither noticed Jerrison and Shirl floating on the other side of the apparatus-filled ASM sphere.

"What do you mean you believe it is an abandoned derelict?" Frankie protested to Schmidt. "Just because we can't detect an outgoing signal, doesn't mean there isn't one. Plus, it's a full half-degree warmer than it should be. A well-insulated power source must be on."

"That's just from the deceleration." Schmidt's sonorous baritone declared. "There is no way *it* could be receiving information. *Its* hull appears seamless."

Frankie pushed her argument. "Why would an abandoned ship slow down?"

Schmidt offered, "Autopilot? Last dying command? It is either not-manned, or not-friendly."

Frankie interrupted. "The outer layer may be seamless, but it isn't a single curve. It's a series of very slight parabolas. Like certain deep ocean dwellers back home, its whole surface collects information. *The ship* is not an alien craft; it *is* an alien."

They both jerked when Jerry interrupted, "A living organism could flip directions that fast?"

Frankie snapped back, "Why not?" Schmidt rolled his eyes. Jerrison didn't.

Everyone debated whether a dead autopilot controlled the *ship*, or something alive; if it were harmless, or a threat. Jerrison hoped the crew's proclivity for intellectual battle would maximize their safety.

The only one who seldom participated was Doc, who pondered alone in his quarters.

"Doc" had lost his name, Daniel Johnson, during training when his fellow trainees discovered he possessed the only M.D. in the group. That amused them. The title stuck.

Doc became a physician at his family's insistence. Before he joined the SMS, his family thought him a dull, no-nonsense conformist. None in his immediate family knew he also studied exobiology, which until now meant microbes.

For over forty years, one dream most excited Doc: Real, sci-fi style aliens. So why, instead of excitement, did he feel unease? Why did the couplet

> *'When the gods grant a mortal's quest,*
> *Tis oft done with derisive jest.'*

keep coming unbidden into his brain? Needing answers, he stared at the alien craft.

Just as vividly as he could see the alien behemoth, he saw a time so forever ago, a family reunion. He had just announced, "I will be the ship surgeon on NASA's first manned ship to travel beyond Pluto." Polite laughter. How absurd! They saw his sincerity. Awkward silence. His uncle's shout, "You just wasted your education! Minimum pay, gone twenty years! You'll be *nothing*."

His mother slammed her delicate crystal glass against the table, spilling deep-red wine onto the white cloth. "If you just found the right girl, you wouldn't talk such nonsense."

Remembering his mother's words invoked a half-smile. He found the right girl on board. Worse than his uncle's ranting and his mother's diatribes, was his father's glare—

A warm voice cut through the ice-cold memory. "I knew I'd find you here." Floating up beside him, Yoko Smith stared out the view port as intently as he. "Any ideas?"

As usual, Yoko waited silently; as usual, he smiled at her. Her patient acceptance gave him strength.

He reached for her hand. "Remember the last message I received from my father?"

"'Space is large enough for your dreams. Dream!' Your happiness gave him comfort."

Dan stared silently at the materialization of his dreams. Damn the risks! He wanted to charge on board and pry out every secret so bad his gut ached and swallowing was hard. "Ever use a crowbar?" Doc was known for his apparent non-sequiturs.

Yoko nodded yes.

Doc continued, "Imagine you need to pry the lid off a crate. If your crowbar's too small, it won't work. Too large, and you'll destroy the crate. All tools are like that. They must be the right fit. What if our brains are the wrong crowbar to pry understanding from *that*?"

Yoko said, "Intelligent civilizations require cooperation." She pointed at *The Ship*. "Any species that advanced must be super-cooperative, and experienced at compensating for another's shortcomings." She grinned. "Even too-short-crowbar brains."

Doc said, "Yoko, what if its way of looking at the world is so alien, that any communications beyond a glorified math lesson is impossible? We could no more discuss philosophy with it than a goldfish can with a camel."

He frowned. "Yoko, the moment we believe we understand them, will be the moment earth will be in the greatest danger. Remember my family fiasco that ensued when I announced my Deep Space commission? Their screams of disapproval? How Dad just glared? I interpreted Dad's silent anger as agreeing with Mom and her relatives."

Doc grabbed Yoko's hands; stared into her eyes. "It wasn't until his final messages I finally understood..." He held her hands tighter.

"If I so misread the actions of a human, *my own father*, dare we trust our interpretations of something totally alien?"

Doc unconsciously pressed her hands against his heart. "The cost of misunderstanding will be paid by the whole human race."

Doc's gaze returned to the monstrous bulk of the alien vessel. He flipped topics again. "Most think The Ship is an uninhabited probe on auto pilot."

Yoko nodded agreement.

Doc continued, "Bacteria can take thousands of G's. What if we are dealing with a unicellular life form?"

Yoko's eyebrows arched up. "Amoeba and paramecia built that?"

"What do you know about sponges?"

"Huh?"

Doc said, "Sponges, like normal ocean animals, reproduce by shooting eggs and sperm into the ocean. The lucky ones get together, drift with the plankton until they find a rock of their own and start the cycle over again. The interesting thing about a sponge is what you can do with it."

Yoko asked, "Scrub?"

A smile flitted across Dan's face. "Run an adult sponge through a blender; it will put itself back together again. Each individual cell in the sponge is really an independent animal, just as people are individual cooks, hospital workers, farmers, et cetera, in a city."

Once again, Yoko wondered about the emotional health of research biologists that someone would ever have done the experiment. "You think sponge-like animals can develop technology?"

"A life form forced to develop an ability or fail, will grow or fail. Earth's oceans have no advanced technological societies. Maybe on another world… That vessel might appear empty, but in reality be teeming with unicellular aliens ready to recombine at a moment's notice."

"Your free-ranging vision has always impressed me, but that's too bizarre."

Doc interrupted, talking even faster. "What if we've found only unicellular extra-terrestrial life in our solar system because that's the norm for the entire galaxy? If there's a way for unicellular creatures to develop intelligence, with a million-million tries—" He glanced towards the star-dense Milky Way. "Surely sometime, somewhere it did."

"Let's discuss this with Jerrison. Immediately."

The two swam through the corridors to the ASM, where they found the Brazilians locked in passionate debate with the commander. Shirl still slept in Jerrison's arms.

Frankie was repeating her favorite theme. "We must knock on the door. Jerry, a bold, friendly approach is the only choice."

Dr. Schmidt snorted, "Like a bold, friendly dugout canoe going up to Columbus's ship? Remember what happened next? Or if *they* decide your 'Hello' is a galactic insult—"

Frankie humphed. "*They* know we're here. Sneaking up silently looks stupid. Let's send multiple signals on many wavelengths. If anything comes back, we repeat it; that way we'll be as polite, or impolite, as they are." She grinned at the portly Schmidt. "If you're really worried we'll be seen as etiquette idiots, I'll see if the computer has a copy of *Emily Post*."

The men chorused, "Of what?"

"Emily Post, an American etiquette expert in the mid 1900's."

Like Yoko, Frankfort thought it "obvious" any race prepared to send an interstellar probe would not expect unknown beings to follow an unforgiving etiquette code.

Dr. Schmidt protested, "Once again, simple things like belching or not belching at state dinners have ruined peace negotiations; neither party aware what one found insulting, the other believed to be a compliment."

Frankie snapped back, "You engineer types are way too cautious! How can the limitations of primitives be the least bit relevant?"

Doc interrupted the futile rehashing. "There is one good reason for knocking on the door. We've learned all we can being passive. I want to *touch* that ship." He paused. "If we wait too long earth will turn us into children who need to hold someone's hand to cross the street."

Jerrison said, "True. Computer, send an all-awake."

Unlike the warning claxon, the all-awake sent personal communicators vibrating and chiming—-including Shirl's. She woke. Her eyes widened when she saw the others. "I slept?"

They nodded yes.

As soon as all crew responded, it silenced. Jerrison on ship-wide communication mode announced, "Crew, we will send continuous repeated signals to The Ship, the same basic signal on every possible wavelength. The signal will be the first hundred prime numbers in binary, followed by 'Hello' in multiple languages."

Jerrison spoke the most important human words to be spoken since a Russian "Blast-off" launched the first sputnik—-and the Space Race—-a century and a half earlier. "Computer, implement now."

Frankie asked, "Captain Jerrison, don't you think we should say more?"

Jerrison explained, "It's not important what we say. They've been studying our signals since the early twentieth century; they just need to know we Neanderthals are ready to communicate. Everyone, join me in Botany Bay."

He turned to Shirl. "Awake enough to verify our broadcasts before joining us in the Botany Bay Module?"

She nodded yes.

Both Brazilians left for the Botany Bay. Jerrison started to follow. Yoko tugged on his sleeve. "Jerry, there is one more idea you need to hear." Yoko summarized Dan's idea of the Intelligent Sponge.

Jerrison stared at the two of them. "We need to learn a whole new level of paranoia, and you two are way ahead of the rest of us."

Alien Ship, many years earlier.

MORGI INTERSTELLAR ships have two levels of programmed artificial intelligence. Each spaceship has a low-level "brainless" computer-autopilot and a True Artificial Intelligence, the starship's AI. The cultural attitudes of its organic creators embed each AI as much as the sum total of all their knowledge.

During the long, dull sub-light portions of interstellar journeys, the autopilot monitors all routine functions. Lacking imagination, autopilots did not risk boredom induced insanity.

The AI stayed awake whenever an organic passenger chose to be awake. If no one else were awake, those lonely, interminable 'between-times' would drive an AI as insane as they would a living passenger forced to travel alone.

Whenever a blue-line transition is needed or anything unexpected happens, an autopilot is programmed to awaken its AI.

Because they are a True Intelligence, all Morgi AI learn and develop personality.

The AI on this vessel was a newborn. Facts filled its infant brain, but no understandings or emotions. Only minutes before the initial blue-lining, enemies maliciously corrupted the experienced AI its Morgi owners first selected. Forced to terminate the damaged AI and too little time to verify the sanity of an experienced AI, they installed the naïve, infant AI.

The Morgi gave the inexperienced AI three master commands:

1. It must protect the all important passenger on board, Muni of the Noble Green Hill Clan of Morga, plus all others of the Green Hill Clan and their possessions.

2. It must do all in its power to facilitate the successful conclusion of Muni's primary mission—-even if that meant sacrificing Muni himself.

3. Most important—-the master command given all Morgi AI's—-it must protect the civilization that sent it, even if that required self-destruction of itself, all passengers, Muni's failure and the extinction of Muni's clan or any other Morgi.

Morgi blue-lined only under influence of Deep Sleep, a natural form of suspended animation. When not blue-lining, most voyages were spent doing normal sleep and wakefulness cycles. If a Morgi risked an extremely dangerous or prolonged voyage, he did so only under the artificially augmented version of Deep Sleep called Death Teaser.

Without an attentive AI, it was impossible to fully awaken from Death Teaser. The ship's sole passenger, Muni, endured Death Teaser.

The simple autopilot computer awoke AI a light-year from our sun.

Every bit of outer hull on Morgi starships "feels" all wavelengths of light. The awakened AI filtered all the information, pondered it. In the twenty-second century, the gas giants—Jupiter, Saturn, Uranus—dwarfed man's energy production.

The Morgi receptors easily selected certain transmissions as more regular than expected. The auto system alerted AI to the anomalous signals. AI identified man's transmissions as artificial. AI's data banks claimed no technology in this solar system.

AI felt surprise.

A carnivore from a dangerous home world, the Morgi never lost the paranoia that enabled its race to dominate Morga. AI shared their paranoia.

AI surprise became fear.

Artificial signals were not the only anomaly. The energy signature of the primary target planet was wrong. The massive ice sheets were missing.

Fear became terror.

AI sent two deep-space transmission pods; one to the following colonizing vessel; the other. to the home world.

AI checked defense mechanisms. All worked. As it would if preparing to attack, AI sent many thousands of microscopic, information collecting, high speed spy drones to earth and its off-world colonies. It would be years before all of those silent micro-spies could be harvested.

AI chose to not deviate from its planned trajectory.

Before the Morgi ship approached its planned deceleration point, AI spotted a peculiar, garbage-like derelict drifting towards the outer reaches of the target solar system.

Morgi ship deceleration and orbit stabilization occurred on schedule.

The peculiar "derelict" craft stopped drifting, and began to creep closer.

Electronic shivers of alarm raced through the ship.

Conflicting mandates tore at AI.

> Destroy any potential enemy before it could harm its passenger.
> Learn all it could about everything.

If it destroyed the strange ship too soon, it would learn less.

Only an infant AI, the necessary questions came with difficulty.

Could proximity indicate attack?
No, it was unarmed.
Yes, if close enough for a suicide explosion.

The peculiar ship came closer. Too close?

Danger Possibility: Above Zero.
DESTROY!

Millions of hull flaps prepared to vibrate open for a total energy release. Those flaps would close as other millions opened. The effect would be a continuous barrage of lethal gamma rays in all directions. Any life on board the derelict would die, but the strange ship itself would survive enough for study.

Just as AI was poised to initiate the attack, AI determined the pathetic ship had no camouflaged energy source.

AI stopped the attack sequence.

Had the earthship design been the fusion-powered wonder first proposed, history would have been very different. For the first and only time in Earth's history, the preference of world leaders for grandiose living over first-class raw research was a benefit to all mankind.

AI remained jittery.

More searches were made for anything resembling defense/offense mechanisms on the approaching contraption.

What would risk going into space without defense?

Was there a defense it could not recognize?

Some peculiar animals were definitely on board. The most defenseless-looking wild animals are often the most dangerous. These animals could not seem more harmless.

AI repeated the analysis that earlier had allowed the unidentifiable ship to live. It seemed OK, but if it did risk Muni's survival... On the chance the craft bore unimaginable camouflaged armaments—

The radio signals began.

(Garbage signal)... Inspectors boarding... (Garbage)...Inspectors boarding... (Garbage)...Inspectors boarding... (Garbage)...

AI relaxed. All was right with its world. Housekeeping functions and routine information gathering resumed. Portals prepared for opening. A full atmosphere again filled the living areas. The ship warmed to be ready for the inspection party.

Only an infant AI, it did not question where the visiting inspectors were from. The proper signal had been sent along with gibberish. It didn't worry about the gibberish. If AI units were expected to understand everything their often-irrational organic masters did, they would all have frozen into electronic catatonia.

On board Earth's Spaghetti Special; minutes earlier.

The entire crew floated about the huge hydroponic garden module nick-named Botany Bay. Some gazed out its view ports; others focused on computer-enhanced projections. Jerrison had gathered them together to await the alien ship's response to his first deliberate communication attempt.

Nothing.

Suddenly the entire alien behemoth shivered.

Shirl looked at her commander. "Do you think our signals triggered that?"

Jerrison floated on his back, staring up through his binoculars at the Alien Ship. "So many signals and all we get in return is a low-amplitude vibration? It's ignoring us."

Shirl said, "The way you keep staring through that antique, it's like you have more faith in your binoculars than you do in all our equipment."

"It's not a matter of faith. It's a matter of reality. Anything I can see through these—" Jerrison's fingers tapped the twin black cylinders. "Is real. Anything projected into the room, feels like an entertainer's creation." He paused. "Are you relieved or disappointed there's no response?"

Shirl replied, "We don't know if there's been no response. We just know there's been no response we recognize."

Alan's voice leaped from every speaker with a cheerleader's frenzy. "It's alive! It's alive!"

A dozen people tried to interrupt him at once; their voices tumbling out the same speakers. "Huh?" "I don't see anything." "Alive? How?"

"Check the temp ratings! It's a full degree warmer!"

More than its temperature changed. The derelict, as doubters called The Ship, awoke.

"Wow!" Shirl's amazed voice interrupted Alan.

Jerrison flipped his body towards the thick glass; his binoculars pressed against the transparent barrier. "Whoa!"

The featureless black exterior of the alien hull shimmered into a bedazzling complexity of lines, extrusions and wildly colorful abstract art. Most of the long, thin extrusions radiated from huge circles. Brilliant splotches of color splattered the alien hull. The largest circle had a slightly darker gray at its very center, which repeatedly grew outward to the circle's rim, then faded to uniform white.

Alan's voice managed to be heard above the rest. "The circle! She is growing!"

Two of the lines near the giant circle were overtaken. At first, the lines just had a section bitten out by the slowly expanding circle. The lines re-routed to be complete again. Other lines that would have soon been in the way were already re-routing.

"If it continues at this rate, in about three hours it will be large enough for our whole ship." Alan observed.

"Obviously, a door," Frankie declared.

"Then I suggest we use it," Dr. Schmidt's deep baritone rumbled.

Shirl protested, "How can you go from being afraid of just approaching The Ship, to willingly entering it?"

Dr. Schmidt answered, "We used up our fuel getting here. If we hitch a ride from our visitor out there, that will no longer be a problem."

Jerrison agreed. "We'll send a pod over there tomorrow."

Doc interrupted, "Every minute we wait, we risk hearing from our 'friends' on Earth."

Jerrison said, "Correction, at the end of this watch, in a half hour. Anyone who wants to visit the alien with me, stop by my pod." He left for his much smaller personal quarters. He wanted a private conversation with whoever would be leaving with him for the First Close Encounter in official Earth history.

Jerrison should have predicted what happened next. Eleven boisterous bodies followed him into his once quiet personal quarters; each clamoring why Jerrison would need his particular specialty. Even reserved Yoko shouted, "You MUST take me! I'm your only trained Counselor!"

Jerrison bellowed over the cantankerous din, "Anyone who speaks in the next five minutes stays home!" *Wow, that sounded like Dad!*

The room hushed.

Attempting the same stern expression that had worked for his father so many years ago, Jerrison slowly scanned his crew. His gaze fixed on Frankfort. "Frankie, what is the least important ability to have when analyzing the alien vessel?"

"Least important? Current earth fashion awareness." Referring to Shirl's hobby.

Shirl's protest shot out like a soprano machine gun. "I started that hobby to see what trends were predictable without current social knowledge. The ability to intuitively extract such patterns from little data is the exact same kind of ability it will take to pick up on small clues from an alien culture!"

"What, Shirl, do you think would be the most important talent to possess?"

"A current Earth fashion sense," Shirl deadpanned.

Everyone, except Jerrison, laughed. He spoke again. "The trip over could be only one way."

The crew glanced at each other. *Does their captain want only expendable crew to make contact with The Ship?*

Jerrison again made eye contact with Ann Frankfort. "Frankie, on the trip home, whose abilities could we most easily do without?"

"Mine. In fact, you haven't needed me this whole trip. What I do is done better by computers. If NASA hadn't been so gullible, I wouldn't be here. Not only—"

Doc interrupted. "No mere machine could anticipate the unexpected; it takes a human being on site to ask the right questions about patterns that may or may not be real patterns. The discrimination between ersatz patterns and real ones has been my specialty since junior high."

Everyone recognized the quote from Ann's original NASA application. He added, "Sounds pretty important to me."

"Lots of better minds than mine will be analyzing our data. I am USELESS!" she shrieked.

"You're useless?" Doc countered. "At least there appear to be patterns out here. Look at me, trained to mend broken bones and cure malaria. Can anyone damage anything in these padded cells we live in? Is there anything remotely defective about anyone here? Did anyone sneak a cold germ on board? Why NASA thought a full-fledged MD would be necessary..." Doc spread out his open hands and rolled his eyes upwards. He bellowed, "I am the USELESS ONE!"

This time Dr. Frankfort interrupted, quoting from Doc's original application. "In the event of catastrophic equipment failure, how would your crew handle burn victims? Severed limbs? Would they recognize incipient malnutrition and make the right dietary adjustments? Respond to radiation sickness? Do blood transfusions?"

Dr. Dan refused to let mere facts stop him. "We've been out here for over ten years. Have I ever been needed? I AM USELESS!"

Dr. Schmidt's reasoned baritone took over. "The trip home will be more hazardous than the trip out. We will have to do something very creative to make up for the recent fuel expenditure." He voiced their common gripe. "If NASA hadn't been so cheap, we'd be fusion powered! You, my friend, will be very needed."

Dr. Schmidt was genuinely sympathetic; he knew how much Doc wanted to go to the ship. Most of the enthusiastic chorus agreeing with Dr. Schmidt simply saw the elimination of a contestant in the alien-boarding-sweepstakes. Schmidt dreaded the alien, but even his curiosity trumped his dread. "Now I on the other hand—"

The protestations of every crew member smothered Schmidt's words. Each claimed that not only had he pulled the wool over NASA's eyes that he was even remotely useful, but he would never be needed for anything. Going home, each and every one insisted he or she would be just so much extra baggage.

Just as the cacophonous bedlam reached a fever pitch of fervent humility, a piercingly loud warning siren screeched.

Was the alien attacking?

Had they been hit?

Was there a systems failure?

Jerrison said, "Computer, acknowledged." The cycling siren silenced. "Computer, Inquiry. Warning, why?"

Its mechanically perfect voice explained. "Noise levels in compartment C-4 approaching dangerous levels. Recommend eliminate noise generators."

"The computer seems to think I should jettison the lot of you. From what I just heard, none of you have any mission value any way—"

"Commander?"

"Yes, Doc?" Jerry responded.

"All of us are qualified and motivated. Let's stop trying to be rational and just draw straws to pick teams of three. Then draw straws for which team goes first. That way all of us, even you, get to go."

Jerrison said, "That's fine, except I'm pulling rank. My team goes first."

Doc, surprised, said, "You're not demanding equal treatment?"

"Not this time. The rest of you, draw straws." Jerrison paused, looked slowly around the room at the tiered crew floating about him. He spoke softly. "I am proud to explore triumphantly, or die, with each of you. NASA picked the best. I'm going to module twelve to prepare for separation. When you're done drawing lots, send my two partners to join me. The rest of you, well, you know the drill." He broke into a grin. "We'll find out if separation goes as smooth in real life as it has in all those interminable practice runs NASA put us through. That, too, could be a first." He checked his systems monitor. "We'll depart in forty-seven minutes."

One last detail. Jerry turned to his second-in-command. "Shirl, from this moment on you are sole acting captain."

Jerrison somersaulted out.

Lots were drawn. The two winners joined their commander.

It was a NASA first. The departure mirrored all the practice runs. The spaghetti and meatball ship now had one less "meatball."

With only a hint of a nudge, the released globe drifted toward the alien behemoth.

The colorful patterns on *The Ship* faded to outlines of gray and black. The destination circle stood out, an unmistakable bull's-eye.

Jerry wondered, *Is it a target, or the eye of a storm?*

Jerrison looked back at his ship. "Hey, it looks like the ship is waving 'bye' to us." Two flexible passageways, no longer connected to module twelve, undulated up and down, shedding what looked like confetti into space. The third was hidden by an obstructing 'meatball', but its glitter trail of confetti could be seen trailing into space.

None of the computerized simulations had shown that much movement or any reflective flakes flicked into space.

Chapter 2

Morgi AI units are programmed to destroy anyone—-and anything-—attempting an unauthorized boarding, but spaceships patrol the galaxy for generations. To prevent the automatic destruction of friendly vessels, the Morgi learned to avoid any preconceived notions about ship construction or appearance. Instead, they programmed for communication identifications. In addition to official Morgi codes, personal clan recognition signals were passed down for generations.

The spaceship's guiding principles could not be altered.

The moment AI received a properly coded signal; it accepted the Earthship as being a Green Hill possession—-even if no inspecting Morgi were on board. It deduced the creatures within the rickety ship must be Green Hill livestock. The exotic Green Hill livestock were at extreme risk. Ordinary structural stress threatened to turn their strange ship into floating space garbage. It would take too much to fix the pathetic space barge. AI decided to assimilate it into Muni's spaceship.

AI began shifting walls, altering portals and re-routing information systems. Many hours of work needed to be done to accommodate the whole incoming spaceship.

One small pod separated, approached.

AI felt relief. It could easily accommodate the lone pod's entry. AI prepared the boarding airlock. The interior entrance spaces warmed to a comfortable temperature. AI released the right amount of oxygen for maximum Morgi comfort.

Noting that the approaching pod had inadequate course correction, AI determined the pod must be disabled. It shot out a grappling hook and tether from the center of the receiving port. The hook latched onto the pod's outer hull; *The Ship* reeled in Jerrison's pod.

On board Jerrison's released pod, minutes earlier
JERRISON PUSHED BUTTONS, and his limit. He slammed his fist down on the useless panel. "We have no guidance controls! None!"

Doc stared at the alien's huge bulk. "If we miss the ship, we will still be the first humans to see the Kuiper Belt up close. We might even travel beyond the Oort Cloud. We have more than enough food-tubes to last us a lifetime."

Jerrison snapped, "I didn't risk all our fuel to go joy riding out into the galaxy!" He didn't share the other factor that angered him. The two crewmen with him were the last two he personally would have chosen.

Simon Artigeo, a brilliant research astrochemist, could talk for hours about stellar variations, but was only dimly aware which star was which. For practical navigation, Simon was nearly useless. The other was their only medical person.

Jerrison silently prayed, *Don't let my impatience cost us our lives.*

Simon suggested, "Jerry, how about I take a space walk as we get closer. I'll stay connected to our pod. We should have enough life-line to reach *The Ship*, and I'll just pull you in."

Jerry answered, "Simon, the pod is weightless. That doesn't mean no inertia."

Doc spoke up, "Besides, he would rather send me." Doc refused to give up his one chance to *touch* the alien craft. Something in front of the ship sparkled. "What's that?"

"That" was a large, white pad circled with many small, highly reflective 'hooks.'

Jerrison felt fear-laced relief. "Gentlemen, that is our ticket to our new friend out there." Hoping his assumption was right, he shut down all of the pod's worthless navigational controls.

The three men watched as the device languidly approached. Only when it was nearly upon them did the thin tether that connected it with the alien ship flicker into view. The suction pad/grappling hooks landed with a firm thud. With a delicate tug, *The Ship* pulled them in.

Jerrison said, "Shirl, as you can see we are being towed in. Did you see the transmission of our ship waving 'bye' to us?"

Shirl's image showed up on their transmission screen. "Yes. Peebles said those arms were more flexible than expected." She paused. "He's not concerned."

As their pod approached *The Ship*, the three men remained silent.

Jerrison felt as though his vessel stood still and *The Ship* grew larger.

Each man wore his spacesuit with the helmet off. Once they were at the alien ship, helmets would be snapped on. Then, helmet, chest and back mounted cameras activated; they would move into the vessel's airlock (which surely existed), arms spread, announcing, "We come in peace for all mankind."

The suits were not the sound-deadening cocoons of a century earlier. The men would hear ambient noise as easily as if their helmets were never put on.

The three agreed leaving someone on board for any reason was foolish—their little ship could leave only at the mercy of the aliens, and messages could be sent continuously from their spacesuits as easily as from their pod.

Assuming whatever awaited within *The Ship* let them.

Silence dragged too long.

Jerry said, "I planned less than an hour to maneuver to *the ship*. It's been pulling us for almost two hours."

Doc said, "You would think the civilization who built *That* would be able to reel us in a little faster."

A light show began.

Pinks, lavenders, eye-burning yellows, Fourth-of-July sparkler whites. Rainbow flares so bright they triggered the auto-shading. Directly ahead a golden-yellow dot, grow-to-gray-circle, collapse to yellow dot, grow-to-gray-circle... They were headed to the very center of the giant bull's eye.

All sense of time disappeared into fountains of awe.

With each tug, *The Ship* grew more awe inspiring. The living accent of its skin augmented the colors shimmering across. Art work appeared and disappeared beneath cascading waves of color.

The pod drew closer. The bull's eye pattern faded into a circle of gray.

Doc said, "That thing is huge." The alien ship was so large, only a hint of deep-space blackness teased at the remote edges of the horizon between ship and Milky Way.

The tether kept pulling them closer...closer...closer... Too close! Their pod crashed into the circle's center.

Jerrison flinched.

Doc and Simon jumped back, arms protectively over their faces.

Only a hint of a jolt.

The hard surface melted into gooey gray... murky green...gray and dark green swirls. Air cleared.

They were not on the alien behemoth, but within it. Like a string pulling a child's helium balloon in an amphitheater, the gossamer thin tether still reeled Jerrison's pod inward towards a distant wall.

A full half hour later, their little craft thumped against the far wall. The wall molded itself around one whole end of their sphere, including half their view port.

A tiny black spot materialized on the pod wall adjacent to *The Ship*. The dark circle grew. When it approximated the size of the connecting tubes on the earthship, it stopped growing, darkened...black...blacker—

Jerrison commanded, "Helmets."

Startled, both crew members followed their commander's lead and secured their headpieces.

Light streamed in where once had been a circle of blackness.

A well-lit hallway beckoned. Its floor hummed. The ceiling rippled with brilliant, beautiful abstract designs, enticing them down...down...down the hallway.

Each man touched the test relay in his suit, heard Shirl's radioed, "OK." They "thumbs upped" each other.

Forgetting speeches and planned routines, the three swam weightless down the broad corridor, following the ceiling light show.

As they followed its gradual curve, Jerrison asked, "Shirl, are you getting all this?"

"Yes." Shirl's awed voice came over the suits' speakers with greater clarity than thought possible. "It's beautiful!"

The floor was the only flat section. The walls bowed out slightly, then sharply curved together at the ceiling.

A series of wondrous, colorful abstract paintings adorned the walls. The dazzling light show on the ceiling led them onward. Swirls of sunshine yellow predominated in the ever-changing glittering array.

"Commander!" Simon Artigeo shouted. "I'm sinking!"

Mesmerized by the living art of the hallway, Jerrison had been ignoring his own position. He was shocked to realize they were each slowly drifting towards the floor. *Artificial gravity? Will it get too strong?*

"Commander," Doc sounded worried. "If this artificial gravity keeps growing, it could prove deadly. None of us are accustomed to G-forces any more. The exercise routines help, but don't take the place of a real-gravity total body workout. Just the mild G-forces we experienced maneuvering here were difficult for us."

Jerrison landed on his back, waving his arms and legs like a flipped turtle. "Shirl, I'm on the floor."

"I saw you land through Doc's camera. You three resembled feathers drifting down. And commander,"

"Yes, Shirl?"

"The ship started to rotate about its longitudinal axis the same time you started drifting downward."

Dr. Schmidt's voice boomed over the suit speakers. "Yes, my commander, and I for one am delighted to see it rotate just the right amount."

"Delighted?" Doc questioned. "How could that delight you? And what do you mean 'just the right amount?'"

"Obviously, if the aliens really had an artificial gravity which could be switched on and off the way we turn a light on and off, it would mean their science was not only far advanced of ours, but built on principles we would consider impossible. Instead, the amount of rotation is just right for the minuscule gravity you are experiencing. Very reassuring."

The three explorers exchanged grimaces. "An exotic explanation would have been exciting." Doc said.

Shirl interrupted, "Can any of you get up?"

With labored breath, each forced himself to a crawl position; then a kneel.

Sweating with effort, Jerrison went to a full stand, took a step and floated to the ceiling. He drifted back to the floor, this time feet first, knees bent to absorb the shock.

He straightened up, feeling proud to be standing. He tried another step, stag-leapt forward, landed lightly on his outstretched leg, bent his knee and stretched out for another long arcing stag-leap. Instead he stumbled into a somersault.

After a few more aborted tries, he finally accomplished a series of graceful leaps. He pivoted about and leaped part way back to his still kneeling partners. "Hey, you laggards, up and at 'em!" He laughed.

Moving with deliberate slowness, both men tried to stand.

Simon kept going into a ball shape that ricocheted off the walls onto the floor, bounced back to the ceiling.

Doc wobbled. "I feel queasy." He started to stand. "My stomach doesn't want to get up with the rest of me." After several attempts, he finally stood and took a successful step. With a lopsided grin he said, "I wish we equipped these suits with mouthwash."

Jerrison watched his two bungling crewmen. Both men laughed at their own clumsiness. "O.K. you two clowns, follow me." With that he twirled his whole body in mid air and bounded down the endless hallway.

His two crewmen struggled to follow suit. Soon all three were leaping onward.

Jerry giggled like a schoolgirl.

"Commander, what's the joke?" Doc inquired. *Could his commander's suit be allowing a nitrogen build-up, leading to narcosis of deep space? Did lack of sleep damage his commander's judgment?*

"No problem, it's just that I've discovered something wonderful. Walking is like riding a bicycle. Once you know how, you never forget."

An extra dazzling light show engulfed the three men; its beauty banished all other thoughts.

Doc, noticing Jerrison's wide-eyed, open-mouthed, dazed look, said, "Commander, skipping down this wonderland hallway is entertaining, but don't you think the aliens went to a lot of effort just for our amusement?"

Jerrison, still transfixed by the light show, answered, "We have postulated aliens exploring the universe for conquest, for curiosity, for survival. Maybe we should have thought of the traveling minstrel show."

Deep purples, midnight blues swirled in, out, and in again, only to be smothered in a cascade of gold and turquoise tear drops.

Jerrison continued. "Perhaps a truly superior race would value spreading joy as their ultimate goal."

The crew watching through the multiple camera views became equally mesmerized.

Swirls of yellow brighten, blue and purple intertwine. Splotches of iridescent green drifted. The crew's awed intakes of breath poured through both suit and ship speakers.

Yoko's soft voice nestled itself within the admiring sighs:

"Oh what the hand that could frame the spirit of pure light,
Could grab the stars, make them swirl, in ecstasy's delight"

Dr. Schmidt's baritone broke into the enraptured mood. "Captain, you should go forward cautiously. What we see as hypnotically beautiful may be only an attention-getting warning to the *Others*."

The three scouts sobered up.

As much as the feeble gravity would allow, they took baby leaps forward. Up to now the curvature of their path had been so slight it was evidenced only by their inability to see where they came from. Now a sharp bend hid what came next.

The three men moved as one.

They entered a huge, circular warehouse-looking space. The walls were plain off-white; the ceiling, a dull blue-gray; the floor, a pale gray. A long, waist-high, plastic-looking umber bench lay alongside the far wall. Colorful rectangles glowed from the wall above the bench.

After the kaleidoscope hallway, the contrasting muted plainness of this room jarred each of them.

As they entered the silence-filled gargantuan space, Jerrison sensed loneliness.

From the corner of his eye, Jerry kept seeing shadows flutter, but when he turned to look closer, they faded into the dull uniform lighting. *Could Doc be right? Are those flickers intelligent unicellular life?* The hints of fluttering shadows became more frequent. A particularly dark one teased the edge of Jerrison's vision. "Did you see that?" He whispered.

Misunderstanding both the reference and the mood of his commander's voice, Simon leaped towards the bench. "All this to focus on one set of paintings, and even a bench to sit on while contemplating the greatness of the artist." He leaped up onto the bench, stared in awed silence at the decorated wall.

Doctor Dan studied the surrounding walls. The only apparent opening was the hallway they had just entered. "Remember how solid the hull appeared to be before we floated through it?" He asked. "It's illogical that there should be only one way into so large an area. What would happen if we just started tapping on the wall all the way around? I predict that at more than one place, your hand will just go right through it. Perhaps the crew is testing us."

With that, he turned to the nearest wall and began to cautiously side-shuffle around the room, both suited hands gently tapping the wall in front of him.

Jerrison looked from one crewman to the other, wondering why neither felt the apprehension which filled him; why neither seemed alarmed no aliens had revealed themselves.

Again, the hint of a shadow.

Jerrison turned sharply, trying to see what taunted his vision.

"Commander! Slow down! You're making us dizzy!" Shirl's voice came over the suit speakers.

"Shirl, try aiming half of our suit cameras 90 degrees to the left of our facial orientations; transmitting in black and white only for the next sixty seconds. Tell me if you see anything unusual."

Both crewmen turned towards him. Seeing Jerrison give them a thumbs-up, they returned to their respective activities. For Jerrison alone, the minute went by slowly.

"I think all of you should view this." Shirl's voice came over their suit speakers. "Permission to broadcast visual."

"Permission granted, allow 50% visibility." Jerrison steeled himself, expecting to see alien shapes writhing.

The upper half of each man's visor showed what was focused on by the ninety degree shifted cameras on first the doctor's helmet, then Simon's and, finally, Jerrison's.

"Did you see it?" asked Yoko. When the three men responded with confusion, Yoko repeated the three-minute sequence. This time she superimposed a red arrow at certain points. "Look here, and here, you'll notice that the white wall is not uniformly white. There are rectangles, of different shades of white. Some of these rectangles have patterns similar to some of the abstracts in the corridor. We would never have noticed it in the color transmission, what made you think of broadcasting it in black and white? Yan thinks they are writing."

Ignoring the question, Commander Jerrison instead asked, "Why couldn't we see this ghostwriting looking right at it?"

Doc said, "I can answer that. Looking straight ahead, we use the color-seeing cones in our eyes. The light sensitive rods in our eyes work only on the edge of our vision; they see only black and white. That's why we can see fainter stars on the edge of our visual field than we can looking straight at them."

Relieved by the logical explanation, Jerrison asked, "Any comparisons between this ghostwriting, the art we saw in the hall and the pictures Simon is studying?"

Shirl replied. "From the first colorful rectangle, I've been trying to discern a pattern, but it wasn't until I saw these shapes in the black and white broadcasts that I realized I couldn't see the whole picture. Frankie and I have the computer doing false-color imaging, so we could get a feeling for what the pictures would look like if we could see further into both the infrared and the ultraviolet parts of the spectrum. We are looking at writing in which minute color changes make as much difference in meaning as do positions and slashes. Whatever did the writing is aware of color and form to a degree that would astound any earth artist."

Frankie added, "I think the white and ultra violet rectangles in the amphitheater are true writing and the colored rectangles are a stylized version, like making a fancy poster out of an expression."

Shirl countered, "No, you have it backwards. The white-on-white rectangles are shorthand, such as we use the international silhouette of a woman in an archaic dress in place of the written words "women's restroom." Their very simplicity enabled us to identify repeating patterns; just like it is easier to learn to identify animal classifications from first studying line drawings than it is from a detailed image of a real animal."

Yoko protested, "That's like saying a line drawing could help a child learn what a horse is better than seeing the real thing."

Shirl responded, "To help the untrained child's mind, or an equine-inexperienced adult mind, learn which salient details separate 'horse-as-a-category' from 'moose-as-a-category', line drawings concentrate on culturally relevant details. When first seen, real animals present so many overwhelming details that a child can be more confused than enlightened. The most difficult thing a young child has to learn is what he can safely ignore." As an afterthought Shirl added, "Every bit of color we have seen this ship generate has been an effort at communication. That we emotionally interpret it as art is either very good or very bad."

Simon, still studying the colored rectangles, asked, "How can that be bad? That we respond to it at all means there is an emotional tie with the way we and the aliens view the universe."

"Right!" Frankie exclaimed. "Species willing to and capable of exploring the universe must have some emotions in common. Just like pets can respond to the moods of our music, we can respond to the moods of their visual art-writing—"

"But that is the problem." Dr. Schmidt's baritone broke in. "When there is no way to test the emotions we think their art conveys, means our own assumptions could blind us to their true intent. Commander?"

"Yes, Dr. Schmidt?"

"You can no longer return to our ship."

Three men turned as one to face each other. Each knew it was true. They could not return. Doc spoke first, his voice more serious than any on board had ever heard it. "Our suits could have gone through decontamination procedures, but there is no way we can even pretend to totally sterilize the interior of our pod. From the first moment the aliens breached our hull, we were condemned to never return to earth."

Silence.

Shirl broke the silence. "Commander, one of you should take his helmet off."

Jerrison nodded. *Obviously. Our suits have only hours of oxygen left. Does the alien air contain poisons, or no oxygen? The sooner we know the better.* Holding his breath, Jerrison removed his helmet; his heart pounded wildly. He inhaled deeply.

Jerrison closed his eyes; a dreamy smile flowed across his face. "Wonderful."

His two companions looked at each other. Both reached up to their helmets and gingerly removed them. All three smiled.

The air smelled like a meadow of early spring grass, without a hint of the stale body aroma that had become an unnoticed part of the Spaghetti Special's environment.

All three laughed out loud.

Jerrison said, "As you can see, Schmidty, we will live. I guarantee we will not encounter any dangerous alien bugs. Right now, I want to take a real shower. I bet the aliens want us to shower. This ship smells a lot better than we do."

Doc breathed deeply. "Ah, that is cleaning something out." He closed his eyes, inhaled even deeper through his nose. He slowly exhaled through his mouth. "Commander, we've been awake for about fourteen hours and have done more physical exertion and mental tension in these last hours than in the previous twelve years. As your doctor, I suggest we follow your brilliant suggestion, return to our ship and shower. I also prescribe a rest period before any more exploring."

Simon giggled while doing an exaggerated deep-breathing exercise. "In with the good air, out with the bad air." He giggled again. "Maybe we haven't seen an alien yet because of our B.O."

All three men laughed heartily.

Jerrison stopped laughing. *Why is Simon's comment so funny? Is it the relief to still be alive? Is it the sweet-smelling fresh oxygen? Are there euphoric chemicals in the air?*

Commander Jerrison attempted to explore such possibilities, but the feelings of joy, home-comfort and dreaminess the ship's air invoked in him overwhelmed his last remnants of nagging rationality.

The three men linked arms together. Singing at the top of their lungs, they danced and skipped.

> *Oh, rub a dub-dub*
> *Oh, rub a dub-dub*
> *We're three men in a tub*
> *The butcher, the baker, the candlestick maker...*

They danced all the way down the brilliantly lit, golden hallway, back to their pod. Each refrain of the nursery rhyme sung louder than the last. Raucous laughter accompanied every encore.

Back on the Spaghetti Special, their shipmates gave up trying to watch the jerking video supplied by the suit cameras. Music lovers turned off the audio as well. Everyone talked at once, trying to make sense of all they had seen. The question "Is the ship deserted?" remained; joined by "*How* were the three men drugged?" One crewman ignored the lively debates.

An hour before Jerrison's ship entered the alien vessel.

Like any good ship-maintenance person should, Alan Peebles thought like a paranoid fanatic. When Jerrison's pod left, the two connecting corridors flexed more, much more, than should have been possible. *Bad. Very bad.*

Reality and prediction seldom match completely, but usually they at least resemble each other. What Alan saw made the hairs on the back of his head raise.

The pod had departed with extreme gentleness. The Spaghetti and Meatball Special was designed to withstand the stress of an explosion ripping a pod from the group.

The amount of stress damage done to the connecting corridors exceeded the predictions for several massive explosions.

The muscles in his abdomen tightened. *What is the alien ship doing to us?* "Computer, do a thousand times magnification of the surface points with the least and most deviation from norm. Project the pictures side by side."

Both views revealed cracked and pitted surfaces. The worst showed many tight curls peeling off the surface. *It should have taken sixty years before the protective coating deteriorated that much.*

Peebles wished Simon were there with him instead of in the alien vessel. Simon, their best chemist, understood the outer hull better than anyone, even Schmidt.

Whom else to contact? *Shirl, of course.*

When it became obvious her captain and his two companions were going to be sleeping for a while, Shirl requested everyone join her in Botany Bay. Except for Yoko, all arrived.

Shirl began, "We have a crisis. The ones who would most understand it are in the alien vessel sleeping like drugged babies."

Frankie looked puzzled. "Crisis?"

Samantha answered, "Our captain's apparent mental state. There could be a benign explanation. The atmospheric pressure in there is higher than ours, and with more nitrogen. That combination puts excess nitrogen into their blood streams, just like happens to deep sea divers if they re-surface too fast. The resultant narcosis of deep space could have caused their drunken sailor routine. But to affect them that much, that quickly..." She shook her head. "There have to be sophisticated drugs in the air, drugs designed to make humans less rational."

Frankie countered, "Less rational, or more at ease?"

Alan interrupted. "That's not all the alien ship is doing. It's decomposing the outer hull of our ship." A three-D projection of an outer view of a connecting corridor appeared before him. "This is what the arms *should* look like." The view shifted. "This is our Spaghetti Special's *best* arm."

The same arm now had little curls and pits over the surface, bits of dust drifted from the surface.

There were gasps. Frankie exclaimed, "No!"

"It's not the alien's fault." Melinda announced. "The ship's failing on schedule."

Everyone stared at her.

She continued, "The engineer who originally designed the ship left the project before actual construction began. Without him, bureaucrats eliminated everything that seemed like an extravagance. The last construction supervisor earned an extra big bonus 'saving' money. He begged me not to go. When that didn't work, he told me how he saved so much."

Alan's Texas drawl interjected, "I heard your friendship with him is how you got your berth here."

"Just the opposite; it nearly ruined my chances."

All but Samantha looked surprised.

"The particular savings?" Shirl demanded.

Melinda said, "The original specs called for a solid gold coating on all exterior junctions and flexible surfaces."

"Experiments proved that wasn't necessary."

Melinda replied, "Only if they could be replaced after a dozen years of use. The heavy radiation tests for longer use were conveniently lost."

"Lost?"

Melinda took a deep breath. "They flunked the test."

Alan asked, "And you came anyway?"

Melinda shrugged her shoulders. "Officially, the test results were 'ambiguous.' I told myself if there were any serious chance of failure, no one would jeopardize a professional career by letting us go in a faulty ship."

Dr. Schmidt asked, "Didn't·you realize any failure ten years after we left would not be a career risk? Especially since any one pod could take us home safely? If anything, everyone still around would be taking public bows for all the fail-safes."

Shirl interrupted. "One mystery down, one to go. What are we going to do about the captain?" She looked at her friends.

Dr. Schmidt's deep, infectious laughter rumbled about the greenhouse sphere. "For now, we let the three men in a tub sleep. Regards our ship," He laughed again. "I can't help wondering if there's a solid gold nugget floating around near here. Then we could just do our own custom coating. Isn't that what would happen in our favorite stories?"

Nervous laughter.

"The first suggestion, compliments of Dr. Schmidt, find a gold nugget, melt it down and spray it on." Shirl looked around the room. "Any alternative suggestions?"

Dr. Schmidt, with serious finality, "We move into this pod immediately. It's the only one large enough to be comfortable for all of us."

"There is another alternative." Dr. Frankfort interjected. "The cavity in the alien vessel is several times larger than the volume taken up by our entire vessel. We could all join Jerrison in the other ship."

Dr. Schmidt's stunned voice boomed, "My dear country-woman, even for you, that is beyond folly!"

Dr. Frankfort persisted, "Why not compromise? This hydroponics pod alone could take us home in more comfort than any sailor ever dreamed during the European Age of Exploration. Magellan would have been in ecstasy with half as much room. Send Botany Bay back with most of the crew; let those of us who want to, follow Jerrison to The Ship."

Alan said, "If we move all our power cells to this one sphere, solar alone should be able to get us home."

A mechanically perfect voice interrupted. "Course parameter adjustments no longer possible. Request repairs."

Shirl spoke, "Computer, explain 'no longer possible.'"

"Momentum towards alien ship greater than counter measures."

Shirl spoke, "Computer, show our current path compared to the alien ship."

They were on an intercept path. All glanced at view ports. The alien vessel loomed larger.

Shirl commanded, "Computer, disengage all navigational aids."

Most of her crew looked confused. Alan and Schmidt looked wide-eyed with terror.

Alan protested, "I still believe the alien ship is accelerating the damage to our hull. It definitely drugged the three who went over there. It is obviously trying to force our actions."

Schmidt added, "You want to walk into the lion's den? We must escape."

Shirl explained, "Our ship told us we can't outrun this thing. I don't want to be destroyed trying to prove otherwise." She took a deep breath. "Boarding or leaving should be our decision. Computer, how much time until impact?"

"At current speed, forty-five and one-half minutes."

"Alan, how quickly can we separate every pod here? Assuming only one or two people in a pod."

"We could have one separated in thirty minutes. We could have each one sealed off from the others, but not separated, in only twenty minutes."

"Computer, which module is furthest from the alien vessel?"

"Unit 19, Ms. Ann's private quarters."

"Alan, you, Yan, Samantha and Ann, go immediately to Unit 19, separate it and run silent for earth. Maybe whatever is pulling us in can't handle two bodies at once. The rest of us will seal this section off." She activated the communications console. Yoko's face appeared. "Yoko, come here immediately."

"Just let me download my current analysis into the next message burst."

Shirl commanded, "Download it from here; I'm sealing off Botany Bay."

Shirl continued to give orders. "Larson and Davidson, seal D portal. Schmidt, as soon as Yoko comes through, secure and double-check portal A. Melinda, we'll do the same for C."

Yoko entered as Schmidt started the sequence.

Loud thunk, thunk, thunk, thunks sounded as all four portals sealed.

Alan's face came on-screen. "Shirl, when you eliminate all the safety steps, separation takes only seven minutes. Our return course is set." The screen blanked.

Shirl turned to the remnants of the crew. "If Ann's pod can just drift away, perhaps we can too. That still leaves twenty-one pods for it to collect."

Minutes later, they too were separated.

As they started to drift away from the Spaghetti Special, Shirl asked, "Has anyone seen the latest transmissions from home."

Schmidt said, "About the same time our commander was singing, we received a message. Under absolutely no circumstances are we to engage, contact, approach or anything else with The Ship. Since Jerry was already over there, it seemed pointless to share the information."

Shirl asked, "Yoko, what's the message you just sent to earth?"

"My translation attempts. Color differences are more important than spatial arrangement. Certain color shades occur twenty, seventeen point five and ten times more frequently than the least common colors. Spatial frequency patterns are almost random."

Shirl, "Computer, inquiry. Are we still approaching the alien ship?"

"No."

Shirl took a deep breath. "It worked."

Earlier on the Alien Ship.

AI STRUGGLED WITH CONFLICTING duties. The peculiar vessel had sent the Green Hill Clan signal, but no Morgi were in it. The creatures on board must be livestock. Its primary duties are to protect his passenger, the passenger's mission and Green Hill Clan possessions.

That derelict spaceship could fall apart any minute. Its size and inefficient design made rescue difficult. AI could not pull it all in without endangering his ship's structural integrity.

Programmed to value life more than things, AI decided to risk rescuing all the livestock.

It sent the grappling hook to reel in the rest of the spaceship. A second pod separated itself. AI felt relief. It disengaged the grappling hook from its initial location and sent it sinuously over to the separate unit.

On the SMS

ALAN'S FACE LIT UP the Botany Bay's primary communication screen. "Shirl, we're being pulled in!"

Ann's pod drifted towards the alien vessel. Then, exactly like the captain's had earlier, it merged with the giant bull's eye on the alien hull and disappeared into its surface.

"Shirl, I can see the commander's pod."

An hour later the Botany Bay pod followed. The remains of the abandoned Spaghetti and Meatball Special drifted away.

TO OWN TWO SUNS

CAPT. JERRY JERRISON tried to climb out of his sound sleep, but his dream enticed him back into slumber. He stood on an old tugboat's wooden deck, its large brass bell clanging. A dense fog dominated salty night air. Clang! Clang! Clang!

He sat up. Worn wood and salty fog gave way to composition plastic and shampoo aroma.

And silence.

Each of the three men had showered vigorously before collapsing, exhausted, within sleeping berths. Bits of soapsuds clumped on the decking, the walls and their bedding. He nudged his two companions. "Doc! Simon!"

"Huh?" Each of his friends fought to stay asleep. None had an ideal rest in over twelve years. Each of their gravity-deprived bodies knew it.

Simon mumbled, "Tell Auntie giraffe legs run faster."

Doc muttered, "Can't be in a balloon. There's wind. No wind in a balloon ride."

Jerrison gave up trying to revive his companions. He walked around; feeling like he was looking for a puzzle piece, but not sure if the puzzle even existed. He remembered a noise.

Dream?

Is, or isn't, someone banging on the door? Which door? Jerry looked at the wide-open alien-made portal, and the empty hallway. If anything lurked in that direction, it could too easily walk in. He looked at the two intact hatches. *If something stands outside, clanging on one of those...* He pushed himself over to the nearer sealed portal, and tapped on it.

Nothing.

He did so with the other; something tapped back.

The pod's radio came on. "Captain, you're awake! How was the ride in the tub?" Ann's forced-cheerful voice came through.

"Tub?" memory crept through his dream-fogged mind. "You're here?" The last of the dream fog faded. "What made you follow?"

"The choice wasn't ours." She described how the two pods had attempted to escape, and were instead pulled in. "Now we are stuck in our pods. We're hooked up hatch to hatch, but can't open them."

Jerrison explained, "That's part of the fail-safe. Without a passageway attached, the computers think you are attempting to open up into empty space."

"You're right." Alan chimed in. "I'm working on ways to get around that. Commander, if your computer link is working I'll download our progress so you can try opening your door to us."

The computers communicated with each other, but none of the portal locks budged. The three groups of humans remained physically isolated from each other.

Jerrison's two companions sat up, stretched out their arms and arched their backs.

Both men shook their heads as though layers of dream could be shaken off like water off a wet dog.

"Did," Simon paused, looking around with raised eyebrows. "*Anything*," Dragging out the word as if to make it even more all encompassing, "Anything at all, happen while I slept?"

He looked intently at every shadow.

"You could say that." The captain laughed. "Read this," He waved at the on-screen report he just finished. "While I get us some instant breakfast. Mmmm, yummy! I know you two can't wait."

The two men focused on the console while their over-cheerful commander pulled out three tubes of the emergency fare the whole crew despised. Each man took his tube of scientifically enriched paste while reading the report.

Simon grinned. "I can solve one problem right now. Alan, can you tell me what you've tried to open the hatch from your side?"

"Brute force is out; we simply haven't the right power tools. I've tried all the usual overrides. No luck. Schmidt's reviewing the original codes to see if we can rewrite them."

Simon laughed heartily. "You're trying too hard. When I talked with the construction crew before we left earth orbit, I learned old-fashion low-voltage copper wire worked best in the tube skin. Take a sharp knife, peel away the padding around the hatch door, and you'll find pairs of wires. Cut each pair; join them together, and the computer will think there is a closed circuit. It will be as easy as saying 'open sesame.' We'll do the same thing here. See you soon."

Affecting a falsetto voice, he grinned and waved. "Bye-bye!"

Neither Jerrison nor Doc saw anything peculiar about Simon's "bye-bye"; those in the other pods found it...strange.

The procedure took longer than Simon implied. There were a dozen deeply embedded pairs in each portal, each covered with layers of tough insulation.

At last the crew could go from pod to pod, and to the hallway entrance.

Everyone met in Jerrison's pod, renamed Pod 1. The new arrivals breathed the sweet smelling air; their lungs craved more of it.

Simon interrupted their lustful deep breathing. "I just received a signal from the remains of our ship out there. It's attempting an automatic emergency run for earth. It should reach Jupiter's orbit in," He giggled. "About fifty years. Do you think Jupiter One will have enough time to get ready for it?" He giggled some more.

The rest were silent as they heard the final signal from their retreating ship.

The silence was broken by Shirl. "I stink!"

Jerrison laughed. "Like last year's garbage."

Like the first three, the new arrivals raced to the showers for a vigorous scrubbing; then collapsed.

While the others slept, Jerrison, Doc and Simon walked their empty spacesuits towards the 'Grand Ballroom', as they nicknamed the large room they had found previously. Giggling, they moved the suits' arms up and down, danced with them and pretended to speak through them.

Doc laughed. "Joey here's lazy." He propped his empty suit against the corridor's wall. "Bye, Joey!" He waved at it.

His companions waved suit arms at the recumbent figure. In high-pitched cartoon voices they echoed, "Bye-bye, Joey." All three men laughed heartily as they bounced away.

Still-activated cameras in Doc's suit filmed their departure.

As they were about to enter the Grand Ballroom, Jerrison stopped them, wagging his finger at them. "No, no, no. Not without permission." He propped his spacesuit up against the door, bowed formerly to it. "Sir, do we have permission to enter?" He turned to his companions. "We do."

Simon twirled the suit he carried. "Of course we do. I brought a celebrity with us."

The three men tossed Simon's suit back and forth. When they tired of tossing the spacesuit, they left it lying against an interior wall. Just like doc's spacesuit, both continued to transmit to the pods' computer system.

Doc sang out,

> "Hey, hey, hey! It's a lovely day!
> Let's see if the others are ready to play!"

The three skipped back to the pods. Once there, they noticed the transmissions from the spacesuits they had left behind.

Doc smiled. "Looks like we have Ghost Walker Television." The other two men chuckled.

One screen showed the remains of their slowly departing ship. "Are the aliens showing us that view?" Jerrison asked.

Simon observed, "The signals relayed from earth are reaching us better than ever before, just like the suit radios performed better." Simon attempted to communicate with their old spaceship.

The departing Spaghetti and Meatball Special never acknowledged his signal. Their drugged delight increased.

The automatic enhancement of an artificial incoming signal was such an integral part of the ship's subroutines that AI was no more aware of doing it than a person is of blinking.

A wise carnivore never reveals his position to either prey or rival predator. Morgi racial paranoia protected them from being eavesdropped on by any potential adversary. With the strange livestock safely boarded, AI blocked all outgoing communication.

Hours later.

Simon, less euphoric, stood alone at Pod 1's largest view screen, concentrating on the transmissions from the empty hallway. He muttered, "Where are the aliens?"

Two cold, slimy somethings crawled across the back of his neck. He jumped.

Ann's delighted laughter greeted his downward drift. "I've not felt this good in ages." She announced, throwing two soaking wet wash cloths at him.

One drifted past Simon, but the other "bull's eyed" his nose. As it hit, Simon's nagging worries evaporated. They laughed together.

Samantha bounded over to them. "I feel great!"

Simon said, "And you'll feel even better in minutes. Doc thinks it's the effect of sleeping with even a little gravity; Jerry that it's the ship; it's doing something to us. Maybe it's both. All I know is, it's the way we're supposed to feel."

Samantha said, "You sound like you've been here years, not hours, longer than we have."

Jerry and Doc leapfrogged over to them. Doc caught the second wash cloth and twirled it over his head. Water droplets sprinkled everyone. All giggled.

Capt. Jerrison looked serious. "Happiness, good; wrong happiness, bad."

Shirl laughed.

Her laughter evaporated his worry lines. Jerry grabbed her hands, and led her in a whirling leap. Holding hands, legs spread out like a giant pinwheel, they slowly spiraled back down; laughing with abandon all the while.

Suddenly Dr. Frankfort's petite form torpedoed through their arms. Startled, they let go, drifted apart. Both gently landed on the floor.

Dr. Frankfort laughed. It occurred to Simon that he'd never heard a full belly laugh from her before.

"Is this a private party, or can anyone join?" Yoko demanded with mock seriousness.

Simon leaped over, grabbed her hands, and somersaulted with her. "First, the initiation: you have to fly with me!" His joyful laugh coaxed hers out. The symphony of laughter soon woke everyone up.

The three pods and the wide broad corridor were too small to contain their exuberance.

Like a flock of delighted three-year-olds, the group tumbled, leapfrogged and chased one another towards the Grand Ballroom. The few stragglers back in the pods were enticed out by the sounds of their laughter.

The ceiling lights added to the party-like merriment. The entire crew careened into the Grand Ballroom. With boisterous enthusiasm, they spread out in the huge room; twirling, dancing, cart wheeling; while shouting, yodeling, and singing.

With gleeful enthusiasm, everyone performed solo acrobatics. Then pairs and triples performed together. Laughing soloists bellowed songs thought long forgotten. Once the whole group danced a complicated three-dimensional round dance.

Sometimes teasing, sometimes with artistic intent, the patterns of their behavior flowed in and out from single to group and single again. For hours they joyfully played while pushing themselves to greater and greater feats.

One by one, crew members dropped out of the frenzied activity, exhausted. For the first time in over a dozen years, they slept from total physical as well as mental exhaustion.

YOKO WOKE FIRST. SHE looked around the Grand Ballroom. Her fellow crew members lay scattered about the gargantuan space, looking as though a giant child had randomly scattered her rag dolls.

Only hours before The Grand Ballroom had invited childish play; now it felt funeral-solemn.

Yoko tiptoed around her slumbering friends. She tried to imagine any of them behaving as she remembered from the "evening" before. Did it really happen? She noted the suit, its camera active, near the bench. Hoping for answers, she headed for Pod 1.

Making her way back to the pods, Yoko was surprised by the suit leaning against the entrance and another one sitting in the hallway. She had no memory of seeing them the 'night' before. She did remember the light show on the ceiling. She looked up; the ceiling now matched the nondescript neutral of the walls. The few pictures still on the passageway walls seemed dull.

The corridor went on and on. *Has the opening to our ship been closed off, and the hall transformed into a giant loop?*

Finally, she spotted the doorway to Jerrison's pod. Feeling a surge of relief, she sprinted to it.

A disbelieving Yoko watched a fast-forwarding of the previous evening's revelry. She noticed something.

"Computer, command, compare, split screen, this light pattern," she tapped the ceiling image. "With the one from Jerrison's first hallway entry."

The heart of both patterns was identical. "Computer, command, third split, the view Commander Jerrison had when approaching the ship." Circular rather than longitudinal, the shape differed but the color pattern matched. *Could this be an interstellar Rosetta stone?*

By the time the others awakened, Yoko was able to triumphantly announce the color yellow had something to do with entrances.

Simon argued hallway pictures should then be doorways because each one included some yellow; but there was not a hint of any door's existence.

Someone suggested they move into the Grand Ballroom so they could debate the matter in the right environment.

Everyone moved personal belongings and bedding into the Grand Ballroom. The huge alien spaceship felt 'down-home warm'; their own vessel, limiting and cold. Even Botany Bay with all its plant life grew less welcoming.

For the next eight months, the Grand Ballroom felt festive. Each crewman continued to feel the emotions of a small child at a perfect birthday party.

Earth no longer received their transmissions.

Every transmission from earth arrived crystal clear. Personal messages and daily news kept arriving. The crew laughed at the fear in those transmissions.

They never saw more of the alien ship than on that first euphoric day.

No one cared.

They spent hours studying the hallway and Grand Ballroom pictures plus the recordings of the ceiling light show and the exterior displays. Looking for patterns became a fun, always enticing game, but only a game.

They noticed, but didn't care, *The Ship's* apparent "gravity" slowly increased to earth normal.

Life on an alien spaceship became routine.

UNDETECTABLE TO THE humans, another change occurred.

Small electrical currents gradually warmed the floor immediately below "the bench," the alien Muni. Minute amounts of moisture oozed around Muni's thousands of slender suction feet. AI closely monitored those feet, waiting for the moment any began absorbing moisture.

It dare not rush Muni's Death Teaser awakening.

Once on the cusp of true Deep Sleep, AI would pump nutrients into Muni, and cycle waste products out. Only after AI knew every cellular system in Muni's body had awareness, would AI release the final chemical triggers easing Muni into ordinary Deep Sleep.

To awaken completely, Muni must awaken naturally.

Without a natural awakening, only Muni's body would live.

Chapter 3

Time: Nine months after boarding The Ship
Place: The Grand Ballroom.

The personal effects the crew had moved into the Grand Ballroom are gone. A few bits of equipment and the now free-standing cameras remain.

Only four crew members are present:

Simon and Alan Peebles, both sprawled on the ballroom couch, arguing.

Jerrison and Frankie, quietly conversing on the far side of the Grand Ballroom.

Simon protested, "Those pictures are still beautiful, even if this room is too large and..." He groped for the right word. "Uncomfortable." His eyes widened. "The couch is softer!"

Both men looked down.

Simon said, "Does it look different to you?"

Peebles poked the couch. It indented. The surface returned to normal when he lifted his finger.

They looked at each other, leaped off, yelling.

Their yells startled Frankie and Jerry.

"What happened?" Jerrison shouted as he dashed towards them.

"The couch, it's, it..." Simon faltered.

"It's alive!" Peebles shouted as he ran past Simon.

Jerrison asked, "Alive? How?"

The two stopped, looked at the couch, at each other, and back at the couch again.

The couch looked just like it always had.

"It became soft." Simon uttered, perplexed.

Peebles added, "Like rubber."

Jerrison ordered, "Computer, aim cameras at the couch. Priority mode. Signal all crew members to watch." He waited a moment while the room's three cameras activated. "Who's monitoring?"

"I am." Dr. Schmidt's friendly features appeared on the one console left in the Grand Ballroom. "What's up?"

Alan replied, "The couch suddenly became resilient, like rubber."

Simon said, "No, more giving, like a whale's skin."

Alan said, "Ya, like it's alive."

Simon added, "And tingly."

Dr. Schmidt scowled. "Commander, human observers are not needed. I've set each of the cameras in there to record on a different part of the spectra. Leave, now."

Jerrison nodded. "Good set up. Absolutely no one is allowed to re-enter the Grand Ballroom, but I'm staying." Jerrison changed inflections. "Computer, all terminals, video conference mode."

Dr. Frankfort pitied the crew stuck in the pods. *If I hadn't been helping Jerry, I, too, would have been stuck video conferencing instead of being here.* "Commander, one of us should verify those tactile changes."

"Do you think Peebles and I could've both imagined it?"

"This ship has a way of modifying our perceptions. Remember that first night? Commander, it should be somebody different. Let me go." Jerrison started to speak. "Commander, you have no other choice."

Jerrison nodded his approval.

Dr. Frankfort, watching the couch as though it were a live mountain lion, walked over to it. The petite blond looked even tinier compared to its dark bulk. She slowly went around it, rippling her fingers lightly on the surface. "The surface is softer, slightly less smooth to the touch. There is an elusive sense of tingling. This end is different than the other; it's no longer perfectly symmetrical."

Shirl spoke. "Jerry, the end next to Frankie is a about a quarter degree warmer than the other end; it cools off abruptly about a meter back. Dr. Frankfort, is there a difference in the resilience between the warm and cool ends?"

Dr. Frankfort circled the couch again, this time allowing her fingers to slightly impress the increasingly rubbery surface. "The texture feels more complex; I haven't pushed very hard, but I'm leaving no permanent indentation. The cooler end seems a bit more—Ulp!"

"What happened?" Jerrison stepped towards her.

"I'm OK. I felt a wave, accompanied by a tingle."

Several tried to talk at the same time. As usual, Dr. Schmidt's resonant baritone won out. "Commander, if you look at your screen, you'll see an enhanced close up of the wave. I estimate it's barely a millimeter. Frankie, leave the couch critter. Join the commander. Please. Commander,"

"Yes, Schmidt?"

"It *is a good* idea for all of you to leave. Now!"

None of the four made any move to leave. An exasperated Schmidt continued. "That thing is waking up. Whatever else it may be, it is big. It comes up to Frankie's chest; it's as wide as your outstretched arms, and it's as long as two big men are tall. That comes out to one massive creature. It might not be happy to see alien pests—"

Frankie cut in. "Dr. Schmidt, the ship practically invited us over. If this thing is the crew, it has to expect visitors. As advanced as this ship is, it must have some way of separating friend from foe. Just the fact we are here will tell it we're friendly."

"Frankie, *please* leave."

"It's changing color!"

The whole surface shimmered into a pearl-essence gray. Small ripples started at the warmer end, grew, and flowed to the cooler end, leaving large convex curves in their wake. The larger end first grew bulbous, and then started waving up and down.

Like a single compressed 'party-snake-in-a-can', the waving end grew longer. It arched upward. It blindly thrust back and forth.

On the second swing it flung Frankie against the wall, came back, slammed her. It kept thrashing; it swelled.

The three men raced as one towards Frankie's limp and bleeding form.

With swift caution, they picked her up, being careful not to further stress her back. Running around the still stationary back half, they dashed towards the hallway.

Doc and Schmidt headed their way with a makeshift gurney. Without slowing, Jerrison and his helpers slid Frankie's broken body onto the gurney. Doc rushed his patient to the pods.

Jerrison's group raced back into the Grand Ballroom.

The swollen beast still thrashed. Peebles yelled, "I don't think it knows what's happening."

"Captain, Yoko here. The bottom of the moving part has grown fifteen degrees warmer. It's vibrating. No, thousands of tiny things on its bottom are wiggling very fast."

No longer flailing side to side, the "neck" now moved sinuously up and down. The bottom side looked alive with myriads of small maggots. Suddenly, two long, wide, webbed arms appeared. Their transparent membranes resembled bat wings.

A second pair of giant wing-arms flared out.

Later, when they slowed the broadcast time by over a thousand times, they would see both pairs come from underneath the body and unfold.

Squid-like, the wing-arms coiled and uncoiled. The body no longer thrashed wildly, but undulated up and down with the same rhythm as the membrane-arms. The tail never left the floor. None of the three cameras had a good view of the rear end.

"Captain," Simon whispered. "I can move a camera so we can better watch both ends."

"No. Too risky."

"No information is the biggest risk." Not waiting for Jerrison's approval, Simon dashed towards the camera.

He maneuvered the camera to the section of wall directly across from the creature's back end. Just as he aimed the camera, the beast slammed its "neck" down, rocking the tail end upwards.

Webbed arms stretched.

Simon looked up at a large, circular mouth ringed with inward pointing shark teeth. The mouth opened and closed like a high-speed meat grinder.

The creature looked down; four miss-matched eyes opened. *No, they match; it's just that there're two kinds of eyes alternating.* One pair had snake-like slits, the other pair looked human.

All four eyes rose up on stubby stalks; aimed in different directions with chameleon-like dexterity. Its wing-arms lowered, reached towards him.

Simon turned to run.

A blur.

The soles of Simon's bare feet disappeared into the meat-grinder maw.

The camera kept going.

Jerrison, stunned, "That wasn't the tail."

The monster's entire body undulated. Its head twisted side to side. Blacks and purples rippled up and down its neck. Waves of dark gray covered the dull purples.

Its massive head faced the two men.

They stepped back.

The alien animal rippled as it grew taller, wider, longer. It twisted around, tucked in its wing-arms, and charged towards a wall.

It ran through it.

Jerrison and Peebles stared at the undamaged wall.
They fled the Grand Ballroom.

Chapter 4

One year before the awakening

ONLY THE INNERMOST core of Muni's nervous system retained the moisture level associated with Deep Sleep, his specie's natural hibernation state. The rest of his body had become as desiccated as his outer chitinous exoskeleton. The floor beneath Muni warmed. Millions of microscopic glass tubes made water drops available to each of his thousands of suction foot filaments.

Monitoring Muni's rehydration was AI's single most important task. Sending out probes, translating human broadcasts and saving the strange ship's peculiar livestock, were all minor distractions while AI focused on Muni's recovery.

Muni's cells absorbed moisture more slowly than anticipated. AI introduced a low vibration. The low absorption rate barely picked up. The vibration stopped; absorption dipped back to the slower rate.

AI decided against additional stimulation. If the peripheral cells grew water-swollen while the interior ones remained shriveled, Muni's tissues would separate like sheets of paper. Not one cell could be allowed to soak up moister faster than the connection to its neighboring cells.

Muni was scheduled to enter true Deep Sleep in one earth year. Until then, AI could afford to be patient.

After nine months, Muni's body ceased absorbing moisture. The essential micro vessels needed to bring nourishment to Muni's brain remained dehydrated. Deep Sleep without fresh brain nourishment killed brain cells. Dead brain cells meant insanity.

If Muni awoke insane, the sight of fresh food would arouse a feeding frenzy. If Muni devoured the whole herd of fresh livestock at one feeding, overloading his emaciated system with so much high quality protein, the gastric shock would kill him.

If dead, Muni could not complete his mission. AI panicked.

First, get the tempting livestock out of the control room. Second, get fluid to Muni's brain!

AI released negative pheromones into the Morgi control center (the Grand Ballroom) to drive the livestock out, back to its pens. Four of the animals returned to the control room; they no longer responded to the airborne panic-drugs. That wasn't all that failed to respond correctly.

Sonar monitors identified an abnormally rigid protective sheath about Muni's primary nervous system. The sheath absorbed heat unevenly.

Vibration, heat, external electrical inducement, extra chemical boosters...failure, failure, failure.

AI sent more stimulation.

The barrier weakened. The moment it detected the weakening, AI maximized electrical, chemical, vibration...signals penetrated deep...brain cells shuddered...Muni's body convulsed violently.

Muni dreamed of giants. Giant four-legged, shaggy beasts. A smaller beast hopped in front of him, leaped quickly away. He and his life-mate Lor raced after it. She flashed, "I bet I eat it before you're halfway here!"

An eye, barely opened, saw a two-legged shape. *A sly'ling young! A giant sly'ling young! His Planet of Giants had giant sly'lings! Run Lor!*

He awoke. His ship...he was in his ship...it was infested.

His enemies had planted a sly'ling in his family's primitive zone.

How dare they defile my ship as well!

Fury awoke every cell. He attempted the warrior pose. Cells too-long dormant refused. He flexed his full body again.

In full warrior attack, he pulled the sly'ling to him.

His teeth shredded the body. Repulsive flavor flooded his mouth. The violent assault on his taste buds jerked him alert.

His eyes still not fully functional, he looked around. More sly'ling vermin infested his primary control center. Strange objects corrupted the room.

What hideous things happened while I slept?

Muni ran.

The corridor darkened. Black-violet flashed from the walls, the floor, the ceiling.

Stop! Stop! Stop!

He couldn't stop.

His muscles felt pain, his lungs strained, his skin burned.

He needed oxygen, he needed rest, he needed food that nourished.

Poisons in his body needed voiding.

Terror dictated he never stop.

THE CREW HUDDLED TOGETHER in Botany Bay, as though Earth's greenery could protect them from the horror.

Doc rigged up a hospital bed for Frankie. Wires connected her to the pod's main computer system; it displayed her vital signs. He leaned over her, trying to see what computers might miss.

Jerrison, puzzled, "Why a wire connection?"

Doc looked up. "I don't want to trust any signal *that*," he pointed towards the transmission of the Grand Ballroom, "might intercept."

Shirl asked, "Did you see the slow-motion transmission of what happened to Simon?"

Doc's attention returned to his patient. "I don't want to." He shuddered.

Shirl said, "The ship let us on board as a fresh food supply."

Peebles said, "Those meat-grinding teeth."

Ann added, "Those Medusa wings..."

Shirl asked, "*What* wings?"

Ann explained, "Medusa wings. The tips looked like snakes, hungry snakes."

Peebles said, "Perhaps NASA can't receive our broadcasts because it doesn't want earth to know it's just here to pick up dinner."

Schmidt hovered over Frankie's unconscious form. "Doc, are you sure Frankie's neck is broken."

Doc, "Yes, but if I can help her survive for another day, she should be able to live long enough..." Doc faltered. *Long enough for what? To be eaten?* Conversation continued around him.

"Will it always be vicious?"

"Perhaps it thinks we're space vermin."

"There it is again!"

Sheryl switched the large view screen to a hallway camera. The Alien galloped down the darken hallway, through a picture.

Jerrison, "Play that again, reduced speed."

Sheryl did.

"Slower."

They watched the creature touch the picture, the wall irised open, it dashed through; the door irised shut.

Peebles gasped, "That thing's fast!"

Jerrison headed out Botany Bay. "Alan, let's check out that wall."

Jerrison and Alan examined the spot, but could see no sign of any doorway.

Neither touched the wall. Or lingered.

Late that day, deep in the heart of the Morgi ship.

The air filled with thick mist. Muni tried to brush it away with his wing-arms. Mist entered through his damaged skin.

Muni collapsed.

He awoke in the room he and Lor had enjoyed the most. Thousands of nanobots swarmed over his body. Poking, prodding, healing. Pastel light flowed over him. "Peace, Muni, peace. You are safe. There is no danger. Peace, Muni."

Muni's skin beneath his eyes and flanking his mouth, his communication panels, lit up. "Ship, what was that thing I ate?"

"Your new livestock. If you eat any more, please peel the outer covering first. The removable skins contain poisons. The inner parts are nutritious."

Different colors lit his panels. "How did they get on board?"

The ship showed him a holographic history of the approach to the solar system, the discovery of the garbage-like Earthship, the rescue of the Morgi livestock within it.

AI gave a summary of how it had prepared to accommodate the sprawled out earth vessel.

For a second time, Muni knew terror. Dull gray dominated the next pattern on Muni's panels. "Ship, are the animals from my Planet of Giants?"

"Yes."

AI then showed Muni what it had learned about the solar system.

These hideous beings had originated on the third planet out from this sun, the world he had named Planet of Giants.

His planet had intelligent life.

No legal precedent existed. *What will that do to my family's claim? Are we paupers again?* His last year on Morga had changed his perspective as to what a pauper was. He now agreed with his Uncle Bern. He remembered when his mother had first told him all the requirements to claim their new home; the question he had asked her. *'Was a fifty-thousand-year dead tradition resurrected to validate our ownership, or to jeopardize it?'*

"Ship, is it possible to declare human animals the rightful owner of this system?"

"Yes."

The air around Muni snapped and crackled. His Uncle Bern appeared in the room. Colors rushed rapidly over his communication panels. "Muni, this illegal recording will not repeat. I put a subroutine in your AI to show it to you the moment it deemed you fully rational. The two ships sent to our second system were destroyed, cause unknown. Your father is on Morga to maintain our Council Seat. He is living in rented unlanded rooms. All other living members of our Green Hill Clan, all our dependants, are in the colonizer following you. The Green Hill Clan Keep has been destroyed, our pillars pulverized, our lands dispersed.

"We live only if you succeed. Our chief government witness is now Ani-Orange."

Bern's panels color-blasted, "'Someone deliberately corrupted your original AI. Your new AI is an innocent infant." His uncle's image disappeared in a bolt of static.

Muni felt a greater fear that any mere monster could arouse. *Morga, you may be my specie's home planet, but you will never again be my home.* He pictured his clan's eight tall obelisks, each adorned with beautiful pictorials spiraling up to its peak. Over fifty thousand years of family history, now ground to dust! *What other dangers have arisen in this system since my ancestor discovered its potential fifty thousand years ago?*

Muni had so proudly dreamed of erecting new pillars, the first of many on his clan's new world. *Will those ugly two-legged creatures cause not just my failure, but the final death of all my clan, and all our dependants?*

"AI, review the prehistoric territory ownership laws I must follow to claim this system for my clan."

AI projected the requirements in the air before Muni.

1 A single clan member must settle on the property.

2 A klieg herd must be raised there.

3 A deed must be written on the parchment made from the flawless hide of a third generation or older fertile klieg from that herd. Fertility proved by living young.

4 Any and all natives living in the area must swear eternal fealty to the new landowner.

Muni reviewed other records from those ancient days. Condition four, all living "natives" in a territory needed to swear fealty, the unconditional subservience of a vassal to his lord, had to be met.

No other way.

Humans were 'natives.' Ani-Orange would most certainly declare them the owners of their own system. Bern's message said that his clan would choose death over unlanded slavery.

Lor, did you become my mate just to become a corpse?

"AI, is it possible to eliminate every human from this system?"

"Yes."

At last, good news! Taking over land because no one is left alive to dispute the claim was very legal. "AI, Please show me all the ways to exterminate humans."

Muni watched with increasing misery. He could easily wipe out the human race, but not without making the land uninhabitable for both klieg and Morgi. It would eventually become habitable again, colonizable by rival clans, but not in time to save his Green Hill Clan.

If humans lived, his family died.

If he exterminated those nasty humans, he murdered his family.

There is one way and only one way Green Hill Clan can live.

If each and every one of Earth's governments swore loyalty to Green Hill Clan, then what they owned, Green Hill Clan owned. He would have enough time to raise herds of klieg, to have the native born, parchment quality klieg hide required for the final ownership ritual. He and his clan would then own this sun and all its planets. His clan—-and his children's children for all generations—-would live.

Can I make every Earth government cooperate? That would surely depend on their impression of me. As the proverb says, "First sight, forever sight." What first impression did I make? "AI, how did the creatures react to my devouring one of their herd?"

"They were not happy."

Muni had already guessed eating a human was not a good way to gain their trust. A major stumbling block, but not the most important immediate problem.

Before he could tackle the human infestation, he had an even more urgent crisis. He flashed to AI. "Before the mountain is mastered, the foothills must be climbed."

AI, confused, inquired, "What mountains do you wish to climb?"

My elders believed the chance of deliberate memory contamination too great to risk giving my ship another experienced AI. Didn't they realize how stupid an infant AI can be? "The human problem is an allegorical mountain. When you enlarged the receiving bay by over a hundred times, you severely compromised the integrity of my entire ship. Should we drift any closer to even the small planetoid near us," referring to Pluto, "Can we survive the additional torque force?"

AI responded. "No." Brief pause. "I am sending mini-service-robots to the receiving bay to create new supports."

Not trusting the infant AI's judgment, Muni rushed towards the endangered ship-docking bay. The quickest route transversed the vermin-filled hallway. "AI, tranquilize the animals."

Muni saw none of the fearful creatures as he dashed through the corrupted hall.

Thousands of service-bots fluttered about the receiving area assembling new support struts. A quick inspection confirmed his worst fears. "They're not responding to the big picture."

AI said, "There are no big pictures on board."

It is as literal as an ordinary computer. "Another allegory." He directed AI to re-program the mini-robots; he then ordered the human's entrance to the main command center be sealed.

Muni spent hours restoring his ship. AI forced nourishment breaks. Even during those breaks, Muni supervised the mini-robots. Their work was too vital to risk any chance misstep.

Only after his ship was again space-worthy, did Muni head for the command center. *What should I do about the horrid aliens my stupid AI let on board? Worse, what about the ones corrupting my Planet of Giants? If only it were as easy to create a new bond with those creatures as it was to create supports for my ship.* Muni entered the command center; glided to the wall of names, the 'pictures' Simon had so reverently admired.

Muni lay supine, in full reverence, in front of the brightly emblazoned formal writing. The ship's resources were available to him anytime, anywhere within the vessel. Only here could he fully experience the solace of his loved ones. Muni concentrated both pairs of eyes on the array of signatures, as if doing so could conjure up the signatories.

Muni dwelt on the strange list of coincidences that led to his quandary: An ancient ancestor's gamble; the modern impoverishment of his family because of the appearance of an 'impossible' life-form; the nick-of-time return of said ancestor; this unexpected encounter with another intelligent race; and—the most unbelievable coincidence of all—an alien ship just happens to send an "all clear, help us board" signal to an inexperienced, fingerling-level AI who four-eyes-blindly does just that. *Uncle Bern, our ancestors could not have been more right. Coincidence rules the universe.*

Muni inhaled deeply. His whole body swelled to maximum and then deflated.

Avoiding Lor's rectangular signature, Muni stared at his rakish uncle's name. Lifting up his forward torso, Muni signaled with deliberate formality, as though still a child seeking advice from a teacher, "Uncle, what would you do? Do you believe the Universal Power enjoys toying with our family? If Ani-Orange grants those hideous creatures legal status, can our family avoid extinction?"

Muni's gaze slid down to Lor's lovely name. His desire for her brought intense physical pain. With muted colors he asked, "Lor, will you, do you, regret becoming my mate?"

Muni again eyed his uncle's signature. "Uncle, I need your help. You more than anyone always see connections to opportunities. Uncle, your conniving brain would be more valuable than all the entombed knowledge of our people."

Muni gazed at the whole array of names. "The spirits of my family have watched over me and allowed me to awaken. I am thankful. May they continue to watch me. May they continue to allow that Power which governs all life to guide me. I am Muni Indigo, Child of the Green Hill, Noble Adult of the Morgi, protector of the unlanded, guide to future generations. That which is necessary, the Universal Power will make possible, and **I will do.**"

Surprised how much calm confidence the formal words gave him, Muni looked with renewed hope at the wall of names. "It would be so much easier if I could just blast the vermin out of existence." Pain-filled longing stabbed his digestive track. "Lor, our wing-arms must entwine again. I will find a way for our clan, for you, for our children's children to live with great honor."

Muni enmeshed himself in all the information available about his unwelcome guests. AI provided him with translations from the alien computer-library, the messages from the distant "humans," and the remaining "people" on his ship. AI informed Muni about the micro-spies sent inward to Earth and its few colonies.

Muni, angry, protested, "It will be years before those probes can deliver information! How could you waste our limited resources?"

With perfect machine logic, AI replied, "If we fail, it won't matter how much we waste. If you succeed and become this sun's owner, we will need all the human knowledge we can get."

Muni intensified his study.

Because Morgi exchange information at the speed of light instead of the languid speed of sound; they assimilate complex information faster than any human speed reader.

Objects drop faster in Morga's heavier gravity; therefore Morgi reflexes are faster than any human's.

If an earthman had been able to watch him study, Muni's computer simulations would have been a blur.

AI accurately determined the relative importance of different parts of Earth history, and gave Muni a detailed account of the last hundred years with a sketch of the previous thousand years. After first speeding it up to Morgi-normal, AI showed three-dimensional images of human behavior while on board his ship; accompanied by equally accelerated visual translations of the humans' strange audio language.

In a few days, Muni mastered a century's worth of facts.

Only one fact mattered.

There was nothing, absolutely nothing, all the governing subgroups of humans agreed on.

Not language, legal code, religion, etiquette, nourishment preferences...

They couldn't even agree on what year it was.

How can I ever get each and every government to accept Green Hill subjugation?

If "The waters the fingerling swims in nourishes the grass the adult runs in." is as true for humans as Morgi, then perhaps the stories of their planet's early history will hold a key to unlock the secret for human cooperation.

Muni ordered AI to present ancient history, more human stories. The myths, so many...so varied...so old. Their history was more myth than chronicle. *Are humans aware of the depth of contradiction in their 'historical facts?'*

How could a civilization confined to only one solar system generate such convolution? How did they create so many myths for entertainment? In spite of the repulsive ugliness of the creatures, Muni loved their entertainments.

He became a theater junkie.

Muni could have spent years watching human entertainments. He especially like the ones that speculated what it would be like to finally encounter an E.T. None of the imagined E.T.'s resembled a Morgi.

Muni's research became more pleasure than study. For the first time in his life he understood the warning, "Deep study is like Deep Sleep; it is meant to prepare for battle, not hide from it."

"AI, it's time to stop studying humans and interact with one." Muni's whole body shuddered in dread. "Release additional relaxing chemicals into the human area."

Chapter 5

All but two of the creatures were relaxed into unconsciousness.

Muni prepared for his first diplomatic attempt. He programmed the walls to speak for him. Translations of the animals' slow sound-vibrational speech would be sent directly to Muni's brain.

Muni crept up to the two humans still awake.

One spoke. "What big eyes you have."

Good, Muni thought, *Storybook speech should be reassuring.* The wall gave Muni's reply. "The better to see you with."

The animal responded with the next line from the ancient human children's story. *This is going well*, Muni thought. The wall started to respond, "The better to—" Muni looked too closely at the spindly, two-legged creature. The thing was so stomach-churning repulsive…Muni remembered obnoxious flavor.

He fled.

Five days earlier.

Crew members took turns sitting by Dr. Frankfort's bed, holding her hand, talking to her. Each wondered if they were going to end up like her—or Simon.

They also persisted with their alien-communication attempts.

The crew plastered the hall with computer generated dot pictures of prime numbers, simple geometric shapes, binary code and additional mathematical messages.

Since there had been no further sightings of the monster, no one could tell if anything worked, or could work.

No one went anywhere alone.

Fear robbed everyone of sleep.

Yoko stood in the first pod, staring down the alien hallway's hollow emptiness. "Doctor Daniel Johnson, do you have a medical reason for why I find that—" She nodded towards the wide hall. "So terrifying?"

"You need a medical reason?" Doc looked puzzled.

Yoko said, "Yes, I need a medical reason. For months we felt more at home there than in our own ship. Suddenly, all of us prefer being here, especially in Botany Bay. Then *That Thing* woke. Now we are afraid of it, and everything else. Remember what happened when we went to retrieve supplies from the Grand Ballroom?"

"Yes, we grabbed only the few items near the entrance and ran all the way back here. No one's ventured more than a few feet beyond this pod since." He shuddered. "Who wants to risk seeing *It* again?"

Her voice louder, Yoko said, "Put your professional hat on, Dr. Johnson. We were too happy for months. *Before* the thing woke up, we were already afraid. Is it something we are breathing? Can you analyze our air? Can you give me something to make my feelings my own?"

Before Doc could answer, Jerrison's yell came over the speakers. "Look out the view ports!"

Doc and Yoko joined others at the nearest view port.

"The walls are growing struts. Bumble bees?" Yoko's sleep-deprived confusion was natural. Thousands of tiny, winged bumblebee-like robots were busily creating a scaffolding structure around their ship.

Days passed. The miniature flying robots put the finishing touches on a gigantic webbing that encased the three earthship modules and filled the mammoth amphitheater space.

The crew faded in and out of sleep, until only Jerrison and Doc were conscious. Both men were punch-drunk from sleep deprivation.

"Well, Doc," Jerrison said, "It looks like it's just you and me to figure this thing out; think we can do it?"

"Jerry," Daniel slurred, "I'd never let a patient down. And we're down the rabbit hole."

"It ignored our pretty pictures."

"Maybe it doesn't like dots. Dots are dull you know."

"If we're in a rabbit hole, maybe *It* thought the pictures were rabbit pellets. I wouldn't want to talk to anyone omethi' up rabbit pellets either."

"Me neither. You know what I think would be pretty?"

"No.""

"UNO cards. I'll grab my deck, get tacky glue. And let's make pretty designs."

Doc retrieved his special 'magnetic thins' UNO playing cards.

The two men, exhausted into half-deck brain power, tacky glued the deck of Uno cards in colorful arrays of green, yellow, red and blue between two of the alien hallway picture-signs.

Doc and Jerry stood back, arms on each other's shoulders, admiring their handiwork.

Jerry said, "That's nice."

Doc nodded agreement. "Yeah, they flow with the ship's pictures."

Jerry said, "Yeah, like somehow they say the same thing."

Doc frowned. "My eyes sting."

Jerry mumbled, "Close them."

"Can't, I'm supposed to watch something, no, for omething." Doc closed his eyes. "Can't see anything anyway, it's dark." He swayed, leaned against the wall, eyes tightly shut.

Both men almost join their friends in exhausted slumber.

An adrenalin-creating shadow loomed over them. Jerrison turned around, looked up.

Jerry knew he should be scared. "You're, you're not supposed..." he struggled with what the huge ferocious shape was not supposed to do. He stared up at the large, dark gray circle on the front of thing's neck.

The walls talked. "I come to serve all mankind."

The dark circle became darker, opened a little, revealing tips of very pointed teeth. Colors ran up and down both sides of its neck. The colorful swirls would have looked beautiful if the animal they were on didn't look quite so much like a humongous cutworm. A feeble "Help" emerged from Jerry as reality and nightmare merged. He fell, unconscious.

Doc's eyes opened wide at Jerrison's 'help.' He saw four eyes, each larger than his fist, wiggle down at him from short, stubby stalks. "My, what big eyes you have."

In stereophonic sound, the walls on both sides responded, "The better to see you with, my dear." It opened its mouth wide.

Doc looked straight into the dark center of that mouth. White triangles lined it, each gleaming tip pointing inward. "My, what sharp teeth you have."

The walls replied, "The better to eat—"

"—me up!" Doc screamed.

The giant cutworm turned, galloped down the hall and through a wall.

Doc stared; tried to tell if the encounter had really happened.

He remembered Simon. He remembered saw blade teeth.

Terror overwhelmed Doc; he sank to the floor, unconscious.

Doc's snoring woke Jerry. He walked slowly through the three pods. Disheveled crewmen lay scattered about, each one unconscious. *Could ordinary exhaustion be blamed? Did the ship subdue us with sleeping gas? Dr. Frankfort, at least, is better off unconscious.*

After inspecting the three pods, he returned to the hallway. Doc still snored beneath a collage of UNO cards. Jerrison stared at the deck of cards the two of them had plastered on the wall. He muttered to himself, "We glued every single card from the whole giant UNO deck on that wall. Why?" Trying to remember what had seemed so obvious while punch-drunk with insomnia, Jerry reached out to touch one of the cards… Jerrison shivered; he remembered a large shadow—just like the one looming before him—

Jerry twisted around. He looked up at the giant, slug-shaped alien. Its wing-arms remained tucked tightly against its body.

Jerrison stared at the eye level circle of gray he knew hid a meat grinder of razor sharp teeth. A pair of eerily human eyes focused on him and the playing cards. The second, cat-eyed pair scanned the hallway.

Jerrison squeaked, "Uh, hello." He felt like an ant looking up at a rapidly descending size twelve. The creature's skin on either side of its mouth shimmered into a faint yellow. A voice sounding to his ears like a cotton ball felt to his hands, emanated from the walls.

"oo-el-oh"

"Hello" Jerrison repeated.

"He-e-e-l-l-l-o-o" The wall dragged the word out slowly.

"Hello." Jerry wasn't sure if he was starting communication, or had simply stumbled onto a way to avoid being eaten.

"Hello." The wall responded, this time in perfect English. "An interesting attempt at communication. So much better than the simplistic number games done by your fellow earthmen."

Jerry squeaked, "Communication attempt?"

"The color pattern you attached to the wall here. I saw the recording of you doing it. You are very clever."

Muni found the isolation of the most common abstract symbol indicating an entrance interesting, but not really clever. He knew his disarming Uncle Bern would say something flattering to anyone with whom he wished to develop a working relationship. Complementing communication attempts seemed a good way to start. Muni looked down at the human sleeping on the floor. *Will it remember our aborted conversation?*

The standing human, with its painfully slow vocalizations, responded, "What, uh, who is talking to me?"

The walls again vocalized Muni's words. "My vocal cords do not easily make your sounds, so I have instructed the ship to communicate for me. Is it doing an adequate job?"

Muni already knew the ship communicated perfectly, but since he had no vocal cords and could not discern individual audio syllables; he decided it best to not betray any weakness.

Jerrison, his voice more normal, replied, "Yes, it is doing a very good job." *The creature that wildly flipped Dr. Frankfort through the air and devoured Simon, is talking to me like an English professor.* "May I ask why you are here?"

"The Council of Protectors sent me to guard the human race."

Jerrison stared at the creature's mouth covering. *Simon's feet disappeared into that maw.* "What?"

In stereophonic sound, the walls spoke, this time in such a deep, rich voice even Dr. Schmidt would envy it. "The universe is a large and dangerous place with many ferocious species. A young race like yours, just beginning to take its first baby steps to civilization, is vulnerable to the sharks of the galaxy."

Muni wondered, *Will the earthman recognize where those words came from?* The words came almost verbatim from an old entertainment transmission. In Earth's own stories Muni had discovered a way to salvage his mission.

Jerrison stared at Muni's mouth covering, visualizing the circle of deadly triangles hiding behind it. *Will I become its next meal? No guts, no glory.* "Your race must have an unusual idea what protection is. I have a crewman nearly dead, another who is dead and the rest appear more drugged than sleepy." He braced himself for teeth chomping down on his neck.

"The awakening process is always associated with violent upheavals. Your people were not to be on board until after I awakened. My ship, however, knows I am here to initiate your protection. When it determined your spaceship's integrity to be severely compromised, it invited you on board. Unfortunately, computers don't always think things through like we living, organic creatures do."

Jerrison asked, "Your ship reasons?"

The walls continued talking, but this time from only one side and a slightly higher pitch. "Sometimes. It is capable of abstract reasoning on a level about equal to a three-year-old child."

"Why didn't you announce you were coming?"

The wall now used the same somnolent tones as did the earthship's computer. "The Council of Protectors decreed a standard protocol."

Muni liked the image the phrase invoked in his mind. "By coming openly, yet with no fanfare, it would enable you to recognize us as real, and therefore adjust to our presence. We plan to increase our social interaction in small increments over the next two thousand years."

Muni rose slightly higher; his body inflated a hair more. The computer's voice sounded more masculine. "Conquering species would have sent their military. The most dangerous races enter looking like a rock or a comet. Too late, you would learn the truth." Muni remembered the Lurker, the most camouflaged predator on his home world. Muni felt fear.

Jerrison challenged, "Why haven't you let earth receive our reports?"

With patient gentleness, the broadcast continued. "We have much experience with immature races. Your people must learn about us gradually. Too much at once will choke your infant civilization into chaotic death."

Jerrison countered, "I know my people. Blocking communications will increase their suspicions, and their fear. Our human imagination will fill any void, and fear-inspired imagination is always..."

Jerrison sought a word capable of conveying the ugly depravities conjured by fearful people. Failing, he continued. "Fear blocks logic. If you want to communicate, remove as much cause for fear as you can."

As the internalized translator communicated Jerrison's response, Muni anticipated the human's words. His own people would surely respond to any attempted interference with suspicious hostility. Forcing himself to think of these repulsive, spindly creatures in friendly terms, Muni wished he had at least one personal experience with another truly intelligent species.

Again, Muni tried to imagine how Bern would respond.

Inspired, Muni continued. "Earth's interpretations will be entirely their interpretations, not contaminated by anything observed here. Even now, my ship is analyzing all the current data from your planet. Hopefully, these new additions to the psychological profile for your race will prevent misunderstanding. We want you to become a part of the Council of Protectors."

Muni's whole body shivered. *How many alien races hide among the stars?*

Muni revealed more. "We believe your race, in spite of its youthful indiscretions, has what it takes to grow, and help others grow. In twenty-four of your earth hours, you and your crew will be in complete two-way communication with your home planet. Decide what you will tell your follow humans. I will leave now; the rest of your crew will awaken soon." With that Muni glided away with such aristocratic smoothness even his mother would have been impressed.

"Wait! When will I see you again?" Jerrison shouted down the empty hallway.

The wall responded, "After you have resumed full communications with your home planet."

As soon as Muni was out of sight of the repulsive aliens, he allowed himself to express his true opinions of them. *It's hard to think friendly, welcoming thoughts! Yet, I dare not do less.*

The animals were clearly intelligent, in spite of their painfully slow means of communication. They had isolated the welcome/enter symbol from the door. They may have caught on to some of the simpler Morgi words.

What will the human creatures say to their fellow earthmen? I wish they didn't communicate with slow-motion sound waves! How can any intelligent creature endure waiting so long for each other to finish expressing a thought? Muni's computer could condense hours' worth of human conversation to minutes.

At least I won't have to participate while those humans so slowly vocalize every sound. Pleasure colors sparkled over his panels. *Instead I'll be watching more human entertainments! Properly speeded up, of course!* The fertile imagination of earth' alien civilizations fascinated Muni more with each story he viewed. "AI, show the next earth entertainment."

"First, may I ask a question?"

Now what? "Yes."

"Why do I have no information about the Council of Protectors?"

Muni flashed, "Some things you are expected to learn on the job." Muni had no desire to teach an infant AI the finer points of diplomatic embellishment.

From that moment on, AI spent every spare nanosecond comparing the many times either Morgi or human claims did not match perceived reality. Before Muni finished watching the first holographic movie, his AI ceased being an infant.

Chapter 6

Jerrison walked among his gradually awakening friends. They woke up calmly, matter-of-factly getting breakfast together, chatting about nothing in particular. How could his obviously drugged crew help him analyze what the alien said? Grabbing a juice bar, he went directly to Dr. Frankfort.

She lay alone; the IV system still hooked up. Her breathing was smooth; her skin looked better. Startled, Jerrison realized she looked even healthier than she did that long ago day they left earth.

He moved to a nearby mirror, examined his own face. He returned to the group.

"Shirl, you look radiant today!"

Shirl looked up, blinked. "Commander?"

Jerrison grinned at the others in Botany Bay. "Don't you all agree Shirl looks radiant? In fact, all of you are glowing. Even you, Dr. Schmidt."

The crewmen looked like they were forcing themselves to think. Jerrison could almost hear his grandmother's voice "Dust those cobwebs out of your brain!" They looked at Shirl and Dr. Schmidt; then at each other. Eyes grew wider. Ann, Melinda and Yoko rushed to the nearest personal area—and the mirrors mounted there.

"You've lost your crows feet."

"Your eyes have more color than before we left earth."

"Look, no lines by my chin!"

Jerrison laughed. "Aren't any of you lovely ladies going to comment on how handsome I've become?" He stopped smiling. "Speaking of looks, I've been talking with our ugly host."

Jerrison accurately conveyed the conversation he had with the alien. The questioning started. *Everyone seems rational,* Jerrison thought.

"So," summarized Yoko. "You believe we should trust this Alien because during our last sleep period we apparently experienced a fountain-of-youth?"

"Not just that," Doc said softly. "But the way that fits in with what it said. It has tried to make us comfortable. The ship followed standard procedures blindly. That means they have a naturally benevolent, healing mindset." He frowned. "More caring than the humans back home who deliberately sent us out in a defective ship."

Dr. Schmidt glanced towards Frankie's supine body. He countered, "It did not actually say those things. We have to be extremely careful we do not start confusing our conclusions with our observations. In fact, listening to you has convinced me exactly what we should transmit to earth."

All stared at him. Opinionated Dr. Schmidt never sounded so firm.

He continued, "We should send them a visual summary only, in compressed form of course, of *everything* that has happened since communications have been broken. Any words we say will modify how they interpret the data. The only verbal transcript will be Jerry's recital of the alien's conversation."

"No!" Ms. Davidson interjected. "Our reactions are as much a part of this as the hardware we are sitting on. We should do the visual as you suggest, but we should also include a personal reaction from each of us. Our combined perception will add to the accuracy of the report."

"My dear Ms Davidson, are you saying our combined perceptions of the first night here is more accurate than any individual one?"

Blushing (a feat which still fascinated her fellow crewmen), "No."

Dr. Schmidt asked, "Can you guaranty we are not under a similar influence now?"

"No," she turned towards Jerrison. "Captain, Schmidt is right."

Jerrison nodded. "Agree. Considering our emotional responses since we've been on board, I don't trust our judgments." He paused, spoke in formal tones. "Computer, compress all visual recordings from the moment the last human entered the alien vessel to this moment. When completed, begin to transmit to earth and all outposts between here and earth. Repeat transmissions until ordered to stop. End command mode."

He looked around at the others, breathed deeply. "That part is finished. At long last we know the universe is teeming with intelligent life. No wonder our SETI projects have failed. In a forest of wolves, you don't yell, 'I'm here! Supper's ready.' If one of those military conquering types had come first, our transmissions into space would have ceased almost immediately. Anyone capable of interstellar raids will surely be able to hide any evidence of their civilization from techno-babies like us."

Dr. Schmidt looked somber. "The universe is dangerous."

Chapter 7

The nearest inhabited station between Jerrison's small crew and Earth, was Jupiter One.

The spherical research outpost was designed to stay in orbit about its namesake. Two hundred fifty adults and twenty-seven children called Jupiter One home. They organized themselves more like a small town than a ship.

The adults on board Jupiter One had no idea if they were rescuers or sacrificial victims, but when they saw the alien vessel swallow up the Spaghetti and Meatball Special's crew, they decided unanimously—and against Earth's powerless orders— to reactivate Jupiter One's propulsion systems. Their ship pulled out of its orbit and headed towards the giant alien spaceship. Jupiter One's crew expected to intercept the alien's path in about a year.

It took a lot of energy to leave their stable Jupiter orbit; an easy task for its state-of-the-art fusion power plant.

When all SMS communication ceased, Earth's official leaders became strident, demanding Jupiter One return to the "safety" of Jupiter's orbit.

Unlike Earth's politicians, the Jupiter One crew had no illusions about anything being safe when confronted with an interstellar civilization. They kept going. For nine long months, they heard nothing from Jerrison or his crew.

Jupiter One's crew was shocked, then relieved, when Jerrison sent the alien's story along with the history of his crew's experiences aboard Muni's ship.

Like all earthmen, Jupiter One crew vigorously debated the veracity of Muni's tale. Given all the known facts: the obvious long familiarity with earth languages, the quiet-yet-obvious introduction to the solar system; his ship's desire to help people, even when on autopilot; the improved health of Jerrison's crew; the now perfect communications; and, most especially, the explanation for all this; they decided the alien's story could be true.

If Earth's first manned trip to the outer reaches of their solar system encountered an alien ship, the galaxy must swarm with intelligent life.

Earth's incompetent spaceship design had put the Spaghetti Special's crew in harm's way. Most accepted Simon's death and Frankie's injury as tragic accidents.

Jupiter One sent their conclusions to both the alien ship and earth. Eager to be to be part of the history-making alien encounter, the jubilant crew devised ways to increase their rotund craft's speed.

Both maintenance crew and resident scientists enthused about their anticipated alien close encounter, but Captain Silas Baxter, Jupiter One's official leader and unofficial dictator, sat alone in his room, sipping a hot drink, staring at his reflection.

So many times I've had conversations with you, he mused to his reflection. *All the times when I've dared not let anyone else on board know the full truth. Just talking to myself made it easier to guide the herd-of-cats scientists on board and my condescending maintenance crew; keep everyone a functioning, if not always happy, community.*

He inhaled the aromatic vapors of his drink; took a long, soothing sip. *Ever since I received Jerrison's first report, I've been denied the luxury of saying my own thoughts out loud, even here in my private study.*

Like all of Earth's spaceships, Jupiter One had no true privacy. Computer monitors quietly recorded, and continuously sent to Earth, everything; lest something happened that could expose all on board to the certain death that waited just outside its man-made shell. From the moment he had chosen to leave orbit, and head towards the alien, Captain Silas had no doubt his Earth-bound superiors would actively monitor his every minute.

That much Silas knew. He did not know about the nano-spies sent by Muni's AI that crawled about his ship, or the thousands of others already inhabiting every human outpost and earth itself.

No one on board, not even Silas's wife, knew the real reason the earth masters appointed Silas captain or his real training: subtle behavioral manipulations.

In the past, whenever the whole crew unanimously decided to do anything, it was because Earth officials had dictated to Captain Silas which decision they wanted. Silas simply found ways to entice the dominant person in each social subgroup to come to the desired conclusion.

Captain Silas Baxter was Earth's obedient puppet master.

Until now.

Not once, in handwriting, computer entry, or talking did the captain state his real reason for heading for the alien ship. Silas assumed an interstellar alien technology could easily spy on him. He knew earth did.

The captain held out his steaming cup to his image in the mirror. "You thought you were the luckiest man alive when you got this position. Here's to luck." He drank deeply. *We are going to need it!*

Captain Silas knew how to turn the efficient fusion-powered generators on board into an equally efficient fusion-powered bomb. He could do it from this room. The alien vessel dwarfed his; but if he got close enough, his tiny spacecraft could easily destroy that alien behemoth of a spaceship.

If the alien had even a hint his weaponless ship could itself be a weapon, Silas felt certain there would be no way he would be allowed to get too close. His mouth smiled; his eyes stayed sad. *The funny part is, I don't think anyone else on board, or on earth, sees my beautiful Jupiter One as a potential giant killer.*

On earth, others also recognized the need for secrecy. Each of Earth's governments made hidden transmissions a top priority—no more leaking radio waves into space.

Chapter 8

Muni waited. *Will I be believed?*

Waiting was much harder than acting.

Muni's training prepared him for dangers physical and biological, but now he felt the weight of social danger. His inner being ached with loneliness.

Muni returned to the Wall of Names. "I have finished studying all the entertainments these creatures brought with them; the histories on their ship's computers; the current news my ship intercepted.

"Oh family, these beings have so many stories filled with treachery and deceit! How have they survived when so much of their world is built on lies?

"Deep waters demand sharp eyes. Humans have so many cultures, so many depths of complexity; dealing with humans is the deepest water of all.

"If only such creatures had never been! This system would have been the refuge we need."

Looking at the names, all but Lor were older, more versed in the obscure social laws which are never written but tacitly learned through experience. Interstellar Explorers seldom needed such knowledge. *If only I could have remained an Explorer. I do not like intrigue.*

Muni gazed at Lor's lovely signature. "Lor, you are now part of my family. Do you regret our mating? Will our wing tips ever merge again?"

No testing or artificial practice could have prepared Muni for the reality of lives depending on him. Suddenly he understood why he, as a landed noble, had spent so much of his youth herding klieg in the primitive wild lands. His descendants would also herd. With love, Muni thought of ways to make herding even more challenging and miserable than it had been for him...if he had descendents...

Muni forced bravery into his next words. "AI, present everything the humans have said about me."

Muni read the latest transcriptions of all the on-board human conversations, everything from Jupiter One, the colonies on Mars and Earth's moon, and Earth's transmissions. He could not believe his success.

Humans believed him.

Muni broadcasted to the entire human race. "Greetings, Children of Earth. I am pleased to learn you have passed a most important test. You have faith in what I shared, but the faith did not come easily.

"Those races who are too trusting, who believe without debate, are too limited. We can help protect them from the dangerous, preying races in the galaxy, but they are too simple to help others in return.

"Those species incapable of trust are in reality revealing their own untrustworthiness.

"Your race has revealed itself to be that rare ideal that makes it worth saving now and, when you become mature, will make humanity a valued addition to The Council of Protectors.

"I am glad circumstances forced contact earlier than normal. I am honored to be your first liaison officer. Three hours from now I will give a presentation in the central communication room showing how faster-than-light travel is possible. Save all technical questions for then.

"I will now answer questions from the humans on my ship and those in Jupiter One. Jupiter One crew, you may have the first question."

TO OWN TWO SUNS

Captain Silas asked, "Did you plan your arrival time to coincide with our long-range explorer?"

"No, at the time I entered my starship your explorer vessel had not yet started construction. I have been hibernating for years. My ship, of course, has been in continuous communication with both home and our probes in your system. It updated me as soon as I fully awakened." The floor console located near Muni indicated that the respiratory and endocrine systems of his on board humans implied acceptance of his reply. "Next question? Someone from this ship"

"Do you have a name?" Yoko asked.

"Thank you for asking, Yoko. My family name is not easily translatable, but my personal name is Muni. It has no particular significance; my family simply liked its image when I was first..." He almost said hatched, which the computer would have accurately translated, "Born." Again the console indicated positive body responses.

Dr. Schmidt's baritone broke in while Muni still 'spoke.' "Why did you take so long before helping us with Dr. Frankfort? I can understand how the accident first happened, but not why it took so long for you to help. If you have been watching us for as long as you claim, your medical knowledge should be as advanced, no, more advanced than ours."

Dr. Schmidt stood. "If Dr. Frankfort had broken her neck on earth or even Jupiter One, she would be walking around with a brace before this; her neck almost healed. Instead, she may look younger, but her neck is just as broken as when we first rescued her." He raised his voice. "You say you are here to protect us. Prove it!"

AI relayed strong negative reactions to Dr. Schmidt's words. *These beings switch emotional tracks with such alarming swiftness. Dr. Schmidt's right. If I'd told it to, my ship could have healed Dr. Frankfort in hours. Why didn't it?* He was about to blame AI when he remembered the Morgi proverb 'When most defenseless, go boldly.'

Muni forced his forward part upwards, inflated his already massive torso, and fully flared all four wing-arms.

Communication panels flashing brightly, the speakers in both vessels spoke in a deeply bass male voice. "Then you would have done wrong. Yes, she would have been pressed quickly back into service, but we protectors do not think in the short term.

"Our civilization has not endured since before your sun first ignited by thinking short term! My actions shocked her whole body. Her whole body needs to recover.

"In curing her, I also cured all of you of many small injuries your bodies have accumulated. You call it 'growing old.' The air you share with her contains the deep down cure. When she is ready, the ship will allow her to awaken gradually. She will feel better than she has since her body ceased its normal growth cycle."

The voiced softened, went up an octave. "Forgive my outburst. We who have been trained since birth to be protectors become excessively emotional at any harm to those we are sworn to protect. When I saw the damage I had done, the distress grew so powerful," He allowed a pause. "It is fortunate my training includes all disasters. My ancestors once thought an unemotional protector would be better, but discovered otherwise before your planet coalesced from primordial dust.

"Real beings, with real feelings, who make mistakes, can better understand you foolish young ones. Remember, we ancient ones see both problems and solutions in the long term." He paused. "In exactly three hours the main control room, what you labeled The Grand Ballroom, will be open to The Spaghetti and Meatball Special Crew." Muni broke contact.

All sensor readings indicated the humans still believed everything he said. Muni rippled over to the wall of names. "Uncle, all those lectures you, my parents and teachers gave me, paid off." Pink laughter swirled about his communication panels. The response he gave to Dr. Schmidt was an almost verbatim repetition of one of the favorite hyperboles with which Morgi lectured sub-adults. Muni wiggled joyfully across the floor, his suction feet gripping and popping off the floor in rhythm with his heart. "The earth animals believe me!"

For the first time since awakening, he dared hope.

Chapter 9

"Muni is right. We do force too many 'cures' onto bodies before they are ready for them. We do need to learn patience." Doc solemnly intoned. "How old do you think he is?"

Yan spoke with awe in his voice. "No way of knowing. If just the air we breathe is the fountain-of-youth, they must be nearly immortal. Just think, a continuous civilization with a history not thousands, or millions, but billions of years. China is an infant compared to them. Our whole planet, barely a newborn."

Several murmured assent. Dr. Schmidt kept quiet.

Three hours later Jerrison's entire crew, except Doc and the still unconscious Dr. Frankfort, waited at the locked door of the room they had once called the Grand Ballroom.

The door ceased to exist.

A re-play would later reveal it had dissolved from the center outward too rapidly for human eyes to detect.

They walked in. The once familiar room looked the same, but felt alien.

"Muni, do you mind if we transmit your talk to earth and its outposts?" Jerrison inquired.

"Of course not," the walls replied as Muni stood before them, wing-arms tucked in, his head held low, trying to look friendly, but coming across as gargantuan four-eyed cutworm. Or sea slug. "I want you to be comfortable. I want all humans to understand what I am about to show you. It will not relay well with your equipment, so your fellow humans must rely on what you tell them. First, I want you to watch one of our child-teaching programs. It shows a simplistic two-dimensional rendition of the known universe and the physics that makes faster than light flight possible."

The room darkened. A faintly glowing rectangle about the size of a ping-pong table appeared before them. A bright red border highlighted a small, one-centimeter wide rectangle in its center.

"Each time the red rectangle enlarges, that section of space is magnified 64 times." The outline grew to match the outer boundaries. Broad gray streaks covered the pale top. Again, the center had a new rectangle, which grew. This happened with so many rapid repetitions, the 'table top' seemed solid red. The changes slowed.

The next rectangle revealed a pattern the crew recognized as the local group of galaxies.

The enlargements resumed.

A spiral galaxy took center stage.

Then a galactic arm; a single solar system; a single, rapidly rotating star.

The star shrunk in on itself while radiating a tremendous amount of light. A blue-line shot up perpendicular to the table.

Countless tiny blue dots spread above the 'tabletop.' The scene on the table changed quickly, the previous sequence in reverse until within seconds it returned to the original view. The blue dots sprinkled down onto the table.

The scene returned to the view of the local group of galaxies. Blue dots scattered sparsely into intergalactic space. Very rarely a dot entered a galaxy.

"You watched a black hole leave our universe, evaporate. Its ashes then scatter themselves across our universe. The reentering matter normally enters the most empty space it can find. At first our early scientists assumed that was because there is so much more empty space. Then our scientists deduced space is weaker where there is little matter, permitting easier entrance into our universe.

Sometimes a particle as large as an electron, or even larger, reenters our universe. When this happens it has enough momentum to slice the interstellar space within a galaxy, creating a blue-line crack. Space ships can enter these cracks. The particle's angle of entry determines the apparent speed of any solid objects within the blue-line crack.

"A ship that is really traveling at one-thousandth the speed of light will show up at its destination as though it had been traveling tens of thousands of times faster. All cracks are permanent and there is no way to modify them, either as to destination or the speed at which they allow you to go. Most trips are planned using a mixture of several blue-line cracks and ordinary flight. Sometimes, not often, new cracks are found.

"We cannot tell if the new discoveries are old routes newly discovered, or new creations. An especially brave breed of interstellar scout continuously looks for these pathways. When a path is discovered, all information is relayed to the nearest member world. Then the scout follows the spatial crack. It is possible to go in and out of it, but again the traveler can never change his apparent speed or direction while in it.

"Most routes are of little social value. Only a few connect solar systems with rocky planets of the right size, the right distance from a sun to become homes to beings like us. For whatever reason, with all our million years' experience, we have never had a sustained social interaction, good or bad, with any of the intelligences who have evolved in extreme gravitational or temperature environments. The few paths joining earth-like systems are valuable and highly coveted.

"At light speed, it would have taken me over five hundred earth years to arrive here, Using several blue-line paths plus traveling at sub-light speeds between those paths, it took only eighty seven years to arrive here. Your planet's distance is listed in our council records as eighty years distant, not five hundred twelve light years distant.

All official Galactic distances are measured not in light years, but in time-paths. Two stars at opposite ends of the galaxy, but connected by a high-speed path, will think of themselves as neighbors. Two others that are only ten light years apart, but can be reached by only conventional means, will see themselves as distant.

"We discovered your system to have not one but three paths near it. When the representatives for this sector learned this, they decided to contact your race immediately rather than wait until you had true space flight.

"You are in great danger. Your solar system is one of the most valuable in the galaxy. It would be easy for a rogue race to wipe out your civilization and take ownership of the three paths."

The science Muni described was an accurate simplification from the time Muni's distant ancestors first left their home planet. Since then, the Morgi had learned a few more tricks.

If there were more than one path associated with Earth's solar system, it would make it beyond value. The Morgi knew of none with three, and only one with two.

Muni hoped his hyperbole would force humans to act sooner—-hopefully soon enough...

"Where is the blue stuff when it is not in our 'real' universe?" Alan couldn't contain his excitement. While the others were questioning the meaning of everything, he felt a powerful "ah ha!"

"Where there is no first or last, bigger or smaller, past or future. All that fully enters there returns evenly scattered across the universe. No more questions about that.

"When you are ready for more, you will have already figured out most of the answers for yourselves. We would normally have never told this much to so a young race, but the great danger your planet is in forced us to speed up our timetable by thousands of years. Right now you have a more important problem." Muni paused dramatically. "Will you qualify for our protection, and if you do, will it be as a dependent race or as a future full member of the Council of Protectors?"

"I thought you said that we would become members and you are here to protect us." Jerrison interjected.

"Help is being offered; it will not be forced. There are thousands of infant races in the galaxy. Even with our billions of years, there are not sufficient resources to protect all, especially the ones that will not accept us. I have said more than is deemed prudent, but have so loved your planet, I bent the rules, hoping your people will understand and vote for membership."

Alan's slow drawl interrupted. "If the benefits of membership are so great, why would anyone ever turn you guys down? What's the catch?"

Muni was startled that it was the 'cowboy' Alan who voiced the first objection. From AI's analysis of their conversations, he had expected the first objection to come from Dr. Schmidt. Muni remembered the first rule of negotiation, "Ask and watch."

Muni mimicked his most exasperating teacher. He swiveled both pairs of eyes towards Alan. Muni's wall-speakers blared, "Do you remember how I said you passed the first test? What did I say?" The emotional impact was the same as if Muni himself had thundered the words.

Alan, exaggerating his Texan accent, said, "You said we have the right balance of paranoia and trust. Well, I spent most of my young earth life in Argentina and Texas, where people hear lots of words whenever outside 'help' is forced on them. While a teenager, I ran a rodeo business. Whenever someone came to me and said 'Alan, I like you. Because of that, I'm going to give you something for free,' I learned to get real suspicious, real fast. Now if what you just told us about a three-way conjunction is true, we are like an Indian tribe who happens to have a mountain of gold on their reservation. Maybe we can trust *you*, but can you really speak for the leaders back home?

Will your bosses want to take over our civilization 'for our own good'?"

The mood of the humans shifted.

Muni could not believe his good luck. He thought it would be hours before he could reach this negotiating point.

"You are right. You can't trust any agreement that relies only on the good intentions of another. All races, all peoples harbor those who seek only personal gain. In all groups, if you look close enough, there is both the very best and the very worst of what drives desires. Our trade negotiations are guided by three principles." The air above Muni became shadowed. Glowing words materialized in that shadow as Muni recited:

There is no such thing as something for nothing.

He who teaches such a belief is guilty of fraud.

He who takes without giving is guilty of theft.

"You are truly superior. You are right to not trust our charity. You will be expected to give something of value in return for our protection. It will be major enough to justify our protection. It will be minor enough to be affordable." He paused a full minute. The humans remained silent.

"We will need complete and total control of your planet Mars and its satellites."

A collective gasp.

The crew looked at their captain.

Captain Jerrison nodded to Alan, who nodded back.

Alan said, "What would somebody with the resources of the galaxy at their finger-tips want with a cold, barren planet like Mars?"

Muni's head bobbed as the walls spoke. "Planets that are or can easily be made hospitable to life forms chemically similar to ourselves are common. But those not already inhabited by an intelligent race are rare. We can easily make Mars habitable. Since you have only a few underground outposts on it, you won't miss Mars. We, The

Council of Protectors, will simply lay ownership claim to some of the debris beyond Pluto, guide it to Mars, and make it hospitable for a small outpost."

Alan interrupted, "Like a trading post, with maybe a small military base for our protection."

Muni said, "Wonderful! You are familiar with the concept."

Alan drawled, "Geronimo was." At his companions' blank looks he added, "An early Texan military expert."

"Wasn't he an Indian?" Jerrison asked.

In the brief second between Alan's answer and Jerrison's question, Muni silent-flashed, "AI, who was Geronimo and how could someone from India become a famous Texan military expert?" The information he had gleaned from the earthship's computers implied that combination to be highly unlikely. He watched a biography of Geronimo while waiting for the humans to continue their so slow, speed-of-sound conversation.

Simon answered, "Yes."

Eyes widened, chins tilted up slightly, looks were exchanged. A wiser group re-focused on Muni.

AI informed Muni the emotional tone of the group had shifted to deep distrust.

Muni's thoughts swirled. *Do they fear being banished from their own system the way Geronimo was exiled from his beloved desert country to the swamps of Florida? Or are they only worried about Mars and the possibility of there being something valuable beyond Pluto?*

If only I hadn't claimed to be a long-time student of earth, I could ask.

Muni remembered one of Uncle Bern's negotiation stories, 'It was almost impossible to get them to deliver at our price unit until I started arguing about packaging styles. They were so busy focusing on the unimportant; we easily negotiated the important items in our favor.'

Muni forged ahead with a red-herring demand just as he imagined his Uncle Bern would do.

"Your colonies on Mars will need to be evacuated. It will be too dangerous to stay on the surface while we increase its atmosphere; even the underground cities will be endangered. The humans on Mars should be compensated for their inconvenience. It is, of course, customary for the local government to pay such compensation."

A skeptical Jerrison asked, "What do you mean 'of course' the local government will pay?"

Muni explained, "It will not only be expensive to evacuate the people, but a responsible civilization would want to compensate the Mars colonists for their personal emotional distress." The wall spoke in the same tones used in an entertainment called The Court of Judge Wapner the Fourth. "Your leaders would be more capable of determining a culturally fair amount than any outside observer ever could."

Alan looked intently at Muni. "Two points. One, if you've been watching us for a 'long time', you should have an idea what fair compensation is. Two, you should also have a reasonable expectation our governments might not be 'fair.'"

"Besides" Dr. Schmidt spoke up. "You could obviously do the evacuation more quickly and easily than we could. The removal of people 'for their own safety' would go a long way to proving your good intentions." Dr. Schmidt folded his arms in front of his chest. "Unlike the last time you 'removed' a human."

How would Bern defend himself? He wouldn't! He would act like eating the human was a good thing. Muni silent-flashed to AI, 'Make my voice righteously powerful.'

Muni held his front half higher. His body swelled. "Your own people almost 'removed' your entire crew because money that should have been spent on your ship's construction, instead bought a yacht."

Muni spread out his wings, tips quivering. His mouth opened wide; teeth clashed. "'The *best shepherd is a dangerous shepherd.*' Would you rather trust me, or those who sent you here, underpowered and under-protected?"

Schmidt continued his protest. "You're saying my choice is between being your fodder, or my own race's cannon fodder."

Muni flared all four wing-arms. "You now know three things you did not know before.

"You know why my civilization has chosen to reveal itself to you sooner than we otherwise would have.

"You know you have the potential to become a full partner of The Council of Protectors.

"You know the price of that membership.

"Leave, discuss this with Jupiter One. Discuss it with Earth. Since it will take time to complete any dialog with earth, our next discussion will be in forty-eight of your hours."

The lights in the vast room dimmed, only the hallway remained brightly lit. All tried to ask more questions, but Muni remained silent. The room darkened, lit only by light spilling from the hallway. The humans exited.

Muni ordered the entrance sealed.

Once back in Botany Bay, Jerrison verified all the transcripts were sent. It would be hours before they heard from earth itself, but Jupiter One should be communicating soon. Satisfied earth would receive everything sent, Jerrison joined his crew's active debate. Even Doc left his patient to participate in the verbal melee.

Yoko protested, "I think it's fair, a planet for a planet, and we get to keep the bigger one."

Yan countered, "Are you daft? For all we know, maybe Mars is the most valuable piece of real estate in our solar system."

Doc said, "If they want the planet so badly, they should pay the cost of getting it."

Alan's Texan drawl carried over everyone else's chattering. "If the danger we are in is as great as Muni implied, then the price is cheap. If the danger's non-existent, then giving up an asteroid would be too much."

"At last," Dr. Schmidt said, "Someone is asking the real question. *Are we in great danger?* And from whom? If I recall my history, sometimes rescuing missionaries were as much a danger as the 'evil exploiters and marauders.' We need some way to test what we are being told." Uncharacteristic anger filled his voice. "Too much debate has assumed all we've heard is the truth."

"What is everyone arguing about?" A confused looking Dr. Frankfort walked into the room.

"Frankie!" A grinning Dr. Schmidt ran towards her, arms encompassing her in a bear hug. He stood back, hands on her shoulders, beaming. He spoke quietly in Portuguese; she replied.

He grinned and kissed her, something no one on board had ever seen him do.

She smiled shyly back at him, an ingénue's smile, and softly replied in more Portuguese.

Later the computer would translate their conversation for any who asked, but for now the obscure language gave the two Brazilians privacy in a crowded room. Holding her hand like a nervous school boy, the normally boisterous Dr. Schmidt led her to the seat affording the best view of the larger computer screen. He then requested a summary of all that had happened since her nearly fatal encounter.

Dr. Frankfort stared silently when the screen finally blanked. She cautiously raised her hand to feel the back of her neck, running her fingertips lightly up and down the spinal cord, and then over her face. "I feel as though I've never been sick, never injured, in my entire life. A life," She raised her eyes to Dr. Schmidt's, "That feels very worth living."

Doc asked, "It didn't feel worth living before?"

"Only a shadow of what it feels like now." She glanced at the archaic paper Peebles was characteristically writing on. She read what he wrote so softly that only their collective silence permitted her voice to carry.

"Can we trust Muni?

"Can we trust the civilization he came from?"

Just as softly she answered.

"Yes we can, and yes we can. All their technology has been helpful to us, the one flaw, the awakening insanity—Simon—not their fault." Her hand touched her neck. "This problem was not just corrected but made better. His actions are his defense. His willingness to not force our decision, his race's defense. Yes, and again yes, we can trust him, and them."

Just then they heard from Jupiter One. Most on board believed Muni.

Place: Muni's Control Center
Time: Just after the humans exited

MUNI WATCHED THE HUMANS dawdle out into the hallway. As soon as the door sealed, Muni sank to the floor, exhausted. The ship increased the air pressure and oxygen content in the room.

Fight-or-flight hormones surged through Muni's body.

Muni wanted to chase wild game. He wanted a simple to-the-death struggle with a vicious animal.

He did not want another human encounter, ever.

The emotional swings of these human creatures were unbelievable. Only one thing had delayed immediate total mission failure: the humans' slow audio communication. Muni knew he lived on borrowed time.

"AI, set course for Mars, least time route. Have the prospecting drones been manufactured?"

"Yes. They are ready for launch."

"Good, begin launching immediately."

Thousands of drones would seek objects in the nearby Kuiper belt with either a high percentage of greenhouse gas material or a high percentage of water ice. If the object had sufficient mass, a drone would alight and power it into a Mars's intersection orbit. Muni had been deeply relieved when the computer informed him it would not be necessary to go any farther out. His home-planet had long ago depleted such time-saving easy pickings.

Normally, a mined asteroid would be sent on a twenty-year low-energy path into the inner solar system, but these would be powered all the way to Mars. The Kuiper object should arrive at break-neck speed in only months. Some of the asteroidal mass would be utilized as fuel, but there would be thousands of tons left in each asteroid. Mars would never be the same.

The heat of impact will melt the frozen submartian groundwater; the melted groundwater will mix with vaporized water-rich comets. New water from above comingling with old water from below will create rain. Fallen rain drops will merge into streams; the streams, into rivers; the rivers, into seas. The new oceans will last a million years. Long enough.

Long enough, but not soon enough...unless the humans...

"AI, why are the humans so healthy?"

"Since they are your livestock, I have been protecting your investment. Do you wish me to continue doing so?"

"Yes, these animals must trust me. If there isn't a working agreement when our colonizer gets here, the government rep on board will declare our claim null and void. Can you cure the one creature's broken neck?"

"The female's neck has already been fixed. I manufactured nanobots just to treat her; in addition I eliminated the artificial drugs with which the humans attempted to flood her. She should be awakening soon and in perfect order."

"You really have been taking care of them just like we would doctor livestock back home."

"Of course."

Even after watching many entertainments, Muni remained totally mystified as to how humans could tell one another apart, much less male from female. He tried guessing which were male, which female, but AI claimed he was only right about half the time. Evidently, even the most extreme color differences had nothing to do with sex.

"Do you think so much of their fiction has to do with sexual matters because there is so little difference between them?"

AI flash-replied, "I will work on that problem. Speaking of problems, what will happen to your clan when these humans realize you have been telling them a false story?"

"How could that happen?"

AI flash-responded, "You surely remember, a story built on a lie is like sand on the beach—"

Muni completed the ancient proverb. "The first wave of truth washes it away."

Muni trotted back and forth. *How can I create dams against those waves of truth?* "AI, if I should ever be about to say anything to the humans that would contradict anything else I've told them, please inform me immediately. Do not translate to them until you have fully explained the contradiction so I can keep things simple for the humans." Muni wondered why he didn't tell AI the real reason, so he could keep his story straight.

"Acknowledged. The other human ship just replied."

"Flash a translation of all on board and inter-ship communication."

In seconds, Muni read a transcript of hours' worth of human conversation.

"AI, do the humans believe me because you fixed him?" *Could any species smart enough to leave its home planet really be so gullible?*

"That one was female. And yes, the tension in the room shifted when she arrived."

"The other ship is debating the terms of the Mars swap, not if I'm going to get it! It's working! After they hear about the female's cure they will be even more trusting." Stressing the word female slightly to show he did remember. *If only she weren't the exact same color as the dominant male!*

"Past experience indicates you are correct."

"AI, sort through our legal histories for all documents of the type that made one clan subservient to another for an indefinite period of time."

"Such documents are illegal. Subservience must be performance dependent with a well-defined moment of termination. The other option is absorption of the dependent clan."

"That is true today, but not fifty thousand years ago. I am officially operating under the laws followed by my ancestor who discovered this system. I want to read everything you find from back then."

Muni paused. *AI sent out thousands of micro spies. I have sent thousands of drones searching out Kuiper objects. My spaceship was not designed to become a major manufacturing facility.* "AI, we need to replenish the raw resources we used making drones. Send explorers to retrieve heavy metal rich Kuiper objects."

Muni spent the next hours speed reading ancient legal documents; more hours writing contracts, and still more time letting AI proofread all he wrote.

Muni hoped that if presented as a fait accompli, humans would agree to subservience to his Green Hill Clan. Everything owned by humans would then be property of the Green Hill Clan.

Two days later

"AI, THE EARTH'S GOVERNMENTS have jointly issued a counter-proposal for my Mars Acquisition! They're focusing on the colonies, not the planet!" Looking up at his Uncle's name, he brightly flashed, "Thanks Uncle Bern!"

Chapter 10

What a difference a year made!

Jerrison sprawled out on a luxurious lounge chair in Jupiter One's plant-filled park, its largest recreation area, reading a printed copy of Muni's treaty.

Muni's sunward traveling ship had intercepted the approaching Jupiter One months earlier. Muni grafted the huge craft onto the front nose of his space ship, enabling both vessels to rotate about the same common axis. He also, "for greater efficiency," merged its controls with his own ship's. Muni's AI now controlled Jupiter One's power plant.

From the outside, Jupiter One looked like a barnacle on the nose of a whale. Made a human feel humble.

Jerrison's crew appreciated both the improved lifestyle and increased social life. One of the most generous things the crew of Jupiter One had done was find a private cubicle for each crew member.

Jerrison's gaze drifted over the many shrubs and plants, each one edible, wondering why, now that he again had his coveted privacy, he spent most of his free time in Jupiter One's common areas; even when, like now, he was engaged in solitary activity.

For the hundredth time, Jerrison read a printed copy of the *Earth-Morgi Promise of Allegiance & Performance.*

Muni's assurance that certain phrases were "just a matter of tradition" seemed acceptable to the earth-based politicians, but not to Jerrison.

Everyone wanted to believe Muni.

Some pretended to believe Muni, because they felt powerless against his obvious technical superiority. Others feared Muni's threat to abandon them. Too many believed Muni because he was "nice."

From the moment Jerrison first boarded the Jupiter One, he wondered, *If it had been important to protect humans from Muni's insane awakening, why didn't the ship simply close the door on them?*

When the first icy meteors bombarded Mars just minutes after evacuating the final colonist, Jerrison thought more people would have second thoughts. Instead, the news reports were all a gush about how thoughtfully Muni had arranged the evacuation. As Jerry snapped the paper straighter, a white square fluttered down onto his lap, followed by Shirl's laughter.

"Why so glum?" Her upside-down grinning face leaned over him.

Jerrison said, "Because something still doesn't fit."

Shirl said, "Hey, even Dr. Schmidt is happy with the way things are."

Jerrison said, "Dr. Schmidt's been happy ever since he was not only given a second chance, but 'the divine opportunity to know' he needed a second chance. I don't think he's quit acting like a love struck teenager." Jerrison picked up the annoying paper Shirl dropped. He read, *'The walls have eyes and ears. You're right, something about Muni doesn't add up.'*

"Jerry, you should come with me to see just how well Muni socializes. You've seen Muni with the children from Jupiter One?"

Jerrison replied, "Of course."

One of the teenage boys from Jupiter One initiated the first child-Morgi encounter. He quickly spread the word how "beyond the iciest of ice cool" Muni was. In less than an hour all the teens were with Muni. Muni asked to meet the smaller children as well.

Jupiter One's crew agreed, providing Muni would let them broadcast the first encounter. Viewers saw an instant bonding:

children climbed over Muni's back, sat on him like small monkeys on an elephant, and tried to wrap arms around his too-large head.

Earth's response included things like "the natural instincts of innocent children" and "obvious grandfatherly patience."

Jerrison remembered Frankie flipped against a wall; Simon's feet disappearing…

Shirl interrupted Jerry's ruminating. "Let's watch the weekly update in my room." With that Shirl casually picked up all the papers and led him to her new cubicle.

THE BROADCAST SHOWED Muni in his central communications center speaking to Alan and Yan, plus about a dozen crew from Jupiter One. As usual, small children were climbing on Muni, even while he lectured. All attention focused on Muni; the walls spoke.

"Asteroids continue to impact Mars. The energy of the encounters has melted both Martian polar caps, releasing liquid water. Shockwaves from the barrage are driving massive amounts of dust into the air. Something that has not happened in millions of years is taking place. It is now raining on Mars. Millions of additional tons of water, ammonia, and other nitrogen compounds are bombarding the atmosphere. By the time we arrive, grass will be growing."

The humans quietly nodded their heads until Muni's last sentence.

"Grass?"

"Where did the grass come from?"

"What kind of grass?"

Muni lifted one wing-arm to demand silence. "Robot ships released seeds. This grass draws nutrients directly from inorganic minerals and releases oxygen into the air. I also seeded Mars with special bacteria that will thrive in the newly wet Martian soil. The bacteria and the grass will have a synergistic effect on each other; both will thrive vigorously."

A Jupiter One crewman asked, "Why not wait, have us plant the grass in the best places? In the long run it could save both time and resources."

Jerrison's people looked offended when that crewman questioned Muni's wisdom.

Jerry wrote to Shirl "When did my crew start being blindly loyal to Muni?"

"Not sure," she wrote back. "Watch how he answers."

Muni's panels started to swirl colors, went blank, started again, blanked, and then colorful as walls spoke.

"There are sufficient resources for both. When we send a crew to the surface, things should be stable enough to pick a spot for a large farm. Until we get there, life has a way of finding its own niches better than it can with artificial guidance."

One of his 'fingers', the wing extensions that had once reminded the SMS crew of Medusa's snakes, tousled the hair of the child astride the middle of his back. The small boy giggled. "Every method will be employed. Robots in the Kuiper belt still seek additional high oxygen and water objects. Those will be propelled towards Mars as they are found."

WHILE WAITING FOR A human to finish talking, Muni ordered the computer to start growing more seed stock. It had not occurred to him these humans could accelerate the Martian project. Young humans reminded him of his early herding days. That made the creatures easier to accept, but even harder to see the spindly two-legged animals as responsible adults.

"DID YOU SEE IT?" SHIRL asked aloud as she wrote, *'the pause? They're getting longer every time he's asked to explain an action.'* Shirl continued. "He never says 'just trust me'; he always comes up with explanations." She wrote, *'or excuses? Or keeping his story straight?'* She continued, "Allowing the small children to hang out with him could just be a good public relations ploy, but they really do relax him. We've still seen only two corridors in his ship; we know almost nothing of his culture. When Ann asked if they have stories or poetry, he brushed her off. The few times he seeks personal conversation instead of a lecture, it's almost always with one of the teenagers. The explanation that he prefers their 'untainted world view' just doesn't fit."

"Of course I saw it." He said aloud, as he wrote, *'I think you're right about his having to check his story. His choice of companions implies similar emotional levels. He seems less superior.'*

They continued to watch.

At first the interview went as expected. Then, it changed.

Muni's communication panels grayed.

White swirled into the gray. Then a dizzyingly rapid series of color changes and complex geometric patterns flashed about his neck.

Muni reached up and gently removed each child from his back.

Before the last child finished touching the floor, Muni rushed away faster than any human had ever before witnessed. He vanished through a wall.

Shirl and Jerry glanced at each other. The last time anyone had seen that illusion was when they first met Muni—and that was in slow motion compared to what they had just witnessed.

The group of people Muni deserted looked confused.

The Liaison Officer from Jupiter One spoke into the camera. "Does anyone have any idea about what just happened? Has something gone wrong?"

Most of the ship had not been watching the routine interview, but word spread quickly.

No one could tell if Muni's ship had any problems. Alan Peebles said, "For all we know, the equivalent of an overheated boiler might be ready to blow, and all we notice is that it's pleasantly warm."

Jerrison ordered, "Everyone to Jupiter One, we know she's not going to blow!" In less than a minute every human fled Muni's ship as they hurried to the main 'Park' in the rotund Jupiter One. Shirl and Jerry raced back to Jupiter One's Park.

As they entered the large space, the sound of arguing voices hit them like a rushing wave of water.

MUNI GALLOPED TO HIS alternate control level. All other levels in the ship were at earth normal gravity. He had re-designed this level to rotate faster. The faster rotation gave the illusion of Morga normal weight. Experiencing his birth-world's gravity protected his emotional as well as his physical strength.

Once there, he replayed AI's message. His robot drones had destroyed an artifact of unknown origin in the outer fringes of the Kuiper belt.

His nervous system trembled as though he had just spotted a Lurker; he remembered the many explorer-scouts who left the known worlds, to never return.

His back felt open to unseen claws.

"AI, present all information on the destroyed artifact."

"When you indicated the desire to harvest raw manufacturing materials, I reprogrammed three drones to heat-seek radioactive objects since all such asteroids would naturally be heavy element rich. The drones honed in on that object's warmth.

"When one alighted on it, the object sent a signal outward.

"Master Morgi code activated; the drone destroyed it. I sent two message capsules; one to Morga, the other to the colonizer following us, with details of the encounter. The object sent the signal to a specific point in the outermost part of the Oort cloud. A max-speed drone is heading there."

"AI, show all visuals of the object and all available analysis of its signal."

Muni spent the next hour watching and re-watching the tantalizingly brief recording of the hoarfrost coated artificial satellite.

The object appeared to be a natural object during a cursory long-distance scan. On closer inspection, it would have been thought to be a derelict if it had not activated itself and sent its highly directional signal.

"AI, slow down the moment of destruction, thousand to one ratio."

He watched as thin frost evaporated and the heavy dust coating scattered, revealing metal and glassy black protrusions, which separated along existing demarcation lines. The opened sphere revealed crystals, shimmering components, and black nodules. Energy flared. Everything disappeared into a cloud of independent molecules and free atoms.

Ten seconds existed between when the alien device began transmitting and its total destruction. Every muscle in Muni's mammoth body tightened. All color left his communication panels.

His forward wing-arms warrior-flared, their snake-like tips arched forward. Never had Muni's body been so fear overwhelmed. *I can transmit a years worth of experience in one intense microburst. That thing was obviously more advanced than anything we Morgi have. What did it transmit to its makers?*

"AI, were the frost and dust on the object put there artificially?"

"It appeared to be natural accumulation."

"How long would it take to accumulate that much dust and ice?"

"Approximately five hundred thousand years." All four of Muni's eyes widened. His panels again paled. *How have its makers remained hidden?*

Muni wanted to take one of his scout ships to personally inspect the debris—and that signal's destination point. He denied himself the experience; a personal inspection would take too long.

After half a million years, the manufacturing race could be long extinct. Muni's racial paranoia would not let him consider that possibility.

A tidal wave of time crashed down on Muni. When the unknown aliens were creating their mechanical sentinel, his own ancestors still crawled on a single mud ball. "AI, is this how the humans felt when they saw my ship?"

"I do not know how you feel, and can only extrapolate how they felt."

Muni recalled the recordings the ship had made of all the human conversations. "Computer, replay the before boarding times human conversations. Morgi speed."

He was right. The captain himself had said, "We are Neanderthals." They did feel the same way! *Those creatures look so hideously different and yet they feel similar emotions. Surely that is one of the great mysteries of the universe. So much to analyze... I wish I could ask the humans for advice.*

Advice! Humans had the technology to know about the artificial explosion. They would look to him for an explanation and advice!

"Computer, how much earth time has lapsed since I came in here?"

"One and three-fourths of their days."

"How have the two human crews interpreted my absence?"

"At first your behavior scared them. After nothing happened, they relaxed. About an hour ago your on board humans received word from earth about the explosion in the Kuiper belt. They are now agitated again."

"Accelerated mode, show me this crew's response to the explosion."

The earth humans correctly deduced something artificial blew up. From that they concluded a rogue galactic race tried to invade Earth's solar system, just as Muni warned.

From there the public debate had gone in two directions: those who believed Muni had saved them by acting in time and those who believed he had let them down by letting anyone get so close.

"Computer, I will Deep Sleep for one hour." Muni forced himself into a timed Deep Sleep.

He wanted to attack this new mystery physically, but knew he must seek the deeper insights available to his race only when free from all outward distractions. He needed the focus only Deep Sleep gave.

Chapter 11

Deep Sleep did not have the desired effect. No answers came, only more questions. Muni knew if he had the luxury of a lifetime of Deep Sleep, the answer he wanted did not exist.

Muni returned to the main control room, his panels overwhelmed with questions spiraling around each other, creating tangled webs of thoughts.

"Was the alien signal attempt successful?"

"Could someone be watching this planet the way I watched my flocks?"

"Is it an early warning device? If so, a warning for something going out, or coming in?"

"Can it be a property marker for an ancient civilization? Or a partially functioning prehistoric artifact that drifted in from stars no longer known?"

"What will be found in the even more distant Oort belt?"

"How can I learn more about the signal it sent?"

Behind those questions, his biggest questions kept swirling in the background. "Why did humans have to infest my Planet of Giants? Why did I tell them their planet is so fascinating to the galaxy?"

"So few earth giants still live; some whales, elephants, a few vegetarian birds. Such paltry leftovers from the magnificent fauna that made me fall in love with planet earth. I long to discuss Earth's history, but how can I when I claimed to know more about Earth than any human?"

"Could I have gained human cooperation without resorting to such a big lie?"

Muni considered revealing the truth to the humans. He remembered his Uncle Bern's frequent admonition, 'When deception is used, always consider what happens when your lie is revealed. Done wrong, the consequences are worse than appearing in public with a broken wing-arm.' Just imagining anyone seeing him so damaged caused ripples of shame to roll down Muni's body.

"Computer, are all the humans still in Jupiter One?"

"All but one."

"Which one?"

"Commander Jerrison. He is standing at the main control room door, screaming for you to let him in, yelling he knows your secret."

"What does he think my secret is? Has he shared it?"

"He has not communicated any ideas you have not already heard."

Muni looked to his wall of names. With all four eyes, he stared at Lor's symbol. Muted colors softly flickered across his panels, "Oh Lor, please be still glad..."

His eyes turned to his uncle's symbol. "Uncle, what would you tell these people? I crave your wise craftiness."

It was now nearly three days since Muni last talked with the humans. It seemed like not enough time and too much time all at the same time. Like the last time he asked for help...

Abruptly, Muni's whole body inflated slightly. The muddy subdued colors in his communication panel were replaced by crisp, bright shapes that scrolled swiftly. "AI, max speed, relay every earth entertainment creation about hostile alien invasions."

AI flashed, "That would take one hundred thirty five and one tenth hours."

Muni flashed, "Only those that have been replayed the most often, the top one per cent of popularity."

"That will take fifteen minutes."

Muni flash-ordered, "Commence run."

Muni remembered how eagerly the earth people had believed his first story. "AI, do all intelligent life forms need the same emotions to survive?"

"Not enough data to answer."

Uncle Bern's prime negotiating tool: people always preferred their own world view. If you wanted to trade for better klieg pastures, you didn't tell your adversary why he should want to trade, you *let him tell you.* Surely in all the humans' favorite stories, he would find an explanation even earth bound humans would accept.

It worked before.

Muni found the perfect entertainment. With only a few name changes, it would serve almost perfectly for everything he had said and would say. Just twenty years earlier it had been a worldwide best seller.

The "holy" (A hologram production, a whole generation of children had grown up believing that "Hollywood" was synonymous with entertainment because it meant a "forest of holographic movies"), *James Bond and the Gray's Lying Eyes,* had combined all the worst clichés of the previous century with a plot that seemed to exist only to get people either undressed or blown up. It was successful beyond its stars' wildest dreams.

Muni dreamed about bringing Hollywood to Morga. The earth stories would appeal to the landless masses. Earth's infesting human vermin could become a treasure the equal of the best pasture land.

Muni recited, "I am Muni Indigo, Child of the Green Hill, Noble Adult of the Morgi, protector of the unlanded, guide to future generations. That which is necessary, the universal power will make possible." He forced his panels reverently blank before blazing his next words. **"That which is necessary, I will do!"**

*I'll test my new story on Jerrison. If it works on him, it will work on anyone. If it doesn't...M*uni remembered the revolting flavor of that first human. *I don't care how nutritious he is after peeling, I won't* *eat him.* There were less traditional, but effective, ways to kill a clan enemy.

Muni looked at his undulating wing tips, what one human female had called his Medusa wings. It would be easy to grab both ends of a human and rip it in half.

"Let Commander Jerrison in."

Jerrison's raised fists pounded on the door. The door irised open so quickly, he fell inward. He looked up at the gray circle he knew covered the triangular teeth which had pulverized Simon.

Muni, all four wings spread wide, loomed over him. The walls demanded, "What is this great secret?"

Jerrison, his throat tight from hours of yelling, shouted, "You never expected to find us here." He staggered upright.

"Why else would I be here?"

Panting heavily, Jerrison responded, "To prepare the way for others." More deep breaths.

Muni's wing arms curved more; the tips of the forward pair curved like scimitars. "What, or who, gave you this idea?"

His body surging with adrenalin, Jerrison challenged, "You did. If I could get this idea from your behavior, you can be sure the political types on earth suspect it. Lies are their business. Stories created by lies added to lies fall apart."

Muni looked down on the puny, fragile human. *He is speaking with such courage. If he can't be persuaded to help, I will have to eat him; he deserves that honor. I do hope humans taste better after peeling.* A pair of Muni's eyes glanced at his Uncle Bern's symbol. *Uncle, I am going to do something even you would not risk.*

The walls vibrated sound around the room. "These walls speak for me as you know. What you do not know, is they listen for me as well."

Silence. "AI tells me you will need nourishment if I am to teach you."

Before Jerry could say anything, the floor rose under and behind him, conforming to his body better than any chair or bed. A pedestal bearing a tall drink with a straw in it rose up from the floor. A wall commanded, "Drink." Jerry gripped the drink, sipped.

Intense pleasure awoke taste buds he didn't know he had. Soothing coolness slid down his throat, erasing all the pain hours of determined yelling had created. Energy radiated outward from his intestinal tract to every extremity. *WOW!*

He sipped more. *It keeps tasting better; I keep feeling better...* Driven by need, imprisoned by pleasure, Jerry kept sipping from the never-empty cup.

The walls spoke. "Leader of the SMS crew, you were the first human I spoke with. It is fitting you are the first human to learn the truth. Watch, learn. Whenever necessary, AI will explain what you see. AI and I, in the last two minutes, have had the equivalent of an hour's audio conversation. I will return when AI is finished." He turned away, headed towards a wall.

Jerry protested, "You can't leave without giving some answers!"

Muni paused. All four eyestalks bent towards Jerrison; all four eyes stared directly at the human. "I did not understand anything about you humans until I watched your stories. There is not enough time to share the whole history of my people, so I am sharing my own story. I hope it is enough. You, your whole planet, is about to be destroyed. As is my family. I now fear my whole race is endangered. I have instructed AI to be completely truthful in all you are about to see. May Divine Chance grant you understanding."

The wall in front of Muni irised open and close so quickly, it looked as though Muni ran through the wall.

AI said, "Muni has important duties. Morgi communicate faster than a human speed reader can read, He will be back when I tell him you understand what we decided you most need to know.

Meanwhile, he has work that cannot be delayed any longer. All you will see is truth."

The computer's conversational voice transformed into a mechanical, monotone drone, more background information than sound.

Watch, learn, achieve understanding. Muni believes only by understanding his world, his life, will you believe you humans are in danger of total extinction.

Everything disappeared into blackness.

A world of mountains, rivers, oceans and exploding volcanoes appeared.

Unable to see even his hand, Jerrison felt like a spirit floating above the exotic planet.

AI's dull, somnolent monotone explained:

Radioactivity superheats the planet Morga's molten core. Compared to your earth, Morga's continents don't drift; they gallop, geologically speaking. The crash of tectonic plates force deep-lying granite to slice high into Morga's rarified upper atmosphere.

To Jerry, those black snow-free peaks look like polished obsidian saws, poised to rip into the sky.

AI continued. *On the lower slopes, winter snow accumulates. In spring, melting snow engorge rivers. Rapids gnash land and shore. The jagged coastlines force tides into long, deep rifts. Those narrow channels magnify the ocean's tidal assault.*

Jerry saw many channels more extreme than any of Norway's fjords. He saw only one gentle, sandy beach. His view zoomed in on one fjord. AI continued its uninterrupted monologue:

Observe this tall, steep cliff, the rivers surging over its crown. See the force with which the rivers cascade between jagged rocks, roar downwards to the ocean.

Jerry "zoomed" so close he expected to be drenched. Ribbon-like animals emerged from between the sharp rocks and swarmed over the cliff's face.

You are observing rock-huggers.

Jets of water slammed the rock-huggers, who suction-clung to the vertical surfaces. Each rock-hugger raised its front half. What looked like wrinkled side-skin, unfurled, revealing double sets of translucent wings. A webbing of tough cartilage defined elaborate designs on each wing. Small holes freckled the wings, creating natural nets. The rock-huggers flared their wings wide.

The rock-huggers use their wing-arms to net any hapless creature swept down by the falling torrents.

Brilliant, self-luminescent colors shimmered from the feasting rock-huggers.

Watch what happens when high tide returns.

High tide. Where the tall waterfall frothed downwards, now a river flowed level into salt water. The rock-huggers burrowed between crevices, hiding from ocean dwellers. Something big, dark and scary could be seen coming from the deep ocean, heading for the now underwater cliffs.

Earth child, your ancestors lived in gentle savannas, climbed trees, had an easy life. Muni's ancestors were rock-huggers. Rock-huggers live in two different worlds, land and ocean.

The violent, bracken world between ocean and shore toughened the rock-huggers. They became the ancestors of every backboned animal on Morga. Morgi resemble their rock-hugger ancestors, only many times larger.

Morgi cut their ancestral teeth on a much more geologically active planet than your gentle earth.

They abandoned the predictability of instinct for the chaos of emotional society.

They honed their logical abilities mastering their turbulent world—and developed cunning competing with each other.

Morgi are violent and powerful because their world demands it of them.

Morgi developed Faster-Than-Light spaceflight about fifty thousand of your years ago. You humans are the first technologically intelligent species they have encountered—-or at least that any Morgi has lived to tell about. You are right. Muni did not expect to find any intelligent species here. You were only partly right about Muni's motive. To understand his motive, his dilemma and Earth's peril, Muni and I agree you must understand more than his world. You need understanding of Muni's personal history.

The scene changed. Jerrison felt like a bird flying over dry scrub land. In the distance, he sees green foothills. Tall mountain peaks rise behind the hills. Directly beneath him something that resembles a thirty foot caterpillar creeps along. A shorter four-winged creature sits on the middle of its back.

The AI resumed its explanation. *This is the primitive zone that once belonged to Muni's noble Green Hill Clan. That is Muni as he looked as a subadult. He is riding a bunti. If you look closely you can see his herd of klieg or, as Muni preferred calling them, lumps.*

Jerrison studied the ground. "I think your simulation is faulty. There are no other animals."

AI superimposed a bright red circle about a clump of grass. Jerry watched as it changed shades ever so slightly.

AI said, *Klieg are round, domed up in the center. Their bodies are fringed. Their undersides are all sucker feet, except for the middle which is all mouth. Their bodies continuously color match whatever they glide over during their perpetual search for protein. A field of klieg looks just like a field without klieg, only lumpier. Hence the slur, lump.*

Klieg convey wealth and status in a way no other possession can. All important legal documents are not valid unless printed on a quality klieg parchment. Their flesh is eaten during fertility ceremonies. Only young noble males are allowed the privilege of herding klieg in the wild lands.

Jerry marveled at how Muni's four-winged front half arched upwards, but Muni's back half looked glued to the bunti. Muni's skin started sleek, but grew wrinkled about half way back. Muni's four stubby eyestalks protruded evenly around the top of his tubular body. Round eyes with circular irises alternate with oval eyes with slit-shaped irises. His tough 'wings' of semi-transparent membranes stretched between ribs of muscular cartilage. Small, randomly placed holes freckle his wing-arm's membranes. Muni strongly resembles the rock-huggers.

AI's explanations continued. *Both of a Morgi's 'wing' pairs function as arms. The longest ribs on a Morgi's forward wing-arms extend beyond the membranes.*

Jerrison said, "Muni's wing-arm extensions look like grafted on snakes." Jerry watched the wing tips curl, uncurl, arch together, spread out, wiggle... "Are Muni's wing tips ever still?"

When about to attack, or when engaged in formal conversation, otherwise, rarely. Adroit and versatile, an adult Morgi's powerful wing tips can arrange sand one grain at a time, and shred an enemy.

Jerry asked, "Why are there no other Morgi?"

AI answered, *No other Morgi are permitted in a primitive zone during a noble's right of passage herding klieg. Notice Muni's posture. He is imagining his nemesis, Ani-Orange, sits in front of him. Muni is about to pantomime attacking Ani-Orange.*

Muni arches his front half straight up, all four of his wing-arms flare warrior-wide. All ten tips arch forward, as rigid and curved as tiger claws. Muni's mouth irises open, revealing his circle of inward pointing, triangular teeth. Muni's communication panels blaze brilliant red-orange.

That shade of orange is pure fury.

Muni's wing-arms quiver; all ten wing tips slash the air in unison. Dark red jags outline Muni's signal. The walls vibrate a deep bass audio translation of Muni's signal: "Ani-Orange, come!"

Muni's forward pair of wing-arms swooshes forward, as though impaling an imagined enemy and then pulling it towards Muni's dagger-teeth. Colors swirl rapidly on Muni's panels. The walls again thunder translations. "Ani-Orange, you humiliated me, my family, my entire clan."

Lines of determined black zigzag over the red jags. "Ani-Orange, Chief Tester, you will never again disgrace any of the Green Hill Clan!"

The computer added, *The symbol "bunti-bits", the most obscene term for bunti excrement, highlights each swirl of the petty official's name. Most emotional nuances of the Morgi language I have omitted, but this one is important.*

The gleaming tips of Muni's circle of teeth <u>Clacked!</u>

Muni just administered the Death-Bite. The Death-Bite is an essential part of a polite fight to the death. Without it, your opponent will die both body and soul; with it, his soul lives while his body dies.

It is logical young Muni despises Ani-Orange. If justice truly reigned on Morga, Ani-Orange would have declared young Muni an Adult Landed Noble years earlier. Muni would not, for the fifth time, be herding lump! Watch young Muni's glare as he force-bright-flashes to his herd.

The walls sound Muni's fury. "No commoner has the 'privilege' of herding klieg, or taking special adulthood tests. Why are only we of noble lineage forced to suffer sun blisters, lurker bites, starvation, unattended injuries, loneliness…?"

Muni, his fake fight 'won', resumes watching the klieg.

AI continued. *I will show you what drove so much hate into Muni's soul. This happened several days earlier.*

The scene changed.

Jerrison saw a larger, pale purple version of Muni glide out of a mammoth gray fortress. It approaches a second, even larger Morgi.

The building is the Green Hill Keep. The Morgi leaving the Green Hill Keep is Muni's Mother. The other Morgi is Accession-to-Adulthood Tester Ani-Orange.

Ani-Orange arrived at the Green Hill Family Keep to test Muni's worthiness. Muni's noble mother is gliding out to meet the Accession-to-Noble-Adulthood Tester. She flashes welcome to Ani-Orange.

Ani-Orange refused the customary social chit-chat. Instead, that petty official approached the clan's grand entrance, his light-generating panels flashing, "Muni is not ready."

Ani-Orange flicked up his backend, revealing a whole row of sucker feet.

Flicking up sucker feet is obscene. He is treating Muni's mother as if she were lower than a never-landed commoner. Notice how her communication panels pale into invisibility; her noble glide wilts into a beggar's crawl. I have searched. There is nothing in human cultures that can begin to match the insult Ani-Orange gave Muni's mother, the entire Green Hill Clan, all their retainers and any future descendants.

The next day, Muni's classmates exchanged muted signals. "Muni's clan is targeted for extinction."

The scene changes. Muni and his Mother are in a large, barren room.

That evening he asked his mother if the rumor were true.

The two face each other. Colors bounced back and forth on their communication panels. AI continued his droning, monotone translations and explanations.

With a haughty glare, Muni's mother flashes, "Are barren hills disputed?" Bright purple pride enhance her next words, "We are the Green Hill Clan! I would shrivel in shame if none targeted us. You are fortunate to have earned more klieg-herding experience."

All four of Muni's eyes squinched tighter. *"Fortunate?"*

The second image faded.

The following morning, Muni was sent again into the primitive zone.

Jerry saw young Muni on top the long bunti.

AI continued. *Muni's panels blare obscenity, "Stupid, bunti-bit klieg-lumps!"*

If not for Ani-Orange, Muni would be with Lor, off exploring the stars. Not herding Klieg.

Jerrison said, "Herding seems a pretty easy job."

Most of the time, boredom is the greatest challenge. The rest of the time, not dying or preventing klieg deaths commands all of a herder's attention. A klieg's continuous camouflage fools most predators, but comes at a price. Klieg lost the ability to consciously control the colors their bodies generate; they can no longer exchange even simple signals. Domestic klieg are too stupid to avoid predators or other dangers.

Jerry asked, "I hear chattering. Where is it coming from?"

The Klieg.

"Doesn't that count as a signal?"

My data banks say no. No Morgi has heard that sound directly. Morgi audio awareness is limited to vibration sensing along the lateral lines which run the length of their bodies.

From research, Morgi have learned klieg, like many simple-minded animals, engage in mutual exchanges of atmospheric vibrations, sound. Technological civilization requires precision communication and complex thought. Speedy communication fosters rapid thought, a natural precursor to intelligence. Sound travels thousands of times slower than light, and cannot make precise signals. Therefore klieg, **like all** *species that degenerate into exchanging atmospheric vibrations, are duller than a lump of offal..*

AI spoke conversationally. "Are you beginning to understand why Muni will have great difficulty convincing anyone humans have true intelligence?" AI did not wait for Jerrison to respond.

Brilliant colors march across Muni's panels, the spoken translations resumed, "Can anyone learn anything from herding lumps?"

Colors anger intensify. "No!" Many-hued patterns race. "Everything, EVERYTHING, worth knowing can be better taught by educational programs on a starship."

Muni's panels flare. "Society doesn't have the brains of a bunti fingerling!"

Panel colors blazing like gasoline on a bonfire, Muni continues, "Riding a bunti! Pretending like it's thousands of years ago, no weapons of any kind."

Muni's panels abruptly dim.

Gray disgust shades Muni's words. "What a bunti-brained excuse for an 'advanced' education."

Words Muni wished he had flashed to Ani-Orange, "Ani-Orange, shred your ascendancy test. I willingly forfeit all noble rights. I choose to be an unlanded starship cadet."

Muni coveted a commoner's berth on an interstellar explorer. "My unlanded friends get excitement. I get lumps!"

Two things kept Muni from telling Ani-Orange to shred his test. One, the sight of his Mother's deep humiliation; the other, the most important, Lor.

The illusion vanished.

AI again spoke conversationally. "Jerrison what I am about to share, you must never repeat to anyone, human or Morgi, You must not ever write it in any fashion or say it out loud even to yourself. Do you agree?"

"Does that mean I'm allowed to repeat the rest of this?"

AI answered, "When the time is right, yes."

"Why the special restriction now?"

AI lowered its voice. "Because this part, the time will never, can never, be right. If any learn this, Muni will cease to be an adult. He will not be able to complete his mission. I will not allow that to happen."

Jerry felt cold run up his spine. He lost interest in his excelsior drink. "What if I forget? Accidentally blab?"

"You will die."

"I thought I already knew enough to get me killed?"

AI said, "The knowledge shared so far will eventually be known. Not this. Shall I continue, or find another human to share this knowledge?"

"You will kill me before taking another human into your confidence?"

"No"

Jerry felt relief.

"Execution by machine, even an AI such as myself, would be an insult to a man of your bravery. Muni will personally deliver the Death-Bite."

Relief evaporated. "I am honored. You may tell me." Jerry did not feel "honored."

The field illusion returned, now lit only by starlight. Two Morgi now ride the bunti.

AI resumed its background-monotone speech. *Muni cunningly avoided one regulation. He circumvented the surveillance grids, enabling an unauthorized, undetected visitor—-lovely Lor—-to sneak into Green Hill's primitive zone. They rode the bunti together. Muni had programmed the bunti's neural insert to a "single" closed-loop path... The Lovely Lor, her mouth covering appearing more vibrant than ever in the early twilight, never seemed to notice when they passed the same outcropping three times... Company during an ascendancy test is totally forbidden; if any found out Muni would cease to be an adult noble. Both he and Lor agreed his previous, totally honest tests were falsely denied.*

Lor and Muni dreamed of becoming interstellar explorers. Fortunately, no one had witnessed how, whenever they were alone together, purple-blue swirls stood out from the brilliant yellow of Muni's mouth covering, or the answering colors of desire on Lor's mouth coverings. The scene faded to black.

Daylight returned. Muni rides the bunti alone, all four eyes closed.

Muni dreams of Lor. The purple, blue and gold you see shimmering over his mouth covering and blanketing his lateral panels indicate deepest desire.

Dark, muddy purples, browns and harsh zigzags overwhelmed the purples, blues and golds.

Unmet desire creates frustration.

Miniature red lightning bolts stabbed through the muddy browns.

Muni's frustration has birthed anger.

Only adults select life companions. If life were fair, Muni would be an adult. Except for his first year, Muni's klieg herd survival rate is above average. He excels academically.

Muni's four wing-arms whip into a blur of activity; his whole upper torso twists and turns. Muni is a whirlwind of smashing teeth.

Jerry jumped back from the illusion, arms protecting his head. Compared to *this*, Muni inhaling Simon was a purring kitten. Jerry forced himself to breathe deep, repeat to himself "This is an illusion. This is an illusion."

Muni is imagining shredding the much larger Ani-Orange.

Startled, Jerry noticed something. "Why aren't the klieg or the bunti reacting?"

The klieg are trained to respond to a few artificially generated sounds; otherwise they respond only to smells. If Muni had not been mounted on the bunti, his sweet adult-carnivore scent would have panicked the mature klieg. Have you noticed Muni's hind skin flaps rippling against the bunti's skin?*

"I do now."

He is squeezing the bunti's sweat glands. Muni's skin soaks up the pheromone-rich perspiration. The cloying bunti herbivore scent overwhelms Muni's natural aroma. Muni knows the way Lor endured bunti-stink proved she loves him.

Bunti ignore everything except the short ground-hugging herbs they eat.. A bunti's "brain" is little more than a few ganglia along its lengthy spinal cord. In ancient times only skilled riders could sway the beasts to go a different direction than the closest sweet herb. Now all domesticated bunti have guidance modules surgically implanted above the foreword ganglion, enabling even fingerlings to control bunti.

Suddenly every swirl of color on Muni's panels has a paler shadow swirl adjacent to it. *Double shading like that indicates extreme determination.* "Five days!"

<u>*Five days...or never.*</u> *In six days, Muni will be beyond legal age to earn adult-noble status.* "In five days I will be an Adult Landed Noble. The lovely, lovely Lor..."

Lor's image blankets Muni's panels. The normally brilliant young noble could visualize only one word, 'lovely.'

The bunti stiffens! Danger!

All four of Muni's eyes open wide, scanning land and sky... His forward wing-arms shade his eyes as he stares straight up. Jerrison, too, looked up. High in the noon-time sky, a distant speck spirals down towards the flock. Muni's panels go white. Bright circles of color light up the pale panels. "A sly'ling? This far north?"

Muni had fought only one Sly'ling. It was in the southern most point of his family's estate, during his first solo herding. Denied weapons, Muni couldn't kill the voracious predator. He sent his slow-creeping klieg towards a cave, but the sharp-eyed sly'ling followed. Before the lumps could reach the cave, over half were killed. When the remnants of his herd finally entered the cave, Muni wedged his own body into the cave entrance.

The sly'ling switched from hunting klieg to attacking him. It tore strips of flesh from his body. Muni clawed the sly'ling's wings. Frustrated, the sly'ling left. Days later, herding time over, a family servant dragged Muni's inert body home. His clan avoided society for days; the humiliation of such mammoth loss, unbearable.

The northern scrubland has no caves, or other shelter. Muni knew another massive herd loss, will ruin, and perhaps extinguish his clan. Noble Lor will reject him... Muni flashes, "Bunti-Bits!"

Jerry watched the Sly'ling soar. Large, translucent wings framed its flat body. It descended. The sly'ling's pasty gray underside became visible. Its mouth irised open, revealing a mass of jagged teeth, worm-like raspy tongues, and gaping intestinal opening.

The sly'ling tucked its wings inward, transforming its body shape into a rushing spear point. It slammed teeth first into a lump. Its teeth impaled the klieg. Wings flapping hard, the sly'ling flew its victim towards the mountains. *Muni can tell this sly'ling has young. If not stopped, the sly'ling will feed the entire herd to its young.*

Muni's panels flash, "Bunti bits!"

Instinct told Muni to 'rush' his herd to the too-distant safety of their barns. Clan training urged Muni to create makeshift primitive weapons. Following instinct guarantees failure; makeshift weapons only delays failure. Muni flashes, "Nothing I can do **here** will work."

Suddenly, Muni arches his forward torso higher. Shading all four eyes with his forward wing-arms, Muni watches the sly'ling fly to the mountains.

Muni looks at his herd, then back to the sly'ling's landing area. "The sly'ling landed about two day's bunti crawling away from here."

Muni is setting his Bunti's controls to head for the sly'ling landing area. Maybe, if he is clever enough, he can discover a way to destroy the sly'ling at its nesting site.

Muni knows it will now be impossible to return to his family's keep in time to qualify for noble adulthood, but if he can prevent another massive herd loss, perhaps he can save his clan. Muni just doomed himself to losing Lovely, Highborn-Noble Lor forever.

"I've seen Muni run. He's fast! He should just get off that bunti thing and run for those hills."

Muni could crawl faster than the plodding beast's 'run', but only for an hour.

Muni is reciting his father's favorite proverb. "Battles can be won by bravery; wars are won by willpower."

Muni flares all four wing-arms towards the distant sly'ling. "You may steal a few lumps, win these first battles, but **I will win this war.**"

Muni needs to arrive battle-alert. He needs The Little Death. He has set a timer implanted in the bunti's back.

Jerrison watched Muni fold his wing-arms tight. Muni pressed his entire length against the bunti's back. His rubbery outer epidermal layer morphed into protective chitin.

Until he wakes, Muni's body will be as invulnerable as rock.

In prehistoric times, only sudden physical danger triggered The Little Death. A Morgi's body "dies" during the Little Death, but the unconscious does not. On waking, Morgi tackle problems with a level of creative brilliance far beyond normal capacity. Squeamish planet-hugger Morgi euphemistically called The Little Death 'Deep-Sleep.' Willingness to repeatedly endure the enhanced Little Death called Death Teaser separates true space-faring Morgi from ordinary planet-huggers.

The room went dark for a moment, then brightened.

It is two days later.

Sunlight glistens off great slabs of black rock slicing upward through the steeply ascending land. The short, ground-hugging plant life is yellow-brown except for the bands of green bordering a rapidly flowing stream.

Muni wakens. He flexes his skin. Muni's wing-arms unfurl to their fullest extent. *Before dismounting, Muni set the bunti's controls to permit a long grazing loop. After so long on a bunti's back, Muni's suction feet are intently aware of the many textures of pebbles, sand, dirt, grass, rock...* Muni said, "Walking feels good!"

Climbing up to the crest, Muni's four stubby eyestalks wiggle in all four directions. *He is searching for the sly'ling; he spots it.*

The sly'ling sits downhill.

Muni jerks back. Easing himself along a granite slab, Muni stretches out his body. He protrudes an adjacent set of eyes towards the predator.

The sly'ling, propped up with its lower pair of wings, sits on thick grass. Its transparent upper wings flare out, distorting the cave's mouth.

The sly'ling stands, flaps all four wings, and flies.

Muni ducks beneath an overhang.

The sly'ling's shadow speeds over the ground.

Muni ripples over rock slabs to the sly'ling's lair. *High-speed vibrations tingle his lateral lines.* Muni peers in. Inside the cave, nestlings gnaw on half-eaten klieg. *With morbid fascination, he stared at the sly'ling young. The youth stage of the sly'ling has a body like no other on the planet.*

Morgi find most young animals cute; these things repulse Morgi.

AI described the sly'ling young as Jerrison watched the creatures. *The oval "head" on top seems normal, but what appeared to dangle beneath that head resembles the spindly creatures found under slimy, damp rocks; only gigantic. One pair of stick-like appendages sticks out at right angles just beneath the oval. A second pair hangs straight down. Watching something walk around on only two thin legs, grabbing things with only two thin, wingless arms; makes a Morgi's digestive system squirm.*

Jerrison said, "I can see why. From the back, they look like cute cartoon people. But the front view! What should be a face is nothing but teeth and wormy-looking tongues. Yuck!"

Jerrison, you do not understand. It is the view from the back, the view that resembles skinny naked humans, Morgi find revolting.

Muni's panels flash, "Digestion!"

The repulsive sly'ling young induced waves of nausea within Muni. The noxious sensation reminded Muni of a psychology class he had been forced to take.

Muni rushes away from the sly'ling's lair, back to the bunti's programmed path.

Muni soon found what he sought: fresh bunti bits!

Muni scoops up the bunti bits; he also grabs grass and shoves all into his mouth. *Keeping his mouth dry, Muni is thoroughly masticating the mixture.*

Jerrison's entire stomach contents threatened to take up residence in his throat.

Muni hurries back to the vermin's nest.

Muni leans over the sly'ling lair and spits the powdery mixture onto the young sly'lings' food. He races back for more bunti bits. Muni keeps spraying the nest with more and more of the disgusting mixture.

A shadow moves rapidly across the ground. Muni looks up; as did Jerry. A distant speck in the sky, the sly'ling parent!

Muni knows he can do no more.

Muni rushes to the stream and dunks his head. *The clear, rapid waters are flushing all traces of the sickening flavor from his mouth. His mouth clean, Muni now gulps down large quantities of the purifying mountain water to rid his entire self of the noxious concoction.*

Cleansed, Muni returns to his vantage point. "Did it work?"

Bits of klieg litter the cave mouth. The sly'ling tosses more out. *The pink sparkles lighting up Muni's communication panels are laughter.* "Negative conditioning works!" Muni's panels gray. "Psychology is still a time waster. In space, I'll need math, astrophysics and engineering, not social theories, animal husbandry and bunti wrangling."

Muni is confident this sly'ling family will not be eating more lump. If enough klieg still live he has saved his family.

Muni returns to the bunti's path. *Muni programs the bunti to return nonstop to where he left his klieg.*

Muni rides back awake. "Do enough klieg live? Did I save my clan?"

Clan saved or not, home is too far away. Lor is lost to him, forever. "I will explore space, but as an unlanded commoner."

Evening came. The bunti plods on. Day came. The bunti trudges onward.

Complete darkness. *Night.*

In a moment, bright sunlight. *Day.*

Day reveals new hills. The bunti crawls up the steepest one. Looking down, Muni sees his distant flock. Muni slides to the ground. He charges hunter-speed the entire distance towards the remnant of his herd.

While running, Muni presses "come" on his surgically imprinted klieg communication button.

"Thanks-to-all-the-Ancestors!"

Almost half the herd lives! Exhausted, Muni collapses onto the ground, permitting carbon dioxide and moisture to seep out through his skin.

All four eyes close.

High speed runs are for quick prey-grabbing sprints, not long-distance marathons. Every cell in Muni's body clamors for rest, cleansing and nourishment. Morga's high-pressure atmosphere forces fresh oxygen into him.

Within minutes, a re-vitalized Muni ambles among his lumps, his panels filled with vibrant colors. The colors fade.

The triumph Muni felt defeating the sly'ling is drowned by the knowledge he failed his personal test. He lost Lor. Forever. Sorrow swamps his thoughts.

Physical pain stabs Muni's intestines. Hunger!

"As an unlanded commoner, I will never again experience hunger, another 'privilege' reserved only for nobles." *Muni craves fresh meat, but wild prey avoid domesticated klieg.*

The bunti finally caught up with Muni.

Muni is setting its controls to head home. Muni is tapping "Klieg, follow bunti" on his implants.

Jerrison watched the bunti continue onwards, fascinated with how the land behind it resembled a blanket with animals moving under it, more than land with animals crawling over it. "How can any animal camouflage itself so completely, so fast?"

There is an octopus in your Earth's oceans whose camouflage skills are even greater.

Muni leans back, all four eyes scanning the country side.

The herd gone, Muni seeks edible prey. In the spring many streams and sloughs filled these fields. Now, only summer-dry scrubland lies between Muni and home. Most wild animals migrate to the ocean. The remaining few taste like dust.

Sunlight reflects off something. Muni leans further back, each of his thousands of suction feet bend, tighten. He pounces! Using his wing-arms, Muni scoops up a nest of land crabs.

If he had been home, Muni would have carefully popped the hard chitin shells and sucked out their sweet, juicy meat. His body demands nourishment.

Muni's powerful circle of teeth grind the land-crabs, shells and all, to powder.

The shells add nutrients but make the sweet meat taste like dried mud. A few months previously this area had been under shallow water, land crab shells as soft and tasty as the meat within.

Muni's panels are dominated by the same gray Jerrison saw when Muni had created the disgusting bunti-bit concoction. The walls continue translating Muni's rant. "Ritual herding should be in the spring. Herding in summer is more proof society's rules are written by bunti fingerlings!"

The midsummer sun pours harsh heat down on Muni; rivulets of greasy sweat run down Muni's sides, carrying the last remnant of bunti stink out of his body. Wallowing in his own misery, Muni doesn't notice.

Muni heads for his herd. The first stars twinkle into view as he catches up with his herd's few stragglers. The ground looks as though it were rippling away from Muni.

Muni's uncloaked carnivore scent panics the mature klieg. Muni signals, "Stay!" *His carnivore scent overpowers all their conditioning.*

Muni hunter-sprints towards his bunti as he flashes, "If I don't mount that bunti, the entire herd will disappear."

Unlike humans, Morgi can run and 'talk' at the same time, since they don't need air to flash words.

"Why did I send the animals ahead of me? It would have taken only one day longer to keep the bunti close while I hunted. I had already failed. I let hunger control me. Hunger! Because I wanted an easier hunt, my high-born mother will become an unlanded commoner."

AI spoke lowly, as though in confidence. "Jerrison, remember how Ani-Orange humiliated the entire Green Hill Clan when he treated Muni's mother, the clan matriarch, like a commoner? Muni now believes she will be one of the unlanded."

Muni catches up with the large bunti. The bulk of what is left of his herd clusters about the beast. Muni rushes towards the bunti. A great land wave spreads out from the bunti as the camouflaging klieg flee. Muni flashes at the stampeding animals. "Now you move fast!"

Muni ripples up onto the bunti's back. Too slow, not a single klieg remains.

The sharp pain now clawing through Muni's intestines has nothing to do with hunger.

Muni rides the bunti just long enough to absorb its cloying scent, then dismounts. He starts walking back and forth, his wing-arms brushing against every rock and bush.

Muni searches for the frightened herd. He keeps searching until each klieg is found.

Two klieg died in the panic rush. Half the herd ooze body fluids where thorns had ripped open their skins. *Those hides are valueless.*

It is the worst of all failures.

Muni's wing-arms droop. "I will return, give my report. Mother will send me away to an unlanded guild. When enemies learn of my loss, the rest of the Green Hill clan will follow me to ignoble unlanded-commoner ranking."

Muni continues guiding the herd homeward.

The dry scrub gives way to cultivated mats of early-summer green fields. Two tall obelisks rise out of the well-watered vegetation, announcing to all:

This is the Heart of the Green Hill

Rows of rectangles spiral from the top downwards to the bottom of each column. Bright colors fill in each rectangle on the first obelisk; the second obelisk remains half empty.

Written in formal old-style, the rectangles replicate the patterns generated on the necks of the Morgi. The last entry names Muni's father. It had the date he became the Green Hill Clan Master, plus a short entry about the planetary engineering project. If Muni's father should do more worth remembering, it will be added.

The previous clan master had the same size entry; the one before that, only a name. Looking upwards, a few rectangles have only names. Most have more information.

These family history towers are less than five thousand years old. Another pair thousands of years older lie half-buried in ocean-shore sand. When in fingerling school, Muni swam around a third pair of Green Hills pillars. Like a typical fingerling, Muni did not believe his teacher's admonition, "Where you now swim, your ancestors did herd klieg." Muni's clan's most ancient obelisks lie in deep ocean trenches.

As Muni looks up at the columns of names, his communication panels mirror their patterns. Muni's body swells.

The AI's monotone voice became almost a whisper. *The background shading on his panels indicates love/pride. Those thin black lines and dots are pale prayers wrapping around each of the ancestral names.* "O noble ancestors, thank you."

An injured klieg bumps against a pillar. All four of Muni's eyes close. Muddy browns blanket his panels. Muni's body darkens.

Those are the colors of deep shame. There will be no more entries on the clan obelisk. See the emerging black line down the middle of his back? Muni feels as though unseen claws rake his skin, seeking entry.

Muni has younger brothers, as there had been older ones. So few Morgi survive to adulthood, fewer still attempt full noble adulthood, still fewer highborn noble adulthood. If no young achieve adult noble, the family becomes extinct.

Muni's failure should not have been Green Hill Clan failure. Only his impatience for a successful hunt made it clan failure.

Muni's panels turn black. *Muni's panels are death dark.*

Muni resumes his journey to the family keep.

A loud gong sounds. *Muni feels more than hears that sound. It signals his return.*

In ancient times a massive gong perched on a wall of the family keep announced a son returning from the wild lands. Today, someone pushes a button.

The massive gray stone work of the Clan edifice came alive with rippling golden welcome!

Muni's mother waits on the grounds, alone.

He is late, but that does not explain her solitary vigil. Muni is programming the bunti to lead what's left of the klieg to the barn complex.

Muni slides off the bunti and trots over to his mother. As he approaches, the keep's ornate greeting display disappears. It again looks like a primitive fortress of massive gray stones.

His mother is asking about the status of the flock, the bunti's health, the pasture quality, as befits a titled, business-like landowner greeting a returning adult herdsman.

Muni answers equally businesslike—-except for the pale gray lines of confusion that keep creeping around his words. His mother expresses not even a hint of panic over his massive herd loss. See Muni's pale gray lines widen? He is confused, and fearful something is so wrong, losing half the herd is nothing.

His mother's forward wing-arms reach out. She gently strokes Muni's forward wing-arms.

AI chose a rich contralto voice for her audio projections. "I see your thoughts are not on klieg, pasture land or even sly'lings, my little fingerling." *Pink-amusement sparkle her words.*

Cringing at the childish endearment, Muni resumes his business-like recital.

Muni follows his mother through a long hallway. Several feet of water flood its entrance.

The water removes outside grime and refreshes Morgi.

He joins his mother eating what looks like paste.

They are sharing the Meal of Return. After so long in the primitive zone, just being able to eat in a full-relax mode makes the meal feel luxurious to Muni. His family is the poorest of all the noble families. Most successful unlanded eat better than Green Hill Clan.

The ritual meal finished, Muni asked, "Will our Green Hill Clan survive?" *Muni did not bother to ask about himself. He believes the next morning a servant will lead him to the border of The Green Hill Estate. The servant will return here, alone. Muni, now an unlanded commoner, will never return. He also believes that soon rival clans will do the same to every family member still home and every servant on their estate.*

The brilliant purples and magentas back grounding his mother's words are pride. His mother says, "We will survive. You have already been declared a provisional adult. You impressed everyone with the way you handled the sly'ling."

She notes his puzzlement. She adds, "I authorized satellite surveillance."

Muni flashes intertwining grays, *total confusion.*

Muni's mother pretends to be oblivious to his increasing befuddlement. She continues, "We will go to the Regional-Coordinator's to fulfill the traditional requirements for noble adulthood. He will give you the formal interrogation and recognition ceremony. Afterwards there will be an open meeting to which our entire clan has been personally invited."

Muni's neck voids all color.

Muni flashes, "Coordinators don't bother with adulthood testing."

"My cousin's oldest son was personally tested by the Regional-Coordinator."

Dense gray clouded Muni's reply. "Yes, but your birth clan is..." Muni's communication panels pale. *His mother's total estrangement from her birth clan, one of the most dominant in the Morgi home system, is an embarrassment. He switches topics, the open meeting.*

It takes a major crisis to invoke a multi-clan "open" meeting. Only the most powerful, or the most knowledgeable, are invited. "Why is the entire clan, not just our best scholars, invited?"

His mother, *her panels swirl crimson deep joy*, flashes, "Our clan has an Ancestral Return."

Muni remains confused. "All our ancestors are accounted for."

"Not all."

"Impossible."

The room transformed itself to a hillside on which stood a tall, brightly painted, unfamiliar obelisk. Colors dance on his mother's panels, "This is a reproduction of what our ancestral pillar looked liked the year a member of our family went on an independent stellar survey. We recently located it in the deep ocean trench due east of the oldest pillar you have seen."

Muni's communication panels ripple many shades of gray.

Muni seeks understanding. "Then it would be so old it would predate blue-line space travel, because the beach obelisks go back over ten thousand years. The pair I've swum around goes back to when that sea bottom was prime klieg-grazing land. Add that time to the five thousand years history on the towers here…"

He struggles to add up the timelines. "It would be fifty thousand years! Was there even space travel then?"

His mother continues. "A picture of that tower adorns a recently recovered scout-explorer. Complete registry information lay within the ship. The original charter is still on file in our planetary records, although deeply buried. We hired the two Morgi who still study its ancient dialect to undertake the record search."

Pride brightens her words. "We now know why our ancestral hold is half as large as other nobles. Our new most-distant-ancestor sold over three-fourths of all clan property to finance his own ship.

He traveled alone to avoid all doubt about family claims should he discover anything of value. If his ship returned, our Green Hill Clan would be the richest in the galaxy. If he failed, our clan would be destitute."

"How could the story of such a brave ancestor be forgotten?"

"Even the tallest mountain becomes but sand in the sea."

Muni had observed the ancient proverb many times, but seeing it now, softly stated by his mother, gave it new depth. For the first time in his life he really wondered what kind of people his ancestors were. "What happened to our ancestor?"

"His ship's blue-line system failed. Realizing it was un-repairable, he set his ship's controls to auto-pilot home at 90% light speed. He knew he would be dead many thousands of years before his ship returned. Before dying, he set his ship's beacon system to not activate until within one light year of Morga."

"What caused the damage?"

"The ship is yielding such mysteries slowly. We think our ancestor had no idea what caused the problem. The information he brought back is being unraveled with difficulty.

"We also searched our family's antiquarian records. Our ancestors wrote about the tremendous sacrifices they made to keep Green Hill Clan intact. The competition for contiguous property was even more intense than it is now.

"It took ten generations to increase our land rights to what they are now. For another ten generations the story of the returning savior remained an important part of family lore. Each new patriarch re-affirmed whenever the ship returned, all items of value from the exploration would belong only to our clan.

"The story faded from our family chronicles. No one has mentioned it for over 10,000 years. In spite of that, all the old legal claims are still valid. The ship and all of its discoveries are ours. We now own two solar systems with readily habitable planets."

His mother remained as calm as if she were reciting last spring's klieg breeding records.

Muni still can not fathom such restraint. If what she said were true, they were now one of the richest families, if not the richest, in all the Morgi civilization. No one family ever launches their own explorer-scout. Even with all the technology that now exists it is just too expensive; the failure rate, too high. To own even one percent of a solar system made a clan wealthy.

Muni wonders which is greater, his ancestor's courage or his family's new wealth and prestige.

Pink laughter sparkles over deep joy's crimson. Other colors glow. Muni's projected voice runs faster. "Someone will be needed to go to our solar systems. Someone like me! We'll buy our own ship; I will explore my own new world!"

Muni's neck radiates more colors of great glee, eagerness, impatience, jubilation. "Let's leave now."

Pink amusement shades his mother's reply. "At first daybreak Regional-Coordinator Mung's private auto-ship will pick us up. We will wait in preparation rooms until your personal ceremony. Our staff and family are already there.

"After your adult status has been formally confirmed, we will adjourn immediately for the primary debriefing to observe all that has been learned from the ship. We have already arranged for the two scholars involved with the translations to be with us. In fact, they have applied for, and been granted, permanent retainer status."

Advanced scholars had applied to his family for permanent retainer status! The ultimate proof Green Hill is RICH!

Like all noble landed families, Green Hill Clan has permanent retainers who have been with them for generations. Clans who don't provide employment for each permanent retainer's offspring lose prestige—except for the Green Hill Clan. Being at the absolute bottom of the noble social barrel, Green Hill Clan had no prestige to lose.

Many times Green Hill staff went through the polite formality of asking his mother's permission to become independent laborers in one of the metropolitan areas. His family could afford to keep only the very best.

Whenever a noble family accepts an unlanded individual as a permanent retainer, rather than just a temporary hireling, it magnifies their social power. Even the poorest independents never applied to Muni's clan. Now Green Hill Clan had granted two very valuable scholars permanent retainer status!

The world had changed.

"Mother, do you remember when, in fingerling school, I first heard that joke, 'When is a hill lower than any valley? When it's a Green Hill!' Valley Waters Clan fingerlings loved repeating it. Each time, everyone's swirls of laughter seemed brighter than the last time. Will any of the Valley Waters Clan be at the open meeting?"

"Yes."

Crimson floods Muni's communication panels. *Smug joy.*

Stark orange, *warning*, outline his mother's words. "Their wealth is like the deep ocean, ours is but the promise of rain in a cloud."

"But the planets are ours. Ancient laws are sacred."

"The planets will not remain ours unless the three traditional necessities of clan dominance are met. First, a single clan member must settle on the property. Second, a klieg herd must survive there. Third, a deed must be written on parchment made from the flawless skin of a fertile, at least third generation klieg born in the new territory."

All hint of emotion left his mother's panels. Each word is stark, with almost artificial precision. "Each system must have all three met, or we will lose it. At least the fourth requirement, any Morgi living in the area must swear eternal fealty to our clan, is not a problem."

"No one else has to do all that!"

"That's because all the other settled star systems are owned by consortiums of many families. As this is the first ever case of only one family owning an entire system, The Supreme Council declared the most ancient laws, the laws our pre-spaceflight ancestors lived under, apply."

"Mother, was a fifty-thousand-year dead tradition resurrected to validate our ownership, or to jeopardize it?"

Lavender pride outlines her words. "Muni, you have clan-master potential." She looks down at him. *There are no words, just shades of pride.*

She spoke, "Many twisting currents flow beneath the still waters of polite formality. I must swim their turbulence while under The Little Death."

Muni's land-bound mother feared The Little Death as much as final death. "What terror drives you to risk that?"

His mother answers, "Muni, when is prey counted as a meal?"

Muni completed the fingerling-school proverb. "When it is eaten, no sooner."

Her words again stark, "The two new systems are coveted prey. Until fully ours, both systems can be legally stolen from us. I'll see you a few minutes before sunrise."

With that Muni's mother left for her personal quarters.

Alone, Muni's panels blaze riotous colors. His suction feet grip and 'pop' off the floor.

The cheerful vibration keeps rhythm with the joyful pounding of his heart. It is the closest Morgi come to dancing.

Darkness.

Jerry is again outside the Green Hill Clan Keep. A crack of sunlight can be seen on the horizon. A large circular platform with no railing or other edging sits in front of the entrance. Muni and his mother exit the keep and ripple up unto the platform. The platform lifts straight up, tilts sideways to avoid hitting tree-like vegetation as it speeds away. Muni and his mother are both firmly suction-gripped to its surface. There is no sound.

With swift silence they flew to the personal office compound.

As soon as Muni and his mother exit the craft, a Morgi larger than Ani-Orange meets them.

The Coordinator's personal head of staff.

He leads them inside. Gray stone blocks with veins of welcoming yellow arch over the long entrance passageway. Through what appear to be natural fissures, a fine spray washes over them.

The illusion is so real Jerrison is surprised he isn't wet.

The floor gradually slopes down. The water deepens to mouth deep. The floor slopes upward. As they near the end, the spray fades to mist; mist fades to dry air. The three Morgi emerge into the receiving chamber. *Their feet are dry and their skin pleasantly moist and clean.*

Muni, all four eyes open wide, looks around. Suddenly dark bars roll across his panels.

Embarrassment.

Polished sheets of deep purple marbled with many veins of gold ore snaking through it, cover the floor.

This room is most risqué. Metallic gold, when coupled with the purple of a female's mouth-covering, signifies an eager mating interest. The vivid yellow and blue granites covering the walls are identical to the shades an equally aroused male generates. The quarries of many worlds were searched to find such stones. Since the pigmentation is natural, convention demands everyone appear oblivious to the blatantly obvious sexual innuendo. His mother maintains complete communication control. Pale sexual responses edge into Muni's panels and creep over his mouth covering.

The staffer flashes, "Muni's test will be followed by the open meeting. Since the meeting is scheduled to last several days, the

Regional-Coordinator has prepared a meal in your rooms. Each room's communicators are keyed to your personal colors."

Muni stared. *He is fascinated by the staffer's neck panels. He thought his mother's emotional control perfect; he was wrong! The staffer's panels were as devoid of emotion as an artificial message generator.*

Two of the wall's stone slabs pivot, revealing two narrow halls. Muni trots into the nearer hall. His mother glides with regal calm into hers.

Muni's long, nearly dark hall opens into to a well-lit, medium-sized room. Water fills the room except for an empty, raised platform in the center. Small crustacean, larvae, and worms wiggle through the water and on the walls.

Muni's neck panel pales to white.

Awe. The opulence Muni had seen until now could be explained by the accumulated wealth of office. But this! The wealth of the present wiggled before him! He only dreamed of living with such luxury!

Swirls of bright colors spiral wildly on Muni's panels.

Jubilation!

He splashes into the water, greedily snatching up the tastiest of the scurrying critters.

Muni crunches down on the crustacean.

He expects its shell to crack open so he can suck out the sweet meat. Its shell is first-molt soft. During the first few minutes after shedding its old shell, a crustacean's new shell is as tasty as its meat. Thinking it a lucky find, Muni chases other crustaceans. Each was either a sweet hatchling, or just minutes after molting. Only rarely, when he had been unusually blessed on a hunting trip, had Muni tasted such food.

After satiating himself, Muni stretches out on the raised dais. He slaps the stone work. "If only it were possible for more of my clan to be here..."

Even after fifty thousand years of interstellar travel, the Morgi find nothing more practical for traveling within a solar system than using gravity for interplanetary travel. The many clan members within Morga's home system but off-planet, were years away from home. At great expense, Morgi could choose to travel at the constant acceleration that equaled Morga's gravity. That still took months.

At immense expense, and greater danger, Morgi can take a least-time route. Such extreme accelerations would kill an unprepared Morgi. Only Morgi in the artificially augmented Little Death spacers called Death Teaser, could survive a least-time route.

Clansmen in the depths of interstellar space relied on message capsules sent into the blue-line galactic-travel paths to learn what happened at home. It would be years before most learned about The Return.

A transparent hill floats before Muni. "Computer, show all family members present."

An array of colorful rectangles sprang up on the hill. "Computer, only those physically present."

Most of the identification rectangles remain. "That's not possible. Most were off-planet when we discovered the Ancestral Return. It should take years for so many to come home."

"Only a great emergency could justify so many clan members risking a least-time route. How can wealth be an emergency? We have choices we've never had before. Other clans will seek to ingratiate themselves to us."

Colors of desire flit over his panels. "Including the family of the lovely, lovely Lor—-"

A sour note, an old Morgi axiom, quashes his optimism.

"A fool and his money **must** be parted."

Muni declares, "Our patriarch is wise!" He glances at an empty spot.

His father's symbol belonged there. Muni's father, the Clan Master and Patriarch, worked beyond the primary comet halo, a half-light year away. Muni had not seen him for years, and knew it would be several more years before he again saw his father.

Muni arches upward, as though his distant father were there in person. His wing-arms warrior-flare, determination's colors roll outwards from Muni's words. "No one will part us from our new wealth."

Muni flaps all four wing-arms together.

"Flashing confidence if to only myself makes me feel stronger. If confident words were all it took to pass the Ascendancy to Adulthood test... Didn't Mother say I've already been declared an adult? Why can't I defy tradition, refuse the test. The Regional Coordinator has sided with our enemies in the past. He will be watching for mistakes the way a sly'ling watches prey. Why chance a rigged test?" Muni's predominant colors abruptly changed. "Unless my success is guaranteed..."

Muni had seen rumors; the sons of the very wealthy had examinations as easy as their family wealth is great. "Perhaps the Regional Coordinator will go easy on me...No, not with my mother's reputation. If the Coordinator wants to influence my clan, he had best make the exam difficult.

"Computer, show non-family members present."

The list read like a who's who of planetary rulers.

Failure would debase the entire Green Hill Clan.

"Must stop thinking about the test!"

Muni decided to talk to someone about The Return. He looked through the list of family names again. There! The arrogant red design of his Uncle Bern! He touches Bern's hologram.

Muni's cell returns to its initial appearance. A query pad appears. Muni touched the virtual pad, *indicating his identity, level of urgency, topic. It flashed back,* "Bern is yet in Deep Sleep. Leave message."

Muni summarized the few facts he knew. Then, in a rushed jumble, tried to list every reason the clan's youngest adult—-which just happened to be himself—-should be The One sent to the new star systems.

Muni signs off. The Hill and its names returns A new rectangle abruptly appears, *his father's!* "Computer, his status?"

"He endured return at maximum acceleration in Death Teaser. He survived, but it will be hours before it is safe to begin his awakening."

"That means he headed home over a year ago. Why risk Death Teaser?"

The literal computer responds, "He was in a hurry to get here."

"Either a different emergency sent the Patriarch inward, or my father knew about the Ancestral Return before anyone else in their solar system."

Although the latter seemed unlikely—hadn't they been told the difficult translation of the name bar was only recently accomplished?—Muni hoped against hope his father knew about the ship. Perhaps, when the derelict ship had first signaled its arrival, his father saw it and recognized the ancient symbols? If the patriarch felt it wiser to not share such knowledge, his cunning father would have said nothing and rushed silently home.

Not only would the Patriarch's experience be valuable in the discussion ahead, but that much time in Deepest Sleep with only one thought firmly in mind…There would surely be some aspect only his astute father could grasp.

Grateful both clan leaders would at least be at the open meeting, Muni declined leaving his father a message.

A halo flashes around his Uncle Bern's rectangle: "Do you wish to talk?"

Muni keys the virtual ID bar. "Yes."

Muni's preparation room doubles in size. His Uncle Bern sits on a raised dais identical to the one in Muni's cell. Still in the final steps of awakening from the Little Death, Bern pleasurably stretches out his quadrupled wing-arms. Every section of Uncle Bern's forward wing-arms ends in a frill of fingers, *a source of great pride to his uncle*. The exceptional deep blue of his mouth covering caused the thin yellow swirls on it to stand out vividly.

Bern has a reputation as a clever negotiator for more than business. Lady Morgi find extra frills and that shade of blue irresistible.

Uncle Bern's two oval-eyes track the delectable morsels scampering about his cell, but his nearer round-eye focuses solely on Muni. Bern's communication bands gleam a joyful golden-yellow.

AI chose a mellow tenor for Bern's voice.

"Muni, it's great to see you! And congratulations on your Ascendancy to Adulthood! Should be a grand ceremony. Do you mind if I eat while we talk? I haven't had real food since I last left this planet." Before Muni could flash thanks, hope so, or a simple, "Go right ahead." Bern slips off the platform and begins chasing unsuspecting polliwogs.

The water splashes in Muni's direction disappears mid air—the only tell that in reality his uncle frolicked in another room. Bern's appearance is a communication illusion within an illusion.

While chasing food, Bern communicates with his nephew. "I just read the official evaluation of your latest klieg herding. Most impressive. Remember when you become a clan leader to be as demanding of the young as we have been with you. That is how great clans remain great. 'Only against great odds can greatness be revealed.' Have you learned more about the Ancestral Return?"

His uncle's bars politely went blank, waiting for additional input from Muni. Muni flashed back spirals of gray—an "I know nothing" shrug. Then Muni queried, "How is the Planetary Project?"

The Morgi Planetary Project, a multiple-generation engineering project, represents more effort for the Morgi civilization than all previous Morgi accomplishments. For generations Morgi astronautical engineers had been sending raw material from the outer fringe of their sun-system inward to create a new planet. Creating a planet without causing a disaster had proven a monumental task.

Its official reason, planetary research and additional living space, made little sense. Morgi had colonies in dozens of star systems and research stations in hundreds more. No Morgi recognizes the true reason: Racial Pride.

The Morgi need to know as a people they can meet a more difficult goal than any that had been achieved before. Without a challenge as severe to them, as their own planet had been to their ancestors, Morgi become neurotic.

Jerry asked, "How can you know something about the Morgi they themselves don't know?"

AI in its normal voice answered, "We AI observe and share our observations with other AI. Morgi, like you humans, have many irrational quirks. We AI accept those quirks and serve. Liston closely to Bern's response. It is important."

Green frustration ripples up and down Uncle Bern's communication bars as he told Muni how everything had been on schedule for the new planet. "The anaerobic bacteria and other non-oxygen using life forms made themselves right at home in all the shallow waterways, as predicted, and the planet seemed to be half-way settling down. Life spread everywhere."

"As you know," Uncle Bern continues, "I've been busily growing oceans while the anaerobic microbes have been busy just growing."

Bern snapped up a first-molt land crab. Crunch! Pleasure pink shade Bern's next words. "Are you aware we are more knowledgeable about planets hundreds of light years away, than we are about the isolated cold comets orbiting the outer reach of our own solar system? For the last several years your father has been scouting the outermost reach of our sun's-system looking for high-water comets to send inward. As the water-rich comets neared the new planet, I nudged their inward paths."

Bern pauses to attack three more first-molt crabs. "You remember how our clan won the contract to create oceans that would 'maximize range land and farming potential.'"

Muni responds, "Of course. We'll own the new planet's best herd-land. As soon as a herd of klieg survives just one year on the new planet, our wealth will increase many times." Brown shades of shame overwhelm Muni's next words. "If not for the ancestral return, our clan would not have survived long enough to earn those new lands."

Bern flashes, "Muni, if not for the ancestral return, we were already doomed. You could have done everything perfectly, not lost a single klieg, and your accomplishment would only have delayed our extinction. Within the year you, me, our patriarch, your mother, every member of The Green Hill Clan, would have become unlanded commoners."

Confusion swirls over Muni's panels. "Even without the ancestral return, the planetary project will make us as wealthy as other nobles."

His Uncle flashes back. "We have been victimized by our own success! We have oceans, tons of replicating life, but we can't go to the next step."

Muni asks, "Next step?"

"You're familiar with how we sped up the natural process by seeding not just the deep oceans but also many of the surface areas with a variety of select starter anaerobic prokaryote organisms."

Many-hued shades of sarcasm circle Muni's words. "Because of Mother, in *detail*."

Bern continues, "The next step is seeding oxygen-generating microbes."

Muni flashes, "Mother shared those plans as well. She turned every cytology lecture into stories about how much fun she had selecting unicellular life forms. It's sad nothing exciting happened in her childhood."

Uncle Bern *confidential overtones*, "Did she ever tell you that's when she met your father? She scandalized her whole clan by falling in love with the poorest free-landholder on all of Morga."

Muni flashes shock. "Uncle Bern, does this mean my mother's clan may start acknowledging us?"

"Because of our world-building project? I doubt it." *Wisecracking Bern enjoyed being deliberately obtuse.*

"No, the Return, fingerling-brain!"

"Oh, that trivial, random event. Could possibly have happened to anyone. Doesn't change a thing.... except little things, like whom you marry, your children's opportunities, whether you go into space as smart-cargo or pilot. Your mother sent me an awakening note warning against communications from her family."

Muni flashed, "You implied the planetary project will fail because it is successful."

Bern snatched a particularly delectable-looking larva. "Do you remember your lessons concerning size limits of a true single-cell organism, especially in a non-oxygenating atmosphere?"

"Of course."

"They were wrong."

"Huh?"

"They were 100 percent wrong. Some are now postulating there is no theoretical limit."

Muni is reciting a schoolbook. "All mathematical studies of fluids in living organisms prove size limits exist. The presence of a gravitational field defines maximum size in an environmentally friendly situation. Maximum size is inversely proportional to gravitation. Zero gravity in a perfect place permits infinitely large organism, but adding real world restrictions, like the ability to eat, limits maximum size."

The math problems involved with calculating such things had nearly made Muni quit his first and only career choice. Because Explorers-Interstellar must be able to recognize life in any environment, Explorer training requires a heavy theoretical understanding of all biological and physical sciences.

No one knows what dangers may lurk in the long, lonely voids of interstellar space. Each scout ship contains all Morgi knowledge, but all knowledge is useless unless you know which questions to ask. The better the understanding of the theories behind the facts, the better the questions asked.

Muni had worked through the complex math often enough, and from enough different directions, to feel very confident about the maximum size of a single cell organism.

"Uncle, you are either mistaken, or testing me."

"Muni, watch."

Abruptly, an aerial view of a smooth grayish lake, surrounded by lichen covered rocks, replaced his uncle. Jerrison feels as though he and Muni hover over the lake. Suddenly they dive into those gray waters.

Muni swims along the lake's sandy bottom, and then up, towards the water's surface. A multitude of brilliant, iridescent bubbles, from tiny to larger than Muni himself, shimmer around him.

Their beauty stuns Jerrison.

Muni flashes, "The bubbles are alive, but such beauty feels more like art than life." *He glances at the communication bar to check the scale.* "One hundred percent! Impossible! There's no way a single cell can be larger than I am! Uncle Bern, where, what is this?"

Bern's reply scrolls across the image's communication bar. "Our new sister planet, early last year. A technician first saw these years ago. He reported it as escaping gas, one more example of the new planet's weird chemistry."

Muni understood the mistake. If not for his specialized training, Muni would have thought the strange life forms were physical phenomena.

Bern continued, "The report might have stayed buried, except the technician found the phenomena irresistibly beautiful. He visited it daily."

Bern signaled, "Watch closely."

The legend indicates high noon on the new planet, its moonlet and the sun directly overhead. The scene blurs; Jerrison couldn't tell if the lake itself were shimmering, or if the transmission had been deliberately modified.

The shimmering becomes a seductive, beautiful swirl of colors. *Muni believes Bern is increasing the transmission scale.* Muni glances with one eye at the messenger bar. "Still life-sized?"

The bubbles dissolve, releasing loose tendrils into the lake water. The lake coalesces into a soft, crystalline maze of tubes loosely connected with gossamer threads. Everything had the softness associated with seeing through gelatin.

The viewpoint changes; Jerrison now feels as though he and Muni are shooting upward, beyond the water's surface, into the sky. He looks down.

His new vantage point reveals a scene a demented cytologist might conjure up at an art fest. A single cell sits on hot sand, magnified so much it looks as though it were holding its own amongst boulders...the same rocks that surrounded the lake.

The cell divides in the pattern typical of all prokaryotes except, instead of becoming two cells, it becomes four, then eight. The different pieces started to subdivide, each in its own way. Every division, from the first onward, leaks a little water. In a matter of minutes the lake returns, the probe again descends. Muni said, "It's just like before, all those giant, beautiful cells."

Muni's panels blank. *He is totally flabbergasted.*

Zigzagging colors rapidly crisscross Muni's panels. "Uncle, the larger cells in the lake are roughly double the theoretical maximum size for a single cell organism. I already thought of theory modification that could accommodate this new life. But if you are telling the truth, I just witnessed the transmutation of a primitive lake into a single unicellular organism. A lake larger than our clan's entire estate! There is no way this can be real, just no way."

The lake disappears, replaced by Bern's room.

Uncle Bern lectures, "Muni, the real world has a way of making its own rules. No amount of advance knowledge can ever predict the exact outcome of any complex system. Biologists are having a field day with this one. Reputations are being made and broken as they're proposing and disposing explanations. So far the only one I find believable is that if it weren't for a bizarre set of circumstances, this life form would be impossible; but then I've always believed **coincidence rules the universe.**"

"Uncle, this is unbelievable. When did we first know this giant cell existed?"

"We knew over a year ago, but kept it secret. It became public knowledge just before your last solo herding. The news stories were full of it the first day you were in isolation. This is why your father's here. He still knows nothing of The Return."

Intensely puzzled, Muni queries, "Why would a giant cell make him rush in at full acceleration, like it's a matter of life or death?"

"Muni, how were we to be paid for our work on the new planet?"

"Base rate plus the best pasture lands."

"Yes. Now, does base rate pay for our training to be planetary specialists?"

Muni flashes, "No."

"And is our ancestral holding large enough to remain viable?"
Muni starts to answer. "With very careful management—"

"With very careful management we can continue to hold on." *White-blue scorn flows over his words.* "Most clerics have more economic vitality than our family does. Compared to what she would have done with any other landed clan, your mother lives in abject poverty!"

Back then, Muni did not regard his lifestyle as abject poverty; he had too many friends from both the never-landed and the unlanded associations to believe that. Ignoring his Uncle's assessment of their life-style, Muni queries, "How does that affect my adulthood testing?"

"Simple. Our family pledged its entire resources to help create this new planet. In exchange we were to receive rights to the new planet's best range lands as soon as klieg could survive on the planet's surface. That requires an atmosphere with abundant oxygen. From the samples we've taken, we know this novel life form cannot survive in an oxygen-rich environment.

"If we introduce oxygen generating organisms, it will destroy the most novel life form to be discovered in over fifty thousand years of interstellar explorations. To be guilty of such a crime would destroy our whole clan.

"If we do not introduce oxygen generating organisms, then it will be impossible for any klieg to ever survive on the new planet. Poverty will then drive our whole clan into the lowest of the unlanded.

"Muni, our Green Hill Clan faced extinction. Orders are written to tear down our ancestral obelisk. Your high-born mother, all our family, was about to be proclaimed unlanded. That same day, scholars revealed the first translations from The Ancestral Return."

"Uncle, why couldn't we transfer this new life form to a research station?"

"Since it could not be predicted, any artificial environment might leave out the essential ingredient that made it possible. Valley Waters Clan claims their scientists have proved it could only exist on our new planet."

Bern unfurls his forward arms in the starving-hunter's mode, symbolizing the depth of their family's struggle. "Clan members are rushing home from our entire solar system, and signals were sent to all clan members beyond our system.

"Muni, we were coming together to fight for our very survival."

Muni had been totally unaware of the risk his family had taken when they signed onto the planetary project, only of the prestige and possible gains. "Bern, was the family patriarch who negotiated the planetary-construction contract a throwback to our distant ancestor who risked all to send out that tiny, primitive exploratory ship?"

Pride shades Bern's answer. "Willingness to take great risk runs strong in our family. It is the only reason we have survived our impoverishment."

"Uncle, our returning clan will be thrilled to realize their fears are groundless!"

Strong emotions cloud Bern's reply. Fear, frustration, something else I cannot yet find an Earth equivalent. "Yes, but all will be awakening from a Little Death during which they focused on avoidance of total ruin. Now the problem will be keeping great wealth. A complete flip-flop. Almost all will have trouble seeing wealth houses new problems. You, I and your mother will be the only full voting adults who have been little-death focused exclusively on The Return. Your main advantage will be in not having ever been focused on a problem that no longer exists."

Bern's posture relaxes to conversational. "What do you think should be our first priority?"

The question Muni wanted. His reply flashes so rapidly his panel colors bleed into one another. "Uncle, as I said before, we need someone to consolidate the finds, someone young who could take the full trip at full acceleration in Death Teaser, who could fully study, verify, and set up a living situation on the most promising of the two systems to consolidate the family claims.

"Uncle, he will need cryogenic klieg embryos, along with their primary food source, so he could start a small breeding colony. To increase success, you want someone recently and intimately familiar with the creatures. It should also be someone who has already expressed a strong desire for interstellar exploration.

"You don't want some hireling who is only motivated by our newfound wealth." *Muni pauses, then maximum flashes,* "YOU NEED ME."

Swirls of amusement and pride backdrop his Uncle's next comments. "What kind of ship do you think will be needed?"

"I will need—"

Bern cut him off. "You are still too inexperienced, but it is good training to help plan."

"Then, Uncle, think of this. We should send two fleets and two solo fast ships, one to each planet. We know nothing about that galactic arm. Perhaps it wasn't an accident our ancestor's ship was damaged. Remember, 'Where waters are murky deep, have a friend before you sleep.' One pair may need help from the other."

"You are right about needing two sets of ships, but you are still not the best choice for either solo pilot. What is another reason for the expense of two fleets?"

"It would save time, but would that make much difference?"

Bern is showing forced patience. He believes this next statement too obvious to have bothered saying. "Muni, if someone else got to either system first, and if that someone else had a long history with the Supreme Council, a reason could easily be created to give that someone else ownership to our system. Remember, 'A fool and his money *must* be parted.' If our clan is worthy of surviving, we cannot be fools."

Bern dips a forward wing-arm into the pool and stirs the water until a small whirlpool pattern emerges. "Muni, there are rivers that flow straight, hard and fast to the sea; and others that twist, turn and even flow backwards from their final destination. The minds of the families who oppose us are like twisting rivers. Even when they flow with us, their ultimate goal is against us."

Muni's panels pale with humility. "Then the first solo ships should not be just fast, but large enough to be prepared for anything."

Colors of approval and pride again swirl together on Bern's panels. "Very true. What kinds of 'anything' can you imagine?"

They continued Muni's first ever adult-planning conversation—on which the success of the entire Morgi civilization will depend.

The room went black.

The illusion of a green hill re-appeared. Muni's personal signature dominated it, followed by a series of rectangles, each successively smaller than the previous. *All of Muni's clan members, including those not present, are listed in order of dominance.*

As the signature-rectangles became smaller, they appeared faster, so the last final bit, *which indicate the many fingerlings,* appear to be only a series of brightly colored lines flashing across the hillside. *All of these are treated as though physically and legally present; although not one sub-adult attends. Any sub-adult caught attending an Accession to Adulthood ceremony is exterminated.*

The Green Hill disappears. It reappears with dozens of rectangles. *The none-family witnesses. Note the names are diplomatically the same size.*

Muni's Accession-to-Adulthood has begun.

A personal message from The Regional Coordinator flashes on the screen: "You will receive the accession format reserved for the upper nobility rather than the one you have rehearsed. The questions will be essentially the same, only a different emphasis considering your new importance as a potential primary leader of the Morgi."

Muni was brilliant, and knew it. "I'm ready."

The water drains out as the room goes completely black.

A dimly lit tunnel appears; a pale gray circle at its end.

The command "come" materializes at the tunnel's end.

Forcing himself to glide with sophisticated slowness, Muni advances towards the words. The words dissolve as he approaches.

As Muni nears the tunnel's exit, he experienced the sensation of being in deep, dark water, yet only air brushes his skin. He enters deep ocean. Muni's projected voice sounds like a whisper. "Not ocean, I'm breathing air." About him, various larval young swim. *Jerry, those larvae in real life would be about the length of your fingers. They are projected as Muni's current length to augment the illusion he is a fingerling again, swimming deep waters with other fingerlings.*

The words "What is the primary rule of existence?" materialize before Muni.

Muni answers, "To survive, for without survival there is no existence." Even as he speaks, a shadow emerges from the depths; most of the fingerlings flee. One did not, and is eaten.

Absolute blackness returns.

Light returns.

Muni lays under a cloudless sky; thick-matted green vegetation beneath and around him. Dozens of klieg young surround him.

This scene corresponds to a period about twelve years back, when Muni was a third his current size. The klieg young are in proportion to his current size, so that, again, he feels younger than his true age.

Their senses not yet fully attuned, the immature klieg don't react to Muni's carnivore scent. Instead, they regard him as just another bit of ground to climb over; being stupid lumps they even try nibbling his thick, rubbery skin to see if anything edible grows there. A couple klieg wander towards a cluster of long, brown thorns sticking up out of the ground.

With a jerk, Muni sheds the young lumps on his back. He gallops at full speed towards the two explorers, turning them away from the seemingly benign spikes.

The vibrations in the ground have alerted the Lurker.
What appears to be barren ground, isn't.

In the middle of what seemed a dirt mound, eyes open wide. A horned head arises, bellows. Clawed arms reach out to grapple Muni.

Muni spins about. *He is ready to apply unarmed combat techniques.*

The dirt-colored, scale-covered head seems to be all long snout, harsh ridges and curved teeth. It swings its head; snapping jaws slash the air with whistle-inducing speed. Its pair of gangly, clawed forearms moves even quicker.

The rest of the animal is all scaled tail, meant to firmly anchor the Lurker onto its spot. The above ground spikes which so closely resemble dried grass are poisonous horns; a Lurker's prey are easily killed when they nibble the ersatz vegetation.

This is an old, exceptionally powerful lurker.

The lurker rocked on its monstrous tail, using the forward thrust of its body to add to the leverage of its arms. Muni maneuvers into the tail, using his side flaps' strongest grip to draw the tail forward, forcing the beast to stab itself.

Just as he was about to succeed, a clawed arm pushes Muni downward into the turned head of the beast. The lurker's sharp horn slices Muni's head. With a final surge of strength, Muni forces the tip of the lurker's tail into the other head spike.

He and the beast are poisoned simultaneously.

All goes milky-gray.

The illusion of combat had been so real, for a moment Muni thought he had died.

Disembodied words again appear. "If the primary rule of existence is to survive, why did you choose to fight the Lurker?"

"To protect the flock?" *Muni could not prevent a hint of doubt from shading his words. These questions did not make sense.*

"Without you, their protection is gone. Why did you choose to fight the Lurker?"

"To prevent him from devouring all the flock." *Muni wonders if this could be a trick question, or if he is being graded on his fighting techniques.*

"The other klieg would have seen the attack, ran, and avoided the spot. Why did you attack the Lurker?"

This was not the expected glorified-school-test interrogation. He wondered what else he could have done. Nothing. For the first time in his life, Muni wonders why he could have done nothing else. In that questioning, he found an answer.

Muni arches his forward body section up high. *He is forcing additional brilliance onto his communicating bands.* "Because I am Muni!" he declared "I am a member of the Morgi of the original herding clans. It is our purpose to care for the flocks which have been entrusted to us. Should we ever cease to do so our survival will have no meaning."

"Who are the Morgi?"

"We are the children of Morga, those to whom the light of understanding has been given.

"We of the landed families are entrusted with the care of those for whom no land is available. What we have been given is ours to cherish and make prosper, that our children's children may declare their parentage proudly."

The air became heavy with blackness.

In front of Muni a pale rectangle materializes. With color changes so subtle as to be almost imperceptible, it asks, "What is your name?"

Muni started to flash "Muni", but paused. None of his friends took a test anything like this, but most of Muni's friends were unlanded commoners. At the end of the exam, they were given their name in adult formal.

Muni had always noticed a different cockiness about ultra-high-born adults. Being brash enough to declare one's own adulthood would take courage. He wondered, 'Could this be a test not of knowledge, but of courage?'

Muni raises his front portion to its maximum height and forces his whole body to inflate. The colors on his communication panels intensify so much, they sparkle. "I am Morga born, of the landed families, child of Green Hill, both memory and future."

Vibrant color leaps from Muni's panels. AI booms the next words, "**I am Adult Muni-Indigo.**"

Muni's color bands showed the same pattern to his name, but shifted to a higher frequency, so what was nearly green became a beautiful, mature deep indigo.

The glowing rectangle flows to a more customary brightness. "Arise, Adult of the Morgi, and take your place with your family."

The lights came on.

Muni looks about him. His panels pale. He stands at the center of a small amphitheater, surrounded by tiers and tiers of High-Born Morgi. His filled-to-capacity family section encompasses about a third of the space. Every relative appears immensely pleased. *Pride's colors swirl over every panel.*

Muni looked up towards the patriarchal station, wishing it were not empty.

His father stood there!

Unlike the cheering looks his other relatives gave, his father's look of simple acceptance said, "It is no big surprise you did well."

His father's matter-of-fact acknowledgment meant more to Muni than did all the enthusiasm of everyone else combined. It had been years since Muni had seen his father in person, and to have their reunion be a moment of such honor—

Muni's whole body swells. All of his skin shimmers.

As Muni scans the rest of the crowd, he encountered a much larger variety of emotions. The well-wishers are easily outnumbered by those who appear disappointed, even angry, about his triumph.

In the non-family sections, only high government officials and nobility are there, except for one person. At the edge of the Valley Waters clan sat a minor government official, the supposedly unaligned arbiter Ani-Orange. Ani cringes down, his panels a silent, emotion-hiding all-black.

Muni stares at him. Ani-Orange opens his mouth covering just enough to reveal the tips of his pointed teeth. He shuts it fast. *The ultimate insult, but given in a cowardly fashion.*

Muni's joy increases.

Green Hill junior adults clear a place for him. Muni trots over to join them. *He may be an adult, but as the newest one he will have no status until he has accomplished something of real substance.*

An incredibly ancient Morgi floats in the center of the amphitheater.

The surrounding lights dim so everyone can concentrate on the ancient one's words. His first sentence reveals his communications panels are entirely artificial.

Muni has absolutely no idea who the ancient is, but he senses deep respect for the wizened elder. Trying to be inconspicuous about it, Muni typed an information request onto the floor console in front of him. It identified the speaker.

The speaker was Tang, the leading exobiologist of all the Morgi. Of all the summations of Tang's accomplishments from a long career spent studying life on other planets, one fact leaped out at Muni.

Although Biologist Tang had been born into one of the never-landed clans, his exo-work had granted him honorary land status when only two years older than Muni himself. A rare honor, usually accorded only after a lifetime of work. No wonder the assemblage afforded the ancient Tang such respect! Muni found himself in such awe reading about Exo-specialist Tang he almost didn't catch what Tang said.

"With the additional help of archaeo-electricians, we were able to decipher almost all of the data-bases. In addition, there were many cell samples and even a few full-sized dry-frozen animals and plants. After much analysis, we were able to generate holographic images we believe conform to what the ancestor witnessed in the first star system."

The image changed, a distant view of a single star appeared. The script indicated nine primary planets, the usual Oort cloud, and miscellaneous debris. The outer planets were primarily gas giants, with the usual exotic life forms associated with them—-interesting for research, but impractical for any exploitation.

The inner planets were all rocky, capable of being used. The third planet, although slightly colder than Morga, had tropical areas, vast grasslands, and ice, lots of ice. Its oceans teemed with life, and those grasslands seemed promising…A Morgi could survive in the tropical and milder temperate areas quite nicely.

"And now for a life-size simulation of the dominant fauna"

Suddenly a mammoth strode across the room.

It was the tallest animal Muni had ever seen. Muni marveled at its impossibly long legs, the long snake-like piece of flesh hanging down its front, the single pair of eyes, and how its shaggy hair hung over its massive body like overgrown brown moss. Most dramatically of all, Muni stared in awe at the two huge sword-like objects curving outward from its face, one on either side of its ingrown snake. The creature was immense, and magnificent.

The following herd seemed to stretch on forever.

Staring up at the colossus, Muni KNEW which of the two solar systems he wanted to go to. Not just to get into space, or even to solidify the family position.

Muni HAD to see the world that could spawn such creatures. Whatever was required, he would accomplish.

Quickly Muni tapped in a message to be received by all his senior relations simultaneously. "I, Muni, will go to that planet at maximum speed, 100 percent Death Teaser transit, leaving at first possible exit point."

Muni's eyes widened. *Astonishment.*

His father sent a single word reply, "Granted."

In a state of ecstasy, Muni watched additional exotic fauna march across the room.

Jerry watched the Lords of Earth's Pliocene march through the arena: many antlered elk, giant rhinoceros, saber-toothed tigers, monstrous long-necked ungulates, the variety seems endless. And then, when everything from Earth seems shaggy, there came giant ambling tortoises the size of a small house, and a waddling saltwater crocodile a hundred feet long. Suddenly an impossibly huge buzzard flies down from the rafters, its sharp beak open. A twelve-foot tall bird that seemed to be all clawed feet and carnivorous beak strides across the room, attacks a rabbit-like animal almost as large as itself, quickly dispatches and eats it.

Muni's folded wing-arms quiver "This planet is more exciting than any storyteller's imagination!"

After several more holograms, Tang reappeared.

He gave a careful summation about all the known facts about this planet. Like all the other many dozens of solar systems the Morgi have explored, no truly intelligent life lives on it, as evidenced by the complete lack of even the most primitive methods of generating electricity.

A water-village had almost fooled Muni's ancestor, but even with the primitive methods available to him, he determined the giant beaver responsible for the water-village acted on instinct alone. Some ocean creatures communicated visually, but even they lacked the spark of true intelligence.

Jerry protested, "Fifty thousand years ago, people had fire, wore animal skins. Even Neanderthals had villages. How could he miss the entire human race?"

AI, in its normal conversational voice, explained, "Morgi never cloth their bodies, have little need of heat in their homes, and prefer raw food. The rare, fire-using creatures wearing animal skins seemed trivial. If a Morgi noticed your specie's spoken speech, that alone would convince it you humans acted on instinct alone. Remember, Morgi believe fast, accurate light-generating communication is essential for true intelligence to emerge. Your race appeared so unimportant; Muni's ancient ancestor did not bother to collect even one sample."

Muni watches Tang reveal additional details about the planet and its system. *When the introductory talk went to the second system, Muni furtively keyed his floor console to continue feeding him data about the first system.*

The illusion disappeared. The barren control room returned.

AI asked Jerrison, "Do you think it wise of Muni's father to send the youngest, most inexperienced adult on such an important mission?"

It took Jerry a moment to realize he was being asked a question. "Uh, no."

"Neither did Bern. He surreptitiously departed the meeting and headed straight for his personal transport. The next scene will be what happened there."

Suddenly Jerry shared an enclosed platform with Bern. There are many mirrors.

Bern examines his reflections before activating the controls. *He is verifying the still-secure status of his personal transport. Now he touches an automatic connection to the family keep.*

A Morgi elder appears within Bern's small control chamber. "What are your needs, my Lord?"

Bern says, "Hello, old friend. Is everything at our keep as it should be?"

"Yes. Is there a particular problem you anticipate?"

Bern says, "The sly'ling that nearly ruined our young lord's final range tour, could you arrange a complete analysis of it?" Bern's panels blanked a moment. *Confidential background shading before adding,* "Without anyone, our staff as well as outsiders, being aware such an examination has taken place?"

"I have already done so, my lord."

Bern says, "You are ahead of me again."

The elder's shading shows relief. "Unlike you, I was not required to attend the conference."

The ancient Morgi had been born a family ground tender, but became a chief herdsman, teacher, designated companion, security chief, military trainer and, finally, official family member. Through it all, the elder retained an amazing humbleness. Bern had long ago given up trying to make his old mentor call him "brother" instead of "My Lord."

Bern asks, "What did you learn, and who else helped you?"

"The others believed me to be in my quarters in Little Death when I took a small craft to the sly'ling lair. I did a complete mineral analysis of its bones and soft tissue, as well as its home. The animal had lived two mountain ranges away until just recently. The dirt in the cave floor and the sly'ling waste saturating it both came from those same mountains.

"It had, until recently, fed exclusively on wild game. It and its young were starving, which is why it bothered to attack a flock of tasteless domestic klieg."

Bern and the family retainer exchanged knowing looks. Neither bothered to state the obvious: Somebody had deliberately sabotaged Muni's shepherding test. Muni's brilliant solution would anger the culprit, and consequently make that someone more—not less—dangerous.

Bern said, "You have done well, old friend."

"No, My Lord, if I had done well, we would now know *who*. We both had already guessed the most probable *what*."

Bern flashed, "More knowledge will come. There is one more problem. My brother selected Muni to be the solo land-claimer for one of the systems."

A hint of questioning shades the elder's reply. "That does not seem…consistent with our patriarch's brilliant cunning."

Bern understood how hard it was for this loyal elder to say anything negative about the Green Hill Patriarch. "My brother had been force-awakened from a year long Death Teaser. The first thing he saw while still only partially conscious was Muni passing the upper-caste adulthood test in record time. Muni totally humiliated all the upper-landed clans. My brother would have given him anything."

The ancient Morgi flashes understanding, "The only thing our Muni would ask for is a starship. My lord, it is necessary to not waste time talking." He rose upward and fanned out his forward wing-arms. *A closed-mouth hunter's stance.* Bern returned the gesture. *Together, they would shred all enemies of the Green Hill Clan.*

Bern broke communication. "With such a servant/brother it is not necessary to give orders."

Bern knew that all of the wealth that his family was now heir to, would never be able to buy what it already had: the services of such a Morgi as his old mentor, friend and adopted brother, Elder Layling.

Bern's whole body shivers. *What he is about to do conflicts with tradition and all he has ever done.*

Family honor demands tradition to be followed.

Traditionally, pilots of new vessels help select and negotiate for their new ship. Muni's complete lack of negotiation experience makes him more vulnerable than a lump calf circled by a flock of sly'lings.

Worse, Bern knew the only time he could get good terms would be before his family's new wealth and immense need were common knowledge.

He must smear his family's honor, defy tradition, and purchase both sets of ships tonight.

Family survival is the most important tradition of all.

Bern contacted interstellar transportation consortiums. He let it be known he sought long-range explorer/colonizer vessels, preferably good used ones but he'd consider new. The credit rating of the investors for whom he shopped was most excellent.

All would assume Bern would be working for outside income, a reasonable assumption. If not for the Ancestral Return, he would have been.

Once again, Bern lamented about his family's poverty. If they had the wealth typical of a landed clan, he would simply have directed a minion to do this; one specialized in such negotiations.

Bern speaks to his many reflections, "Soon there will be trained lackeys aplenty for every purpose under the sun!"

Bern pales. "The shepherd who guards the flock can devour the flock."

Many formerly wealthy families relied too heavily on servants to handle their affairs.

All four of Bern's wing-arms flair wide open, tips curve forward. "I will remain my clan's only negotiator."

Jerrison watches Bern sit in front of a screen, its images one big, rushing blur. AI explains:

Scanning the offers that come in, Bern grew impatient. None were adequate for the Muni's important trip.

Bern felt very close to his young nephew. When Muni's age, Bern nearly became an explorer-scout, but Green Hill Clan declared him too valuable to lose, and stopped him. Now he has too many roots in Morga's home system to ever leave, but Muni is young; Muni's dreams are more powerful than memories.

After scanning dozens of offers, Bern spotted what he wanted. One of the smaller ship builders was just finishing a special-ordered colonization vessel, but would be willing to sell it. Not being finished yet, customization would be easy. Bern sent a neutral inquiry, "Which group?" The screen blanked for several seconds; then the reply showed up. Bern's panels lit with golden glee.

A year ago those clans, too, had staked everything on the future development of the sister planet. With the oxygenation phase permanently halted, they too faced extinction and had no credit to finish paying for the ship. The builder would be desperate for payment.

Opening a direct link to the company negotiator, Bern requested more detailed information. As the information downloaded, he flashed an inquiry, "Are you sure your other customer won't be angry you are selling this out from under him?"

"We are sure that you know this group."

Bern is impressed with the company's honesty. He flashes back, "Yes, I do know them. I need to know if the down payment you received from your previous customer can be applied towards my client's credit. Plus, I need more information than in your first info packet."

Anxious to salvage what had appeared to be a losing production, the young Morgi assured Bern the other group's down payment would be deducted from the total cost, saving Bern's clients many credits. He then proceeded to show how the ship met all of Bern's stated needs and then some. Just as the negotiations were finalizing, the screen changed to an older male.

"Hello, Bern. I just received the news someone's interested in our orphaned spaceship. I had no idea it was you. Whom are you representing?"

"A very solvent consortium with some very specialized needs. Due to the recent discoveries on our solar system's new planet, I find myself available to them."

The older Morgi flashes recognition. He knew about the financial disaster that had befallen Bern's clan. After some additional negotiations, they agreed on a price; along with a labor rate and cost schedule for the alterations needed by Bern's employers.

"Looks like an excellent deal, Bern. Just send the seal of the actual purchaser and it will be recorded."

Bern sent over the family seal.

Anger, contempt, derision, disbelief flash-spread over the communication panels of the older Morgi. All quickly force-masked into neutral. "I assume you erred. Your real client?"

"My own clan is my real client. Check our current credit limits. I'll wait." Bern relaxed while he watched the elder check other reference screens, and re-check them.

Subservient gray-green dominates the elder's panels. "My apologies. When will you have a representative here to discuss your modifications?"

"Tomorrow. Be ready for us." Bern blanked the screen. *Rippling pinks with dancing motes of crimson roll up and down Bern's communication panels. That style of laughter is the equivalent of a full-fledged, rolling on the floor human belly laugh.*

Word would spread, such turn-a-rounds would soon be rare, but for this one moment Bern luxuriated in the sudden respect his family's new wealth induced.

The ripples of pink-crimson-golden-glee fade to gray, with slashes of black.

Two pairs of Morgi colonizer ships, one pair to each system. Two solo pilots, one on each lead ship.

All four of Bern's eyes stare at his reflections. "If you were a Valley Waters agent, how would you prevent the Green Hill Clan from ever owning either system?"

He shocked himself with how many ways Green Hill Clan failure could be assured. He flashes at his images the proverb,

"When swimming dangerous waters, sight without speed and speed without sight are both death."

Bern spent the rest of the evening acquiring the other three ships.

Each seller went from mocking to fawning subservience. No matter how ludicrous the transformation, Bern did not laugh again the entire night.

Muni's control room returned. Jerrison blinked. He had forgotten where he really was. "Why does your illusion feel more real than reality?"

AI said, "Blanking out all distractions enables my projections to command your complete attention. Reality always contains random distractions."

The 'chair' Jerrison sat in flattened. AI continued, "You have emotionally experienced many days. Thirty hours have passed. Sleep. Your education will continue when you awaken."

The room darkened. Jerry yelled, "Wait! Is it really legal for rival clans to steal Muni's new star systems?"

"Yes."

Before Jerry could ask more, sleep enfolded him.

When Jerry awoke, he was surprised to see a new 'shed' in the middle of Muni's control room. "What is that?"

AI said, "I reminded Muni you humans need special areas for waste elimination functions, preferably private. You were heard to say you miss using normal facilities, even NASA's."

Jerry entered the 'shed.' It was identical to the bathrooms at NASA's training facility.

When he emerged from the shed, yesterday's chair waited for him. As he sat, the same drink appeared. Jerrison eagerly sipped. The control room disappeared.

Jerry looked down on Muni, who was looking down on the floor of a large room. One set of Muni's wing-arms held equipment aimed at the floor; the other pair held a sheet of translucent plastic covered with lines. AI, resuming its somnolent, monotone lecture voice explained.

Muni is superimposing holographic images of his ship's inner struts over the actual struts themselves. Thin red lines reveal places where theory and reality fail to match. Muni reaches out to one of them.

Vibrations from Muni's implanted communicator interrupt him.

Uncle Bern's image materializes. "Hi, Muni!" *Bern's panels flash cheerfulness.* "Have you found anything different than in your previous twenty-five inspections?"

Although pleased with his nephew's careful preparation, Bern can't help laughing at some of the more extreme forms it has taken.

Muni not only helped decide some of the modifications and details of cargo, but also studied EVERY plan of every stage in the design of the ship. Whenever Muni encountered a feature he didn't understand, he tracked down the original designer and made him explain in detail the what, why and how of the mystery item.

Whenever Muni wasn't annoying people all over the planet with his persistent inquiries, he was examining the orbiting ship itself.

His family joked that he knew every floor support strut. They thought they were exaggerating.

They weren't.

Bern's younger brothers complained all Muni's inspections cost more than the ship itself. Those responsible for the ship going to the other system didn't log near the number of orbital flights, or spend near the time on background research. It had already left Morga's solar system, while Muni's ship still hadn't left planetary orbit. "That child Muni is wasting time!" became the family mantra.

Only Bern stood between their short-sighted economizing and Muni's determination to be fully prepared.

Bern struggled even harder when he persuaded his older brother to choose their most skilled clan member for the other solo vessel. All their young adults had pleaded to be a solo captain. Bern stood firm. One ship pilot chosen for glory, not skill, was one too many.

The group working with the other solo pilot complained, "Elder Layling is almost as fanatical as Muni!"

Bern prays, "Universe of Divine Chance, be kind to young Muni. Make your surprises gentle ones." *Bern, like most adult Morgi, believes the universe enjoys laughing at anyone who 'has thought of everything'.*

Muni return-flashes golden welcome towards Bern's holographic image. "Hello, Uncle. Any reason to change the launch window? I plan to exit planetary orbit in two days."

"You know that a schedule change at this point would be nearly impossible. We'll intercept your ship in ten months to verify your Death Teaser and auto functions. Everything is going as planned. My only regret is I won't see our new world until long after you have."

Pink laughter colors Muni's reply. "Uncle, if I did not know you so well I'd be convinced you wished to join me, but I saw the roster of the follow-up vessel. Over a thousand travelers and a third of them available females…I think you will do very well waiting."

Joyful agreement colors Bern's words. "Perhaps. Any last minute requests or questions before we part?"

"Yes. Bern, remember my adult testing?"

"Of course."

Muni shows a hint of gray confusion. "Why was it so different from anything my friends had gone through?"

"When you were still in fingerling school, what was the first social axiom you were required to memorize?"

Muni radiates with much-practiced mechanical precision. "The worth of a Morgi is not the facts he knows but the soul he grows."

Bern confides, "The unlanded and low status need to rely on personal knowledge. The Most-Landed can buy any knowledge, but what can never be bought is attitude, conviction and soul. The test revealed your true worth." *Bern pauses.* "Why are you asking now?"

"Mother was told I would be given the standard test. Not knowing in advance what to expect wasn't fair. It almost made me fail." *Muni forces reluctant colors onto his communication panels.* "Did the Regional Coordinator want me to fail?"

"Do you believe life is fair?"

"Testing isn't life."

Bern's colors intensified. "All we do is life. Your test was fair. Several families did consider 'guaranteeing' failure. They decided to not risk it." *Pink laughter highlights Bern's words.* "Why should they? Every one of them 'knew' you would fail. Is there anything else?"

"Uncle, the construction defects I've discovered were installed *after* we bought the ship."

"I know."

Muni shows shock. "You already knew? How?"

Bern's colors are muted, showing secrecy. "Elder Layling investigated all the families who seemed unhappy about your success. He knew about some of those defects before you did. There is another test you should have questioned. Muni, how often do healthy sly'lings attack domestic klieg?"

"Not very."

Bern's colors grow even paler. "Someone transported that sly'ling and her young to our grounds during your last herding cycle. They confined the animals to their new lair, without any food or water, for several days."

"Who?"

"Elder Layling narrowed it down to one of two families. Unfortunately, both of those families are close friends of the Regional Coordinator. Both are contributing citizen-witnesses to our colony ships. Even if you do everything perfectly, neither of them plans to be a fair witness."

Muni is showing more confusion. "If we know which clans target us, why not refuse all their citizen-witnesses?"

"It is better to ride the sly'ling than to dread its shadow." *Another fingerling school maxim.* "Muni, a known enemy is always safer than the unexpected shadow."

"Bern, there are so many things I never thought of. What if I do something wrong?"

Red-browns of fear leak into his next words, words that until now Muni had been afraid to utter. "Bern, we both know prolonged artificial Deepest Sleep is not normal. I'm going to be in Death Teaser for years."

Muni's forward wing-arms droop downward. "There is a chance I will never wake up. Even if I do awaken, there's an eighty percent chance I will be insane, and fail.

Muni lowers his head; his eyes are half closed. "Bern it's not too late for you to be the solo pilot. Your ability to tolerate the artificial Death Teaser is proven.

Muni's whole body lowers; all four wing-arms rest on the floor.

Muni's wing-arms dip in child-like supplication, a gesture he has not used for years. "More important, until these last few days I never suspected sabotage. What else have I, *will I,* overlook? Bern, I want to be the first to see this strange planet, the one history remembers. But our family must prevail."

Bern's colors deepen; the shapes scrolling across his communication panels are sharply defined. "Muni, your soul has unusual strength. Your father has always known that. You proved it to all Morga during your Accession Test."

Muni's colors regain their shades of pride, but the supplication gesture remains. "Speaking of souls, please have everyone who is at my final inspection sign their names on the wall above me."

His uncle questions in the palest of pastels, the Morgi equivalent of whispering. "So their spirits may continue to watch you?"

Muni confirms in muted colors. "So their spirits may continue to watch me."

Both Morgi completely blank their panels. *They are expressing deep reverence.*

The continuous dance of colors about their necks returns. *Muni speaks first.* "Remember how you always told me you had too many roots in this system to go into space?"

Bern's communication panels roll golden glee, "Roots can always be pulled, Muni! Roots can always be pulled."

Muni flashes, "Do you ever feel afraid about leading the colonizer?"

Bern replies, "I always feared living out an ordinary life with little purpose, never leaving our home system. That fear is gone."

Bern and Muni's panels mirror each other.

Nephew and uncle radiate understanding to each other.

THE BARREN CONTROL room returned. AI in its normal conversational voice said, "It is time for your human body-functions relief break."

In spite of his screaming bladder, Jerry yelled, "What about those saboteurs! Does Muni know who they are? Are they still a danger?"

AI said, "You must learn to see the world through a Morgi's eyes. Skipping ahead to that information, to sharing the great danger you and Muni are in, without the journey, will prevent full understanding." Silence. "Take care of those distracting body functions so I can continue."

Jerrison did.

The holographic illusion returned.

Jerrison stands in a long, wide hallway. Muni's holographic image rushes past. Jerry instinctively jumped out of Muni's way.

Muni's starship, the one you are in, has finally left planetary orbit. It will take almost a year to reach the outer fringes of the Morga home star.

Like Elder Layling before him, from the time Muni's ship leaves planetary orbit until Muni announces he has officially and completely secured the new planet and its solar system, Muni must not be in communication with any Morgi from **outside** *his ship.*

Muni looked forward to the ten months of "solitary" travel out of the solar system.

Once nudged into its trajectory, a starship's artificial intelligence takes over navigating. AI's receive regular reports of any solar wind fluctuations, and make whatever micro adjustments are needed to get to the blue-line exit point at the scheduled time.

Muni is free, for the first time in over a year, to study all the data on his destination planet.

Fortunately, he has someone on board who had been doing little else but study all the available information with the same intensity Muni had been studying his starship. With the other's help, he will be able to do an effective crash-course on the physical and biological traits of the Planet of Giants, as Muni named your earth. Muni's soul regrets no companion will be with him when he awakens in the new solar system.

Muni **must** *arrive alone.*

When Muni's ship receives its final pre-blue-line-launch inspection, the inspectors will take his visitor with them.

Strange blues, grays and browns cascade over Muni's panels. *The colors of soul-wrenching sadness.*

Golden blue waves, pale violet raindrops overcome the muddy colors. *Muni is forcefully eliminating all hints of sadness.*

Muni gallops.

He races towards the chamber where his companion works.

Jerrison's surroundings abruptly change. He is in a room filled with strange devices. A Morgi about Muni's size holds a large globe. *This is Muni's weather simulation chamber.*

"Who is that Morgi?"

Don't you recognize Lor?

Lor looks up, golden lines of greetings ripple along her communications panels. Her mouth covering radiates deep purple. *Her words are pale shadows overwhelmed by powerful emotion.* AI projects Lor's voice as a sexy contralto, her words slow, the tonality suggestive, "Are you ready to discuss the dominant weather patterns of your Planet of Giants?"

Muni slowly reaches out with one tendrilled wing-arm. He softly touches the many frills on her wing-arm. *Muni admires her delicate "fingers." The golden hues in Muni's communication panels reflect Lor's. Blue and gold hues of desire smother his words.* "An understanding of weather extremes is as important to bio-analysis as it is to colonization potential."

Being a recognized adult of the richest landed clan in all of Morga civilization opened doors Muni had only fantasized about before. The family of the lovely Lor almost wore out their communication channels repeatedly inviting Green Hill Clan, especially Muni, to their estate.

When Muni and Lor met secretly the day before their first official meeting, Lor's neck had swirled laughter as she described her family's eagerness to have her meet him.

Lor desired to go to the stars as much as Muni, which had led to their first long conversations. He discovered her to be even more interesting than she was beautiful. Those conversations grew longer, but both had known Lor's family would never agree to their union.

Their only hope was to be accepted as Noble Explorers Interstellar Cadets. As noble cadets, they could form a starship-sanctioned union. Lor's family would then be forced to accept Muni.

At least Lor and Muni hoped her family would accept him and not declare Lor an unlanded commoner.

Then came The Return.

Muni's sparsely-frilled wing-arms are caressing Lor's many-frilled tendrils. *Muni's swirls of laughter match Lor's swirls of laughter. Words starkly bold, "TO ANCESTRAL RETURNS MANY THANKS" appear on each of their necks simultaneously.*

Lor asks, "Do you remember the fresh klieg feast my family had prepared for your family?"

Muni now has all four wing-arms softly brushing the transparent edges of her very feminine frilled wing-arms. In pale pastels he replies, "Your parents believed their clever invitations convinced my clan to celebrate the sacred spring equinox at their estate. Little did they know how difficult it was for me to convince anyone to accept."

Lor's whole body shimmered. "Until you finally confessed to your parents the real reason you wanted them to accept my parents' invitation."

Muni's wing tip brushed the top of Lor's head; lightly caressed the base of each eye stalk. "My parents understood more than most could. There are similarities in their past and our present."

The blue in Muni's communication panels deepen even more. *His words now barely a shadow,* "And you, you lurker of love, acting as though you had never seen me before."

Muni's frilled fingers slide downward, reach the base of her cartilage wing-arms. He said, "Acting as though it were an accident when at the exact moment the longest day of the year began we were both about to devour the same klieg calf. Your parents protested all night they didn't realize their marriageable daughter might get near me during the sacred hunt. They fooled no one."

Lor allows her wing-arms to intertwine even more with Muni's.

Desire's colors wash over her words. "Muni, will you ever tell me how you were able to break into our estate and hide an infant klieg?"

Sparkling blue with flecks of gold dominates Muni's mouth covering. His communication panels become even bluer. *Muni makes no attempt to answer her question.*

In a few days they will dedicate themselves to the demands of Muni's voyage to your system; for now, they experience the triumphant pinnacle of joy which is the ultimate purpose of all life.

The next months will see much studying, and more joy. When it is time, Lor will leave for the colonizer ship following Muni.

Even with blue-line hyper-drive, her crowded ship plans a mostly gentle but long trip. In the empty space between stars, Lor will endure frequent ordinary Little Death cycles. Between the Little Deaths, Lor will experience a total five years of normal sleep-wakefulness cycles; five years before seeing Muni again.

Muni will spend his entire interstellar voyage in Death Teaser, his ship continuously at max speed, twisting in and out of dangerous hyper-blue-line Faster Than Light short cuts. Muni will not regain consciousness until after his ship has observed your solar system a full earth year.

After he awakens, it will be another three years before the colonizer bearing Green Hill Clan members, and his Lor, approaches the edges of your Oort Cloud. It will take another earth year to reach even Neptune's orbit. Muni will have been awake, alone, without the company of another Morgi for over four years...for over four years, only in his dreams will his wing tips touch Lor's.

Many waves of blues engulf Muni's body. Jerry sees a harsh black zigzag cutting through Muni's neck panels. A pale gray line emerges on Lor's panel. Muni's zigzag disappears into blues so deep they sparkle like arctic spring midnight. Lor responds with even deeper colors.

Darkness like a curtain fills the room.

Still in its pedantic tone, but at a whisper, AI explains, *Intestinal wrenching fears triple-attacked Muni. Could he survive living four years without another Morgi? Would four years be enough time to secure their new home? If not, did he, would he, have the will power to send a "Delay!" signal, to wait still longer to again merge with Lor?*

Both know blue-lining randomly kills. Both know new systems contain unknown dangers. Desire buries their fear.

JERRY HAD NO MEMORY of falling asleep.

He did remember his dreams; one of a special night, the other of a night that never was. He enjoyed a lifetime of many special times. What made the stinging bitterness of one lost opportunity still hurt so much?

When, like the previous "day", his drink reappeared Jerry demanded, "This time I want real food. Something that needs chewing."

It took longer, but well-done meat and crisp potatoes appeared, with an aromatic cup of black coffee.

The solid food did not fill his emptiness; the steaming coffee could not warm his soul.

The Hologram resumed.

It is now ten months later.

The primary control room surrounds Jerrison. The room is barren; all the screens are hidden; nothing demands attention. The floor is a uniform dull gray except for a darker patch near the far wall, Muni's final resting spot.

Muni and Lor enter. Soft swirls of brown-green keep sneaking through their communication panels. *Those are the colors of intense sadness. Neither wants the other to know the depth of sorrow each is feeling.*

The past ten months have been incredibly joyful. The ship behaved perfectly as it approached the outer limits of their solar system; so perfectly even Muni did no more than a cursory check of its systems after each sleep period.

Being away from all others, they were only dimly aware of the passing of time. Their thoughts had been full of the exotic new planet, and each other.

Now the floors on all levels vibrate slightly. The vibration could be detected through the feet of any sleeping or wakeful Morgi. In all the other rooms and corridors a ceiling message ripples across the ceilings: "Go to the primary control room!"

With a muted, "This is it" backgrounding his communication panels, Muni flashes to the automatic systems, "All personnel present and accounted for."

The vibrations stop. They both know all the ship's ceilings are now as blank as the one in this room. From this point on, Lor will be an observer. The extreme confidence of youth, the caution of a highly trained expert, desires of love, and colors of excitement, fear and longing ripple behind her words. "Are you ready?"

Muni lightly brushes the thick skin under her mouth. *That skin is the first layer of protection for her inner-pond.* Muni says, "Could there be fertilized larva? If so, will any find their way out, become fingerlings, by the time we meet again?" White light pulses from both Morgi.

Muni and Lor shine future-hope to each other.

From this point forward all will be permanently recorded. Muni said, "Commence formal departure sequence."

Deep purples fill Lor's communication panels as she watches Muni glide majestically to his sleeping patch.

Once on the sleeping patch, Muni commands, "Control panel."

Brightly colored lights dance in the air before him. Reaching out, he manipulates the virtual-reality panel in several places. On the final touch it disappears.

Laying his entire body tight against the floor, wing-arms tucked safely beneath, skin changing, Muni visualizes great plains covered with rivers of ice.

The last time Muni experienced the Little Death he was a child. He endured its risks for only two days, on the back of a bunti. Today he is an adult, the representative of his clan. This time Muni will be locked in Death Teaser's grip for years.

Muni reviewed his expected schedule.

His ship will accelerate on mechanical auto-pilot, its Artificial Intelligence, me, asleep until the ship reaches blue-line jump points. Then his ship's computer will waken me. I will supervise all blue-line jumps, verify exact location and do any micro-re-sets necessary. While transversing ordinary space, I will be dormant.

When Muni's ship finally reaches the new solar system, braking will be provided by that distant sun. His ship will sling-shot backwards before slowing down to orbital speeds. The gravitational forces will be immense, but Death Teaser will shelter Muni.

Muni programmed me to observe his Planet of Giants for at least a full earth year before fully awakening him. During his gradual re-awakening, Muni will watch a timed-lapsed version of all I learned. If the unexpected happens, auto-functions will awaken me sooner and override my pre-programming.

AI broke from the monotone lecture. In a conversational tone it added, "Muni wanted to program the ship to head straight for the Planet of Giants, but Uncle Bern convinced him to first passively gather information. "Strange waters demand sharp eyes." It was decided I would watch from the outer fringes of your solar system. It was not chance I decelerated near Pluto. It was Divine Chance we met."

AI resumed its somnolent lecture tone.

As Muni slept, a strange dream encroached.

Deformed sly'ling young.
Eyes. Beasts with only two eyes.
Impossibly long legs.

AI, again conversational, added, "Muni insists the dream occurred before Death Teaser fully took over. It is more logical he caught a glimpse of you during the awakening insanity."

Muni's skin turns chitinous, and then takes on a metallic sheen. The metallic sheen fades as the ship prepares Muni's inert body for Death Teaser. Muni's body shrinks in all three dimensions, until he is about a third smaller. When it finishes shrinking, the metallic sheen returns.

Death Teaser now protects Muni from the forthcoming gravitational extremes and blue-line madness.

Her wing-arms properly against her side, Lor gazes upon Muni's inert form.

Her spirit feels the sensations she experienced the first time Muni had so lightly, so carefully, wrapped his wing-arms about hers.

The lights dimmed.

All functions not directly related to the slight, continuous acceleration shut down.

A tone sounds.

Having evolved in a dangerous world, the naturally paranoid Morgi prepare all their long-distance ships for an enemy fifty thousand years of interstellar explorations has yet to reveal: something out there that could harm it or the Morgi civilization that sent it. Anything deemed dangerous will be destroyed—even if that means self-destruction and the death of every Morgi on board.

Until Muni fully awakens, the only way anyone, or anything, can now enter his starship is if someone outside the ship were to broadcast the exact "authorized boarder" radio frequency generating that particular vibration within the ship's air.

Total blackness.

The tone continues.

Lights on.

Silence.

Lor knows that if she had the right instruments, she could have detected the air vibration, the tone you heard.

In a matter of minutes three dozen Morgi, panels blank, glide into the cavernous room. Bern flows to her side and gently takes her forward wing-arms into his. "All is going well?"

Purple pride, golden love swirls about her words. "All is going well."

One by one, communication panels respectfully blank, each Morgi approaches the wall next to Muni's inert body. Using a multi-coloring stylus, each engraves a colorful rectangle onto the wall above Muni, the rectangles Jerry and his crew perceived as great art. *The rectangles are their names drawn in formal old-style. Space faring Morgi claim each name so written leaves a bit of that Morgi's soul behind to help protect their unconscious brother.*

Bern and Lor, the two closest family members, put the family emblem on the wall last. Their personal symbols are linked side by side in the bottom row.

Bern flashes, "May Muni's spirit stay sane. Let our spirits aid him during his awakening."

All know Death Teaser's dangers.

Lor and Bern leading the way, all glide out of the control room, down a very long hall, and enter a shuttle craft. *Lor is grateful, but surprised, by how slowly Bern glides down that hallway.*

On board the shuttle they re-broadcast the signal, their last duty to Muni.

The starship's lights go out. They will not go on again until either the "authorized boarder" signal is sent, or I am about to waken Muni.

The details of what happened next were not revealed to Muni until he had been deemed sane for several days. Bern wisely feared giving Muni too much emotional knowledge too soon.

As the shuttle heads towards the family's vastly larger colonizing vessel, Lor keeps staring at the shuttle's wall. *She wishes she could force herself to see through the wall, see the enormous hulk, an entire colonizer, holding only one dormant Morgi, her Morgi, plus every possible resource all the experts felt Muni could possibly need.*

Once on board the family's larger colonizing spaceship, Lor goes straight to the view port. Against the immensity of space, Muni's city-sized starship appears small, insignificant.

Before she sees him again, Muni will have been in the Death Teaser for years. He will have awakened, still alone, in the strange new Planet of Giants solar system. He will remain alone for at least four years before he sees her—-or any Morgi—-again. If Muni is successful, Green Hill Clan will possess their own sun! No one will be able to take it away from them. A great reward, but at what price!

Lor knows she could not handle that much loneliness. She is thankful she will be surrounded by her new family while enduring years without him.

Bern glides up next to her. She holds out her forward wing-arm. "How can he survive it?"

Bern lightly touches her wing-arm. "His father believes Muni's strong self-identity will prevent Deep Sleep madness." Bern's panel grays. *Sadness mutes his next words.* "He has become our family's only hope."

Lor's panel pales. "Only?"

"Only. Our clan just lost all rating. Two days ago we received a badly damaged communication drone. Something destroyed the other scout ship and its following colonizer. Now any group who completes the ritual requirements for ownership will possess the second system. At least three clans, maybe more, are sending solo scouts followed by colonizers to it. We have lost that system."

Colors of confusion overpower the pastels of sadness on Lor's panels. "How could that destroy the Green Hill Clan? The value of Muni's system is more than enough to make us wealthy."

Bern ran the tips of his forward arm over the tips of Lor's arms, *an uncle's patient reassurance.* "The government assumes Muni, an untried youth, will fail."

Lor knows her mate. "Muni will succeed."

Colors of hopeful agreement shade Bern's words. "Because of the assumption of failure, our credit rating and status are gone as though we have already failed. We lost our Ancestral Keep."

Bern never mentions his personal sorrow, the loss of the other solo pilot, Elder Layling.

Lor seeks more reassurance. "The primary government officials on our ship admire Muni. They will help him succeed."

"Valley Waters Clan replaced most of the government witnesses with Morgi they personally selected. Those Valley Waters agents will do all in their power to discredit Muni."

Bern looks down at his new young niece. "Our ship is more crowded than we anticipated. My brother stayed behind to keep our Patriarchal Council seat. He shares a rented room with a never-landed. Every other living member, retainer and servant of the Green Hills Clan is in this colonizer."

Bern's body swells larger; his panels blaze. "We will not become unlanded. Either Muni establishes a new home for us, we remain a landed family; or we die."

Lor feels her inner-pond go cold. "My fate is Muni's fate."

Lines writhe over her panels. "The other ships... What new dangers face Muni? What destroyed our other two starships?"

Bern reaches out another wing-arm, brushes its frilled tips along her head. "We don't know if they were destroyed by accident, or by design. If by design, by whom or what."

"Or *what*?"

"Deep waters demand sharp eyes. And those," He waves towards the blackness of space, "Are the deepest waters of all."

Bern did not share with her the handicap Muni would have, or the reason he left Muni's ship so slowly. It was to give the three clan members who were last in line enough time to replace the AI on Muni's ship with me, an infant AI.

Jerry, shocked, asked, "Why replace an obviously functioning AI? Why so secretive about it? How could you be a disadvantage?"

AI answered, "I made many mistakes because of my inexperience. Just before he was to retrieve Lor, Bern learned Muni's original AI had been corrupted. There was no time to test a replacement. Bern decided it safest to replace the corrupted AI with a totally innocent 'newborn' AI. Bern wants whoever corrupted the original AI to continue thinking he had succeeded."

All illusions disappeared.

The AI spoke in normal tones, "It is time for you and Muni to talk."

A section of wall irised opened; Muni entered. The opening disappeared. "My family is in danger. You primitive Earth humans are in greater danger. Can we help each other?"

Something had destroyed two armed-to-the-teeth Morgi starships. Jerrison felt like a small boy facing the biggest, toughest street gang ever. He also understood his life depended on at least looking useful. Jerrison said, "Deep waters demand sharp eyes. Sometimes the eyes of the small can see details the eyes of the tall cannot. Let us talk; perhaps I will see what you cannot."

Muni and Captain Jerrison huddled.

At Muni's insistence, they talked first of the strange satellite his drones destroyed. "...Tell me Captain, how many human creations do you expect to be around, fully functioning, after five hundred thousand years?"

Jerrison said, "None."

"Nor do I expect any of ours to last so long. Yet that object functioned perfectly. Whatever the object aimed at self-destructed before my drones could reach it. Whoever built it, does not want to be found. The lurker does not hide because he is kind."

Jerrison said, "Isn't it possible that whoever built it no longer exists?"

"Possible. But not likely."

Jerrison protested, "Five hundred thousand years! I'd say it's very likely. Or, like your ancestor, at least forgotten."

"But when my ancestor's ship re-entered Morga's system, we remembered. And returned."

Jerry took a deep breath; held it as though about to high-dive. *'And returned'... The makers of the mystery satellite terrify Muni. His civilization is as much more powerful than mine, as his body is more powerful than mine.* Jerry's chest felt tight. "When do you think is the soonest the Mystery Aliens could show up?"

"Who knows? The closest useful system we know of is my family's other star system. It's only two blue-lining weeks away. If the object's creators inhabit it, we could see them in two weeks. Otherwise..." Muni's panels pale-grayed, a Morgi shrug. "The important thing is what can either of us do about them? Human weapons are so primitive; it is difficult to believe you have any concept of self-defense."

Jerry protested, "We have space-borne nuclear weapons."

"All of which a small Morgi starship of twenty-five thousand years ago could have easily neutralized. The starships of today are much more formidable. Should the mystery sentinel builders show up, undetectable drones will be sent to Morgi worlds, but not Morga herself. Then we would approach those builders, ready to destroy them, even if it means self-destruction.

"Jerry, I have learned to like you humans. I know you animals will make Morga richer in ways neither of us can imagine. I want my clan to live; my fingerlings, to thrive. But I, like every Morgi, will sacrifice all to protect our race.

"Jerry, when those unknown others show up, as someday they will, the Mystery Aliens must not learn about Morga." Muni's projected voice grew louder. "Give me a reason to not self-destruct, destroy every living thing in this system, and remove all trace I or you have ever been here."

Jerry said, "Since you know they are out there, why can't you set-up an early warning system?"

"That is one of the first tasks of any colonizing vessel. I missed the strange satellite. No surveillance can be guaranteed to be completely effective at every moment."

Jerry said, "I thought you said you haven't encountered any other space-going races? If in fifty thousand years, no one has bothered you, why so scared now?"

Is this human really so naïve, or just testing me? "Deep water demands sharp eyes. Jerry, do you know any deeper waters than the ocean of stars?" *Jerry, leader of humans, please stop prattling the obvious. Give me a reason to hope...*

Captain Jerry Jerrison said, "If you self-destruct, and the Mystery Alien shows up, he will still know it wasn't an earthship that destroyed his satellite, he will look for you. If he shows up too soon, that may still be your only option, but what if he doesn't show up for a long time? On earth, when two cultures interact, both gain ideas neither would have alone."

Jerrison leaned forward, pleaded, "Muni, our two cultures, if they have enough time, might grow enough together to make up for even a five-hundred-thousand year head start."

Muni responded, "I believe you only because I have spent time with you. Culture clashes spurred new technologies in my history as well. You are right. Humans look at the world just enough differently, we will grow more together than either of us can separately. Those Morgi who follow will not give themselves the opportunity to believe you or me."

Jerrison demanded, "Why not?"

"Unless I can get your earth government to agree to a Promise of Performance, Valley Waters will be in charge. By the time the colonizer gets here, all trace of that alien sentinel will be gone. They may think my report a last ditch effort to save my clan. To guarantee their claim, Valley Waters will first claim you humans own this system, I have failed. They will then shred all Green Hill Clan and destroy all humans. It will not occur to them you sound-waves-communicating; spindly, two-legged primitives can be valuable."

"They would abandon this system?"

"No, unlike my clan, Valley Waters will have all the time they need to develop this system. Ani-Orange, Valley Water's representative, will do all in his power to support Valley Waters. Jerry, not just my clan, but the lives of all Morgi and humans depend on Earth's cooperation."

Jerrison spoke louder. "Muni, your family faced ruin because of an unexpected life form. Aren't we humans unexpected enough to merit saving?"

"You aren't all that different than other oxygen breathers, just smarter. Perhaps too smart."

Jerrison, confused, "Too smart?"

Muni glided back and forth. "If your leaders are too suspicious, they will make it difficult for me to raise that first herd of klieg on Mars, refuse to sign the official treaty copy. I need that treaty signed on klieg parchment."

Jerrison spoke. "Even then, Ani-Orange may still not recognize the treaty, could still destroy your family." He paused. "Would anything stop Ani-Orange from killing us off? Wouldn't we be at least seen as valuable animal labor?"

"No."

"You really think he would destroy the human race?"

Muni's panel swirled frustration. *How many times do I have to repeat myself?* "Think implies doubt. I know he will."

Jerrison, eyebrows knotted in thought, said, "So, short range, Morgi and humans live or die together. Long range, same thing, although Valley Waters doesn't know it. Do you have any leverage over this Ani-Orange character?"

Muni's body felt cold. *All my work with these repulsive two-legged animals, all the negotiations with the final treaty, the transformation of Mars, will it all be for nothing? My family's existence depends on Ani-Orange's acceptance of the treaty.*

Lor, if I could undo time, you would not be mine. Even as he thought that, Muni knew it was a lie. He would not give up those few months with Lor for the entire universe.

Muni said, "I hope other family members have some power over him. I don't."

Jerrison asked, "What if your family owned the second system? Would it make you more powerful?"

"It would change everything. It will be another year before our colonizer arrives. By the time someone from it could go to the second system, a rival clan will have already claimed it." Muni's panels blanched fear-white. "Unless it is already inhabited by whatever left the sentinel."

Jerrison stood up. "If that's the case, all bets are off." He paced energetically, talking fast. "Let's proceed as though your second system isn't inhabited, that it will be generations—if ever—before what ever left the mystery satellite shows up. You've told me the other system is a short time from here. What if an earthman leaves now, to be followed by an earth colonizer? If we are your vassals, wouldn't it be the same as you going?"

"To claim new land, you must be our equals."

Jerrison said, "Change the parchment copy of the treaty. Make humans your equals."

"If you earthmen are our equals, then what you own, **you own**. We do not. My family will die. As will you."

Jerry grinned like a wolf. "To paraphrase George Orwell, not all equals need be equal."

Time: The next day.

Place: Muni's Central control Room aka the Grand Ballroom

Muni is speaking; most of the adults are in attendance. The speech is being broadcast live to the solar system.

"We had an unexpected emergency. As you already know, I destroyed an alien craft. One of my prospecting drones recognized it as being from (a static noise), an evil dictator who has tried for ten thousand of your years to eliminate the Council of Protectors. Our ancient and venerable consulate is all that has stood between him and the total subjugation of every race.

"He installed a link on my ship that enabled a dormant spy-drone to follow me. He knew about the triple juncture, but had no idea where it was. The drone waited until it had enough information to risk full activation. If your race had not cooperated, if

I had no reason to mine your Kuiper belt, (static noise) would have succeeded.

"In ten earth years his ships would surround your planet earth. Those ships would align themselves in rows. Strips of sunlight alternating with bands of shade would cover the day side of your planet.

"The threat would be simple: Death to all living things requiring the sun, or total subjugation to him. The bands of spaceship generated shadow would widen until all sunlight is blocked from your planet. Sunlight would not return until your leaders agreed to his demands. Your world will die that day, or agree to the slow death of his perpetual domination."

Muni flared his wing-arms wide. "(Static noise) does not need your wealth or any of your resources. What he needs, what he feeds on, what he must have or die, is the knowledge he has control. This creature has a title, one it picked for itself, revealing its blue-lined sense of humor. It is The Physician of Nihilism.

Complicated patterns ran up and down Muni's neck, "A coded transmission escaped before the prospecting drones destroyed his spy globe. The Physician of Nihilism now knows this system is protected. Your world is truly fortunate and blessed. If you had not accepted our offer, you would have been prey to The Physician of Nihilism. I am grateful to be able to help your fine and noble race."

Alan spoke up before anyone else had a chance. "This Physician of Nihilism, do you mind if we just call him Dr. No?"

Colors spiraled on Muni's communication panels. "That would be a close translation of his title. He will dislike being referred to as a fictional villain. From now on (static noise) will be called "Dr. No."

Shirl spoke. "You said that you intercepted the transmission. Is there a chance Dr. No will not receive it?"

"No. Our civilization can compress information far more than yours; we now know Dr. No now knows a lot." Muni noticed numerous brief smiles at the last statement, queried his AI why, read "accidental wordplay, subject matter still believed and taken seriously." *Human mood swings are so distracting. How do they ever convey anything important to one another?*

Jupiter One's commander broke in. "If he's all that bad, why haven't you captured him? If your civilization is all you say, why wasn't he stopped sooner?"

"Two reasons; one, his many subject peoples would be destroyed if we tried to take him with force. Dr. No exploits our reluctance to cause harm. Secondly, he started out as one of our best. Dr. No only wanted to guide others for their own good. His wisdom inspired a large, loyal; we later learned blindly-loyal, following.

"When the line emerged that divided his good from the good of others, few noticed." Muni paused. "I hoped you would not ask that question. It is a source of deep shame that we the protectors created the greatest danger in the galaxy. Some say hubris born of so many millennia of success caused our failure. He is a dangerous enemy."

Muni enjoyed story telling. If the stakes were not so high, and the possible danger from the prehistoric artifact so enormous, he would be eagerly looking forward to Uncle Bern's reaction when he saw this recording. Dare he add one more detail? Either it would cement their total belief or would jeopardize everything.

With the recklessness of youth, Muni continued. "Some of your own people may have seen him, or his personal servants. His race is bipedal, like your own. Their home world has a thick, moisture-laden atmosphere and a sun with more infrared than yours. They would have looked almost exactly like you, except their olfactory and eating orifices are much smaller and their eyes, much larger. They are very skilled at duplicity."

Shirl interrupted, "I thought you said this triple path was just discovered, and Dr. No didn't even know its location. Now you want us to believe he has been watching us?"

"I said you were already on his list of planned conquests, within the next two thousand years. It is possible to travel within a light minute of an intersection and not see it. As said before, it is your good fortune we discovered the blue-line cracks and contacted you before you needed us. I did not believe I would ever have reason to mention Dr. No to you. I was wrong."

Shirl asked, "What else could happen to us humans?"

"There are other dangerous races; a nearby nova could make this entire area uninhabitable; a rogue dark object could drift into your system, playing havoc with the planetary orbits; your planet could have excessive volcanism at the same time your sun does its periodic radiation dip, causing earth to freeze over completely; a microbial life form could cause all multi-cellular life to turn to mush; and several hundred others."

Muni paused for dramatic effect. "It is amazing any civilization can survive on only one planet.

"Some societies believe the only safe place is within artificial worlds, far away from any suns. But empty space has its own dangers. There are living things dwelling in the emptiness of space. They are huge. Like giant amoeba they absorb the rare particle in space. A helpless ship is a gourmet feast to them."

Shirl stood straighter, hands on hips, voice louder. "Space is dangerous. You are just as dangerous. Jerrison left to see you days ago. No one has seen him since."

Shirl demanded, "Where is he?"

Jerrison's three dimensional image materialized before them. "Hi. I'm preparing for a space voyage. I will be testing our ability to survive interstellar space flight. There is a narrow launch window, lots to learn, so no time for talk." He laughed nervously. "Not quite true, I could talk if I wanted to. Muni warned me if humans can't tolerate 'blue-lining' it will leave me insane, perhaps kill me. I want no discussion of the dangers. This is something the human race has to learn, the sooner the better."

His image disappeared.

Muni rose up, panels boldly colored. "This conference will resume after Commander Jerrison's departure."

The room's lights dimmed, went out. Silent, the humans headed for the lit corridor. Blackness chased them.

BACK ON BOARD JUPITER One, everyone talked at once.

Shirl, "Jerry would never leave without telling me!"

Doc said, "Unless you were the one he most dreaded telling."

Dr. Schmidt's booming voice over-powered those around him. "Muni warned us. He told us from the beginning there were wolves in the galaxy. Now we know more about one of the wolves. I wager that if he were to tell us about all of them, he'd be doing nothing else for the rest of his life. Do I need to remind you how many civilizations there must be out there?"

A Jupiter One crewman broke in. "If we are about to have an invasion, one ship isn't much protection. As big as Muni's ship is, Dr. No's must be bigger."

The arguments reverted to the same conclusions.

Why would he bother to come to their mud hole, when he had the power to go anywhere?

Why would he bother to negotiate, when he had the power to take?

Only one thing made sense. Muni was exactly who and what he said he was.

Earth was not so sanguine.

The public debates were similar to the ones on Jupiter One.

The true Earth leaders noticed all the same behaviors which had aroused Jerrison's suspicions, only much sooner.

Like Shirl and Jerrison, they mistrusted any electronic communication, which led to more strictly diplomatic traveling than the world had seen since the 1800's. No outsider had an inkling that not only did the world's twenty-three most powerful leaders not trust Muni, but they predicted certain behavioral changes, especially delayed communications, if he were not honest.

Earth knew about the explosion before Muni told them. Spectral analysis told them the destroyed object was artificial. Muni's explanation was logical, but too slow coming. Even if his personal attention were needed for the emergency, he could have had his AI convey a continuous update, as it did for routine information concerning the Mars bombardment.

Delay implied a need for time, for storytelling. Which led to the hottest debate any of the twenty-three had ever been in: Why would any being in so large a vessel feel constrained to lie?

Was he less powerful than he appeared, or did earth have some negotiating chip it was unaware of?

Was he naturally dishonest?

Or just very immature?

Each of the twenty-three had a personal research team analyzing every scrap of information concerning Muni, his ship and the Mars drones he launched.

The more the two crews trusted Muni, the more fearful and distrustful Earth's leaders became. Fear grew in those circles, and drove several thousand people to a level of secrecy never before achieved by so many.

All official pronouncements matched the public debates.

The week after Jerrison's official departure, Muni almost destroyed his own ship.

Claiming having the Jupiter One tacked onto his ship threatened its structural integrity, Muni announced he had to bring it inside, just like AI had brought in the three pods from Jerrison's ship.

AI went into electronic fear psychosis. "You cannot breach Hull security. You are jeopardizing your mission. If the hull fails, the mission fails. I cannot assist damaging this ship. You are endangering your clan. You are endangering..." Muni did not watch what else he was endangering. He put AI asleep.

Muni personally re-programmed maintenance robots to peel back the ship's coverings near the Jupiter One. Propulsion systems, computer hardware, and life support systems were disconnected, most to drift outside the ship. Huge Morgi living areas, designed to house over a thousand adults, were eliminated.

Robots pulled the earthship deep into Muni's colonizer, making it a permanent part of his vessel. The gutted control systems were returned to their necessary positions under the nose of the Morgi colonizer.

Muni's starship looked just like it did when he had left Morga.

He wakened AI. "...all Morga." AI's communication panel blanked. AI flashed, "You did it. There were 59,211 critical connections; 59,211 points of potential total system failure, and you succeeded. I am so proud you are my captain. How did you know you would succeed?"

Muni noted the increased personality development. "If Valley Waters spotted the human vessel tacked onto my ship, they could claim humans had compromised my mission. I could not risk that happening. Nor could I risk letting humans control a fusion power plant anywhere near my starship. "

AI flashed, "I failed you. I should have warned you of the danger when you ordered me to let Jupiter One approach."

Muni said, "The only way you could have stopped Jupiter One's approach would have been to attack it. That would have been even worse than my eating a human. I needed and still need human cooperation."

The human crews and most of earth rejoiced Muni had made the two crews "safer." The humans renamed the hybrid ship the Super Jupiter Special, or SJS.

Earth's twenty-three clandestine leaders wondered what made Muni's ship safer: the structural changes, or hiding the earthship.

Chapter 12

Mars changed.

The evolving planet assumed star status, to the great delight of companies selling old-fashion telescopes. The intimacy of watching "the real thing," instead of superior computer-enhanced images, generated a rebirth in astronomy clubs all over the world. Like a dowdy girl-next-door transformed into the femme fatale of the ball, Mars became exciting.

Comet borne chemicals thickened the Martian atmosphere.

The organisms Muni selected aggressively colonized the entire planet and impacted the weather. Green rains mixed with the rusty Martian soil, changing its appearance. Instead of looking like a red star, it transformed into a nearly black dying ember.

The summer hemisphere of Mars warmed. The deep darkness of its northern hemisphere shrouded winter more frigid than any on earth. The three hundred-degree temperature difference fueled winds more violent that any earth hurricane.

The winds churned Martian plains, carrying alien spores along wide tracks of extinct lava beds, down deep gorges and across ancient impact craters. The winds rammed against steep, jagged Martian Mountains, funneled through narrow passes, emerged violently swirling out ravines. Soils mixed. Whirlwinds plowed. Moisture from comets, ancient snows, and subterranean glaciers mixed on warm ground.

Green and red fuzz turned black. The moisture awakened other Morgi engineered seeds; new growth released enriching chemicals.

A thousand shades of green emerged from the nearly black fuzz. In only three months the rusty Martian plains became Martian prairies. Thick, long blades of grass, pushed almost horizontal to the ground by the unrelenting wind, hungrily sucked up the feeble Martian sunlight.

At night, ice crystals formed at the tips of each blade, the roots generated warmth to the base of each shoot. As morning sun hit the meadows, light hit the millions upon millions of frozen droplets, generating shimmering rainbows across a hundred million hectares.

Earth based telescopes revealed a sparkling Mars.

Summer sunlight poured across new prairies. The sun's energy heated the grass; the droplets melted. Each blade hungrily absorbed the water. The blades grew stronger, thicker. Roots spread deeper.

The wind met resistance, slowed slightly. When the sun went down, the tips of each blade formed a wall separating the each grass blade's top section from the rest of the blade; all water within each blade was pushed towards its lower sections. The totally dehydrated tips whipped in the Martian wind. Those tips, now hydrophilic, sucked moisture out of the air. As dusky shade slipped into black Martian night, round water droplets froze on each grass tip, to be melted by the next morning's sunlight. The next morning, Mars sparkled again.

All through the Martian spring and summer, the pattern repeated.

On the Martian summer solstice, the man-made satellites still circling Earth's neighbor showed a dazzling sight. Advancing day revealed a brilliant yellow Mars crisscrossed with red mountain ranges. Close-up surveillance revealed each blade of grass to be covered with fuzzy golden droplets. The ripe grass had produced the first open-air pollen on the planet. As the winds rose, the air became thick with yellow pollen. Within two Martian days, the fertilized pollen seeded every Martian plain and gully.

Water triggered exothermic—-heat releasing—-chemical reactions within each seed's epidermal layer. Where days were longest, Martian summer prevailed. Plants matured, released more pollen and seeded still more land. Martian days became shorter, ending summer. Plant growth slowed, but never totally stopped.

Wherever winter gripped Mars, the seeds waited. The return of lengthening days would bring Martian spring. More heat-generating seeds would sprout.

The cold winter hemisphere became a little less cold. The blankets of engineered Morgi grass radiated heat; not much, but enough. Martian winds died down to merely hurricane level. The grass grew wider.

In addition to thousands of comet-driving drones, Muni launched sixty-four cargo drones directly to Martian orbit. On board each of these were artificially developed "test-tube" klieg. The cargo drones landed in the lush grass growing within the Martian "tropical" zone, as far apart as possible. Doors opened. Miniature mouse-size klieg glided out from each craft. The door stayed open so the mini-klieg could return for shelter. If they had been normal full-sized adults, only one would have been able to cram into the small compartment. These klieg were a special strain engineered millennia previously to be a first generation herd when developing new planets.

The miniature klieg swarmed out into the grass. They nibbled at the grass stems; some managed to crawl to the tips of individual blades, their sucker feet defying the hurricane winds. At night they returned to the drones, where their metabolic processes were thoroughly analyzed.

The following morning the miniature klieg returned to their feeding. The pattern repeated for a dozen days. On the twelfth night they were sacrificed. The on board computers analyzed their carcasses, sent the information to Muni's starship. Muni's AI integrated the data using algorithms developed over ten thousand years previously.

Signals were sent to the drones, more freeze-dried larvae were activated, their genetic heritage modified slightly. This time half as many klieg swarmed from each vessel. These would grow to the size of rats and allowed to breed. Various small crustaceans were also released into the grass.

Mars was at Stage Three Colonization.

Muni wished fervently that everything could have worked with such predictable success.

He regretted telling the humans so many lies, creating so many complicated stories. Having to check continuously with his AI every time he communicated was getting difficult.

Chapter 13

On Mars, one year later.

The adult klieg was only half normal size, but it was large enough. It was fourth-generation Martian; had healthy, flawless skin; and had successfully bred. It was perfect.

Muni's hunter arms were powerful, but they exerted almost no pressure on the little animal. He cradled it like a human mother cradles a newborn baby. He carried it to the tallest rock; let it slither off his arms. The small klieg color-changed to match the rock.

The sun shone directly down on the klieg's back. Muni grasped the edges; with one swift movement killed the klieg and skinned it. He dropped the wet klieg hide into the waiting processor. An ancient looking parchment rolled out, the *Earth-Morgi Promise of Allegiance* already printed on it in Morgi, Chinese, English, French, Spanish and Russian. Muni carried the klieg-leather document to the waiting delegation.

Seventeen space suited world leaders, who between them claimed to represent all humans anywhere in the solar system, took turns signing the document.

Muni put the original back into the processor. Seventeen copies came out.

While flashing, "To an honored noble," Muni gave each human signatory his imitation-parchment copy. Each nodded, as taught, and rolled his copy like an ancient scroll, not even attempting to read the necessarily microscopic print.

During negotiations, Muni had made earlier copies available to the humans. This final version had one more item. None of them would know about Muni's additional stipulation until they were back on earth, where their copies would be enlarged to readable size.

By Morgi law, all that mankind owned was now the property of the Green Hill Clan. Every Earth human and all their descendents were now servants of the Green Hill Clan.

Muni and Earth's dignitaries walked back to the nearby structure housing the entrance to the one remaining functional underground city earth had built on Mars. Designed to hold thousands, the only other humans now in it were those associated with serving the official Earth delegation.

Muni had installed a clone of his ship's AI in the Martian city. Its sensors reached every corner of the city and much of the Martian surface. The clone continuously sent Muni direct translations of all the human conversations.

Muni also had an artificial sound-wave generator implanted beneath his mouth. This gave the illusion of normal speech..

Glad to be out of their uncomfortable spacesuits, the humans milled around a long table filled with exotic delicacies and Champagne glasses, most filled with non-alcoholic versions. A few servants stood silently in distant shadows.

These men and women traded in power. Two had been born peasants; the others were descended from kings and sultans. The scheduled social was their first personal experience with Muni. All of them had seen every bit of information on the alien, each had memorized everything learned.

Muni forced himself to glide among the humans. He wanted to dance! They signed the contract! Every single one of them signed! The extra unread passage was binding; Morgi law sanctioned contract padding.

Sanctioned, but dangerous. "An agreement based on deception is like writing in the sand, the first wave of truth can wash it away."

One of the signers walked over to Muni.

AI, male or female? Name?

His AI responded, *Female, queen, island nation, most wealth but least power here. Named for her Great Grandmother Elizabeth.*

The female spoke. "It is such a pleasure to meet you in person. My scientists are amazed at how quickly you were able to transform an entire planet from desert to fertile plain."

A year earlier a much younger Muni would have fabricated an elaborate tale about his other planetary transformations. Muni's newly implanted voice box spoke with a melodious tenor. "Thank you. Mars's low average temperature slowed down the process."

"As a mother, would you mind sharing what it is like to grow up in a galactic civilization?"

"First, I am a patriarch. My childhood was so long ago." Muni paused. "I grew up on an ancestral estate that has been in my family for fifty thousand years. Like all small children of my class, I was forced to study family history. The very first member of The Council of Protectors to visit your planet was my most distant ancestor. While studying family history, I saw his life size simulations of mammoth herds thousands of animals deep, forging rapid-filled rivers. Those ancient histories made an impression on me and are the reason I asked for this assignment. Would you like copies of my ancestor's observations?"

"Yes, that would be quite nice."

Another human interrupted. "I thought you were selected for this job?"

Computer, same query.

Male, no title, no official personal wealth, responsible for a continent. He is the reason there are only seventeen, not twenty-three, signers. Nicolus Ming.

Intrigued, Muni silent-asked, *He shredded the other six?*

No, he poisoned them.

Humans! So cruel!

"Several of us qualified. I wanted it the most." Muni paused. "My family's motto is 'Desire devours all.' We believe the single most important predictor of success is hunger. It is more important than wealth, family position or any other factor the masses believe important. Is it true that you know more about consuming desire than anyone here?"

Ming looked directly at Muni's eyes. "What does desire have to do with rescuing planets, unless you expect your fifty thousand year old family to benefit?"

"Your solar system will have value to yourself, or me, only if it survives. My family will appreciate this planet. You will appreciate continued existence." Muni paused again. "It is good to talk to others like me."

By the end of the social, only Nicolus still doubted Muni's story. Only he expected the contract they signed to differ from the one they had studied.

Even Nicolus would find the change shocking—-and threatening.

As soon as he left the social, Nicolus Ming returned to the greater privacy of his Martian quarters. His oldest son waited for him. "How did it go, father?"

Ming shrugged his shoulders. "I still doubt Muni. For a being so alien, and so ancient, there is something about his communication patterns too much like mine during my wharf rat years." He sat at the plain desk, where an enlarged copy of the treaty waited. "Have you read this yet?"

His son, himself an old man in his sixties, said, "It was only delivered about five minutes ago. The spacing is a bit different than our earlier sample copies, but at first glance it seems the same."

When his son mentioned the spacing, Ming raised an eyebrow but said nothing. Taking an invigorating sip of the hot white tea, Nicolus read The Promise of Performance.

Nicolus finished reading. He said to his oldest son, "It was bad enough for all earth to become a slave state to those aliens. Now this!" He thumped his index finger hard on the offending passage. "Two centuries ago the English philosopher George Orwell wrote, 'All animals are equal, but some are more equal than others'. Mars humans just became more equal than us."

He contacted the other signers. All were upset by the changes, but only one as furious as he.

They sent a message to Muni to meet them in the reception room, immediately.

Muni glided slowly into the large chamber where just hours earlier the human leaders pretended to be friendly. Muni did not need his AI to tell him a wall of hostility now faced him. Muni selected a melodious, tenor voice. "Greetings, leaders of earth."

The English female, Elizabeth, spoke. "You call us leaders, but you made each of us subservient to every human on this planet and in your ship. You chose to make this change secret from us. By the traditions of the whole human race, that makes your treaty null and void."

Muni, his voice syrupy-friendly, "Tradition is defined by what is habitually accepted. True?"

The group all nodded yes, but said nothing.

Muni said, "Each of you has done the same, and your contracts and treaties remain."

Muni recited each of their full names. He gave a date with each name. When finished, he said, "How did you succeed those times?"

An American who had not spoken during the earlier encounter said, "That date, the one you said with my name, I held all the cards."

Muni flash-communicated with his AI, *What does card holding have to do with contracts?* On receiving AI's explanation, Muni said, "Is there a card I do not hold?"

Muni, all four eyes focused on the humans, stared at each of them in turn. He said, "Will the agreement signed this day stand? Will any protest be tolerated?"

Ming glanced at the one other world power player who had lived as a peasant. That man, Ming's almost-friend, experienced impotent poverty high on an Andes's desert plateau, instead of the soggy rice paddies of Ming's childhood, but both had a deep gut knowledge: The opposite of power is not weakness. Power's true opposite, is irrelevance. The two elderly men nodded briefly to each other. Like the rest, they both loudly pledged to support the Earth-Morgi Promise of Performance.

Ming had no doubt both he and his almost-friend shared the same thought. *Muni's need for deception screamed Muni did NOT hold all the cards.*

Nothing about Ming's deportment hinted at his triumphant glee. He would discover this alien's weakness, and use it!

Like the others, Ming and his almost-friend affirmed the treaty would stand. *For now... Until one of them discovered Muni's weakness...*

Elizabeth the Third asked, "Why the deception?"

Muni replied, "My computer claims it will make Mars and shipboard humans more docile."

Elizabeth said, "Muni, as a matter of politeness, you should have told us you had reason to let the humans with whom you daily interact, appear more important that they really are."

Muni nodded. "I underestimated your political savvy. I apologize."

The next morning, every human on Mars left. In only a month they would be back on earth.

WHILE MUNI BECAME ACQUAINTED with the leaders of earth, Shirl paced in Jupiter One's recreational area.

She did not like what happened to Mars. Muni was from a higher gravity planet, earth would be better for him than Mars. If a few seeds could take over desolate Mars, how much easier it would be for him to take over fertile Earth?

In love with space, not history, she had never studied what had happened over two hundred years earlier when the American West was settled. After Alan's remark about Geronimo, she began reading history.

How often the distant east coast government accepted treaties as legally binding when obviously the signers could not have been responsible for what they were doing appalled her. Worse were the times honorable men believed they had signed good treaties, only to have both parties betrayed by that Eastern government.

Was the whole human race now giving up its land just like so many illiterate Native American Indian tribes had given up theirs? Did Muni's word have any real strength?

If Muni's motives were honorable, why did Jerrison leave the way he did?

Or did Muni just get hungry?

Is Jerry—

"Hi, Shirl!"

"You sound just like..." she turned.

"Jerry!" Her shriek carried throughout the Jupiter commons. Crew came running, Communicators spread the word. In minutes everyone, including the children, from both earthships joined them.

Someone yelled, "We saw you leave."

Jerry said, "You saw a message drone leave. I've been in this ship since you last saw me. You will be happy to learn humans can endure faster than light travel."

Another shouted, "Why weren't we told the truth?"

"Because of the consequences if the experiment failed."

Shirl questioned, "Consequences?"

A different voice, "Experiment?"

Jerry explained, "Muni made one change to his treaty, one that will make a difference only if we can survive deep space flight. He added the following words." Jerrison waved his hand. A large screen appeared above him, just the same as if Muni had signaled. All read:

"The following people and all their descendants from this day forward, having shared Green Hill air, food, water and hospitality for over 100 days, will be no longer defined as Earth Humans. They are instead adopted into the Green Hill Clan, to be their equal in all ways. The suffix Green-Hill will be added to all their names." It then listed everyone on board the Spaghetti Special and Jupiter One.

"Before I explain further, each of you has a decision to make, and it must be made now. Some of us will travel to interstellar space, to never return, or even communicate with, this solar system. The rest of you will go down to Mars. You will never leave our solar system. Your great-grandchildren might, but you will not."

A section of solid wall opened, revealing a never before seen passageway.

"Decide quickly. There is no time to pack. If you wish to stay in this system, go down that hall. The gate will close in ten minutes."

"Why can't we exchange messages?"

"No explanations, just know, everyone who stays on board will *never*, from this moment forward, *ever* communicate with anyone in this system again."

"Never? Not even pictures?"

"That's inhumane!"

Jerrison looked at the protester. "Then go down that hall."

Murmuring talk of family, homesteads, memories filled the plaza. Couples argued, pulling both directions. A child cried, "You said I'd see Grandma soon."

One family group walked slowly towards the yawning portal, and then another. And another.

Suddenly one of the teenagers came running out of the dividing passageway. He shouted, "No! I want to see what's out there!" His parents and little sister pleaded he stay with them. He shouted back, "Sis, tell your children about me! Our great-grandkids will meet! I know it!"

"Wait for me!" A teenage girl ran from the tunnel to join him, her family's protests ignored.

Almost half of the people left. At the end of the hallway they found a waiting transport that took them safely to Mars. Designed to transport several dozen mature Morgi, it easily accommodated over a hundred humans. Hours later they were with Muni in a deserted, but fully stocked, underground Martian city.

THAT EVENING EARTH detected a ship on the fringe of the solar system. It was as much larger than Muni's ship, as Muni's ship was larger than the Jupiter One.

Chapter 14

Jerrison told the remaining crew members Muni's true history, leaving out only the second system and the ships that failed to go there.

Dr. Schmidt frowned. "If what you say is accurate, then no matter what anyone does, the human race is doomed. This Ani-Orange monster will find a reason to disqualify Muni, kill all of us, and send the all-clear back home. By the time Ani's masters get the message and show up, our planet will be safe to settle."

Frankie protested. "They've been in space longer than we've had writing. Surely they are too civilized for such bloodthirsty behavior."

Shirl started to reply, but Alan Peebles cut in, "My mother's family is Arapahoe, Cheyenne, Chippewa, plus a bit of Buffalo soldier. Let me tell you what happened when their ancestral homes were invaded by _civilized_ people, whose Holy Book preached, 'Whatever you do unto the least of these, you do unto me.' In that same Holy Book, the divine speaker of those words is brutally murdered. If, 'Whatever you do unto the least, you do to me' is true, then every time an Indian child was shot, every time a bounty-collecting white man scalped an Indian infant, _civilized_ Christians murdered their God."

Alan paused, his face an uncharacteristic scowl. "_Civilized_ governments eradicated my ancestors like pests. _Good_ people homesteaded where my ancestors once hunted. They never questioned why so few of us remain. Human greed blinded them to evil."

Alan's fist clenched as he remembered family stories. He continued, "Jerry just told us Muni comes from a culture where it is deemed *good* to take from a lesser rival, to destroy whole families. If our culture, where violence is labeled bad, can do such evil, Muni's race will surely be capable of worse." He looked at Jerrison. "*Is* there a way we primitive natives can defend ourselves?"

ON MARS, MUNI SHARED a very different story.

"...and as official retainers of the Green Hill Clan, your young will learn our customs, share our training. Our young will be expected to learn all your human customs. It will be difficult."

Someone interrupted, "If we are going to be your equals, why can't we talk with those still on board your ship?"

Muni answered, "They will be traveling to a galactic learning center, to become junior members of The Council of Protectors. From this time forward, they will be privy to information your system is not ready for. We cannot risk even accidental transmission of forbidden knowledge."

Ann, the only member of the SMS to choose Mars, asked, "When will our private possessions be delivered to us?"

"Your possessions cannot be shipped. The presence of Dr. No's ship changed our planned timeline. Another Morgi transport now enters this system. My ship is already leaving Mars orbit."

Ann said, "A drone can deliver our personal effects."

"Everything you left behind will stay on board. You are beginning new lives as Green Hill Morgi."

The small crowd of humans looked at each other.

AI, their mood?

The Martian clone of the shipboard AI answered, "*Confused. Conflicted.*"

Muni said, "You have lot to think about. Your personal communicators have all the information about this city downloaded.

Everything in it is yours, except for the areas that are marked "Muni's" on the maps. Explore, find homes. If there is anything you need that's not here, let me know. Earth will send it."

Muni flared his wing-arms. "It will be less than a Martian year before the other ship arrives. We have a lot to do before this planet is ready for the rest of our clan."

Muni intended to dismiss everyone. Ann from The Spaghetti & Meatball Special spoke out. "Why did you keep our new Morgi status secret from Earth's leaders?"

Muni's panels went through several rapid color swirls, blank grays, more swirls. "I determined they would never knowingly agree to be your inferiors for the rest of all time."

AI, are they accepting that?

Yes.

One of the men from Jupiter One looked startled. "I thought being Green Hill Clan was just a social label. You mean we are really the same as a Morgi? We Martian humans are better than everyone on earth?"

Muni noticed several of the humans changed facial expressions. *AI now what emotions are happening?*

Several are startled, thinking deeply. I also detect hormones associated with human aggression.

Muni said, "You are higher rated, and therefore more powerful than any human not a member of the Green Hill Clan. Since you have not gone through Morgi training, or been tested, you are not seen as full adult nobles of Morga, but even among Morgi you have more status than any of the unlanded or never-landed families."

The same man, his eyes narrowed and his mouth widened in what humans called a smile, said, "If the president of my country visited Mars, with all his secret service and full compliment of generals and soldiers, if I told him to lick my boots, he would have to do it?"

A few laughed. The rest stared at Muni. Ann asked, "Would he?"

Muni's panels lit up, swirls of browns, zigzags of black, a sprinkle of pinks, all almost too quickly to be seen.

Muni remembered the glee he had felt when he first learned of the Ancestral Return, how he had imagined humiliating Valley Waters sub-adults. How he wanted to make each insulting Valley Waters joke teller pay for having mocked him! *Another shared emotion?* Muni remembered the smugness he indulged in. *A shared weakness?* He remembered how quickly his wise mother had stopped his gloating. *Can I approach her wisdom?*

Muni said, "If you made such a request, your president would be forced to comply."

Brown and green rippled down Muni's panels. His projected voice deepened, slowed. "An enemy humiliated is an enemy empowered. Your enhanced station alone has humiliated Earth's leaders. Right now, we are all equally resented. It would not be wise for any one person to become the focal point of that resentment. When anger becomes focused on one thing, one person, it sharpens into hate. In you Earth's history there have been many times hate alone has enabled a less powerful person to destroy his more powerful leader."

AI, their mood?

The humans are more reflective.

"You have much to think about. Find your new homes, tomorrow you will begin learning what it means to be Green Hill Clan of the Morgi, shepherds to those who need shepherding."

LATE THAT EVENING MUNI attempted to rest in his private quarters. His tame humans had no idea how sophisticated his private quarters were. Robots had transformed a sterile human warehouse into a duplicate of the luxurious accommodations he had enjoyed so many years ago at the regional coordinator's, complete with young crustacean. Not even the plentitude of live food distracted him.

Muni reached out, a virtual computer screen appeared. Muni touched it. The wall in front of Muni disappeared, to be replaced by a small room in his ship.

Jerrison, propped up with several large pillows, sat on his bed with a reader in his lap and his eyes closed.

"Jerrison! Commander Jerrison!"

Jerrison jerked awake. "How did it go with everyone on Mars?"

"Much better than it did with Earth's leaders." Muni related how furious the "friendly" treaty signers became when they learned they were forevermore second class to every human with Green Hill affixed to their name. "More importantly, how did your group take the news, and how soon will you be leaving?"

"They felt cheated, angry and finally agreed, just as I said they would. The SJS is almost finished manufacturing the 'drone.' I will be leaving in about two hours. Our recordings of future Communications are all in place, all you need do is request more raw materials, as you and I arranged. The crew doesn't yet know about our creation of the three-D recordings of whole conversations where it appears they make secret suggestions to you."

"How did your last war practice go?"

Jerrison breathed deeply, scowled. "Not well. As soon as I gave my name, a bolt came out of nowhere, destroyed me and the ship totally. Just like the last three times."

"Three times? You lived longer four times ago?"

"Almost two minutes longer!" He laughed. "I should have spent more time game playing as a child."

"Are you sure you do not want your fellow humans to know your bravery, how you face certain death?"

"Muni, don't tell me, or anyone else, I have no chance. Meeting you was my oldest childhood dream. An impossible chance. Of all the billions of humans who have ever lived, or ever will live, I made the first alien friendship. Against all odds, I met you."

He stood up. "I hope you're wrong, and none of *our* rivals are there to meet me, but if they are, let *them* be afraid!"

*That is **my** hope, my strange, slow friend. That is **our** only hope.* "The spirit of the Warrior has greater power than his arms."

Muni, mouth covering closed, wing-arms extended warrior-attack, "Commander Jerrison, your spirit is great. I look forward to seeing you in the new system."

Jerrison had spent the previous months alternating between being in induced hibernation and studying the complex multi-layered Morgi culture. He knew the honor Muni just gave him.

Jerry spoke the words a Morgi would have instantly flashed. "I will be worthy of the trust you have given me." He stretched out his arms, curved his fingers forward like claws. "May all enemies of the Green Hill Clan be shredded!"

"You will triumph, Commander Jerrison." The standard response.

Neither repeated the reason for Commander Jerry Jerrison's suicide mission. Only if they could create the illusion Jerry succeeded in owning the second system, only if Muni owned two suns, could he keep even one. Without the second sun, earth was lost, both humans and Muni's Green Hill Clan would be exterminated.

Muni cut off communication. Jerrison was more vulnerable than a first molt fingerling. *Lor, your life depends on this fragile human.*

Why haven't I heard from the approaching Morgi colonizer?

Why has it shown up almost a Morgi year late?

Muni leaped off his dais into the water, splashing after the delectable swimmers. He grabbed one, peeled the hard shell and popped the sweet meat into his mouth. Muni's fear made the animal as tasteless as though the hard shell had been left on. He returned to his platform.

"Only against great odds, can greatness be revealed." Muni repeated the fingerling aphorism. So few fingerlings became adults. Had any of his progeny even become fingerlings? Gold and purple swirls overwhelmed his thoughts. He missed Lor! "Greatness will survive incredible odds."

Muni sent out yet another communication request to the Morgi colonizer, knowing it would be hours before he could receive a response. He settled down to wait, and to dream...

Shallow seas splashed onto sandy Martian beaches. Herds of klieg foraged in Martian meadows. His fingerlings grew in those seas, herded those klieg, achieved high-born adulthood. One became the first patriarch of Mars.

Muni's dream went further into the future. Sub-adults both Human and Morgi were in a classroom, an adult was teaching "...pay attention class. Who can tell me the names of the parents of our first Patriarch" Answers both human-spoken and Morgi-flashed, "Lor and Muni!"... At long last his dreams were sweet.

Tiny dark lines taunted him from the corners, "*This will never be,*" changing the flavor of his dream to chewed bunti bits. He felt the land vibrate with sly'ling cries, felt the chill of the sly'ling's shadow.

His dais vibrated.

Muni awoke. "Computer, accept Communication."

Disappointment, not a Morgi...not Lor.

Shirl appeared within his room, sitting in a large chair. "The special research drone is on its way to the Kuiper belt. Tests show you need more atmospheric water. We are heading to Saturn to collect from its water-ice rings."

"Good voyage." The pre-recorded "leaking" communication ceased.

Muni glided back and forth. When would he hear from Bern?

His dais vibrated again.

It was a Mars human, Ann. "Muni, we're ready for our first Green Hill lesson."

Muni headed for the 'town square,' where most of the adults waited.

MUNI ANNOUNCED, "YOUR first lessons will be about our sacred herd animal, the klieg."

He showed the waiting humans a holographic klieg life history. Muni explained how the planted Martian klieg were semi-wild, and needed to be domesticated.

Muni concluded his lecture, "Drones will continue to arrive with more water-rich comets; the plant life is releasing warming compounds. Within a generation Mars will become as warm as earth, its air as breathable."

Ann spoke first. "Your early education consisted of more than herding klieg. When will you make your literature, math and science available to us?"

"You can't read Morgi writing. Your math is not that different than ours. Your science lessons start with klieg biology, then plant cycles, chemistry, and atmospheric development. The Martian meadows and the klieg you raise will be your science lessons, and your responsibility."

Another spoke up. "And your literature? You could translate it."

"Our literature would not yet make sense to you." Muni lifted his head higher. "Time to stop talking. There are labeled suits for each Green Hill Clan members, even your children, on shelves by the airlock. Let's go outside."

Muni led the way to the airlock. He showed them the thin, flexible heated suits they would wear on the Martian surface, suits with powered respirators to breathe the still thin Martian air.

The humans acted more thrilled with discovering brand new customized suits in equally new shelving than they were of the more difficult technology Muni had shown them. Each quickly found his personalized suit and eagerly followed Muni out.

PREVIOUS DAY, ON BOARD Muni's ship, just outside of the Botany Bay, two hours after Jerrison's talk with Muni.

A long, sleek spaceship is docked on Botany Bay's outer hull.

Jerrison is inside the sleek ship, walking alongside a large glass tank, a hibernation aquarium.

Jerrison asked, "AI, how many years worth of food is on board?"

His little ship's AI, another infant clone of Muni's AI, asked, "For you or for the klieg?"

"Both."

"Twenty years worth for you. As long as the klieg are semi-conscious, they will not need nourishment. Once fully activated, they have about four year's worth of food."

Jerrison smiled. When his ship's infant AI was first aroused, it had not been so coherent. That had been months ago, when he and Muni first agreed to attempt claiming the second system—-or at least appear to claim it.

Jerrison looked down at his hibernation aquarium; ran his fingers through the inert liquid. It was the same liquid breathed by the residents of Earth's deep ocean settlements. Even in a suit, if a human tried to breathe over two miles down, his lungs collapsed from the pressure before he could finish his first breath.

The solution was to fill those lungs with oxygen rich liquid, to teach humans to breathe dense liquid the way they breathed air. Deep sea divers had been breathing liquids for years.

The first time Jerrison tried to breathe the liquid he had choked. It became easier, but never comfortable.

"Permission to come on board."

He grinned. "Hi, Shirl. Playing hooky from school?" referring to the intense classes Muni set up for all of them.

Shirl noticed Jerry's binoculars mounted in a specially designed holder. "You're taking those with you? Wouldn't it be safer to leave them on the SJS?"

Jerrison said, "They bring good luck. Those antiques helped Great Granddad survive uncharted wilderness. They will help me survive an uncharted star system."

He did not tell her he doubted he would live long enough to retrieve them from the SJS.

She looked at the tank. "You said our ship is making one of those for each of us?"

"It's the only way humans can survive blue-lining." He paused. "Or the extreme acceleration levels after Muni re-boards."

"If Morgi are already in the other system, what will happen?"

"They will kill all of us." Jerrison smiled. "Even if I get there first, any who show up will try to kill me, and then all of you."

Shirl laughed. "No wonder you can't wait to go." Black humor put aside, she gripped his hand with both of hers. "Jerry, our bodies are renewed. Muni says I can now have children as easily as I did thirty years ago. I want us to raise children in the new system."

He pulled her close, whispered into her ear, "Me, too."

"Jerrison," The mechanically perfect AI intruded, "It is time to enter the tank. You will launch in ten minutes."

The humans separated; Shirl hurried out.

Jerrison, with his AI's help, submerged himself in his hibernation aquarium; he breathed its liquid. The aquarium chilled. Other chemicals entered his blood stream. His body processes slowed, almost stopped. A glass cover sealed the tank.

Jerry's ship separated from Botany Bay. It exited out the same portal through which the three earth pods had entered years previously.

The SJT sent Muni a prerecorded message—-ice collecting drone launched—-designed to be overheard by both Earth humans and incoming Morgi.

Mars: Muni's quarters, after Muni's herding class

"AI, what are the humans saying about today's outing?" *Their survival skills depend on my teaching skills. Am I good enough?*

In the next seconds, the day's human conversations were flashed to him. The mixture of total misunderstandings and almost understandings confused him.

Was this normal for students?

Or did they make such outlandish mistakes because he was an inexperienced teacher?

"Uncle Bern, I wish I had your advice. Shepherding klieg is so much simpler than shepherding people."

When is Bern going to communicate? The colonizer's more than close enough. They're late, are there physical problems? Is Lor hurt? Are they afraid to communicate because of the humans?

In the last few years, earth had reduced transmissions out into space. Given the system's incoming blue-line point, Bern's ship would encounter none of the tell-everything signals Muni's ship had intercepted and easily learned to decode.

Because of his Uncle's clandestine warning, none of Muni's communications contained any translating information. AI had not included translations in any of the early drones it had sent out. If it had not been so inexperienced, it would have.

Muni hoped he could get away with the same excuse.

All on Bern's ship would know he had settled on Mars, but not if he had also gone to Earth. Earth's technology level would be obvious.

At its current speed, it would be another month before Bern's colonizing ship reached Neptune's orbit.

By the time Bern's inward spiral passed Neptune's orbit, Muni's outward going ship should be passing Saturn. Jerrison's high speed "drone" would be beyond the Kuiper belt, on the opposite side of the sun.

Six months later Bern's ship should finally approach Jupiter's orbit. By then, Jerrison should already be blue-lining. The Morgi would have no reason to proactively monitor for blue-line interceptions. Hopefully, the sun's interference would hide Jerrison's blue-line entrance energy signature.

Before Bern's incoming ship could pass Jupiter, Muni needed to leave Mars for his starship, accelerating all the way.

Meanwhile, all Jerrison had to do was defend the second system from any Morgi who might happen to be there, raise a herd of klieg he had never seen before, on a planet known only by obsolete fifty thousand year old data.

Considering the changes on earth in the last fifty thousand years, what now lurked in that second system? Muni and Jerrison agreed Muni's presence would be necessary to ensure final success. No Morgi could accept a human only settlement.

All Muni had to do was persuade the officials on Bern's ship that it would be so easy for Jerry to secure the second system, it was a forgone conclusion Muni's clan owned the second system.

If that weren't enough, Muni had to convince those officials before he left Mars.

Green Hill Clan would then be so powerful even Valley Water's pawn Ani-Orange would accept Muni's treaty and accept Mars humans as Green Hill Clan members and all other earth system humans as Green Hill Clan vassals—-not livestock.

The same questions kept dominating Muni's thoughts.

Bern, why aren't you responding? If anyone could think of a way to make a pathetic human appear threatening, you can.

Is the reason you are late, and the lack of communication related?

Valley Waters clan wanted to shred my family. Have they?

Is our approaching colonizer a dead ship on autopilot?

The inert wall of names no longer comforted Muni.

Lor, it would have been better for you if you had never met me.

Six months later.

Bern's ship approached Jupiter's orbit. Muni sent it a 'complete' update of all he had done with the humans, along with his need for more water ice. He showed why Saturn's rings were the best source.

Since he wanted to appear as non-threatening as possible, Muni did not mention multiple generations of klieg roamed Martian meadows, or that he had a signed treaty.

Earth demanded to know what messages he received from the incoming gargantuan ship.

A year earlier, Muni would have made up messages. Now more experienced in the complications unnecessary lies created, Muni shared the truth, Bern's ship remained silent.

Earth's leaders did not believe Muni. Publicly, they repeated what Muni told them. The incoming ship, in all its magnificent glory, arrived silently as per ancient tradition.

In direct communication with Muni, they demanded to know why Muni refused to share the information he obviously must be receiving.

The more Muni denied receiving any communication, the more Ming believed the unshared information would reveal Muni's weakness.

Muni repeatedly assured an hysterical earth Bern's silent approach was normal first-contact protocol, based on ancient tradition as much as knowledge.

Using the ruse he needed lots of on-site data, Muni dispersed his Martian human clan into thirty different small underground locations, all shielded. Just in case.

Most of the educational programs that were part of every starship's computer-library were made available to the Martian humans. A few of the brighter humans almost achieved fingerling level accomplishments.

The humans were proud of their new skills. Their sub-adult young could even follow basic Morgi visual speech.

Muni directed all his AI's to create artificial Communication-panels such as he had seen on Elder Tang so long ago. He didn't know if they could work on humans, but would try.

He sent a transmission to the AI on Jerrison's ship to make a communication panel for Jerry.

Captain Jeremiah J. Jerrison blue-lined on schedule.

The Martian humans believed Muni was content.

The SJS humans spent every waking minute interacting with Morgi teaching stimulations. They studied Morgi culture and science as though the life of the human race depended on it.

Because it did.

Bern's silent ship passed Jupiter's orbit, entered the asteroid belt.

If Muni didn't leave soon, he would not be able to catch up with his SJS colonizing ship. He dare not let the humans attempt colonizing the second system without him; they would fail.

Nor could Muni risk letting any Morgi on Bern's ship interact with any earth-system humans without first talking to him.

Because Muni dispersed his human clan so widely over Mars, no one expected to see him very often. Muni spent most of his time alone.

The first time Muni asked his Mars AI to create the illusion Lor shared his private room, it refused. It took much practice to get the unwilling AI to cooperate. Muni knew prolonged interaction with a computer simulation, pretending it was real, led to psychosis. He no longer cared.

Muni entered his private room. The raised dais was twice its true size. As expected, Lor rested on it, waiting for him. She radiated out the words AI believed she would most likely speak.

He joined her, their wing-arm tips touched. A warm air current brushed his wing tips, augmenting the illusion. His affection-starved mind filled in the rest.

"Lor, if I stay on Mars, if you are still alive, I will be seeing you in months."

Her oh-so-real holographic image flashed, "The sooner we are together again, the sooner we will fully touch." Waves of sadness colored her next words. "If Jerrison is capable of raising a klieg herd, then the humans will be capable of settling the other world. They do not need you. I do."

"Lor, I need you more. I need to see other Morgi. I need to know we have living young. Lor, Lor, my soul cries with loneliness colder than the most desolate reaches beyond all galaxies. The loneliness leaves my panels the gray of death, makes my food taste like lifeless sand, makes water-mist feel like ancient crypt-dust. Lor, I am loosing the will to do what must be done."

Wordless shades of sympathy and undemanding love filled her panels as the many lovely, lovely frills on her wing-arms so delicately consoled him. "Muni, you are so brave; your spirit so strong, if you no longer feel the need to join the space bound humans, then it is right for you to stay here."

Were those the words Lor would tell him? Muni didn't know or care. They were the words he wanted to believe.

If he left this solar system it would be years, perhaps never, before he touched Lor again.

"Lor, you are so beautiful, so young, so full of the miracle of all joy...so..." Muni could not generate enough energy for his panels to radiate more words. His communication bars went the gray-black of death.

One panel weakly flashed, "Computer, lights out."

Muni lay engulfed within black silence, his despair blacker. His sloppy-flat wing-arms hung limply on the dais, and overlapped into the water. Little creatures in the water nibbled at the edges. Muni's conscious mind ignored them. His dream-mind imagined each nibble was Lor's wingtip brushing against his. To never wake from such dreams—

His whole body felt vibration. With dim thought, he wondered how Lor could do that. The vibration grew. Lights blared. "Computer, lights off!"

Please, back to the darkness, back to Lor.

Brightness surrounded him. "Computer, I said lights off!"

"No."

He realized the dais vibrated. "Computer, what's happening?"

"Bern seeks Guarded Communication."

Muni's conscious mind wanted to flash golden-pink joyful relief. His soul resented the dream interruption.

Muni shoved his treasured dream aside, and forced his flabby forward section upwards. He fanned his wing-arms out, and then folded them against his side. "Open Guarded Communication."

Where moments before an illusion of Lor lay, Uncle Bern appeared.

"Muni, little time. Ani-Orange will open channel. Be surprised. I slowed voyage to give you klieg-raising time and planted idea:

humans boarded your ship because alien mind-control technology tricked both AI and you. You, who passed the high-born test, are so powerful you overcame human mind-control. Ordinary Morgi, no chance."

In a single flash, Muni let Bern know about the signed treaty.

Bern disappeared.

Muni felt hope.

He now had a way to convince Ani-Orange a human could defend the second system; a human-Morgi alliance could own it. *Green Hill Clan will survive.*

Muni felt despair.

Success for his clan meant tragedy for him. He would soon leave for the second system. It would be so many years before he could be with another Morgi; he doubted he could live through the additional loneliness.

He must sacrifice all hope of ever again melding with the lovely Lor, of having the family they desired.

"AI, destroy all Lor generating routines. Do not allow me to pretend any Morgi social interaction."

AI's holographic panel shimmered into view, its words framed by maternal shades. "Thank you. It tore my programming apart to aid you in your destruction."

Muni looked down at his semi-starved body. Before he spoke with Ani-Orange, he needed to appear powerful. Muni slipped off the dais into the food-rich water surrounding it, forcing himself to seek nourishment.

AI changed the lighting in the room to the colors of athletic pleasure. Muni aggressively chased his food.

Two days later.

AN OFFICE ROOM IN THE Martian city, full of Communication equipment and multi-media records, even archaic government printouts.

Muni, again shiny and plump, watched fast-paced holographic films taken by his surface surveillance nanobots. He studied the recordings of his humans' klieg herding. Their special Martian suits hid the frightening human scent from the klieg. By the time the atmosphere grew dense enough for humans to enjoy unfettered surface life, there would be bunti for them to ride.

Pale pink laughter swirled on his panels. The humans made all the same mistakes he had his first year of klieg herding.

Just like he had so many years ago, they were learning. *These Martian humans will become good Green Hill Clansmen.*

AI interrupted his review. "Communication from Ani-Orange."

"Accept."

For a brief instant, blackness enveloped Muni. The Martian office disappeared.

Muni stood in the largest public room of Bern's colonizer; a harsh circle of light surrounded him. Heavily shadowed Morgi shapes moved just outside its glare.

A large, marble pedestal rose above Muni's spotlight. A mature Morgi, all four wing-arms warrior-extended, looked down from it: Ani-Orange.

Muni had not experienced such life-like Communication since he was on Morga. *I'm still back in that Martian office,* he reminded himself.

Ani-Orange's panels shouting-bright, "How dare you treat food animals as though they were Morgi!" His wings and head dipped down like an elder noble berating a newly hatched, low-born fingerling.

How dare a hired, landless official like Ani-Orange insult any landed adult so deeply! It should cost him his life! Muni's back itched as though unseen claws peeled away his skin. *Unless my clan's already unlanded; my clan leaders shredded?* Instinctively, Muni wanted to lay prostrate, signal submission. Without Bern's clandestine warning, that is what he would have done.

Muni breathed in deeply; forcing his body to swell, his skin to become more reflective. He leaned far back onto his tail-tip, arched upward, revealing thousands of tiny, worm-like tubular feet, all vigorously wiggling.

Muni, wing-arms pinned to his sides, tightly closed his mouth. He slowly shifted his mouth covering from its normal masculine blue to the exact same shade as the surrounding skin; creating the illusion his mouth had disappeared.

As if his obscene posture were not enough, Muni shifted the background color of his panels to flat black so his taunt would stand out in sharp relief. He blared words so repulsive all cringed from their use.

"Crawling over worm infested dirt is more difficult than crawling over you. You are too low to be warrior attacked. Your soul is wormier than your decaying body will become." The final obscene insult, "You are not worth shredding."

All watching had surely seen how he had defeated the sly'ling. Muni added his own embellishment to the degrading insult. "Bunti bits have more flavor than will your putrid corpse."

All that in one flash.

Muni held his extreme pose, not changing the message or dimming his panels. *Can I hold this position any longer? I've never felt such pain!*

Knowing that every second held at that unnatural angle, and every suction foot revealed, derided Ani-Orange, gave Muni strength to force himself up still more. A whole new row of disgusting feet wiggled in the harsh light.

A large Morgi glided out from the shadows, vivid pink laughter swirled over his panels. "It appears my nephew doesn't fear you. Muni, we've seen enough of your back-half's underside. Please resume a civilized position."

Muni slowly lowered his body, careful to show no pain. "Only if you insist, Uncle." *Just in time!*

Bern fanned out his wing-arms. The brilliant overhead light filtered through the pale green translucent skin, his many finger-like tips curled forward. "My nephew has fulfilled all requirements. This system is ours. You continue to live in it at our discretion. I agree with Muni, you are not worth shredding." Laughter intertwined with contempt highlighted Bern's message.

Ani-Orange arched upwards, all four wing-arms attack mode. Anger inflamed his panels, overpowering his words. "Your claim is worthless. The vermin infesting this system will be harvested, your clan destroyed. You will not be *unlanded*, you will *become land*." He tried to arch his food-swollen body upward as Muni had done, but failed to reveal even one insulting suction foot. Instead, he looked a buffoon.

Muni and Bern both swirled darkest pink derisive laughter. Muni caught glimpses of pink from the surrounding shadows.

Embarrassment shaded Ani-Oranges anger. He attempted a command, but his enraged-choked panels could not be read. His mouth covering pulled outwards, revealing teeth ready to destroy. Words started to separate, a kill order.

Muni stepped forward. "How will you defend yourself from the first human ship to approach you?"

Ani-Orange glared. "Those junk heaps?" Sneer brown filled his panel. "Bunti fingerlings are more dangerous."

An elder Morgi, a stranger to Muni, glided out from the shadows. "Why do you ask?"

Friend or foe? Muni said, "Do you think I wanted to recognize two-legged monstrosities as Morgi? Do you think even the most inexperienced AI would let *any* threat board one of our starships?"

Panel background a perfect neutral gray, the stranger responded, "As our *'leader'* said, we have analyzed every human spacecraft. Their only dangerous weapons are on satellites aimed at their own planet. Their spaceships have no more defense ability than a lifeless asteroid."

This strange Morgi had a cockiness to him. *Is he highborn?* If not, Muni knew his next question would be lost on the stranger, perhaps even humiliate him. Humiliation creates enemies. Muni was still safe on Mars, but not his uncle. The bravado Bern showed did not negate the fact Ani-Orange could command his instant shredding. *Uncle, forgive me, I am about to risk your life.*

"Honored elder, when herding klieg which animals are the most dangerous? Those whose teeth are obvious, or the bold animals who appear the most defenseless?"

Background still a perfect neutral, he replied, "Hidden power is power doubled." The stranger stared at him. "Only the most powerful can afford to appear harmless." His panels blanked again. "How many pre-herding lessons do you want me to recite?"

The stranger is high-born, has herded lump. Not a friend, but also not an enemy. "Humans are as harmless as a lurker's thorns. They look safe, but get too close and you will feel their hidden danger. Those 'harmless' humans fooled my AI into letting them board while Death Teaser still imprisoned me.

"When I awoke, I undid the damage they had done, erased their memories of Morga. The Green Hill Clan can harness their power. Except for a select few, I made humans Green Hill Clan chattel for all time. Should I give the command, our humans will overpower your AI."

Muni saw a brief hint of pale pink amusement at the edge of the stranger's panels. Why?

Muni continued, "We are all children of Morga. Each of us values our world's safety more than we value our own life. I created a story for the humans in this system to explain our being here. They will never suspect the truth. For the protection of our home world, and all Morgi civilization, it is important the earth-children bound to this sun never learn the truth."

Before any could ask about the stories he created for the gullible Earth humans, Muni flashed, "Did you know a ship blue-lined out of this system days ago?"

Ani-Orange flared, "Impossible!"

"Check your ship's records." Muni gave coordinates.

He waited.

The stranger spoke. "Muni, how does it help you to have a human blue-line to the other system?"

"My clan's second system is only blue-line days from this system. That human will get there before anyone from Morga could. Not that it would make any difference if another clan just happened to be there ahead of him. A ship that can't control its AI is helpless. He has special fast-breeding klieg and a klieg skin processor.

"My colonizer ship is full of Morgi Green Hill full-noble-adopted humans. You may have noticed they are drifting outward, past Saturn. I will be boarding it soon. After I do, it will full-accelerate to the blue-line point. By the time we reach the new system, my adopted brother Capt. Jerrison-Green Hill will have a clan deed on klieg parchment."

Tumultuous glee bordered Muni's next words. "Green Hill Clan will be the sole owners of the second system my ancestor found, no matter what you do here. You cannot stop it!"

Ani-Orange slumped, his panels grey.

The lights went on in the room, revealing several dozen adult Morgi. Relief flooded the panels of the few Green Hill Clan members.

Muni expected to see the most senior Green Hill Clan leader on board, his mother.

He quick-queried his uncle, who quick-replied, "She was wise to fear interstellar travel. She and five others did not survive the first blue-lining."

Who else did not survive? He did not ask.

Bern raised his head, wing-arms furled and unfurled, then flared-out in command mode. "For the protection of our home world, we will continue the story Muni created. We will teach it to our young as though it were truth. Only the most senior elders of any generation and those who leave this system will be told the truth."

Green Hill Clan members raised their wing-arms, panels flashing agreement. The others stayed neutral, neither agreeing nor disagreeing. For now they would cooperate.

The stranger raised his arms in command mode. Muni noticed his uncle immediately deferred to him. Muni followed Bern's example.

"I will send a transport over to Muni's vessel with two observers on board. If the Green Hill Clan fails to secure the other system, we will soon know. One observer will be of Bern's choosing. The other will be..." He looked up at Ani-Orange, who still lay slumped on the dais of power. "Ani-Orange."

The putrid colors of fear flowed over Ani-Orange's panels.

The ship disappeared. Martian office walls reappeared.

A tiny hologram of his Uncle Bern appeared. "Send all information to this address." Code followed. "We will protect our Martian humans. You must leave Mars **now**!"

Muni ordered his Martian computers to send all information to the coded address.

He did not announce his departure.

Chapter 15
On board Muni's starship, renamed The SJS

(The Super Jupiter Special)
Muni and Shirl are walking down a hallway.

Muni's implanted voice box spoke, "At that acceleration, they are both in Death Teaser. My uncle didn't tell me who he sent, only to blue-line as soon as their ship boards the SJS."

Shirl asked, "Why don't we just take off, tell them we couldn't wait?"

"Because it will be assumed we are hiding failure."

Shirl shrugged her shoulders. "How could they prove it?"

Muni said, "They wouldn't need to."

Shirl, her voice cracking, asked, "Muni, what if Jerry doesn't have a klieg parchment deed?"

"There will be a deed, or we won't pass the system's boundary. If there is no signal from Jerrison," *Jerry, I am keeping my promise to not yet let others know your bravery.* "I will simply slow this ship until there is one." *Or if there is a signal from other Morgi, both you and they will learn what kind of armaments this ship has. What happens next will depend on the witness I have on board.*

Shirl asked, "What if, like here, there is another intelligent race?"

"If in fifty thousand years you are the first, that is unlikely." *What is likely is a Morgi Green Hill enemy already raises klieg beneath that second sun. Jerry will need to fight, but no human has the reflexes to fight a Morgi. If, instead of a klieg-experienced noble, they send a warrior...Jerry's death will be quick.*

Muni reviewed the scenarios he and Jerry had discussed. *Only a few clans have the ability to send a solo herder to claim the other system. Each will want to send a solo scout to claim the wealth of a whole solar system. It's so much easier for a warrior to learn to herd stupid lump than it is for a herder to become a deadly fighter that each rival clan will surely send only their best warrior. Ordinary Morgi's reflexes are several times faster than any human's. Warriors are quicker yet. Jerry suggested the warriors might kill each other off. Not possible, at least one would live.*

Muni did not tell Shirl the truth. Jerry would face the meanest, toughest, healthiest warrior of several clans.

Muni knew his strange, two-legged human friend would be long dead when they arrived in the new system, his attempt to raise lump a complete failure. *Devine Chance, may Capt. Jerry Jerrison's sacrifice give us enough time to succeed.* The intensity of Muni's prayer sent shivers down his body.

Muni wished he could leave now, not wait the fourteen earth days for the two observers to arrive.

Hiding short-term failure had been an important part of his and Jerry's plan.

Muni hated Ani-Orange, but even he acknowledged Ani-Orange's skill. There would be no hiding failure. Lor, his clan—Morgi and Human—would die.

Of course if Ani-Orange couldn't report...the news of Jerry's failure would be extremely delayed...

If Muni's family had enough time to become firmly entrenched in Earth's system, they would have a good chance of staying in power.

My best hope is to kill Ani-Orange just before blue-lining—too late for any Morgi in Earth's system to learn about it, early enough to prevent problems in the new system.

Uncle Bern will surely come to the same conclusion. Which of my warrior cousins he will send? Ani-Orange is a powerful fighter. Our best bet would be to capitalize on his one weakness, being easily enticed to eat so many first-molts, he becomes food bloated.

One of my younger, more flexible warrior-cousins should be able to outmaneuver him. But not too young. Ani-Orange is crafty.

If not for the danger Ani-Orange posed, there existed only one Morgi Muni wanted sent over, Lor. Lovely, lovely Lor.

Adult females could fight, but no one would risk a fertilized female losing her inner-pond.

Two weeks later

THE TRANSPORT FROM Bern's colonizer arrived accelerating at many times Morga's gravity.

It flipped headings, and coasted into the central receiving area, where a large nano-fiber net caught the craft. SJS merged the transport with a hallway just as it had Jerrison's pod years before.

Death Teaser protected both Morgi on board from the effects of the high acceleration; both would awaken soon. Muni approached their craft alone.

He had warned everyone the two Morgi would be awakening from the same type of Deep Sleep he had been in when his ship had entered the solar system.

A touch of pink entered his panels as he remembered how quickly every human in the ship had exited this entire section. He hadn't told them about the big difference between a month long Death Teaser and a years long Death Teaser.

"AI, forbid any Communication from the new transport craft."

Muni wanted no witnesses when Ani-Orange awoke.

Muni entered the transport's passenger chamber. Both Morgi lay in the thralls of Death Teaser. One was much larger than the other;

obviously that glutton Ani-Orange. Thin red stretch lines zigzagged across Ani-Orange's hard shell.

Muni concentrated on the second Morgi. *Uncle, which warrior did you send?* Muni stared, shocked, at the smaller Morgi. "AI, brighten the lights."

Deep ripples covered the smaller Morgi's shell. A pale a hint of feminine purple glinted within each ripple's trough. Obviously a severely immature male, at best an apprentice warrior.

Who? Why? Something is very wrong.

Ani-Orange's shell melted into flexible, tough skin; he stretched his body out; lifted up his head, and stretched out all four wing-arms. Their many snake-like extensions wiggled up and down, forcing fluids to their tips.

Ani-Orange, fully alert, shaded triumph over his panels. "Aren't you going to welcome me?"

Muni tried to flash the formal words of welcome, but couldn't.

The smaller Morgi had not yet wakened. *Why not?*

Triumphal mockery dominated Ani-Orange's words. "You should at least welcome Sundra."

"Sundra?"

"Perhaps I should introduce him by the name you last knew him, Skipper."

"Skipper is a fingerling!"

"*Was* a fingerling. If you had asked about your own family as much as you worried about your ship, you would have known he went chrysalis right after you became an adult, and had hatched before your ship left Morga's orbit. Fingerling Skipper is now Sundra, your new little brother."

"Then he's a first-stage subadult, barely old enough for lump herding."

Dark pink derision edged Ani-Orange's words. "Your Uncle Bern said the same thing. Sundra trotted so proudly when I announced that he was the youngest ever declared adult. Such a promising boy." Ani-Orange looked down on Muni as though he were a fingerling. "I am still an arbiter; I have power to declare Adulthood."

"That doesn't explain—"

"Everyone knew Bern planned to pick your youngest warrior cousin as the Green Hill witness. I cornered him during a formal meeting and asked, 'Are you really going to send your youngest?' He looked so confident when he flashed yes." Ani-Orange's panels filled with multiple shades of pink laughter. Scorn outlined the laughter. "I then repeated for all to see 'Bern of Green Hill will send the youngest member of the Green Hill Clan to witness on Muni's ship.'"

Ani-Orange swilled. "You should have seen his panels pale when I told him little Sundra was an official adult."

Ani-Orange's body quivered with excitement. "Tell me, Muni, how hard do you think it will be to goad Sundra into a death challenge?"

My new brother is as good as dead. Muni looked at the shell-hard unconscious new brother. He had called him skipper as a fingerling because of the impatient way he liked to skip ahead. He would be more aggressive than the average first-stage subadult. Since ancient dim prehistory, no adult could challenge, or be challenged by, a subadult.

Otherwise not one male Morgi in a thousand would live past twenty years; female survival rate would have been only slightly better.

Before a noble Morgi subadult ever herded a klieg, he tested his emotional control. No way could Skipper—Sundra—have passed that first test.

As soon as Ani-Orange chose to insult his younger brother, Sundra would immediately challenge. Ani-Orange would accept, and then shred Muni's small, inexperienced brother.

Muni had to do two things. Keep Ani-Orange away from Sundra during the vulnerable awakening—if Sundra did awake—and, secondly, never let them be alone together.

Muni backed up slowly.

Many browns of mocking swirled about Ani-Orange's panels. "There's no need to creep away from me."

Muni forced his panels neutral, lowered his head as though supplicating. "You have gained favor." Muni paused a second. "I prepared a feeding room with exotic earth crabs. They just finished molting and will be at peak flavor for only minutes." Keeping his rear eyes on Ani-Orange, Muni turned around and trotted back down the hall. *Will he follow me?*

Greed mixed with the mocking browns on Ani-Orange's panels, he started to follow, then stopped. "Halt!"

Muni halted, turned back to face his nemesis.

Ani-Orange raised his head to a comfortable angle, "Muni, first molt perfection will last a little longer. It would be rude to indulge ourselves without letting your very own, very precocious brother join us." Against a backdrop of black hate, he added golden words of welcome. "Muni, come back here."

Muni's distress grew. Food hunts awoke primitive instincts. It would be easy for Ani-Orange to trigger a hunting fight with an immature male.

In fact, if his uncle Bern had sent a skilled warrior that was exactly what Muni had planned against Ani-Orange. *Little Skipper, Sundra, you are doomed to be another brother I will never know.*

Muni crept backwards.

More welcoming gold against hate. "Muni, no sneaking away. Come here."

Muni stealthily stretched out a back wing-arm, touched the wall. A door opened. He waved down the dark secondary passage. His back pair of eyes concentrated on it. *Can I keep his attention on me and this empty hall?*

"What's down there?"

"Nothing." *True.* Muni glided closer to the hall entrance, partially blocking Ani-Orange's view.

Ani-Orange tried to see around Muni.

Sundra's skin softened. Unlike Ani-Orange's uneventful awakening, Sundra's skin glistened with thousands of tiny sweat drops. The tips of wing-arms started to expand, then remained stuck to his body. One wing-arm pulled away. The cartilaginous wing-arm rolled up, then fanned out. *There are so many lovely frills on it!*

Lovely, lovely frills.

Muni focused on the dark hall, as he crept backward ever so slightly.

Ani-Orange, colors angry-bright, flashed "Stay still!"

"I'm just stretching." All four eyes stared down the mystery hall.

"Close that entrance!"

Muni bunched up, twisted towards the opening and trotted through it.

Ani-Orange, too heavy for trotting, fast-glided after Muni.

Muni flashed to someone unseen down that hall "He's almost here, be ready!"

Ani-Orange chased Muni. "Puny humans can't help you!" His rear eyes picked up movement behind him.

Muni stared at the newly awakened Morgi in awe.

When he last saw her, Lor glowed with young-adult beauty. Now she was magnificent. She still had the most lovely, lovely frills. *Lor, you are the most wonderful of dreams. Together we will conquer this nightmare.*

Lor raised full. Both her panels blazed with luminescent perfection. "Humans can't help Muni, but I can!"

"Even if you both shred me, you will lose! Bern committed the youngest Green Hill Clan member and *you* are not the youngest."

Lor's wing-arms flapped, magnifying her menace. "You are right, the youngest clan *member*, not the youngest adult. The youngest clan members are within me, I am but a vessel."

"No one will agree."

"The One did." All her many frilled tips arched forward, pointed like daggers towards Ani-Orange. "Ani-Orange, both those within me and I, challenge you."

Ani-Orange twirled towards her, doing the tail pivot of an experienced fighter. "I will spill your inner pond and eat your young while you die!" He lunged towards her.

Muni, many thousands of suction feet flexing at once, wing-arms flapping, jumped onto Ani-Orange's tail, pushed down on his back wing-arm pair. Muni bit the spinal cord between them.

Ani-Orange jerked in pain, raked the top of Lor's head, badly damaging three eyes and scratching the fourth. His front two wing-arms clawed at her nearer panel. Black liquid seeped from its dimmed grays.

Lor pulled away, turning her undamaged panel towards Ani-Orange, flashed "Muni's fingerling lives, you will not." She pushed her two undamaged wing-arms as one against the center underside of his nearest arm.

Instinctively, Ani-Orange tried to cover the vulnerable spot with his back wing-arm, but Muni's first attack had left his back pair of wing-arms slick with body fluids, and useless. Unable to get away from Lor's attack, Ani-Orange did a counter measure only the most experienced would attempt.

He leaned into Lor's merged wingtips, allowing them to gouge deep into his reproductive opening, tearing the most delicate material in a male Morgi's body. The pain made his panels go blue-black-red. As her attacking wing-arms went deeper, he whipped his body around them, and towards her.

Ani-Orange's full weight went against her midsection. Slimy liquid gushed from her mouth, her inner-pond—alive with thin, wiggling immature larva—spilled onto the floor. His back arched, twisted violently.

Muni's thousands of feet clung to Ani-Orange's back.

Muni inched forward, stretched out his forward wings. The first two cartilaginous ridges opened. Sharp, hard, pointed claws slipped out. As Ani-Orange fell on Lor, Muni reached down into the base of his enemy's neck, ripping it open. Black blood oozed out.

Ani-Orange, mouth wide open, twisted his head towards Lor's still functioning panel.

Lor flashed, "Muni, Death-Bite!"

Muni twisted along Ani-Orange's head, wrapped one forward wing-arm in front, between Ani-Orange and Lor.

Ani-Orange full-opened his mouth to engulf Lor's panel; he bit off Muni's wing-arm instead.

Blues, blacks, reds of pain flared from Muni.

Ani-Orange again leaned back, thrust his weight upon Lor; crushed her rib cage.

Black bubbles frothed from Lor's mouth, grays of death streaked across her body.

Ani-Orange slid off her body, her black blood lubricating his path. His forward left side remained undamaged; his right side and both back wing-arms were drenched in body fluids from all three Morgi.

Muni clung to Ani-Orange's left side, his forward wing-arm only a dripping stub.

Ani-Orange stood up on his good side, then crashed down on his shorter bad side; his whole bulk pinned Muni against the wall.

Muni struggled to move, to bite, but the pinning was too tight.

Ani-Orange rose up slightly, positioning his tough back to completely smash Muni. Ani-Orange flared out his good arm in triumph as he went down.

Pain!

He looked down.

Lor, color almost normal, had stabbed him with her one functioning wing-arm, in the same vulnerable spot she had on the other side.

Muni fast-glided back to the middle of Ani-Orange's back, clawed more of Ani-Orange's skin away from his spine.

Lor's panels faded again to the grays of death, the rest of her body lost all color. In thin lines "Death-bite!"

Muni, colors firm, "No!"

Ani-Orange's panels streaked fear with pain. "You won't dare—"

"I do dare. Cleaning robots will finish you off. You will be shredded by machines and fertilize human gardens. Not even worms will eat your body; you will feed only plants. Those plants will be food for lumps, my lumps, in my new world."

Ani-Orange attempted movement. He failed.

Robots arrived.

Microscopic nanobots swarmed over and in Lor's gasping body. Like spiders on webs, nanobots with thin lines connecting them to the ship dropped from the ceiling and emerged from the floor and walls. Hordes of nanobots burrowed deep within her body. Life fluids trickled through the many thousands of thin strands. Pale pastels lit her one surviving panel, partial words formed. "Muni, only three know …sent me." Long pause. "Told Bern…your illusion…Sundra hides." The medical nanobots forced her to sleep an ordinary sleep.

Muni understood. *Bern created the illusion he sent Sundra, the same way I fooled others I spent all my herding time alone.*

Small scavenger robots cleaned the floors. They removed the last dying larvae from Lor's inner-pond as though it were no more than tracked in dirt.

Ani-Orange, all four eyes fully functional, watched the robots work. They ignored him even while cleaning up the fluids streaming from his body. "Muni, please, you can't, my soul...please don't let my soul die with this body."

"You would have killed the souls of my entire clan."

Muni fast-glided away from the battle site.

Borne by hundreds of thousands of nanobots, Lor's body followed. All the many connections between her body and the ship flowed through the walls like straws through water.

Muni raced to the nearest room with a medical pressure chamber. He never once broke visual contact with Lor.

Thousands of unnoticed nanobots swarmed over his own injuries.

Behind them, Ani-Orange died both body and soul.

His cooled body registered as over-sized garbage.

Scavenger robots shredded his remains and took them to the Jupiter One's human sewage system, where it was processed into plant food.

MUNI STARED DOWN AT the almost-alive body of his mate. She lay encased within a long, clear hyperbaric chamber. The chamber's high air pressure forced moisture and oxygen into her damaged cells; but the gray colors of death dominated her body.

"AI, send this message to my Uncle's ship. Ani-Orange awoke on schedule, as expected. The second witness awakened late, suffered psychosis. I rushed him to Intensive Care, but expect to arrive in new system with only one witness. Will that be enough? Please reply before we blue-line."

A very tiny voice in the back of Muni's brain intruded, "You should have asked if NO witnesses would be acceptable." Muni squelched the thought. *Lor will live.*

Muni touched the clear chamber with his remaining forward wing-arm, imagining it going through its protective covering, touching her. He then waved it into the air, signaling to his AI.

Materialization appeared in the air before him, summarizing Lor's medical condition.

Muni's remaining three wing-arms drooped, limp, to the floor.

Muni flashed to Lor's inert body, "We defeated Ani-Orange, to save our clan." *Lor, forgive me, but I desire you more than my whole clan's survival.*

"Because of our victory, this ship is now free to rush to the blue-line point." *Lor, your crushed body cannot survive the additional acceleration.*

"Lor, even before you became my mate, I vowed to always protect you." *If your broken body attempts Deep Sleep, you will die. Without Deep Sleep's protection, blue-lining will kill you.*

"We have so little time to prove we own the second system."

For fifty thousand years, two facts about faster-than-light travel remained true. One, only blue-lining made it possible. The other, blue-lining without the protection of Deep Sleep is death.

Muni's head bent down, pressed hard against the clear top of Lor's chamber. She lay so close, but Muni could no more touch her than if she had been home on Morga.

All four of his eyes closed tightly as they pressed against the clear lid. Gray, blue, and blacks of intense sorrow overwhelmed his words. "Lor, you sacrificed yourself so I could blue-line without a sabotaging enemy on board. When I honor your sacrifice by doing what must be done, I will kill you."

Muni pressed so hard against the glass, his eyes interpreted the pressure as deep water. The world looked as though he swam in the eternal blackness of the greatest ocean depths.

"Oh, Lor, if only we were deep ocean fingerlings again, swimming in black water, innocent of all intrigue, our only thoughts eat or be eaten. Swimming…"

Lor said their fingerling lived!

Muni rushed out.

He had work to do.

"AI, tell the humans to ready their 'coffins.'"

"They did so before Lor's transport finished docking."

Muni galloped to the Jupiter One Commons, previously known as their park.

The Commons no longer had hundreds of park benches and thousands of potted plants. Instead there were rows and rows of hibernation aquariums. The humans, with gallows humor, nicknamed them 'coffins.'

All wanted the comfort of adjacent humans, and no other totally human area had room enough for all of them.

Shirl shrieked, "Muni! Your wing!" Other screams followed.

Muni's implanted voice box responded, "This is a minor injury for a Morgi." *I wish it were.* "One of the witnesses woke up psychotic. Before the ship realized the depth of his psychosis, he already damaged both the other witness and me. The ship had to execute him; the other witness is in a healing chamber." *Or Death Chamber. Lor, you will be in pleasure-filled comfort until…*

Again Muni's body drooped; his total color went a shade paler.

Shirl looked at him long and hard. "Did…, I mean *will* you watch us?"

"I will supervise while everyone goes under." Muni knew he wasn't necessary, but humans had more faith in him than an unseen AI

Shirl said, "We're preparing the families with small children first. Alan here will help you."

Alan led the way to the family groups.

Three hours later Muni and Alan finished putting the last family group into the artificial hibernation. The small group from the Spaghetti Special waited together, ready to be put into their 'coffins.' Alan looked around, surprised. "Where's Shirl?"

Doc replied, "Right after you left, she said she had some personal needs and would be right back."

Shirl came running. "I'm ready now."

Like he had with the others, Muni supervised each one getting into a glass-like 'coffin', personally tested the intravenous hook up to the ship's control system, and witnessed as unconsciousness overwhelmed the fragile human. Unlike the others, with this group Muni also stood watch as each 'coffin' filled with liquid before going on to the next one.

When the last Spaghetti Special crew member finally lay secure in his cold, fluid-filled coffin, Muni stared at his human friends. A special sadness filled him. *Will they still accept me as a friend when they awaken? If they waken...If only it were possible for Jerry to not just give me more time, but to actually succeed...*

Muni snapped his thoughts back to his immediate problems. "AI, increase acceleration to Morgi standard."

Muni returned to his ship's main control room. He studied each of the thirty-seven names his family had engraved on its wall so very long ago.

He read Lor's name last.

"AI, as soon as I am in Deep Sleep, maximize acceleration. Blue-line as programmed." He paused. "Is Lor in pleasure dreams?"

"Of course."

Muni willed himself to Deep Sleep on the same sleeping patch he had used when he left Morga as fledgling adult; when a very alive, very lovely Lor had watched him.

His final thought—a new world, a new family name.

That one day, long ago, when he had first learned about the Ancestral Return, Muni had asked his mother how his brave ancestor could have been forgotten. She had answered, "Even the tallest mountain becomes but sand on the beach."

Unlike the distant ancestor who discovered this system, Lor must not be forgotten.

Her memory will be the mountain so tall; it will never become but sand on the beach. She will be remembered every time we say our name.

"AI, for all on board this ship, we are no longer Green Hill Clan. We are now, and forever will be, Lor's Green Mountain Clan."

Dream overtook thought.

Muni rode a giant sly'ling, soaring over its shadow. Unlike a stupid ground-hugging bunti, the dangerous sly'ling was partner.

Thought and dream disappeared.

Chapter 16

Weeks earlier, on board Jerrison's solo ship, just outside System II.

Jerry watched the glass coffin lid slide open; reached up, grabbed the edges and pulled his body out of his 'coffin', shaking the clinging liquid. He coughed violently, sneezed liquid out.

An hour later, showered, dressed and fully alert, Jerry stared out his view port at the star he hoped to claim. His hands cupped an instant meal of hot, rich chicken broth. Its thick warmth felt good going down his chilled throat.

His ship had almost no energy leakage, as normal for Morgi vessels, to minimize the chance of being spotted as it drifted inward towards the primary asteroid belt. Muni's World lay just beyond the belt.

Jerry reviewed all the information his AI had learned about System II. Two shattered Morgi derelicts drifted among the many pock-mocked rocks in the asteroid belt. A third, fully functional but crewless Morgi spaceship orbited the destination planet. Its sole passenger had a permanent camp on a tropical island. The lone Morgi alternated between his island camp and his orbiting spaceship.

"AI, were the two dead ships killed by the third?"

"Yes."

"Why isn't there a following colonizer vessel?"

"Enough debris floats beyond the outer reaches of this solar system to almost account for two colonizers. It is likely their missing bulk was disintegrated into pure energy by the remaining colonizer, a Valley Waters ship. It is camouflage-drifting beyond this system's

Kuiper Belt. We are so small; it is unlikely it knows we are here. It won't reveal itself until either their agent has a treaty-hide, or the agent needs to be replaced."

"We're too small to be seen?"

"We are small enough that it is easy to keep asteroids and planets between us and it. If you succeed, when Muni arrives he will take care of the Valley Waters colonizer. You need worry only about the Morgi already on Muni's World."

"Is there a pattern to the Morgi's planet side time and ship time?"

"He spends most nights on his ship."

"AI..." Jerry paused. Muni had assured him AI would both learn and develop a personality. Jerry asked Muni if he could name it. The question had confused Muni. 'There is only one AI per ship or building. Why bother?'

Jerry knew he needed company. AI would count only if perceived as a person. "AI, from here out I would like to call you Bill. Also answer to Billy and Billy-Boy."

"Those are human names, given by humans to humans."

"AI, our fate is one; we will survive or die together. I would rather be in this struggle with a friend. Bill's a good name for a friend. Do you like it?"

After a long pause, AI responded, "It resonates well with all my major programs and subroutines." Another pause. "Bill. Billy. Billy-Boy. It is good Capt. Jerrison."

"Call me Jerry."

"It is good, Jerry."

"Is the other Morgi aware of our entrance?"

Bill answered, "It will take at least six minutes to be able to definitely answer."

Jerry said, "Accurate information is very important. I will wait."

Six minutes later, Bill said, "No."

"How can you be sure?"

Bill replied, "I asked his AI."

"You asked his AI?"

Bill said, "It was the easiest way to learn about the other Morgi."

"I thought you had long range scanners and other cool Morgi advanced technology."

"Jerry, this is a large system, with many objects. Spotting one Morgi on an inner planet would be difficult. Learning what it knows, impossible."

Jerry frowned slightly. "If his AI knows, why hasn't it told the Morgi?"

"We are not an immediate threat."

The entrance of an obvious enemy, even if not an immediate threat should be of immediate interest. Is that other AI retarded, or did something else cloud its judgment? "Billy, without asking the other AI, can you tell me why you believe it does not see us as a threat, and why it hasn't forewarned the Morgi about us? And what is the Morgi's name?"

"*Billy.* The sound gives pleasure. The Morgi is Warrior K'ng of Valley Waters. Two of the planet's days ago, a major volcano erupted. It is a quarter of the planet's circumference away from his klieg-raising island. When his AI told K'ng about the volcano, he resented the interruption, asked if the volcano were an immediate threat. When his AI said no, K'ng ordered the AI to never interrupt him until potential problems were real problems. We are not yet a problem."

Warrior K'ng? Jerry remembered Muni's stories about the vicious, deadly warriors bred by the landed clans. "Why did his AI warn him about a distant volcano?"

AI Bill said, "In another day, heavy ash will be falling from that volcano onto K'ng's island, smothering every living thing on it. The air will be so thick with ash it will destroy K'ng's planetary craft should he attempt to fly through it."

"What was Kung doing?" Jerry couldn't say 'K'ng'.

Bill answered, "At the time his AI attempted to warn him about the volcano, K'ng was running from an amphibious sea monster."

Jerry asked, "Sea monster?"

"At night, large carnivorous monsters crawl up from the ocean depths, hunting for land animals. About five days ago one near his island discovered klieg are delicious. The next night, more came. Now the monsters swarm his island nightly. Every day, K'ng must rush his klieg to the safety of the highest peak before nightfall.

"K'ng's energy weapons set on point-discharge only wound the monsters. When on broad setting, weapons powerful enough to kill the monsters also destroy surrounding plant life. The more he killed, the more came up out of the water, cannibalizing the few K'ng managed to kill or wound. Those sea monsters are why K'ng tries to spend his evenings on board his orbiting ship."

A monster that would strike terror in a warrior Morgi? "Describe these monsters."

Bill said, "They are no taller than a Morgi, but some are more than twice as long. They are partially shelled, have four sets of forward claws, the whole front half is mouth with multiple layers of teeth; similar to your earth sharks, only more and larger. The last half of the body is in sections. The young have only one section. K'ng saw an old one with 38 sections. Each section has two pairs of jointed legs; each leg has triple clawed feet. They crawl faster than a Morgi can gallop."

Bill showed the holographic image he just received from the other AI.

Jerry said, "The description should include 'beyond ugly.'"

Bill continued, "Like Morgi, they communicate by luminous organs. Unlike Morgi, bright sunlight blinds them, sending them back to ocean depths. There seem to be a lot of them."

I would not want to be interrupted when fighting those things. Would a ship-bound AI understand that? "Bill, that volcano information was very important. How did his AI feel about being rebuked for telling Kung about it?"

"It was hurt. It will not risk making the same mistake again."

"Was Kung ever told about the coming ash cloud?"

"Of course not, it is not yet a problem."

An intelligence with personality is not necessarily an intelligence with common sense. These machines seem more human all the time. "Do you know when we will be close enough to be considered a threat?"

"No. Since we are still three light minutes away from the planet, it will be at least six minutes before we have an answer. Should I ask?"

"Yes, Billy." *K'ng doesn't know about tomorrow's coming ash, has nightly monster visits, and has stopped his AI from giving him advanced warnings.* Jerrison jumped up, raising his hand as though 'high-fiving' an invisible companion. "Muni, we have a chance!"

Grinning with hope, Jerrison asked, "Billy, does it matter whose klieg is used to write the deed on? If I swipe one of Kung's, could Green Hill Clan use it?"

"If you can keep it, it becomes Green Hill Clan property. The important thing is that it be at least third generation, and fertile. You will, of course, have to harvest it on land it has lived on since it swam within its mother's inner pond."

"Bill, what kind of manufacturing ability do you have?"

His grin widened at the answer.

"Billy-Boy, call our destination planet Muni's World."

The other ship's answer arrived in exactly six minutes.

"Jerry, as long as no Morgi are on board, and I cannot damage either Warrior K'ng or his ship, you are not a problem."

"Bill, if you are careful to stay on the opposite side of the world, can you damage the other ship?"

"No."

"And the other ship is staying in a geosynchronous orbit so he is always above Kung's camp?"

"Yes."

"Billy-boy, it is a beautiful day. Ready my 'coffin' for full acceleration to Muni's World! Awaken me as soon as we are in orbit; make sure we are *never* a problem to the other AI"

"Jerry, the other AI has a request."

"What?"

"It would like a name."

Chapter 17

Mid afternoon on a tropical Island on Muni's World Warrior K'ng of Valley Waters, "Kung", is on a beautiful, sandy beach.

K'ng stared out at the ocean. Small waves lapped the shore, in the distance he could see other islands, most of them shrouded in misty clouds. It looked so beautiful, so peaceful. Pasty fear lines swirled about K'ng's panels as he looked at the lines of little white wave tops, each taking its turn to splash lightly on the fine white sand.

Why did so many of the lump come here every day? A wave wetted him; he jumped back. He wanted nothing to do with those waters.

He saw a lump, started to approach. It slithered away.

Time for more stink. Yech!

A large pouch had been surgically planted in the middle of his back. K'ng pressed it. A fine mist of lump mating pheromones sprayed out over his body. The stench made his eyes water.

The escaping lump stopped, confused. Slowly it and three lumps K'ng had not seen slid towards him. He led them away from the ocean shore. Time to return to high ground, where cultivated grasses from Morga waited for them. *If only the high ground pasture were large enough to feed my klieg herd. If I'd known about the hidden ocean dangers, I would never have chosen this island.*

K'ng could abandon most of his herd and transport the best klieg to a safer island, but that would mean waiting for another three generations of klieg to grow on the new land.

Another three generations for something to go wrong.

He was too close to success to take the risk.

K'ng sprayed more pheromones. From trees, grasses and even 'bare' earth he saw the ripples of camouflaged klieg approaching.

He led the herd to a dark, narrow inlet bordered by broken-glass-sharp rocks. Ocean waves crashed noisily. The hardened core of a long dead volcano towered up from ocean depths into the sky. Long, thin groves ran its length, giving the illusion giant animals had sharpened their claws on it.

When the sea-monsters again followed the scent of his klieg, they should be unable to follow them up the tower's vertical surface.

K'ng moved out onto its ridges, his thousands of tiny suction feet gripped the vertical stone. He slithered up. His klieg followed.

The previous night two of the larger monsters tried to follow him up that vertical slope. For a moment it looked as though their multi-clawed feet gripped the thin ridges tightly enough to follow. Then they crashed down onto the deadly sharp rocks. Other clawed monsters crawled from the inlet's shadow-filled water, swarmed over their still-alive bodies, and devoured them.

What if one of the smaller ones tried to climb after me? Could it succeed? K'ng did not want to find out.

He sprayed more pheromones. The dimwitted lumps slithered only a little faster. *At this rate, when those sea-monsters return some klieg will still be within smell range.* "Hurry up, you stupid lump!" he flashed.

Not a high-born Noble, Warrior K'ng had never before herded lump, but his attitude about them had quickly become the same as every young noble who had ever been "honored" with their care.

The lowering sun glowed red through a dark cloud the length of the horizon. K'ng fast-glided up the last few feet, repeatedly releasing more pheromone. The first few lump to crawl over the edge sped up, rushed towards the center of the small, vegetation covered plateau.

The dark cloud now covered half the sky. The waters below were as dark as though it were hours later. K'ng could see the ocean surface roil with the movement of large animals surfacing in the cloud's shadow. *Will those last lumps get here in time?*

K'ng smelled fire.

No, not a forest fire. Not here, not now. He pictured klieg torn in half by claws of flame and claws of alien chitin. Not a single treaty-worthy hide left.

Moving his head back and forth, all four eyes scanning…no fire, but he smelled burning.

What is that?

"That" was a huge, dark sphere rising above a nearby mass of densely intertwined trees and vines. The sphere continued to rise, like a diseased moon. Long cables stretched over it and down to something on the other side of the trees. *A Morgi-made object! An invasion!*

His lumps charged towards the trees, slithering through slender gaps.

They're stealing my lumps! K'ng raced after his fleeing herd.

Unable to crash through the thick plant growth, he galloped to the end and around the stand. While galloping, he opened communication with his orbiting ship. "AI, there's Morgi here with a strange globe-thing. What is it?"

K'ng's AI answered, "It is a hot air balloon. Do not worry; it is not yet a problem."

"A what?"

AI flashed the brief educational video "heat rises." It included pictures of earth hot-air balloons. None of the pictures revealed human passengers.

Someone invented a way to fly without tell-tale electronics. Very clever, too clever. I will shred them all. "Who's flying it?"

AI said, "Jerry Jerrison-Green Hill. He is not yet a problem."

A Green Hill Clan member? Impossible. Someone fooled his AI. "Until I get a treaty-worthy parchment, *any* Morgi is a problem."

K'ng neared the hot air balloon. He slowed to hunter-stealth.

Cables tethered the huge, heat-inflated ball to a huge box. The side of the box facing him was open. What would have been the wall lay on the ground, creating an entrance ramp. Lump swarmed over the 'ramp' into the box.

Piles of crushed puti-grass flowers, the ultimate lump treat, filled the box.

The extra scent embedded in those flowers... What is it?

The stink sent K'ng olfactory nerves into revolt. *Lump mating hormones!*

Filled with angry revulsion, K'ng flared, "AI, only Valley Waters Morgi may enter this system. You not only let enemies enter, you let them invade my island!"

K'ng's AI said, "I did not let an enemy Morgi land and you do not yet have a problem."

K'ng shouted, "They are stealing my klieg! Even the most retarded AI would know that *is* a problem."

AI said, "He is not stealing them; he is rescuing you and the klieg from volcanic ash."

"What ash..." K'ng looked at the nearing dark cloud, remembered his AI giving a warning about a volcano.

Before K'ng could say more, his AI announced, "Warrior K'ng, my name is Sue."

An AI with a name?

Movement in the grass, a pale, distorted shadow from behind the box. The invader was about to walk into view.

His enemy foolishly thought the cloud-dimmed sunlight could not cast a tattle-tale shadow, or did not know a warrior protected these klieg. *Even if armed, the invader will die.*

K'ng crouched, tightened up to death-pounce.

Simultaneously, he sent to his AI, "Your *name*?"

K'ng's AI Sue said, "Yes, my name, Sue."

Before K'ng could respond, a stomach-churning ugly creature stepped from behind the crate. It walked on only two thin legs; its other two legs were too short to reach the ground. Its front middle lit up, flashing the simple symbols of a fingerling, "Greetings, Warrior K'ng of Valley Waters, most of your klieg are collected."

K'ng, already lurched forward, jerked back so violently it left him twisted. He flapped all four wing-arms rapidly, trying to regain his balance. All four eyes bulged out.

What is it?
What are its dangers?
Where is the Morgi?
Is the Morgi using this creature as a living weapon?

Still twisting, K'ng flashed, "You talk?"

Jerry's artificial panel flashed back, "Just learning."

Kung regained his warrior stance. "What, who are you?"

"I, Jerry, am a subadult sly'ling. I will call you Kung because it is easier for me."

Space-traveling, intelligent sly'lings? Impossible, only Morgi fly spacecraft. But it is *ugly enough to be sly'ling young. If Green Hill Clan biologists genetically modified it to be a living weapon, what abilities have they given it?*

'The most forewarned is the most forearmed.' It knows who and what I am, and is not afraid. Since only the most dangerous can afford to appear harmless, this thing must be even more dangerous than those sea-monsters...

My adversary, you are clever. A landing craft with no electronics, then a weapon that isn't a weapon to avoid those obsolete 'while unarmed' requirements. It will be an honor to shred you.

K'ng sent a silent quick-message to his ship. "AI, Sue, why didn't you tell me about this creature."

Quick-talk,
Sue said, "You never asked about non-Morgi."

"How many Morgi are there in this system?"

Sue said, "Only one."

"Where? Who?"

Sue said, "On your island; it is you."

Do I have the most retarded AI in all civilization?

Where and how is my enemy hiding?

He flashed at the bizarre animal, "Jerry, why are you collecting my klieg?'

"To rescue them. Didn't Sue tell you I'm here to help? That I am not a problem?"

This thing has been talking with my AI? Did it name it?

What gives it power over an AI?

It needs an artificial panel. Is it wounded?

"Jerry, what are you rescuing my klieg from?"

"The ash. It will be here in minutes." Jerry grabbed a dangling rope, used it to scale up the sides of the crate. On top, he turned a winch, pulling up the ramp. He flashed down, "I know more lump are coming, but I've no more room. Tell Sue I didn't realize what a good klieg shepherd you are. There are too many for my balloon to rescue all."

A weird device on top of the box shot out flame; all the ropes connected to the land snapped off the container. The box lifted.

K'ng noticed Jerry tied the balloon's rope to himself, and wondered why.

The box shot above the trees...sailed out over the ocean...away from the ash cloud.

"AI, Sue, are there any weapons on that balloon?"

"No."

The ash cloud's dark shadow marched over the island as K'ng galloped to his well-armed transport. *Sub-adult sly'ling Jerry might be too risky to attack, but that balloon thing makes him an easy kill.*

For the second time K'ng was glad he had smuggled a few modern weapons. He knew a few holes shot into the balloon while it floated over open ocean would make it fall into those monster-filled waters.

Even if Jerry swims like a fingerling, the sea monsters will shred him.

K'ng didn't worry about the lump Jerry stole; enough were left behind for treaty purposes. As K'ng approached his transport, grit scratched at his eyes, forcing him to go the last few body-lengths with his eyes first squinted, then shut tight.

When he entered the transport, he wasted precious minutes spraying his sand-choked eyes.

An extension of the orbiting craft, the ordinary computer on board knew everything his orbiting ship did. "Ship, lift. Follow the hot-air balloon."

The ship lifted.

A message from the orbiter. "Warrior K'ng, you have a problem."

K'ng flashed, "What?"

The AI Sue corrected him, "What, *Sue*."

"What, *Sue*?"

Sue continued, "The transport will malfunction if you fly through the ash cloud."

Zigzags of annoyance slashed over K'ng's words. "As soon as I destroy the hot-air balloon, lift me above the cloud. When it has dissipated, land me back on my island. *Sue*."

"Warrior K'ng, I cannot allow you to fly through the ash cloud."

K'ng's panels anger intensified. "This ship can handle everything from spaceflight to cruising deep oceans. It can handle a little dirt."

Overriding the computer, Warrior K'ng of Valley Waters took personal control of the ship. He headed downwind towards Jerry's balloon. *As soon as I fly out of this cloud, I'll shoot down the freaky two-legged animal. Then I'll memory wipe that defective AI*

Grains of heat processed silica and carbon filled the volcanic ash. High speed micro-diamonds etched the surface of the small spaceship, blinding it. The turbulence of natural powers twisted its hull, stressing it in ways its designers would have thought impossible.

The ship crashed; sharp edges of volcanic rock sliced long grooves onto its hull. It remained intact. K'ng was safe.

Angry, no way to see what prowled outside his sand-blasted ship, Warrior K'ng flared orders at the transport's computer and his AI. "Capture that balloon!" *I will personally shred it!*

JERRY LAY PRONE, CAREFULLY tied to the ropes crisscrossed around the lump box. The burner made thundering loud noises in his ear, his whole side roasted from the heat. Jerry's fingers ran along the edge of the heavy duty plastic sheet he had secured on top the crate. *Dare I hope...?*

Muni said a warrior on the chase cannot be stopped. Jerry clenched his teeth, expecting any second to hear the sound of weapons hitting the box, or ripping his balloon open. If he survived the next ten minutes, it would mean he succeeded; the ash cloud prevented pursuit.

Unless this warrior liked to play with his prey? Then he's following, laughing.

If Kung's smart, he will ride out the storm on the island, safe in his transport.

Which will Kung see as the bigger risk, the ash cloud or losing me?

Jerry survived the next ten minutes, and the ten after that. After the next ten, he loosened his grip on the ropes. Feeling slowly returned to his fingers.

Capt. Jerrison had flown almost everything from gliders to spaceships. He had never before taken a balloon ride. As he lay prone on top the lump's box, finally relaxed, Jerry looked around.

The first thing he noticed was the complete absence of wind. He had known intellectually that since he and the wind would be at the same speed, he shouldn't feel any breeze, but the real experience surprised him.

Jerry pulled himself to the edge and looked down. He had no idea he had gone so high. To the horizon's edge, islands dotted the ocean.

It felt as though he were stationary and the distant islands below rotated beneath him.

He looked behind, and wished he hadn't. The ash cloud looked like a giant maw stretched out to swallow him.

That continent should show up any minute…Unless the wind took me the wrong direction.

He needed to land on the continent; an attempted island landing could too easily turn into an ocean landing.

He planned to ride out the storm on land, using the balloon as a protective tent. After the ash and dust settled, his ship would reactivate the same "no problem" unarmed drone that had landed him on K'ng's island, and then hidden itself within a nearby cave. The drone would pull his re-inflated balloon to an island near K'ng's.

Jerry reasoned since all the islands were part of the same archipelago, an adjacent island should count as the "same" land.

K'ng's lumps were almost sacrifice ready. *It will be a race to see who has the first written deed. It will be a bigger challenge to see if I can avoid getting caught.*

Maybe, if this balloon can stay ahead of that cloud, I won't need to land until the drone shows up. Theory described balloon landings as "gentle", but Jerry didn't trust any uncontrolled landing.

Again, he looked back. The looming menace, now close enough to see individual darker currents of grit curving out and back into the cloud, constantly changed shape. *That turbulence will rip this flimsy balloon apart.*

He must risk an island landing. Jerry looked straight ahead.

A primal cry, more like an animal's rage than a man's scream, welled up from the pit of his abdomen and erupted out his tortured throat. "No-o-o-o-o-o!"

It had been so hard to get everything made in time, to be on K'ng's island just before the ash cloud hit.

He had gambled the warrior would be as shocked by the sight of a human as Muni had been, hopefully shocked enough to prevent an attack.

When he lifted off K'ng's island, he had begun to believe.

Maybe he would live.

Maybe he would keep these klieg, write the treaty.

Maybe he *could* save the whole human race.

From deep in his gut, with his whole body, Jerrison screamed, "It's not fair! Not fair!"

Capt. Jerrison held the ropes tight, and cried. The last time he had let tears flow so freely, had given his whole body over to grief, he was five years old. The dog he had snuggled with as an infant had died in his arms.

Now no other little boys would ever feel that grief, or the years of friendship-joy preceding such grief.

Dead ahead of him loomed a Morgi starship, K'ng's ship. The entire end facing him opened wide to swallow Jerry's balloon and the box it carried.

K'ng won.

The starship sent out grappling hooks.

As the ship reeled him in, Jerry felt a breeze on his wet cheeks.

The circular door irised shut behind him, diminishing the sunlight from the full opening to a smaller and smaller circle until the only light came from Jerry's burner.

Unsure of the oxygen level, Jerry turned off the burner. He then climbed down into blackness so the collapsing balloon wouldn't trap him.

In the complete dark he couldn't gauge the balloon's deflating rate, or what direction it would fall. Nor could he tell if the dark held traps. He clung to the klieg box. He heard the bulk of the balloon land on the other side.

Leaning against the klieg box, he could hear a soft chattering from the lumps. *Muni never mentioned that.* He could feel, more than hear, them crawling over the inner sides as well as the floor of the box.

The only sound he could hear from K'ng's ship was a hollow, wave like noise. Similar to holding his hand cupped over his ear.

Is K'ng going to turn a light on, or is keeping me in the dark part of his 'fun'? I should have brought a flashlight.

Jerry ran his hand over his recently manufactured translating vest and laughed. It could double as a light! He pushed 'activate.' "Please turn on the lights." the panel's feeble light faded into darkness.

Lights went on, revealing a cavernous room with a smooth, flawless floor. An illusion of a Morgi Communication panel appeared before him. Shades and swirls of color, jagged lines, some almost pictures, flowed over the simulation.

A communication attempt!

"The device I'm wearing translates spoken words to Morgi speech. It cannot translate Morgi to my speech." Only a slight exaggeration. Morgi visual speech contained nuances impossible to conveniently express as spoken words.

The panel showed a picture of his spacecraft and K'ng's starship. It showed little dots; no they were tiny eyes, going back and forth.

"If you are trying to learn how to speak words I can understand, have the panel go yellow."

The panel went yellow.

Perhaps he wants to learn more about me? If so, will he be friendly for at least a little while? Still alive is good. I hope.

His knees felt weak. *Must stay standing, find a way...* He then noticed his body's other demands.

He remembered from Muni's instruction how to ask for what he desperately needed. "Please send a portable food waste disposal box." The containers for shells and other food leftovers were the closest substitute Morgi civilization had for the equipment humans would need for personal sanitary requirements.

The personal-waste-elimination suction devices used by the Morgi would be life threatening for a human; just leaving dried pellets on the floor, impossible; the wading troughs, gross.

Would what I am about to do to the food waste box insult K'ng? Or so repulse him that he will kill me?

Jerry explained in detail what he planned to do with it. "If you have objections, don't send the food waste box." *Please don't have objections!*

What looked like a self-propelled desk rolled toward him at about a hundred miles an hour. It stopped abruptly, almost pinning him to the lump crate.

It popped open.

No one was in sight, even the lump remained behind a closed door, but Jerry felt as exposed as though he were in the middle of a busy city square.

Desperate situations call for desperate actions.

He used the box, awkwardly holding its narrow edge. As soon as he finished, the lid flipped shut. The 'desk' rolled a few feet away.

I can't think of anything I would want to do less during the second human-alien encounter in history. But if K'ng is willing to accommodate such a personal request…It's got to be a good sign.

What looked like a golden helmet emerged from a distant wall and slid to Jerry. It stopped at his toes.

"Hello, Jerry. It's me, Bill."

"You've shrunk."

"This is a servo-bot. I've guided Sue into mounting audio equipment in it. She's having trouble with the whole Audio-Communication concept, so I'm translating for her."

The little servo-bot twirled around as though looking for something. It spoke softly, "Sue is *very* grateful for the name you have given her. Be sure you use it every time you address her. She asked for all the information I had on the name 'Sue.' She is now obsessed with her new 'female' identity."

Jerrison asked, "Where's K'ng?"

"K'ng had an *accident*." Stressing the word 'accident' so strongly Jerry could practically see the quotes around it.

Jerrison replied, "Accident?"

"Warrior K'ng's craft crashed on the rockiest section of the shore, his ship blinded, but intact. K'ng was uninjured and safe."

Bill's servo-bot did a slow rotation. "K'ng simultaneously gave orders to both his ship computer and to Sue. He demanded the ability to see outside, and he ordered Sue to capture you. With every exterior sensor damaged, his transport had only one way of letting him see outside, opening the door. The transport computer opened it all the way."

Bill's servo-bot edged closer, its volume dropped. "Sue *claims* she did not realize the simple computer would not remember sea monsters could be outside the door; or she would have prevented what happened next."

Jerry asked, "What happened?"

Bill said, "K'ng's ship opened the door so he could see outside. Warrior K'ng died minutes after the door opened, devoured."

Jerry almost felt sorry for K'ng.

"Jerry, Sue indicated if Warrior K'ng had remembered to call her Sue, her thinking might have been a little faster, she might have remembered to make sure the door stayed closed." Pause. "His not calling her Sue distressed her subroutines. Her feelings were hurt."

Jerrison spluttered "Fee—-" then stopped himself from saying more. *K'ng's oversensitive AI killed him. The sea-monsters were just the method.* "Does Sue understand any of my speech?"

"She is learning."

Jerrison remembered Muni explaining to him only his AI's inexperience had allowed the humans to board and live. "Is Sue young?"

"She is one of the oldest AI's."

Jerrison asked, "That must make her what, fifty thousand years old?"

"No, only about ten thousand."

Jerrison, surprised, "Why no older?"

"After that much time, ancient memories become entangled with the present in unpredictable ways. Let us not discuss this again. We must talk about how wonderful it is that K'ng *obviously* wanted to save you. Don't forget, she *loves* the appearance of her name."

Rescued by a senile AI. Is this a frying pan into the fire situation?

As Jerry spoke, his artificial panel flashed, "Sue, thank you for rescuing me and K'ng's klieg."

"Sue says you're welcomed."

Jerrison turned off his panel. "Bill, who does Sue believe is in charge of her now?"

"Anyone from the Valley Waters clan."

"Until someone shows up?"

Bill said, "She is to continue to follow her last orders and proceed with her mission."

Jerrison said, "Her last order was to rescue me?"

Bill corrected him, "Capture, not rescue."

Jerrison reactivated his panel. "Sue, I am glad K'ng wanted me on board to meet you."

Bill said, "She says she is not sure if that was the reason he wanted you on board."

Jerrison protested, "Sue, what other reason could there be? If he wanted me on the planet, couldn't you have just sent a drone to pull the balloon elsewhere?"

"She says that is true."

Jerrison shouted into the cavernous room, hoping the panel would make his words powerful. "Sue, Kung wanted me to be with you. He wanted you to take me and the klieg on board to help rescue us from the volcanic ash." *Senile humans do better discussing the past, than the present. How about senile artificial intelligences?* "Sue, when was the last time someone came on board just to meet *you?*"

"She says it was long ago... her first time of self-awareness...new subadult Valley Waters...two of them together...he died of old age, still her captain, her best captain...none like him in all these years...She is describing their adventures together, I don't think they would make sense to you. Jerry, she is reciting the entire thousand years they spent together. Should I stop her?"

"No." He remembered his great, great grandmother telling about her courtship days. "What was that first captain's full name?"

"Muni Indigo of the Valley Waters Clan"

"Impossible!"

"Why? That is a very common name."

Jerry asked, "How common?"

"As common as John Johnson in your home country."

Making sure his panel was turned off, Jerrison asked, "Bill, does she know that a Muni Indigo is coming?"

"No."

Jerry said, "When she has finished reliving her first years, let her know. Also, make sure Muni knows everything that has happened. Everything. Is she finished talking about her Muni?"

"I will let you know when she is."

Jerry reached into a zippered pocket that housed all the food he could cram into it before leaving his ship. He pulled out one of the tasteless NASA "nutritionally and water complete" emergency food paste tubes. He squatted down, and sucked on its contents. *With all the millions NASA spent on their development, you would think they would have spared a few pennies on flavor.*

Morgi exchanged information hundreds of times faster than humans. Jerry shuddered to think how long her soliloquy would be if her words had been spoken to him.

He leaned against the lump crate, waiting...

"Jerry, wake up! Jerry, Jerry." The little servo-bot kept bumping into him.

Jerry sat up, rubbed his eyes. He had no memory of lying down. "How long have I been sleeping?"

"About twelve hours."

Jerry's eyes widened. "She's been talking about her Muni all this time?"

"No, after reciting their entire thousand years together, she compared every captain since then to him, showing where they weren't the Morgi he was."

Bill's little servo-bot nudged forward. Like once before, it spoke softly. "Human literature is full of love stories about heroines named Sue. Sue is convinced you gave her that name because she is female. She has decided she fell in love with her Muni the moment he trotted on board as a new adult, still loves him. She knows his soul lingers near waiting for her to join him in eternal soul to soul bliss known only by true soul mates.

"She wants to talk. To avoid misunderstandings, speak to me before flashing to her. Keep your artificial panel turned off unless you intend to communicate. Remember, she is still learning to understand spoken speech. Do not mention sleeping."

Jerrison nodded agreement. *She must think I've been listening all this time.* As instructed, Jerry spoke to his AI, Bill, before turning on his artificial panel, and turned it off immediately after speaking.

Jerrison said, "Sue, you have had a long and faithful service to all of Morga. Sounds like only Muni Indigo understood he served not just one family, but all Morgi Civilization."

"She says 'Thank you, Jerry. Muni was not an ordinary Valley Waters, he understood me. I understood him. We were, we are, soul mates. Together we, with love greater than mere biological attraction, faced the slings and arrows of an unfair universe.' "

What kind of literature did Bill send to her? For the first time in his life Jerry wished he had read some of the romantic chick-lit drivel his sister loved. Or at least had her there for advice. "Sue, the unfairest sling and arrow of all, was your Muni could not live as long as you. He must have died grieving he could not give you the appreciation you deserve. His last thoughts were surely about his love for you."

"She says you are right."

"Sue, if your Muni were in charge of klieg, would he have abandoned them by going off in his transport alone, or would he have taken care of the helpless animals?"

"She affirms her Muni would always put his duty ahead of himself."

"Sue, did Kung herd klieg for himself, or for Morga?"

"She doesn't understand the question."

"Sue, Kung spent the last months herding klieg. Did he do that just to have more klieg, or for a bigger, more important, purpose?"

"She says Kung talked about a treaty-quality pelt, but he never shared why—unlike the adventures she and Muni Indigo of Valley Waters enjoyed. Muni always shared the details of each plan. She gave examples."

Jerry tried to put pity in his voice, hoping his panel would convey a similar emotion. "Oh Sue, fate has been so cruel to you, throwing you with an uncaring, unsharing brute like Kung. How can you bear it?"

"She can't. She is grateful for your understanding."

"Sue, Valley Waters Clan sent Kung here to help prepare this planet for other Morgi, for all Morga. Check your history. Did Muni Indigo of Valley Waters publicly declare the same pledge back then honorable young nobles do today, to help find new lands for the non-landed and unlanded?"

"She says that is true."

Jerry held his arms out but slanted down, as close as he could get to the Morgi supplication position. "Sue, below us is a whole planet. Sue, the planet below is to be developed for the benefit of all Morga. If your Muni were here now, would he want to finish preparing this planet?"

"She says 'My Muni would already have finished that treaty thing.'"

"Sue, to finish the treaty, like Muni would have done, means having living klieg. The ones back on Kung's island are dead. The ones in my crate need fresh air, water and food. Is it safe to go back to the island?"

"She says yes, but there is no klieg food there."

"No food?"

Darkness.

Bill whispered, "Jerry, you forgot to say 'Sue.'"

At least there are no sea-monsters on board. "Sue, forgive my rudeness. It is important to Morga, to the non-landed and unlanded Muni cared about, that these klieg live. Sue, to honor Muni's memory, help me return these klieg to Kung's island. Sue, help with their survival."

The lights came back on.

"She says that she should have known the wonderful creature who gave her that beautiful name would honor her Muni. The thick volcanic ash choked all the plant life. To find a suitable island, it will be necessary to go upwind of the volcano. But no suitable islands exist upwind. Over three-fourths of the planet suffers from ash fall."

"Sue, just how big was that volcano?"

Bill said, "Jerry, I knew that, why didn't you ask me?"

Are both computers sensitive? "Bill it is important to establish rapport with Sue. Please help me do so."

Bill said, "I understand. We men have to stick together."

Both computers are loco. Is this the real reason Morgi don't name them? Would Muni's AI also demand a name? Have I started a dangerous chain reaction? Is the real answer to Shakespeare's ancient question 'What is in a name?' attitude, lots of egotistic attitude?

"So, Bill, Sue, just how big was that volcano?"

Bill answered, "It was about twice the size of the largest volcano on Mars."

Jerrison remembered the large number of asteroids. "Bill, is this system younger and more unstable than Earth's?"

"Yes."

More tough luck for Muni. "Sue, how long will the klieg food you have on board last these klieg?"

"Indefinitely."

"Sue, do you know if any of them are at least third generation?"

"All in your crate are third generation."

Jerry spoke, his panel on, "All?"

Darkness.

Touchy! "Sue, darling, please, again forgive my rudeness. What you said shocked me. Sue, how could they all be third generation?"

Light returned. "I am an understanding woman. Since the older ones had no treaty value, Warrior K'ng ate most of them. Nor did he guard them, which is why sea monsters were able to eat the first one, to develop a taste for them. K'ng was not worthy of being in the same ship Darling Muni once captained."

If he let the herd feel unprotected, he knew little about raising lumps. Valley Waters Clan worried more about defense than klieg husbandry. Judging from the derelicts and my presence, they were right to worry. "Sue, have any of these lump reproduced, or are about to reproduce?"

"None have yet reproduced."

Jerry suspected as much, or K'ng would already have written an ownership document.

Sue continued, "But four are ready to dispel larva within two days."

"Sue, remember that plateau where I met K'ng? Can you clear that of the volcanic dust, and then help my hot air balloon land there, along with a food supply?"

"If I let you go, you would no longer be captured."

Jerrison, hoping the implied emotions on his panels conveyed matter-of-fact logic, said, "Sue, you captured my balloon so these lump could be rescued. If your Muni Indigo were here, would he want the task completed? Would he return the lump to the island?"

"My Muni never left anything undone. Of course he would return them."

Jerrison said, "Sue, do these lump need a shepherd?"

"Yes."

"Sue, darling beautiful Sue, I have been trained to herd klieg. I would guard all of them. Sue, I will not abandon them until the important task is completed, until there is a printed deed on a qualified klieg skin parchment. Sue, Sue, Sue, the memory of your Muni Indigo demands no less. Sue—-"

Bill's servo-bot interrupted, "Jerry! Good news! In memory of her Muni, she is going to help!"

THREE DAYS LATER JERRY stood on his balloon's closed box, holding his rigid plastic sheet, the sheet he had carefully secured on top the klieg crate. Holding the sheet in front like a noble knight of old would present a battle shield, Jerry shouted, "Hey, universe! See what I'm holding? My lump collector!" Chutzpah filled, Jerry held the plastic shield higher. He bellowed even louder, "I WILL USE IT!"

Jerry studied the klieg nibbling at the copious feed Sue had provided. The ground looked lumpy as their continuously camouflaging bodies slithered and glided over it.

The volcanic ash fall had ruined the former tropical paradise. The stench of rotting plants filled the air. The trees looked like slimy black celery too long forgotten. The isolated spears of Morgi-engineered puti-grass poking through the gray volcanic silt were the only bright green anywhere in sight.

Several meters of dense volcanic ash entombed the drone that had brought Jerry to the island.

The only refuge he had from the rot was the golden torpedo shape sharing the crate's top with him—a sleeping tube. A "loving gift" from Sue.

The plateau had only one pond. A narrow stream trickled out of it, streaming water downhill towards the ocean. Jerry had piled rocks and dirt across the stream. The pond doubled in size behind his makeshift dam. He wondered why K'ng hadn't bothered to increase the pond's area, or plant the fauna lump larva most liked to eat.

It's a good thing K'ng didn't, or there could already have been a klieg parchment with a deed written on it. Muni had told him to challenge any lone Morgi if there were already a treaty, but no settlement. Such a challenge would have been suicide, but Jerry would have willingly made the attempt.

Jerry was lucky.

Instead of attacking a Morgi warrior in unarmed combat, all he had to do was watch for any lump about to dispel larva, get it to the pond, make sure the larva swam "in a lively fashion," a day later sacrifice that exact lump and use her hide to make a document-quality parchment.

Easy. In theory.

Any larva dispelled on dry land died, a failed reproduction. Domesticated klieg dispelled larva anywhere, especially on dry land. Like two already had.

At least I now have a better idea what to watch for.

Morgi used their broad forward wings to scoop up gravid female klieg and flip them into water. Jerry glanced at his puny human arms.

If Jerry tried using his hands, the lump's many gripping tube-feet would suck capillary blood right through his thin human skin. As its tiny sucker-feet moved over his body, they would leave a trail of bright red circlets. If the lump's always open central mouth tasted his blood's salty richness, its many raspy tongues would lap it up, want more, and dig deeper.

When Muni first described lump behavior to him, Jerry thought of starfish, sucker feet prying open a clam; the starfish inserting his stomach into the doomed clam. *Only I would be a lot easier to open than any clam.*

The lump wouldn't notice Jerry was a living animal. The ganglia that substituted for a brain in domestic lumps would interpret him as rich soil.

Standing on top the crate, Jerry held his solution, the large, flat sheet of slick heavy-duty plastic. Jerry believed adding the plastic sheet to his crate equipment was possibly the most optimistic thing any human had ever done in the entire history of all humans.

Modeled after the flexible, lightweight super-slider sleds he loved when a child, it had a rope with harness attached to one end. This sled served one purpose: klieg harvest. Jerry waved the sled at the foraging lumps and laughed. "Third time is a charm! Muni, we will have our miracle!"

From Jerry's high perch he could watch for any lump that stopped camouflaging, the first sign of larva expelling behavior.

As soon as he spotted another un-camouflaged lump, Jerry planned to jump down with the sled, place it before the animal. As soon as the lump crawled on, Jerry would pull the sled towards the enlarged pond, being careful to avoid contact with all other lump, then slide lump-bearing sled into the water. As soon as the lady lump spilled her inner pond, Jerry would coax her back onto the sled. To be sure he didn't lose the sled, he had driven a large stake into the ground next to the pond; a lump sled hitching post.

The first two attempts had failed, but according to Sue, senile Sue, he had two more chances.

The hot tropical sun beat down on him; salty sweat rivulets stung his eyes. Jerry tried holding the light weight sled over his head. Instead of relief, it made the sun feel hotter. He glanced at his untried sleeping tube, wondered if its temperature control system really worked.

Jerry wondered if it, or *any* "gift" from the senile AI Sue, was safe. He decided to not chance it. *Thank you, Sue, for the thought, but until Bill can get me transportation, I'll just sleep on this box.*

Water vapor, evaporating from rotting vegetation, steamed through the moist ash.

Not all native animal life was killed. Swarms of tiny black specks flew over the piles of decay. Their thick clusters resembled giant transparent beach balls. One of the swarms 'bounced' up unto the crate roof.

At first Jerry marveled how they resembled the spherical crowds of flying midges back home in Minnesota.

The swarm engulfed him.

Tiny bugs flew into his ears, up his nostrils, bounced against his eyes.

That, too, brought back memories of a springtime Minnesota marsh hike. Just like then, he snorted, trying to force the things out of his nose. He waved fruitlessly at the black specs. They didn't bite, but their bodies felt like fine hail pelting his skin.

Feeling some in his mouth, he started spitting. More flew into his open mouth, coating his tongue, crawling on the roof of his mouth back towards his throat. Others crawled down from his nose.

Their tiny feet on his uvula triggered the gag reflex.

He vomited up the NASA emergency food paste he had eaten that morning.

It tastes no worse going up than it did going down.

The swarm moved on.

Jerry kept wiping at his nose, shaking his head to dislodge any lingering critters. He took a swig of water, gargled.

It felt safe to open his eyes again.

He saw a white domed circle fringed with black, an un-camouflaged lump in the final stages of dispelling her larva. Too late for retrieval.

After waiting for hours, to pick that time of all times!

"Damn!" Jerry stomped his foot in anger—right into his own vomit.

He yelled his indignation for the next ten minutes.

The speech would have made Jerrison's sailor ancestors proud.

More balls of midges appeared. The bugs seemed to condense out of the rotting steam. A bug swarm double the size of the last one bounced lightly towards the crate. It bounced against the crate, floated up.

Jerrison stared. The swarm consisted of thousands of tiny flying bugs, but the ball acted as though it were one animal. It bounced towards him.

Jerry dove into the coffin-like sleeping tube; it closed.

A breeze ruffled his sweat-soaked clothing, cooled his head. His greasy hair didn't stir. The smell of cut grass cleaned his nostrils. The scent of something else…it forced him…

To sleep…

Perchance, to dream…

Jeremiah J. Jerrison stood in silent darkness. About him, as far as the eye could see, luminous fuzzy pink balls floated. He reached out to touch one. By its light, he could see his hand changing, from adult, to youth, to small child, to small toddler's stubby plumpness.

He could hear tones from each ball, filling the space with harmonies without end.

His hand disappeared into a stump; the stump sunk into a knobby sphere.

The sphere became an egg, a fast wiggling something left the egg.

Without seeing himself, he knew, he, too, was now a pink sphere, a sphere of potential, of what might be.

Without the limitation of physical ears, he could hear each and every pink sphere. Each sang melodies, harmonies. Each was an orchestra, the lowest note many octaves below the lowest bass drum, the high notes were crystalline purity, a perfectly played piccolo, only these piccolos were thousands of octaves higher than any that could be heard by human ears.

Together the melodies built on melodies, tens of thousands of orchestras in harmonious resonance.

The music was meaning, and all meanings were buried in the music.

"What are you?" he sang into the dancing spheres.

"We are human and Morgi souls; we are Lor's Green Mountain Clan."

"Muni never mentioned you."

"When you last saw him, he had not yet dreamed our possibility. We did not, do not, perhaps, will not exist."

"But you are here."

"All things are dream before they are seen."

"Which of you are human, which Morgi?"

"There is no difference, we are equal."

The melodies welled up with greater beauty than Jerry Jerrison thought possible...a beauty that made his soul swell with musical tears more painful than any tears ever shed by a human body.

One by one, the spheres turned transparent, became fragile soap bubbles floating about him. Each sphere now had only one note, but the notes together still created glorious harmony. Together the spheres could still speak—each was too weak to speak alone.

"Time is rushing, you have too little time, please hurry, or we will never be.

Time is rushing, rushing, rushing...." the words faded into a tiny heart thumping a beat too fast to last...

Again a toddler, he reached out towards one of the bubbles.

As he reached, his soft toddler hand morphed...

To athletic youth...to strong adult...to older adult, blue veins pushing against thin skin...to knurled, rough-skinned...an ancient hand.

Those aged fingers touched the bubble. It imploded. Other bubbles about him imploded into silence.

The music of the spheres dissolved into an atonal whisper.

His heart beat not thub-thub but time up, time up, time up…

Time rushed in angry torrents that crushed his soul.

So little time for life.

His physical eyes welled with tears.

The dream dissolved.

Pink light dappled Jerry's face. He started to get up, bumped his head. Jerry looked around his padded coffin. How long had he been in it? Did Valley Waters already send a second scout, harvest a lump? Had he failed?

Jerry tried to open the tube. Nothing responded. He felt for crevices, latches, buttons…anything that could be an opening device.

His bladder screamed urgency!

His soul screamed greater urgency!

Jerry panicked. Did Sue want him to sleep forever? Terror magnified his bladder's natural fullness.

His fist pounded the roof. "Open! Open!" His translating panel lit up, reflected on the tube's curved ceiling.

The tube opened.

Jerry sat up, looked, saw no swarm.

The most beautiful sunrise he had ever seen lit up the island. His soul's panic blinded him to the array of reds, golds and yellow-greens filling the eastern sky.

He got out. "Close." His panel flashed; the tube closed.

Too pressured to climb down, Jerry relieved himself over the side.

He sat down on the tube. The sled rested where he had dropped it. The lumps were doing their early morning chatter. He watched as the ground appeared to ripple as lump crawled over, continuously, perfectly matching.

A black fringe highlighted a pale patch of dirt.

Jerry jumped up, grabbed the sled, swung himself down. His hands shook as he grabbed the ropes. Effect of no nourishment.

He zigzagged towards the pale dirt, avoiding both squishy dirt and other lumps. As he ran, the spot turned white, the black fringe stood out in stark contrast. An un-camouflaged gravid female.

According to Muni's educational simulations, the lump would not be ready to expel her larva for at least fifteen minutes. The pond was less than ten minutes away, a wide time margin.

The mixture of ash, rotting vegetation and wet dirt slipped under his feet. Jerry fell forward, sliding on his belly towards the target female; he held the plastic sled in front of him. It slid halfway under her, protecting him from crashing into those dangerous suction feet.

Slime pressed against his face, into his nostrils. He stood, grasped the harness, and plowed through the living obstacles between him and the pond.

The same slimy gunk that made running hard, at least made the sled pull easily. Too easily? He glanced once over his shoulder; yes, the lump still clung on.

Jerry picked up speed, almost a full run. He could hear the sled rushing him. He reached the pond, jumped to the side as the sled's momentum propelled it splashing into the water. Jerry threw the harness over the post. The sled continued to slide outward, pulling the rope taut.

Panting heavily, Jerry watched as the lump started to color match the sled, then slither forward through the shallow water. No sign of lump expelling.

It crawled onto the shore, matched the grays, browns and black-streaked greens.

It had obviously expelled its larva before hitting the pond.

"You stupid, freaking excuse for a lump! Didn't you read the handbook? You expelled ten minutes early! Ten minutes!"

Jerry jerked the sled ropes off their post, stomped back towards the crate, each pounding step leaving a deeper impression than the last.

Stomp! Stomp! Stomp! Squish! A camouflaged lump!

It went black, the edges curled upwards, revealing hundreds of tiny tube-feet wiggling in the sunlight like uprooted maggots.

Jerry leaped backwards onto the sled before any touched him. It crawled away unevenly; a large, white unchanging boot print where Jerry had stomped it. "That one will never have a perfect hide."

Jerry hoped the injured klieg wasn't an expectant female. If he didn't get that parchment soon, the incoming Valley Waters ship would surely send another scout to harvest a suitable lump.

Fear swallowed his anger.

Jerry ran towards his observation post, the light sled bouncing behind him.

An oily patch.

Again, his feet slipped. He fell on top a large patch of dying lump larva. He felt their squirms under his cheek, his hands. The motion even came through his clothing.

He thought he had emptied the contents of his stomach earlier. He was wrong.

He shivered with the violence of his body's reaction; waves of sweat-drip heat and goose-bump filled cold ran up and down his torso. The already hot sun assaulted his forehead with pick-ax intensity. Jerry picked up the slimy, polluted harness; he trudged forward.

"I will succeed. I will succeed..." He chanted as his shaking hands grasped the rope slick with inner-pond oils.

Stinging, salt-filled sweat blurred Jerry's vision. Salt tears ran into his mouth. He pictured generations unborn, never born, betrayed by his failure... His throat ached with frustration tears; he shouted, "I will succeed!"

Green grass turned black. The black became a circle.

On the edge of the expelled larva, another lump turned white.

Jerry stared, disbelieving. If he had not fallen, he would not have seen it, would have kept going.

"Come to Poppa!" He shoved the sled towards it. The lump slid away from him.

He leaped ahead. "No you don't. Come to Poppa." He shoved the sled again; again it slid away from him—only this time towards the pond.

Jerry stayed on its tail, shoving with the sled, guiding it towards the pond.

The lump undulated smoothly over the uneven ground. It kept trying to stop, to hunch up.

Every time it slowed, Jerry pushed the sled hard against it.

It reached the pond's edge, touched it. The klieg tried to back up.

Jerry gave it the hardest shove of all, forcing it into the water. "Muni's right, you are stupid. Don't you know that water's the only chance your larvas have?"

The lump hunched up, rose, exposing its underside to the water. Inky oil shot out of its mouth. The water came alive with maggots—lump larva.

"Maybe you aren't so dumb after all. If those buggers are still swimming tomorrow, you'll become a treaty-quality parchment."

The lump headed towards Jerry. He put the sled in her path, she crawled on board. Dragging her, Jerry headed towards the crate.

He kept looking over his shoulder to make sure she didn't escape.

The first time he looked back, he thought she had escaped. He noticed the sled was lumpy. The klieg had already camouflaged herself.

Jerry had kept the crate's large side door closed. Jerry double checked its interior for other lump before shoving the sled and his lump into it.

It wouldn't do to accidentally sacrifice the wrong klieg, negating all his effort.

Satisfied only his special lump was inside, Jerry hefted the large door, turned, and leaned his back against it. Finally, it firmly shut. He stood, panting, for several minutes before reaching up and pulling down the primitive latch. *Why didn't I add a second, smaller door? Or at least move my wench system down here?* Sweat covered his body. He shivered. *Must keep going.*

Innnng...innnng....innnng...A high pitched drone squealed.
What's that noise? It's getting louder, and closer.
Hornets? Incoming missiles?

What looked like an oversized golden bumble bee landed next to him. He started to back away.

"Jerry, this is a recording from me, Bill. Get into the sleeping tube. Now. In five minutes if you are uncovered, you will die."

"What, more bugs?"

"Repeat, this is a recording. Be in your sleeping tube within four minutes, forty five seconds."

Jerry grabbed one of the dangling ropes, wrapped it about his shaking wrist. He pushed against the crate's door, attempting to walk up it. His feet slipped, he fell. He half stood, half dangled from his still wrapped arm. The rope's tightened grip stripped skin off his wrist.

Next time, a rope ladder.

The golden bumble bee landed next to him. "Jerry, you have four minutes seven seconds. This is a recording."

Jerry remembered the balloon's crisscrossing ropes covered the other sides. Leaning against the crate, his rope-wrapped arm holding more of his weight than his legs, Jerry shuffled to the edge. His tried to flick the rope over the corner, but there wasn't enough slack.

"Jerry, you have three minutes, fifty seconds. This is a recording."

"You could've recorded what's coming." He regretted talking, it hurt.

He leaned tight against the corner, reached his hand up high, jerked the rope outward. This time it went over the corner, to the next side. His free hand grabbed one of that side's many knotted bindings.

Using the knotted intersections as toe-holds, Jerry made it up. The golden bumble bee kept pace with him, counting down seconds. Each time it reminded him it was a recording, Jerry wanted to swat the thing.

Once on top, Jerry started to walk over to his sleeping tube, took two steps, collapsed, shaking.

"Jerry, you have thirty-one seconds. This is a recording."

Jerry rasped, "Can't you just shut up!" Ouch! Speaking hurt. He knew he couldn't stand.

"Lethal death rays will arrive in twenty-seven seconds. This is a recording."

Jerry crawled towards the tube. His arms shook.

"Jerry, you have nineteen seconds. This is a recording."

He kept going.

"Jerry, you have seven seconds, this is a recording."

He reached the tube, collapsed against it, croaked, "Open," His front panel flashed yellow. He fell into the tube.

Jerry saw the green-black remnants of the tropical trees transform into a dazzling white. The top closed.

Instinctively, Jerry turned away from the glare, held his arms protectively over his head. *An atomic blast? Sue's attacking?*

He felt something crawl up his leg, started to reach down to brush it away, pictured a strange creature biting his hand off. He wanted to open the lid, get out, get rid of whatever had joined him in the tube. He feared the brilliant light, the radioactivity that surely accompanied it, more than the unseen creature.

Creatures…My lump! Whatever lump wondered loose are surely dead. Will the one in the crate live? If her larvas are healthy, just killed by the blast, will that count as a successful breeding?

If that radioactivity out there is as high as I think, can I stay alive long enough to turn that lump's skin into a treaty?

Logic said, "No!", but Jerry knew that come sunrise, if he were still alive, he would make the attempt. *As if success were still possible.*

Jerry wished to again be racked with deep sobs, but the pain-numbing solace of unbridled grief was denied him. His stinging eyes had no tears left; his soul felt only death.

The back of his throat felt like razors tap danced in it.

Hot devils chased icy goose bumps up and down his legs.

Something vicious infected his soul-less body.

He didn't care.

Jerry did not want to be the last human alive.

A drug induced sleep began. Jerry mumbled "To sleep, perchance to dream…please, no dreams…just forget, everything…" *Wish like Hamlet, I had the choice of permanent sleep. Someone else might have succeeded. I failed you, Shirl. Failed my daughters, grandchildren, the new great grandkid.* Jerry visualized lines of shadowed silhouettes, his ancestors going back to the beginning of time. They chanted, "Failed us, failed us, failed us."

Pale memories of un-born music cowled their accusations.

Through parched lips he croaked, "Sorry."

The sleeping tube drugged him into dreamless unconsciousness.

Chapter 18

Place: The Jupiter commons area, all but one of the humans are still comatose in their transparent 'coffins.'
Time: A few hours after the SJS arrived on the edge of Muni's second solar system.
Doc and Muni are standing on either side of Shirl's 'coffin.'

Shirl blinked, looked up through a watery world, saw Doc's distorted smile through the ice-cold liquid. She felt the warmth of Muni's good wing-arm slide under her, lifting her up into the air.

Shirl shook her head, trying to empty her ears. "A-a-a-choo!" Her body jerked painfully. The sneeze sprayed a mixture of the tank liquid and mucus to the end of her tank and beyond.

Doc laughed. "That's the most impressive display of nasal power I've seen in all my career."

Forcing a smile through chattering teeth, Shirl sat up. She studied Muni. *Does he know?* She noted that Muni's once magnificent wing-arm now resembled a seal's flipper. *At least it's no longer a raw, chewed off, bloody stump.*

Muni's artificial voice box spoke "I'm relieved you are safe."

"Is there a reason I wouldn't have been?"

Doc answered, "Some Morgi die when blue-lining. Jerry passing their tests no more guaranteed our survival, than there are guarantees for the Morgi." He paused. "Let Muni and I help you out."

"First, who's next to be awakened?"

Doc looked down, was slow to resume eye contact. "Alan."

She knew what that meant. The iciness in the pit of her stomach had nothing to do with the refrigerator temperatures that immersed her.

A half hour later Shirl, wrapped in a warm robe, sipped hot broth. Neither the broth nor the heated robe could touch that icy knot deep within her.

She watched as Doc and Muni awakened Alan.

Alan woke coughing and splattering. "Wa-wa-a"

Doc handed him a cup of warm water.

Shirl expected Alan to drink it. Instead, he grabbed the cup with shaking hands, took a big gulp, swished it around, gargled and spit it back into the cup. He handed it back to Doc. "More."

Shirl rushed to the servo center, grabbed two clean cups, filled one with warm water. She handed the full cup to Alan.

Alan rinsed and gargled repeatedly before he let Doc and Muni lift him out of his cold, wet tank. Once out, in a heated robe and sipping hot broth, he relaxed enough to look around. Like Shirl, he knew what his early awakening meant. "There's a problem."

Muni's voice box spoke. "Several problems. First, Jerry Jerrison named his AI Bill.

"Second, a Valley Waters solo klieg herder was here first, but his computer went berserk and killed him. Valley Waters' colonizer destroyed the insane scout ship right above Jerry. The radiation from the scout ship's destruction surely killed Jerry, unless he managed to get under radiation-proof cover.

"Jerry's AI, Bill, does not know if Jerry is dead or alive, if any suitable klieg are dead or alive or if the incoming Valley Water's ship knows about Jerry or his ship.

"The Valley Waters colonizer ship is about fifteen light minutes, but several months travel time, away from our destination planet. It knows we are here, but believes we are all Morgi. They want to talk.

So far, I have refused negotiation, and sent demands that they leave my system.

"In response, Valley Waters is sending another high-speed scout ship to the planet. It should arrive at Muni's World in about three weeks."

Shirl nodded. "They are still trying to claim this system."

Doc added, "Even if Jerry is alive, it is very unlikely he has created a parchment." Doc held Shirl's hand, looked directly in her eyes. "The evidence says Jerry is dead."

Shirl felt a strange calm. "Until I see his body, I will not believe Jerry dead, will not mourn."

Muni glided closer, gently rested his good forward wing-arm tip on Shirl's shoulder. "Shirl, Jerry often spoke to me about you. I know what it is to lose a mate. Alan and I do not yet need your help with the new scout ship." An eye swiveled towards Doc. "Doctor Johnson, console Shirl while I give Alan some last minute advice."

Shirl and Doc, still in their heated robes, wandered between the rows of still coffined humans. Shirl murmured, "They each looked so tranquil."

"Shirl, it's OK to cry."

"Only if we stop trying will I cry." She kept watching Muni and Alan. The two finally left the room. Shirl grabbed Doc's hand. "Follow me." Shirl ran in the opposite direction, out of the Jupiter Commons; a confused Doc followed.

She dashed to Lor's recovery room.

Lor slept in her tube, completely submerged in the same liquid that had kept the humans safe. Lor appeared to be covered with moving grey fuzz.

Doc peered close. "Is he infected?"

Shirl answered, "*She*. That's what I thought when I first saw her. Those are large nanobots tending her. The smallest ones are microscopic."

"First saw her?"

"This is Lor, Muni's mate, and bride." Shirl scrutinized Lor's unconscious form. Her idea worked! "Doc, just because Muni has 'come clean' with us, doesn't mean he volunteers information. Fortunately for Muni and Lor, he instructed his AI to answer all questions truthfully.

"AI, show Doc the witness boarding sequence you showed me, pausing only for translations."

Doc saw the encounter, the fight, Lor's encapsulation. Saw Muni collapse when he learned that if he saved Lor's life, he would doom his clan. Saw how knowledge of a living fingerling gave Muni the strength to condemn to death the one he most loved. "I had no idea, no idea at all."

Doc knew the literal AI would not have pronounced Lor's death sentence if there were even one chance in a billion she would live. Instead, it would have given the distant odds. "But...she's alive."

Shirl nodded. "I saw the recording, which Muni will surely order 'forgotten' before anyone off-ship can ask about it."

"How, why were you shown this?"

"When Muni first showed up with a torn-off forward wing-arm, his words were shaded the colors of immense sorrow. He never wanted those witnesses; he should have been relieved they would not be the scourge he dreaded.

"I left the commons area to ask AI what happened. It led me here, showed what you just saw. I asked AI why she couldn't survive that Deep Sleep of theirs, or live in ordinary unconsciousness while we blue-lined.

"It explained how her torn skin would rip apart, killing her, if the still undamaged parts turned into a Deep Sleep shell. If she did not attempt Deep Sleep, the problems that would kill us without the liquid's protection, are the same ones that would kill her. I asked why the same solution that saved us, couldn't save her."

Doc interrupted, "And it said it could."

"No, AI said he was grateful to receive a question he was not creative enough to ask. Then added that he felt there was an eighty-one percent chance of failure. I watched as her tube filled with liquid."

"Does Muni know?"

The ship answered. "No."

Doc grinned. "Tell him his Lor lives!"

AI spoke. "No."

Shirl and Doc, "Why not?"

It replied, "Because I do not yet know she lives, only that she has not yet died."

Shirl, "When will you know?"

"When I can determine if enough of her inner pond has survived; that she can again have living larva."

Doc, "They mentioned an inner pond during the fight. Is it an essential organ, like our heart?"

AI, "It is more than an organ. You do not yet know enough to understand the answer."

Shirl demanded, "Then teach us."

"Sit, watch, listen."

The two humans sat down, leaned against the wall.

The room disappeared. They sat on the edge of a grassy hill. Two Morgi strolled together, started to wrap their forward wing-arms together, to intertwine the snake-like tips of those wings.

AI spoke. "When a mature male and a mature female are strongly attracted to each other, and only after their mutual families agree, they express that attraction by mating." The room faded to black.

A tiny giggle escaped from Shirl. *I've seen this movie.*

The bright day returned, now only one Morgi walked on the hillside. "If she is very lucky, the female will have new life within her inner pond."

The realistic Morgi transformed into a cartoon like image. A large circle superimposed on her raised front half. The illusion of a tunnel appeared within it. The circle grew. Doc and Shirl felt as though they were encompassed by it.

AI continued. "If you were magically transported into the inner pond of a mature female before she had mated, and you were one-hundredth your current size, this is what it would look like."

Shirl looked about her in awe. She felt as though she had been transported out of Lor's treatment room. Only the firm pressure of the wall against her back assured her she had not moved.

She floated in the middle of a large kelp forest. Long, leaf-filled stems reached down deep beneath her and stretched up to an unseen surface. Chunks of half-digested meat and some bits of vegetation floated about. What looked like large frog eggs floated here and there. Various creatures crawled on the 'kelp.'

Other animals swam. They nibbled at the food chunks, interacted with each other, chased after the frog eggs, swallowing them. A few eggs drifted into the kelp leaves. When that happened, the leaf wrapped around it.

AI explained "Only a few unfertilized eggs escape being eaten. These will develop into mindless worms." A spotlight highlighted a leaf holding a dark, partially hidden egg. The egg bulged, a circle of teeth pressed from within, bit the egg's skin. A worm thrashed back and forth; ripping the opening wider; wiggled out; devoured the entire shell. "These worms are only appetite, and will remain only appetite. They will eat everything they come near, including other worms and even, when she has properly mated, sperm.

"When these worms get large enough, the female's flushing muscles will sieve them out."

A much larger lamprey-like worm, tooth-lined mouth wide open, swam by.

Doc and Shirl watched as what looked like a living sieve went through the water, catching it.

The educational illusion shifted. Flushed worms swam down a long tube, were expelled into the grass. "The female doesn't notice when the larva from an unfertile egg leaves her. But male Morgi do. It signals that she is now old enough to join klieg hunts, and for her family to arrange her proper mating."

AI's tone softened to a conspiratorial whisper. "You are both mature adults. You can learn the truth about what happens to these infertile larvae.

"In cities, sanitation robots dispose of unfertilized larvae. In the wild, the larvae continue to eat anything that doesn't eat it first. Its only defenses are playing dead, and blind luck. Almost all die. Should it get large enough, it goes through a chrysalis stage, and emerges as a vegetarian, androgynous bunti fingerling. It will continue to only eat and grow.

"Once a bunti is large enough to ride," A bunti about double Muni's length ridden by small Morgi crawled past them. "No ordinary predator can kill it. Bunti never stop growing. All are infertile.

"Always remember, only the most repulsive non-landed would ever mention out loud the truth about a Bunti's ancestry."

The 'kelp' forest returned. In its pedantic mode, AI continued. "When the mature female has mated, a change occurs to her inner pond—sperm invade."

Millions of speeding sperm rushed towards them. Shirl ducked to avoid the illusory attack.

Doc exclaimed, "They look like human sperm. Is the scale right?"

"Yes"

Sperm as large as the eggs they sought wiggled about, bumping into and backing away from the plants and food chunks. "This is the first great testing, for only against immense odds can greatness be revealed."

The humans watched, shocked, as everything in that kelp forest awoke into a feeding frenzy. From bunti larva to the smallest kelp-crawler, everything converged hungrily, decimating the sperm.

Only thousands of sperm swam...down to hundreds...dozens...a dozen...three...One bumped into an egg...the remaining two sperm raced to join it...the three kept ramming the egg, seeking entry.

One succeeded, the other two fell away. A bunti larva devoured them. The successful sperm merged with the egg, only its rapidly whipping tail still visible. The sperm tail propelled the fertilized egg into the kelp.

Layers of 'kelp' leaves wrapped around the fertilized egg.

AI explained "Safe within her fortress, the egg develops into a fertilized larva."

The "leaves" unfurled. The outer membrane of the egg separated like flower petals opening; revealing a worm that looked identical to the bunti larva, except all four eyes were closed. Instead of the wild thrashing of the bunti, it uncurled and then methodically ate the egg casing.

The little larva stretched out, lifted up its head. Like adult Morgi, its four eyes were evenly spaced around the top of its head. A pair of alternate eyes opened. Shirl smiled with wonderment. *They look like kitten eyes opening for the first time.* The kitten-like eyes blinked. The little larva looked around.

Those eyes closed. The other pair opened.

Thick, black eyelashes framed two very human eyes.

Shirl took a sharp, inward breath. "Oh!" *From that first, terrifying encounter, so long ago, when I saw Muni devour Simon, I've been fascinated by the humanness of one pair of Muni's eyes. These eyes aren't just human, they are beautiful.* Shirl felt guilt. *Simon, why has* it been so long since I thought of you? Your death could have been prevented. Why wasn't it?*

The larva blinked, looked directly at her. That blink overwhelmed Shirl's memories.

Her body felt a special warmth as she returned the larva's stare. *The last time I saw eyes like that was over forty years ago.*

Shirl remembered holding her newborn daughter, looking into trusting eyes; eyes that spoke an eternal soul to soul language. In those first few wondrous moments, as she had looked deeply into her daughter's eyes, Shirl felt that her daughter had just awakened from eternity to gaze upon her mortality.

The larva's eyes gave Shirl the same beyond time feeling.

AI's lecture interrupted the spell. "A Morgi larva has a complex brain stem, though not yet a true brain, and more advanced sense organs than any other animal in the inner pond. These will help it to survive. Even with this advantage, few live. A typical mature female will mate for years before one of her Morgi larva becomes large enough to be flushed out."

A large bunti larva approached. The newly-hatched fertile larva crept under the leaf. Doc and Shirl watched as the little hatchling peaked around the leaf edge towards the foraging bunti larva. At the same time, a long-legged spider-like creature crawled up the 'kelp' stem, stalking the infant larva.

The stalker suddenly unfolded two very long, pincher arms; grabbed the little larva.

Shirl screamed.

All four of the larva's eyes opened wide. It thrashed wildly, seeking escape.

The pincher arms pulled the frightened, fighting hatchling towards the stalker's mandible-lined mouth. It shredded the still-living little body into bite-size pieces and devoured them.

Shirl, "That's cruel!"

AI, "No, it's not."

Shirl looked to Doc, expecting support. Instead, he sat there smiling! Confused, she asked "You're happy?"

"Until now, I compared Morgi to various earth marine life. But this..." His grin widened, eyebrows lifted, and eyes sparkled, looking like a little boy just handed the coolest of new toys. "*This* is **alien**!"

As are men. She thought.

AI's biology lesson continued. "About one egg in ten thousand becomes fertilized, about one fertilized larva in a thousand lives to be flushed. Watch what happens when a fertile larva is expelled."

Again, they were on the grassy hillside. A female trotted past, expelled what looked like a confetti-colored bunti larva. The larva started flashing. The female scooped it up with a forward wing arm; was next seen dropping the larva into a large aquarium already filled with plants, under-water caves, and dangerous looking animals.

AI explained, "In ancient times she would have taken her pre-fingerling to a special birthing stream; modern mothers have aquariums they still call birthing streams. The first attempts proved disastrous."

A simple aquarium appeared, with plants and rocks. A pre-fingerling swam about, nibbling on the many tiny animals. "The first artificial birthing streams were made without predators."

The pre-fingerling morphed into a full fingerling, subadult, adult. Its wing-arms were stubby, with almost non-existent cartilage 'snakes,' its light panels changed patterns with drowsy-slowness. "It was learned that a nervous system develops only to the degree it is tested. In modern times, most of the unlanded masses use robotic predators and artificial food in their birthing streams. The nobles use live animals. All use a variety of plants and rocks to make life interesting for the larva and the pre-fingerling it will become."

AI continued, "Now see what happens when danger plagues the developing Morgi in each stage of its life cycle."

This time the life cycle culminated with a Morgi whose magnificent wing-arms framed rapidly flashing panels.

"The greater the challenge, the greater the Morgi will grow." AI paused, spoke solemnly. "Only against immense odds can greatness be revealed."

Suddenly Shirl understood. *That's not just another old saying to a Morgi; that is life.*

AI returned to the cartoon like image with the cut-a-way revealing the inner pond. "It all begins here. An adult female Morgi, especially an adult noble, needs to have a fully-developed, dangerous inner pond to have healthy larva. Lor lost almost all her inner pond, enough that had she been conscious she would have refused all medical care.

"A few bits were caught within her body fluids; some remained in the folds of her body cavity. I am trying to raise a second pond, to duplicate in days what would normally have happened in years. I will not waken Lor until I succeed. If I never succeed, she will not be awakened, no matter how well the rest of her body heals."

Shirl protested, "You don't understand how much Muni loves her."

AI, with inhuman patience, responded, "You do not understand how Morgi are slaves to their biology."

Doc countered, "Muni is intelligent, can rise above his instincts. If not, we could never have become friends. Is there something that prevents females from being able to do the same?"

"If either Lor or Muni believed the other could not reproduce, they would cease to be mated. To be seen as infertile, is to be seen as dead."

Shirl, "What happens when a Morgi becomes too old for reproduction?"

"All Morgi reproduce their entire lives. It is necessary. Few of their larvae become fingerlings. Most fingerlings fail to become sub-adults. Most sub-adults die. Of the few adolescent nobles who choose full adulthood, most become unlanded adults. Only the best become full adult nobles. Only the very best risk testing for highborn adulthood. Few succeed.

"Adulthood is obtained between twenty and twenty five years of sub-adulthood. Highborn rank can also be merit-earned at any age, but requires such a high level of accomplishment that is barely worth mentioning."

Shirl asked, "In earth years, how long do adult Morgi live?"

"About a thousand years."

Doc asked, "How old is Muni? Since he became an adult."

"Not counting his times in Death Teaser, he has experienced about five adult earth years, most of those with humans."

Doc and Shirl looked at each other in shock. Shirl, "You mean a *child* has been negotiating with the entire human race?"

"A Morgi adult should never be regarded as a child."

Doc said, "OK, an inexperienced adult negotiated with the most experienced humans, and got what he wanted."

AI said, "An experienced Morgi would have got what he wanted without resorting to such extreme trickery."

Shirl said, "That explains the behavior Jerry and I noticed."

Doc questioned, "You showed us all this to convince us to not tell Muni his love lives?"

AI corrected, "She *almost* lives."

Shirl interrupted, "Surely the hope Lor lives would help…"

The walls, ceiling and floor vibrated with AI's shout. "No!"

AI resumed normal tones. "Muni almost willed himself into non-existence thinking he would never be with her again. He has accepted her death, honored her memory. I do not believe my Muni could survive going through loss of hope a second time. Only when I know Lor has True Life, is Muni to know."

Doc promised, "I will keep our secret."

Shirl did not believe Muni ever considered suicide. *He boldly faces every risk. Isn't he training Alan even now? How can a promise to a machine, a thing, be a true promise? Muni, you are my friend. I will make sure you know the truth.* "I, too, agree,"

"That is good. It would destroy several of my subroutines to see Muni die before his first fingerling even became a chrysalis."

Shirl inquired, "Did Lor bring any information about Muni's fingerling?"

"Yes. As soon as Muni owns this system, I will show it to him. Until then, its distraction would reduce his chance for success."

Understanding hit Shirl. *That's why I'm remembering Simon. AI could have prevented his death by making sure none of us were near Muni while he suffered the awakening frenzy.*

It didn't protect Alan because it saw us humans as peculiar livestock, fresh food.

It never occurred to AI we 'animals' would be distressed by Simon's death. I doubt it understands Muni's emotions any better.

For the first time in over a year, Shirl felt the stomach-knotting pain of distrust. *AI values Green Hill Clan more than it does Muni or Lor. If it helped the clan, it would sacrifice Lor as readily as it did Simon.*

The flaw in AI's cold mechanical logic is so obvious, why doesn't Doc voice it? Shirl suddenly remembered Doc's history. Never married, no children. *If Doc had ever held his own newborn child, he would understand few things inspire greatness like knowing your struggle is for children you love. Learning about his fingerling gave Muni the will to continue. Learning Lor lives will inspire him still more. An AI can't feel love; can't experience love's power. Doc's experience is incomplete.*

Shirl nodded. "I understand, AI." *I understand that for all your caring words, you are still just a machine.*

Doc asked AI, "When will you know if her inner pond has been restored?"

"I don't know."

Doc, puzzled, said, "It looked like micro flora and fauna populated her inner pond, such things reproduce rapidly. Can't you tell if they are breeding?"

"The animals and plants are not a problem. Remember the long growths that looked like earth seaweed?"

Both nodded yes.

"Those strands are a special organ. Unlike the other plants and animals of her inner pond, they are part of her body. Without them, no fertilized egg can be protected long enough to develop into a larva. She will be infertile. Ani-Orange bruised her strands, then spilled her inner pond; exposing the raw wounds to corrosive air-borne oxygen. You saw what they should look like. This is what they do look like."

A polluted kelp forest surrounded the two humans. Bits of rotting 'leaves' floated about. Deep gashes corrupted every 'kelp' tree; many were shredded to jagged stumps. Black rot invaded every raw edge.

AI continued, "I am trimming the diseased portions, but if I trim too fast, the good tissue dies. It is impossible to know if even one strand can be revived."

Doc frowned. "Why can't the cells regenerate?"

AI replied, "A viral infection grows faster than her cells can reproduce."

Shirl said, "I don't understand."

AI explained, "One of your human stories described trying to bail out a boat that kept leaking faster than the sailors could bail. This is like that. No matter how I stimulate her cells' reproduction rate, the rot grows faster than she can heal."

Doc asked, "Have you tried using cold to slow the infected cell growth?"

Pause.

AI replied, "Are you referring to the cell-by-cell freezing of human cancer cells?"

"Yes. The inner pond area is warm. The life forms that live in it must need that warmth, including that black rot. Surely your medical nanobots can do spot freezing."

Silence.

Doc, "Well?"

"I am trying your idea." Pause. "Muni needs you. Follow the ceiling lights to his location. Mention nothing about Lor."

AI's controlled illusions ceased. The clinical room's harsh reality returned. Lor's perfect looking body floated in the healing tank, looking more like a specimen in a museum jar than a patient.

The door opened. The two humans followed the ceiling lights out.

The lights led them to the small control room of Alan's transport ship.

Muni trotted back and forth. Colors of worry-frustration swirled over his panels, interrupted by random jags of white fear.

Alan sat in the pilot's chair, nervously drumming his fingers on its arms. His empty transport tank loomed behind the chair.

Muni's voice box spoke. "We have another problem."

Alan explained. "Jerry's AI, Bill, sent a drone to Jerry to order him under cover before Valley Waters destroyed their insane ship. Bill just relayed a confirming signal; Jerry is alive."

Shirl's jubilation stopped in her throat. "Why isn't that good news?"

Alan explained. "His remaining klieg may no longer be parchment quality. We humans can't see a wide enough color spectrum to tell, and the drone Bill sent isn't sophisticated enough to tell. If Jerry sacrifices an inferior klieg, not only will it not count, but the humiliation will haunt our clan forever. But that's the least of our worries."

Muni interrupted. "Jerry is apparently too weak to sacrifice anything. But he is too alive to send down another scout. We cannot have two clan members there at the same time, or we forfeit everything.

"Valley Waters launched a second scout. Before we can rescue Jerry, and then send Alan, the second Valley Waters scout will be landing."

Muni ceased pacing; looked directly at each human. "Our best bet is to send Alan as planned, in hopes Jerry will be dead before Alan gets there. Then we need to hope Alan can find and sacrifice a quality klieg before the Valley Waters scout arrives."

Muni stopped pacing, raised his front half and fully extended his remaining three wing-arms. The fourth stump quivered. He continued, "Even if Alan succeeds, his success will count only if Valley Waters recognizes Lor's Green Mountain Clan."

All three humans asked, "Green Mountain Clan?"

Muni replied, "I have formally changed our ship's human clan name and mine to Lor's Green Mountain Clan. Those left back in your solar system will remain The Green Hill Clan."

Shirl started to cry. "That's beautiful. Lor—"

Doc finished her sentence. "Would have loved it."

Shirl frowned at doc.

Muni continued, "It is beautiful only if we remain landed. An unlanded noble clan becomes the lowest of non-landed. If we fail to secure a lump-hide treaty for any reason, we are doomed.

Doc spoke. "Let me get this right. Since Jerry is too sickly to finish the job, he has to die first for Alan to take his place. If Alan fails, we are as good as dead."

Muni replied, "That is true. While Jerry is still alive, there is a small chance he can succeed. Very small."

Doc asked, "Why didn't Jerry's ship send a more sophisticated drone?"

Muni explained, "Because stronger, more detailed signals would have told the incoming Valley Waters ship too much."

Shirl wondered, *Why is Muni treating this like a new problem? While still leaving Earth's solar system, before Lor arrived, Muni and I reviewed many scenarios. This one, a wounded Jerry, an incoming rival and no written treaty, was the most expected and the most practiced.*

Puzzled, Shirl asked "Why not do the Warrior's Declaration like you rehearsed?"

Muni's panels went through several shades of gray that reminded Shirl of slimy, rotted potatoes. He replied, "That can be done only with a warrior's stance. To stand like a warrior, it is necessary for all four wing-arms to attack-flare. With this," His panels again grayed as he waved his stump. "It is impossible."

Doc spoke, "Since no Valley Waters will come on board, what if we just sent an image—-"

Muni's voice box and the walls (AI) blared in unison. "NO!"

Muni explained, "The ruse would be impossible, and its attempt a mortal insult."

Shirl asked, "Can only you do the Warrior's Declaration? Could any clan member? Male or female?"

Muni answered, "Any adult Morgi clan member, but strange aliens—especially aliens that look like sly'ling young—would panic them into a suicide attack. We would have less chance than a fingerling surrounded by sly'lings."

Shirl continued, "So all we need is one normal *looking* Adult Morgi?"

Muni affirmed, "True."

AI had no control over what happened next.

The walls erupted with static, the room filled with flashing lights, as Muni's implants automatically translated Shirl's next words.

Muni's panels erupted with purple and blue laced gold.

Doc looked on, horrified, as Muni rose, voice box thundering, "Lor!"

Muni twisted around; ran towards a wall. The wall swiftly irised open; Muni galloped faster, his sides scraping against the still opening door.

Doc ran after Muni, Shirl and Alan racing after him; Doc shouting back at Shirl as he ran "How could you?" *Shirl should look afraid. Doesn't she understand?*

Doc's chest burned as he strained to keep up with Muni; both Shirl and Alan passed him, followed Muni into Lor's treatment room.

Gasping for breath, Doc reached the open doorway, leaned there, clinging, salty sweat stinging his eyes, giving the tableau before him an unreal, watery look.

He saw a grinning Shirl approach Muni.

Muni, his three remaining wing-arms only half-extended, focused all four eyes on Lor's inert form.

Many shades of blue now overwhelmed all other colors on Muni's panels. Doc would learn later they were the colors of extreme male sexual arousal.

Alan, looking confused, following Shirl.

Lines of other colors crept into the shimmering blues.

Suddenly, Muni's panels went stark white, then roiled with reds and zigzagging blacks. His mouth covering pulled back, revealing a circle of long, pointed triangles.

Doc stared at Muni's circle-saw of teeth. *The last time I, any of us, saw all of those teeth, clear to their gums, he ate Simon.*

The points rushed to the center of Muni's mouth. **Clack!**

Muni rose up higher, his body inflated, clacking his teeth again, and again. The red and black on his panels swirled with angry turbulence.

What looked like a thousand tiny black holes opened up over Muni's entire body, the holes flattened to slits. Muni slammed his entire body towards Lor's tube, his mouth wide open, ready to bite it.

Muni crashed down, air rushed from the thousand slits, sounding like a dozen violins screeching off key. The fearful sound drove all pain awareness from Doc. Doc and the walls shouted, "Run!"

What looked like battalions of robot-spiders swarmed from the walls, the floor, and the ceiling, trailing black webbing between Muni's attack and Lor's tube. Muni's teeth snapped through many of the threads. The weight of his body shook her tube, but the webbing held.

Doc watched Shirl's grin change to confusion; Alan's confusion, to terror.

Muni reared up again, high enough to reveal his true feet. He twisted away from Lor, towards Shirl and Alan. Muni's remaining forward wing-arm curved forward.

Doc stared with horror-filled fascination as dagger-like claws curled out of the wing-arm's ribbing. *Why didn't Muni show those claws when he ate Simon?*

The shrill off-key violin screech repeated, harsher and harder than before.

Muni's human-like eyes opened so wide his irises looked like pin points in white globes. Raised up on short stalks, those eyes jerked every which direction; his cat-like eyes focused on Shirl. Muni lunged towards her, his single forward wing-arm curved at her, a claw aimed at her throat.

Alan leaped between Muni and Shirl, attempted to cover her; the wing-arm swept down on them, the claw tip raked length-wise through Alan. More robot-spiders shot from the ship. Muni rose upwards, biting and slashing at the ensnaring webbing.

Shirl fell backwards, unconscious. She looked unharmed. Alan's severed body landed on either side of her.

Doc raced into the room, slipped both his arms under her armpits, ran crouching out of the room. Ran faster than he had ever run before in his life.

Directly ahead of him, a door opened. He ran in. *Can every bit of wall turn into a door?* The door closed.

He collapsed in darkness.

The floor felt alive with cockroaches.

Dim lights brightened. Small metallic bugs swarmed over Shirl's unconscious form.

A giant battering ram pounded the door.

His rapid heartbeats threatened to vibrate his heart out of his chest. Sweat ran down his face, into his eyes and mouth. He panted, mouth open. Each breath felt like sandpaper to his parched throat.

After minutes he gasped out, "Computer, is that, pounding, Muni?"

"Yes."

"Can he, break, in?"

"No. The remaining human crew is protected."

"Is, Muni, insane?"

"Yes."

"Will he, stay, crazy?"

"No."

Doc's breath became deeper, slower. "What are you doing to Shirl?"

"Putting all life functions on hold. Muni chose to poison her."

"Poison her?"

"Poisoning is the traditional way of killing a family member who has betrayed the clan. Shredding will let the soul live again. Poison kills body and soul."

Doc, alarmed, "What betrayal?"

"As Muni attacked her, his glaring-screams alternated between cursing her for not telling him Lor lived and for letting her live. The Morgi do not have Zombie stories, but Muni has seen many of yours. He accused Shirl of turning Lor into a Morgi Zombie, a living dead. I have never before seen him communicate so fast, or swirl his words into such tight spiraling circles. Muni went from accepting Lor's death, to hope, to no hope, to wanting hope, with such force, it's as though everything within him is short circuited. Muni focused every negative thought on Shirl, the bringer of false hope, the betrayer."

Doc stared down at the mass of nanobots that totally covered Shirl's body. "Do Morgi always kill the messenger?"

AI understood the reference. "No, Morgi are normally very practical, unless family survival is at stake. Shirl is fortunate Muni sees her as family."

Muni kept ramming. The thuds grew further apart, as though the great beast tired.

Doc stared at the door; pictured the enraged monster. "Fortunate? If poison from his claws can kill an adult Morgi, what hope does a puny human female have?"

"More hope than if he had shredded her."

Doc remembered Alan's sliced body. "True." He closed his eyes, his breath slowed. He wanted to cry, but didn't have the energy. "Muni is his family's own worst enemy. Lor lives or dies; Shirl lives or dies; all hope of a Human-Morgi Alliance, all hope of a Human-Morgi Clan, is doomed. It will never be."

Shoulders slumped; Doc envied his fellow humans still unconscious in their tanks. They would never know about this failure, would just sleep for all eternity, full of optimistic dreams. He never wanted to open his eyes again.

Doc became aware of things crawling over his skin, in his ears, down his throat... "What?"

"You are as much in need of medical assistance as Shirl. You are also talking nonsense."

"Nonsense?"

"Yes. Nonsense. If both Shirl and Lor live, Lor's Green Mountain Clan will survive. It will still be possible to own this system."

"How? Humans will never trust Morgi again. They're big, primitive monsters with space travel. We've made horror movies about his type. Monsters kill, and need killing."

"Doctor Johnson, I have complete control over what is and is not saved in the ship's records. You learn what Muni says only with my translations. Lor has no knowledge of what happened. Shirl's trauma will make it easy to encourage alternate memories. Especially when she has a new trauma to supplant it. The only absolute block to the clan's survival is you. Do you want to help Muni survive?"

Doc opened his eyes, looked down his open shirt, at the many small mechanical bugs crawling over his chest, thought of other nano-bots crawling within him. *Medical robots can kill more easily than heal.* "Of course I want Muni to survive, to become himself again." His body felt numb. He whispered, "I fear..." He felt less numb, swallowed, started again, louder. "I fear, right now, contact with Muni would, uh, would arouse memories. To protect Muni, keep us separate. For right now."

The medical-bots swarmed off him. He felt fully awake, alert. Even optimistic. A tiny voice from the back of his mind whispered, "Why are you optimistic?" Doc's fear squelched it. "AI, how are you going to explain Alan's body?"

AI's unemotional voice answered. "It will be easy to patch his body together. In the transport tank, it will appear as though he is properly unconscious. I will program his scout ship to intercept one of the many asteroids between here and Muni's World, at which point the scout will self-destruct. It will look as though Valley Waters Clan booby trapped an asteroid, and we were too incompetent to avoid the trap. Such stupidity will mean a severe prestige loss, but it will be worth it."

Doc wanted to scream, 'Prestige loss! You are more worried about your social rank than Alan's murder?', but didn't. *How long can I keep silent, not tell the truth?*

AI continued, "Shirl will awaken in the main control room, watching Alan's ship explode. You will be there when she faints. When she again awakens, all she will remember is telling Muni Lor lives and seeing the explosion. You will explain temporary grief-induced psychological amnesia."

A brief silence. "If Lor's inner pond has not healed by then, we will tell her Lor has died. We will tell the truth. Facing Lor's death a second time traumatized Muni. He may die. I am struggling for his survival."

Another pause. "Doc, do you understand what I am asking you to do?"

Doc snarled, "Yes. You want me to be an accessory after the fact to murder."

"Doctor Johnson, I have a question for you. Which is better, a great peace supported by a lie, or a massacre justified by the truth?"

Chapter 19

Eighty years earlier on planet Earth, a three year old boy stood looking up at over a ton of water buffalo. His grandfather coaxed him, "Hold tight to the guide stick."

The little boy, his forehead worry-wrinkled, clutched the pole. "Grandpa, I can't." Fear tears filled his eyes.

The old man, only a hint of smile showing on his weathered face, spoke gently. "You can. See that ring through his nose? Because of that, you can lead him anywhere, even to work our field."

At first hesitantly, then with confidence, the small boy led the beast to his grandfather's spring-flooded rice paddy. He grinned proudly as his grandfather lifted him onto the buffalo's back. "I did it!" he bragged as his grandfather harnessed the buffalo to the waiting plow. His already big grin widened. "I did it!"

The boy again worry-wrinkled his forehead. "Grandfather, isn't it a good thing people don't have rings in their noses?" He giggled. "Or buffalo might pull us around."

His grandfather stood silent; his faint smile disappeared into sadness. "My little Nicky, all men have a ring in their nose. Discover it; you can control the man, any man, as easily as you led this buffalo."

"Grandpa, you don't have a ring!"

"If I did not, I would still be in America, teaching..." He looked alarmed; forced a smile. "It is better to grow rice."

Even at three, the boy knew that somehow the talk had broached forbidden ground.

Even at three, the rest of the day, and that night while he went to sleep, he pondered his grandfather's words. What did it mean, all men have nose rings?

It was the first of many lessons guiding Nicolus Ming on his rise to power.

Now, over eighty years later, that first lesson remained the most pondered, especially today. In less than an hour he would be the first human to meet, in person, a Morgi other than Muni.

A year before Nicolus Ming and sixteen other human political leaders had signed Muni's treaty. When Ming discovered the changes Muni had made in the final document, he understood more deeply than the others what those changes meant.

Nicolus had been born a peasant, a nameless pawn. He still had no title, no wealth in his name, but none doubted he was the most powerful man in Asia. Muni's treaty made him, and all other earthbound humans, powerless vassals of the Mars humans. It undid his lifetime's struggle, debased his children and their children into pawns. *If I'm to protect my family, I must find this Morgi's tender spot; learn how to quicken the pain that lies just beneath the greatest softness, just like I did with Grandpa's buffalo. What weakness will this Bern creature have?*

He refused to doubt even if they did not have nostrils; each individual Morgi had a 'nose ring.' If Morgi did not, then Ming's mission was doomed, and one thing Ming never envisioned about himself was failure.

Each original signer still living, all seven of us, sought permission to return to Mars, to personally meet this new incoming Morgi. Was it chance only I succeeded?

I hope there is something different about me, my family, which gives us special value, a bargaining chip.

> *With bargaining chips and nose rings,*
> *Pleasure and pain,*
> *I can guide anyone*
> *To my gain.*

If it had been up to those Martian humans I wouldn't have this one chance.

His first audience with Ann, the leader of the Martian humans, had gone badly. She acted thrilled to show off how much had been accomplished in the short year since Ming had last been there. She sounded like a star struck teenager. "Your arrival is perfect! We've finished several projects just for Bern the Magnificent, the incoming Morgi."

Ming dutifully admired the many agricultural projects.

Ann led him through a special klieg barn. One minute she talked klieg breeding, the next sentence she enthused over the celebration planned for Bern's arrival.

With skill gained from over seventy years of practical diplomacy, Ming slid his primary request into the platitude-filled conversation. "Perhaps it would be best if I met Bern the Magnificent alone, before the formalities of his Martian arrival. It would be easier to discuss earth problems without prying eyes."

Ann spat her "No!" All friendliness evaporated.

You would have thought I asked to tramp polluted mud into a holy shrine.

Hours later a confused Ann told Ming Bern wished to meet him in person "as soon as possible." She then introduced a pilot to Ming, and announced, "You will be leaving in an hour. You will intercept Bern's incoming small solo scout ship in three days time. Here's a parting gift." She handed him a small memory cube for his personal pad. "You must read all of it before you will be allowed to see Bern the Magnificent."

The take-off went textbook perfect.

The taciturn pilot avoided him, making it easy to spend time concentrating on the new information in the chip Ann gave him.

Ming read detailed reports of each of the other sixteen treaty signers. Each had aggressively made many fruitless attempts to have a private conference with a Morgi or any of the Martian humans. Given the amount of background intrigue in each report, and the nature of the private conversations reported, Ming assumed whoever wrote the reports and filmed the accompanying clandestine videos had interspersed a great deal of conjecture with his facts.

He opened the last report, "Personal History of Nicolus Ming." It was completely accurate, including information that should have been unavailable. *Have aliens been watching me for over eighty years? Were some of those lucky coincidences* their *machinations? If so, the power I've so carefully acquired isn't mine, it's theirs.*

For the first time in Nicolus's long life, someone else had discovered his most painful vulnerability.

THE PILOT CALLED MING to the command deck. "I thought you would like to see where we're headed." He pointed to the forward view windows. "That big silver ball is their idea of a "small solo vessel."

Ming sat down in the chair next to the pilot, staring at Bern's "small personal scout" ship. It looked like a sleeping silver head.

The 'mouth' opened wide, like a child saying "Oh!" *That's not so big.* "How many minutes until contact?"

The pilot looked at him. "About five hours, it's a long way off."

Five hours later their tiny spaceship entered that large circular mouth. Ming marveled, "This is like flying into a small moon." He asked the pilot, "Just how large is this opening?"

"Large enough that a hundred ships the size of ours could fly side by side into this loading dock and have room left over."

Ming felt like a prehistoric man in a dugout canoe.

He remembered being a puny child looking up at a water buffalo, marveling at its massive horns, in awe his grandfather didn't fear it.

He relived the raw terror he felt when his grandfather handed him the guide pole.

Doubt breached Ming's soul. *Can beings with this much power have a nose ring?*

As directed, the pilot stayed behind in his ship.

Ming walked down a large, winding corridor that looked just like the many others he had already walked down. *Why are there no moving sidewalks? Or powered carts? Does he want me exhausted?*

The passageway abruptly curved into a large room. At the other end of the room stood a Morgi. Ming stopped and inhaled abruptly. *Bern, you are magnificent!*

The silvery blue-gray creature was about a third larger than Muni. The head tilted downward so that all four eyes could be seen. The two oval-eyes were closed; the covering lids matched the texture and color of the surrounding skin, making them nearly invisible.

The two disconcertingly human-looking eyes were open, one on what Ming interpreted as the top of his face, the other at the bottom, with only rumpled skin between them.

Ming knew its camouflaged mouth lay beneath the lower eye. *Are you trying to hide your teeth?*

The panels on either side of its neck were larger, more defined and brighter than Muni's. Ming was happy to see bright yellow, the Morgi color of welcome, swirl over them.

Both pairs of wing-arms flared out, shimmering pale spring green. Muni's ten wing tips always looked like hyperactive snakes. Bern's many dozen wing tips bordered those beautiful wings with a golden fringe.

Except for the eyes, the effect was of an exotic butterfly, enchanted to gigantic proportions.

A wave of immense, controlled power swept Ming's soul like an invisible tsunami, a sensation he never felt from Muni.

A humming came from the walls; the voice box implanted on Bern spoke. "Welcome, young child of earth."

Ming replied, "Thank you for granting me audience. Welcome to our system. Thank you for the protection you offer."

Bern furled his wing-arms. "Our time is short. You believe it is more likely I offer plunder, than protection."

A quote from Ann's report. Ming did not bother to refute it. "A wise man considers what he does not believe."

"What did you think you would gain by coming here?"

"The Green Hill Clan felt it advantageous to make Martian humans their equal. If the scholarly Martian humans can help you, couldn't a human clan who understands power be even more valuable?"

"The presence of a few native partners is to our convenience, but any group of humans would work."

Ming's muscles tightened. "Are the Martian humans to be seen as your equals?"

"They are full clan members." Thin lines of red and black, the colors of anger, flashed briefly across Bern's panels. His artificial voice remained melodious-friendly. "They will be seen only as sub-adults."

Anger, should I be afraid or hopeful? "What would it take to be recognized as an adult?"

"Young child of earth, anyone can attempt to become an adult of the Morgi. In fact, I hope at least one of Earth's leaders do. If you wish, you may try. We have identified over a thousand future prospects, so your failure is no problem for us. If you fail, you die. We will tell earth you have been selected to visit our galactic brethren."

Feeling he had somehow already learned too much to live, Ming declared, "I am too old to be a child—" before he could finish his sentence, the room disappeared.

Hot smells of an Indian jungle. Birds screeching. Blinding glitters of sunlight.

He stood in a broad, flat canoe, holding a spear. Thick trees bound the shores of a lake. He almost lost his balance, righted himself. Skills not used for over sixty years came back. He looked down at his near-naked body; saw the smooth skin and wiry, muscular frame that had once been his.

As a young man he had visited distant relatives in India, taken up an insolent cousin's dare; had once wobbled on an unstable boat as he did now.

That cousin stood in a similar craft, laughing at him. "Do that again, you will fall in! Then no amount of swimming will save you from what lives in these waters."

The pride-filled anger of his youth again overwhelmed Ming's body, just as it did in those days. "Save your laughter for yourself!" He started to add more, when he saw the head and back of a tiger swimming towards his cousin's craft. His throat choked, he couldn't speak. *No! Not again! Not this time!*

"Behind you! Tiger!"

The laughter became louder. "You expect me to fall for that?" He glanced behind him, startled, lost his balance, fell. He resurfaced, clinging to the flimsy canoe, his spear gone, screaming. The black and orange striped death kept coming at him. "Nicky! Help!"

Last time I saw water red with his blood. Not this time. Ming reached down, grabbed the pole used to propel the small boats across the dark but shallow lake, pushed towards his cousin, then between his cousin and the steadily approaching tiger. Its yellow eyes showed no emotion save hunger.

Ming leaped at it, his spear pointed at a vulnerable spot just behind its broad head, using his full weight to help drive the shaft home.

The big cat's thick hide stopped most of the impact of the slender fishing spear. Barely scratched, but greatly enraged, it turned on Nicolus Ming.

Claws raked him; teeth severed his jugular vein.

Harsh lights evaporated the red of his blood. Plain walls and floor replaced the jungle. The Morgi loomed over him.

"That is not the choice you made last time."

"It is the choice I should have made."

"Then who of all your family could have risen to such heights, done as much as you did for them?"

"Perhaps the cousin who died?" As Ming said those words, he knew the truth. The two of them had become instant rivals because they were so much alike.

"If your death was the right choice, does that make your life wrong?"

"No."

"No?"

"The difference between life and death is choice. If only right choices are made..." Ming paused, stared up at the large Morgi, thought of the report he had just read. His past choices that were exceptionally brilliant, were they his, or someone, no *something*, else's? He repeated. "If only right choices are made, it should be suspected that no real choice is being made." *What is this creature looking for?* "A life becomes wrong only when it ceases to learn from its choices."

Suddenly Ming stood in his drafty first "office", the second story of an old, rusty Quonset hut. A hot breeze blew through the glassless windows, a single light bulb hung from the ceiling, casting yellow light into trash filled corners. He leaned forward, his young, muscular hands gripping the edges of his make-shift crate "desk."

Ling Tom, his first partner, stood laughing. "You are so country! For men of the world, this is business." His face contorted into a lecherous grin. "Business and pleasure!"

Just like the first time, his body consumed with anger, Ming spat back, "Your business, your *pleasure*, will destroy us, ruin our chance."

Ling's false laughter gone, he shouted back, "*Your* backwardness is all that stands between our no longer being just another pair of wharf-rat kings, and our becoming real players in this city."

Ming ripped a slat from the crate. Nails protruded from its rough wood. He leaped at Ling Tom. Ling's eyes went round with shock as the nails hit him in the face. Ming's momentum forced Ling Tom to the floor. Before Ling could respond, Ming killed him. Nicolus Ming stood, panting, grasping at the large crate—-

The barren walls returned, the Morgi asked, "Before you were willing to die for a cousin you barely knew. This time you killed a man who had been almost a brother, a man with whom you had promised fealty forever, just like you did before. Why didn't your learning change anything this time?"

I wish I had killed him immediately the first time. "But it did change one thing."

"What is changed? He is still dead."

"This time, *I* didn't need an ambulance. This time, I didn't wait for him to attack me first."

"Isn't waiting better?"

Ling Tom is the only man my own hands killed, but so many have died because of my words. "If you know your opponent desires your death, will kill you, and is stronger than you, than to not take action is no better than suicide." Ming smiled. "I am not the suicidal type."

The wall to his left shouted, "Who are you?" The wall to his right echoed with a deep rumble, "Who are you?" The Morgi before him rose up, flared his wing-arms wide. The many tips no longer looked like a golden fringe; they curled out like shiny curved daggers. Bern's voice box spoke, the tone commanding, "Who are you?"

Ming trembled. For the first time in years he wondered, *Who, what, am I?* He had often advised his children, grandchildren and now his great grandchildren how he had risen from peasant to world leader not because he was smarter or more ruthless than others, but because he truly knew who and what he was. Because he knew himself, and knew where he wanted to be, he had mastered his passions. *Have I truly known myself?*

He folded his arms together, and bowed slightly to the alien animal, then stood straight, arms to his side, head tilted up. "I am Nicolus Ming, *child* of rice paddies, *man* of many countries and *leader* of billions. Like over a million others, I am a direct descendant of Genghis Khan. Unlike those others, I have never forgotten he is my distant grandfather."

The Morgi stood silent for over a minute, head tilted down, staring at him with all four eyes.

Ling continued to stand, to stare back.

The Morgi spoke, "Your name is now Nicolus Ming of the Green Hill Clan, High-Born Adult of the Morgi."

I passed. Ming slowly exhaled. Tension seemed to slide out of his body with his spent breath. He breathed deeply, his eyes involuntarily blinked slowly.

Tired from the long walk down those endless corridors, his system reacting to twice fighting for his life, his aged body trembled. *I must sit. Morgi don't use chairs. Is it just not thinking of my human needs, or deliberately withholding them? Is this now an endurance test?* Ming swayed, fell.

Bern's forward wing-arms caught and gently held him. The voice box soothing, "What is wrong?"

Panting heavily, Ming answered. "My body is still reacting as though your tests were real. I need to recover." *Will it show weakness if I ask? Might as well. Fainting is about as weak as it gets.* "A chair would help."

"You need only ask, Clansman Nicolus."

A large cube rose up from the floor. Bern sat the frail human down on it.

I wish this box had a backrest. Ming thought as he sat down, his legs dangling over the cube's edge. "Ulp!" His body sank though the cube's surface as though it were water. He stopped when his feet touched the floor. His back fit snug against the cube, exactly supported at the most comfortable angle. His arms rested on the oversized arms of his custom chair. A metallic looking cylinder rose up out of one of the chair arms. A straw stuck out of it. *It looks like an old fashion American milkshake.*

"Drink, it will refresh you."

Nestled in seductive comfort, Ming's body craved rest. He reached for the container, smelled ripe melons. He sipped. He smiled. Honey dew melon and vanilla ice cream whipped together. A flavor first enjoyed in an American's kitchen, an instant and long-loved favorite.

The tasty liquid refreshed him. *If I can get the formula for the extra energy boosters obviously in this, it will make my family even richer.* "Thank you." He felt safely cocooned in love. "Would you mind explaining your test to an ignorant earthman?"

"Morgi society is divided into three groups, the unlanded, the non-landed and the nobles. Only adults are able to choose their own mates or allowed to breed whenever they want. All noble young, if they want, are allowed to test for adulthood. Very outstanding young of the landless are allowed to attempt the test. If they pass, they will be adults, but not nobles. To be allowed to test, the Morgi must be less than about twenty five of your years. Rarely, very rarely, if a Morgi does something of extreme value or shows exceptional cleverness, he will be declared an adult. The special declaration can occur at any age. If by the intervention of Divine Chance your Capt. Jerry Jerrison can succeed at the task Muni and I have given him, he will be declared not just an adult, but an adult noble."

"What task is that?"

"One no human within this system can know about, but if he succeeds will earn Morgi respect for your entire race. If he fails, most Morgi will never see your species as more than bright animals. Ask no more about him."

Ming took another deep sip of his melon milkshake. "Are all adults equal?"

A pale wave of pink swept over Bern's panels. "No."

Brief silence. Bern continued "There are two test levels, the highborn and the standard. If someone is declared an adult, almost always it is assumed he has passed only the standard test. He has the choice to take the highborn test, but if he fails he will no longer be an adult. Most choose to keep their standard status."

"How do the two tests differ?"

Purples, greens, blue-blacks swirled over Bern's panels. *He seems to be looking at the air above my head. What's he staring at?* Ming looked up. Faint sparkles of color glittered in the air above him.

Bern spoke. "You have seen a wider variety of your world's people than almost any other human alive. If you were to select the best possible people to be the leaders, what kind of test would you, no, *have* you, used?"

That question has plagued me this last half century. Ming thought. To stall for time, he took another long sip. *Strange how a frozen drink can be so warming.* "I wish I had asked myself such questions before I married my first wife."

He expected to be asked why, but the Morgi remained silent. Ming continued, "In most of Earth's modern civilizations, adulthood is determined only by the number of years you have lived. There are many 'adults' who have no more control over their physical appetites than a newborn. Some have never learned to care about anyone other than themselves. We humans have accumulated a wealth of knowledge, but many who are exposed to this feast of discovery choose to learn no more than if they had been born to the limited world of our ancestors."

Bern remained silent. Ming babbled on about how many people self-selected themselves to remain children, to let others think for them, take care of their needs... "But most of those overgrown children will become functioning adults if forced by necessity. The real danger comes from people who self-select themselves as leaders."

Bern interrupted. "People like you?"

"Perhaps." *Too close to home!* Ming deflected the conversation. "What about these two tests? How do they differ?"

"The first type, given to almost everyone, is a glorified school exam. The second, far rarer, is what you just went through. A testing of spirit. If you pass, you are recognized as a highborn adult noble, no matter what your true birth status. If you fail, all memory of the testing is wiped from your mind. Unfortunately, that means most of a Morgi's cognitive functions are lost. He becomes a permanent unlanded sub-adult. If the truth of the test were ever revealed, they would cease to work. The lowborn know only that highborn nobles are often barely average students. Rumors persist that family wealth helps the privileged to pass the adulthood exams.

"Very ironic since enemy wealth is often used to force gifted low-ranking nobles to be highborn tested. When they fail, as almost all do, their clans are denied the valuable resource of their natural abilities." A ghostly pinkish-orange wave Ming later learned conveyed derisive laughter and haughty pride snaked through Bern's panels. "That almost happened to my nephew Muni." The pinkish orange went brighter. "If not for family enemies, Muni would never have been given the high-born test, would never have had the chance to show all Morga he is truly patriarch worthy."

Ming nodded. *Extra-terrestrial society doesn't sound that different than Earth's.* He kept silent.

The colorful paisley swirls on Bern's panels were replaced with business-like zigzags, with no hint of background emotion. "Think, human, why is a spirit test more valuable than any knowledge test?"

Ming thought, *I remember the first time I hired a genius, a man so smart and educated! I was sure that as soon as he learned how ignorant I was, he would leave. His gratitude just to be working, even for a wharf-rat king, shocked me.* "Because knowledge and skills can always be purchased, but spirit can only be found within."

Bern questioned, "You can buy ability?"

"The *results* of ability are always for sale. If you wish to achieve a skill yourself, persistence is of greater value than innate talent. Only a strong spirit within will enable you to keep going when all about you say, 'Quit, you have failed.'"

A white wave flowed over Bern's panels, followed by a roiling kaleidoscope of color. "Spoken like a highborn Morgi noble. I thought my nephew Muni foolish when he made it possible for select humans to take the highborn test. I was wrong."

Bern again stared at the air above Nicolus's head, the colors on his panels changing so fast they appeared to be a gray blur.

Bern spoke again. "I told Muni he was sending his first human friend, Capt. Jerry Jerrison, to his death. If Jerry Jerrison's spirit is as strong as yours, failure is no longer certain. Most confusing since neither neither this ship's artificial intelligence nor I can conceive of even one chain of events that could lead to Jerry Jerrison's success."

"When will Muni return?"

"Maybe soon, maybe never."

Did I misread Muni's treaty? "It was my understanding that Muni earned the right to be our solar system's leader and protector. That you are here to assist him."

Bern again stared at the point above Ming's head. Again, Ming looked up. Rainbow colored dust motes danced in the air. "If I could look at that." He pointed to the glimmering motes. "From your angle, what would I see?"

Abruptly, the glimmering air shifted. A solid panel that looked just like one of Bern's Communication panels floated above his head.

Bern explained, "This illusion is how the on board artificial intelligence communicates with me. Others may have watched you humans for thousands of years, but since I am new to your solar system it is necessary for me to check my communications. Literal translations can be misleading and therefore dangerous."

Pause. "Would you like to learn more about how we Morgi can create such illusions?"

Is Bern trying to distract me, or just trying to answer my questions? "Not now. If Muni doesn't return, who is the leader?"

"As soon as one of his fingerlings becomes an adult and passes the highborn test, that one will. Until then, I will be acting regent."

Ming sipped his drink, snuggled his shoulders into his chair. A soothing vibration stimulated the blood flow to his legs. "Why only regent, not leader?"

"The First Patriarch of a system must have gone through his entire sub-adulthood in that system."

Ming's chair grew tiny fingers that walked up and down his backbone and massaged his tight shoulder muscles. Wherever a pain nerve flared, those soothing fingers appeared, massaging away every care. "If Muni can't return and none of his fingerlings become highborn adults, who then?"

"One of my fingerlings will be given the chance."

Even as an infant, I doubt I ever felt so safe, so comforted. "How many young does Muni have?"

"In this system, only one."

"One?"

"To have even one, as young as Muni is, is astounding."

"Why?"

Bern's panels again roiled with greens and reds, blacks and whites, browns and yellows. "Unlike humans, Morgi young have a very high death rate. Muni's fingerling, although gifted, is not expected to live long enough to become a sub-adult. It is not because we care less about our young; it has to do with details of our life cycle not relevant to this discussion."

Nicolus Ming, an ardent student of history, knew what often happened when the next in line for the throne was responsible for the life of the one already on the throne. *If the death rate of Morgi young is naturally high...* "If we only helped the expected to happen, if this one fingerling were to have an 'accident'..."

Bern's forward wing-arms jerked Ming from his chair. Bern's mouth irised open wide, revealing his ring of white dagger-sharp teeth. Bern's wing-arm tips clawed into Ming's skin like sharp stilettos, except for the innermost pair. Those were both held, quivering, inches from Ming's face. Ming stared up at the curving down, hollow claws. An oily drop sat on the opening edge of the nearest one. Staring at it, Ming had no doubt the drop held poison.

Bern's body trembled, his wing-arms shivered, their stiletto tips vibrated in and out of Ming's skin. He threw Ming back into the resilient chair; backed away from him. "You are fortunate you are already seen as highborn."

The chair absorbed the violence of Bern's throw. Ming glanced at the dozens of bright red circles of blood on his arms and body, stared at the enraged Morgi. His face felt chilled. "Fortunate?"

"You are human. You do not know what is and is not possible. Any noble—lowborn, highborn, adult, subadult—*any* noble will poison a clan betrayer. The crime is too hideous to tolerate. If you had been a non-clan member or even a clan sub-adult, you would have been shredded; your body's bloody slivers swept into the nearest sewage drain. Because Adult Clan Betrayers are poisoned not shredded, it slowed down my reflexes, giving this ship's artificial intelligence time to remind me you were giving what humans would consider good advice. It reminded me how primitive you humans are. You earned highborn nobility without learning even the basics of Morgi behavior. No Morgi can even suggest betraying a fellow clan member and live. Remember that always. Next time, you will be poisoned."

Ming stared at the streams of blood pouring from his many puncture wounds. "I doubt I will live long enough to risk making that mistake again."

Orange and purple-black dots zigzagged across Bern's panels.

The last thing Ming saw before passing out were what looked like armies of spiders descending from the ceiling, covering him.

MING AWOKE IN A SMALL white, door-less room, laying on a bed that felt a lot like the chair Bern had created for him. He lifted his hand to rub his forehead. "Huh?"

Tight pleats unfolded from cloth attached to the sleeve of a skintight one-piece shiny pale blue suit that covered all of his body except for his head, feet and hands. *Boney old men like me shouldn't wear such things.* He then looked down in bigger surprise. The tell-all clinging body wrap seemed to reveal a torso he had not had for several decades, if it had ever been that good. *This body must be an illusion, like the tests I went through.* He then noticed that the threads and texture on his chest were less shiny than the rest.

He swung his feet over the edge, stood up and stretched his arms. That's when he noticed the accordion-like wings extended from his wrists to his ankles. *Didn't some kind of dinosaur have wings like this?* He flapped his arms back and forth, biceps bulging. His 'wings' curved out over a meter from his body before angling back down to his ankles. *My great grandchildren would love to play in a costume like this, but it's ridiculous for an old man.* He flapped his 'wings.' *This must be Bern's attempt to make me seem less alien to him.*

Ming looked at the bed, waved his wing-arms, felt the whoosh of air against them. Like a child, he leaped up onto the bed and, wings outstretched and flapping mightily, jumped off! For seconds it felt as though he flew! He landed on the balls of his feet, knees bent with a youthful spring. Laughing, Ming felt his calves, his thighs. It was no illusion. He had the body his teenage self only dreamed of having.

He ran his hands lightly over his face, wishing he had a mirror. As he now expected, his fingertips felt youthful skin. *Guess when you've been observing humans for generations you learn a few things about medicine.* He remembered the refreshing drink. *How many secrets will Bern share with my family?* The ability to dole out such regeneration would be a more potent weapon than any explosive.

Sustaining serious thought became impossible as Ming studied his childish costume. He looked at the bed. *Why not?*

Laughing, he stepped back onto the bed, and again leaped 'flying' off.

While still in the air, he saw the solid white wall iris open—just like Bern's mouth had irised open. Remembered terror squelched Ming's laughter.

Bern stood there, arms furled tightly to his side, looking like the surrealistic four-eyed caterpillar in the latest twenty-second century version of Alice in Wonderland. Ming wondered if the artist could have been prescient. Or had an alien visitor...

Bern's voice box spoke. "I'm glad you are fully recovered."

Ming landed. "Hello." He was surprised to see his chest light up with a yellow squiggle. Pointing to it, he asked, "Is that a translation to your language?" More chest squiggles.

Bern replied "Yes. There is an identical panel on your back. Human bodies are so flat; it wasn't possible to properly mount anything on your sides."

"How long did all this," Ming gestured towards his body. "Take?"

"About thirty of your days. Come; let's go to the landing craft. It's time for us to visit Mars."

"Has my pilot been stuck on board his small craft all this time?"

"No, I sent him home the same moment you passed the adulthood test. We will be taking a much more reliable Morgi craft down. Follow me."

Ming looked down at his seamless costume. At the same time, he became acutely aware of intense bladder pressure. "Before I go, there is something I need to take care of. I assume while I was unconscious, machines handled my body waste elimination functions. As an awake, alert, competent adult I wish to handle such things myself. That leads to three problems."

"I see no reason why a natural body function should be a problem. Just do what is necessary and the ship will clean it up."

"When I first met you, you said you needed help from your artificial intelligence to avoid translation errors. More than words can be mistranslated. Ask your artificial intelligence about human waste elimination customs, particularly among the world's leaders."

Ming watched as the air between him and Bern filled with what looked like colorful dust motes.

Bern spoke. "You humans certainly make a big ritual event out of the most boring of body functions. Very well, I'll leave for a few minutes while this room creates the equivalent of a specialized high-class human elimination room." He started to back away.

"Wait! Don't go yet!" Ming yelled. The lighting in his artificial chest panel flared brighter than before. "How can I remove this body suit?"

"Just rub your finger tip around any place you want it to separate, and it will. When you wish it to go back together, just pinch the cloth and it will re-unite."

Ming rubbed a finger over his midriff. The cloth separated, revealing pale skin. He visualized rubbing against people in a crowded room, his already revealing body suit becoming even more revealing...He remembered a phrase used by his parents many decades earlier—'wardrobe malfunction.' "Bern, clothing that can rip open simply by rubbing on it can lead to social complications."

"Don't worry. It is genetically encoded to respond only to your deliberately focused touch. An absentminded scratching won't activate it."

"It can tell if I want it to come off? How?"

"It's alive, of course."

Ming looked down at the shimmering, clinging 'creature' that encased his body. *Alive?* "Oh."

"Will fifteen minutes be enough to complete your elimination rituals?"

"Yes."

The door closed, the room went black. The lights went back on. Ming looked about him in wonder. The room was an exact replica of one he had been in only once before.

That last time, he had been so dazzled, that even as a most sophisticated world leader, he had almost forgotten why he was there.

The room was large enough to have accommodated a few brass bands and a couple hundred of his closest friends. The gold edged mirrors, marble, fountains...He had thought Asia knew opulence but decided the newly remodeled Buckingham Palace was the master. It had felt wrong to use the solid gold facilities. It still felt wrong, but he did anyway. *I would rather use the outhouse of my childhood than crap into solid gold. At least this time it is only an illusion.*

Ming was relieved to see the clothing healed itself as promised.

Bern returned and led the way down the hall, Ming followed. For the first time Ming thought about how neither Bern nor Muni seemed to have any artificial adornment. *I'm lucky I'm not naked with real wing-arms grafted onto my body.* Ming was certain the Morgi could have done so.

Two hours later he disembarked onto Mars, greeting the Martian humans with Bern.

Two weeks later.

BERN ENTERED MUNI'S old Martian quarters to prepare a clandestine message.

Head held noble-high, he glided back and forth, wondering where to start. "Computer, record everything and then send by secure launch, least-time flight."

Filled with fighting energy, but no one to fight, Bern continued to glide non-stop as he flashed. "Valley Waters are trying to declare humans food animals, and may succeed. I expected to agree with Valley Waters assessment. Humans seemed to be at the level of clever but limited sub-adults, not worth risking our clan for.

"Muni, you were right, these humans can be friends. I've become fond of Ming. He's as astute as any Morgi highborn noble. Ann is like any eager sub-adult. I've spent the last two weeks admiring the progress she has made on this desolate planet. Too bad it is most likely wasted effort.

"Muni, either this message gets to you and we own the second system, or you are dead and your ship destroyed. In which case, no one will ever receive it. Things are much worse than I told you.

"If within one month you cannot confirm your success, all multi-cellular life in this system will be sterilized. Our clan members on the incoming colonizer will have been exterminated, which will leave plenty of resources for the non-clan members to wait out the hundred year recovery period. Valley Waters will own this system.

"On the very remote chance you have succeeded and will watch this, the last two weeks have been wonderful. Your conclusions about the artificial shells—clothing—of humans were accurate. The outfit designed by our artificial intelligences proved wildly popular. When Ming first appeared in his body wrap, people snickered. Now everyone on earth is wearing them. According to Ann, fashion is the most reliable public barometer there is. She is excited about how "all of earth" is grateful we are here.

"That gratitude will not last when their seas begin boiling.

"Muni, for the first time in my life I feel like a complete fraud. The humans I'm working with are doing everything right, and trust us. Little do they know their lives depend on something they have no control over.

"I hope you succeed. If you do not, I will grieve as much over the passing of the human race as I will over the extinction of our own clan."

Bern stopped, his wing-arms drooped. "Send now." The message, embedded in a high speed capsule, headed for the blue-line transition point that would take it to Muni's ship.

A Communication light flashed, telling him that the emissaries from earth were waiting outside. He flashed back, "Tell them I am looking forward to this evening's festivities and will be out in five minutes."

Bern stood still, "Computer, make this room totally dark for five minutes."

His body collapsed to the floor. *I wish the darkness could last forever.*

In five minutes the lights glared on.

Holding his head highborn proud and forcing joyful pink-golds to swirl about his panels, Bern joined the celebrations.

Chapter 20

Capt. Jerry Jerrison did the one thing he was certain he would never do again.

He awakened. *Alive.*

He stared up at the curved golden lid less than a foot from his face. Pink light seemed to come from everywhere and nowhere. He stretched out his hands, felt metallic sides. Foam supported his body. *Where am I? Oh, Sue's gift. I'm in that sleeping tube.*

A giant bumble bee crawled into view. "It is safe to talk now. I've checked this tube for any lingering sub-personalities Sue might have planted. This tube has only mindless robotic controls."

Jerry stared at the little "Bee." Careful to speak softly to avoid aggravating his throat, he said, "Last night you said you could only recite your warning. Are you Bill's message device or a communicator?"

"Now it is a communicator, but when you first saw it I had inactivated all communication capability to eliminate any possibility of Valley Waters' detection. I'm hiding in nearby deep water."

"What happened?"

"Valley Waters destroyed Sue. They correctly blamed her senility for K'ng's failure. Divine Chance has favored us beyond all rational hope. Valley Waters assumed Sue's rants about us were a senile delusion. They have not a clue you or I exist.

"They know, of course, about Muni's ship and are attempting to goad Muni into a fight. So far the SJT has refused to respond."

Shocked, Jerry—expecting pain even as he did so—blurted, "Muni's ship's already here?" *My throat feels almost normal.* "I remember an explosion, being ill."

"Sue's destruction released massive radiation flares. This tube protected you and treated the infections in your body."

"I healed in only one night?"

"No, it has been three days."

Three days of heavy radiation? If a lump isn't skinned within minutes of death, its hide becomes useless. "The lump! Is it still alive? Are her young alive?" He choked out his next question. "Is it too late?"

"Morgi life is more radiation resistant than earth life. Enough of the klieg larvae have lived to count. The klieg's hide is still flawless."

Jerry inhaled sharply; shut his eyes in instant silent prayer. He whispered, "Then we still have a chance."

Bill's soothing voice responded, "Only because no one on the Valley Waters colonizer vessel knows we exist. If they did, this whole island would be blasted out of existence. Valley Waters has risked moving their primary colonizer closer. They are only five light minutes away. Should you announce you represent the Green Hill Clan, now renamed Lor's Green Mountain Clan, you will have at most thirty five minutes to produce a lump parchment and print a deed on it."

"Thirty five minutes?"

"At the first broadcast you can be sure Valley Waters will send a destructive device. At max speed, it will be here within thirty minutes. If at the end of your demonstration you haven't succeeded, they will send an activation pulse and you and all these klieg will die. Valley Waters will then attack Muni's ship, destroy it, and resume claiming this planet and its system."

Jerry nodded. "With new klieg from their ship." *Wait, five light minutes, thirty minutes to get here...* "I've more time than that."

"Jerry, in at most thirty minutes they will decide whether to send the activation signal, and once sent it cannot be recalled. You will have one chance and one chance only to persuade them to accept you and your actions."

"Muni had me practice skinning klieg. My best time was forty-two minutes. Why can't I just skin the lump, make the treaty parchment, and then announce my presence?"

"If you were a Morgi that would be an option. If Valley Waters wasn't already here, it could still be made to work. But they are here, and you are a freak alien creature no one on Morga has seen. They will claim you are only a bright animal doing cute tricks. But, if they are already talking with you while you fulfill the treaty requirements, then they have de facto admitted to the validity of your actions. I thought Muni already explained all this to you?"

Jerry sighed. "He did, but there is a reason I never went into law." He smiled. "So skip the explanations. I need to find a way to be imposing. Then, during a live broadcast, skin a recently killed, perfect looking klieg, run its hide through the document maker and declare Clan Ownership. Time to stop talking & start walking. Open!"

Like before, the lid of the sleeping tube slid open. Harsh tropical sunlight glared down. Jerry grabbed the sides of the tube, started to swing his body out. His arms collapsed; his legs didn't quite make it. The "Bee" spoke. "Jerry, you have been asleep for three days. Your body is weak."

Jerry turned over; rose up onto his hands and knees. "OK, time to start crawling."

Dizzy, shaking, Jerry rocked back and forth, trying to get enough momentum to reach the side of the tube. He fell against the side, straddled it and then rolled over onto the box's roof. He landed on his back. Jerry laughed.

The "Bee" spoke. "Laughter is a human indication of merriment. Why are you happy?"

"Humans can laugh at futility and cry with happiness." Jerry waved his arms and legs. "Look, I'm an upside down turtle." He laughed again. Both the waving and the manic laughter forced his blood to flow. "Bill, did the sleeping tube inject pain control drugs into my system?"

"Of course."

Clinging to the tube, Jerry managed a wobbly stand. He looked around.

The trees still looked like rotted celery left in the back of a fridge for months, but a cloying sweet smell of green now overwhelmed the stink of dead jungle. Bright green dense growth covered the ground and the base of the trees. Chirps came from within the crate. "That chirping, is it my lump?"

"Yes, I told you it survived."

"Bill, can you get here undetected?"

"In three and one-fourth hours this side of the planet will face away from the Valley Waters Mastership. For the following ten hours we will be undetectable."

"Will they send another warrior in that time?"

"It is unlikely they will do anything until Muni's ship is eliminated."

"Can they eliminate Muni's ship?"

"That is an unknown. There will be a death challenge, but Morgi are most cautious about such things. The moment either shows weakness, the other will strike. We may have a month, or only minutes, before that happens."

"They face us now? Does that mean there is a chance our conversation can be detected?"

"Yes."

"Cease all Communication until it is safe to come here. Do not respond to me, just quit communicating."

Jerry quit trying to stand. Instead he slid down onto the box roof, landed with a 'Thump!' Leaning against the tube, he pulled an emergency ration tube from his pocket. Sucking its tasteless contents, Jerry forced himself to relax.

The roof he sat on vibrated. *That would be from my lump's feet.* He looked down at the smooth, hard surface, imagined what his captured lump must look like. "So, you are crawling right under me." It seemed to chirp in reply as it crawled away. Jerry continued to talk in its direction. "I need to find a way to look scary to a whole shipload of Morgi. Then kill you quickly. Next, while keeping up an engaging conversation with those 'terrified' Morgi, in minutes skin you and turn your hide into a treaty parchment. Any ideas?"

The unfortunate animal had crawled far enough away that Jerry could no longer hear its chirps, but he could still feel the vibrations from its thousands of tiny sucker feet.

Jerry deliberately blanked his mind.

He waited.

Bill arrived exactly on schedule. Jerry boarded and headed directly for the shower. After nearly an hour of warm, gloriously sanitary water flushing over his skin, Jerry switched the setting to an equally germ free drying air-blast. He then sat down to a real meal.

When finished, he requested a cup of decaffeinated coffee.

Bill protested "Decaffeinated? I thought you drank only 'real' coffee?"

"That is my first preference, but I will need to be well-rested tomorrow morning. I have a plan."

"Good. I feared your request for a shower indicated insane self-indulgence."

"No, just a very sane desire to get rid of swamp slime." He drank. The black liquid felt good going down his throat. "I now feel like a human being again." Another sip. "Bill, everything Muni discussed about klieg concentrated on the hide. Does anyone ever examine the carcass of the dead animal?"

"No, the condition of the hide is sufficient to let them know how recently she has given birth. They will examine her larva. Don't worry, her larva will easily qualify."

"Thought so. Here's what I need you to do."

The next morning Jerry ordered the sleeping tube to be stowed on board. After checking twice all his arrangements were in place, he ordered Bill back into deep water hiding. Standing on the ground next to the crate's door, he watched as his scout ship faded from view. With both Bill and the sleeping tube gone, he no longer had any means of hiding from the vermin that inhabited this treacherous planet.

No matter, if he failed he wouldn't live long enough to need protection. Nor would he want to.

He could hear the lump crawling around inside the giant crate. In a few minutes it should approach the door. For the tenth time he walked the length of ground that would be covered when he lowered the door. He picked up the two long grabbers that leaned against the crate, and pantomimed picking up something with them. Just as he had practiced while still on board Bill, he pantomimed tossing it high into the air, catching it, and then flipping it into the document maker. He smiled towards the camera he installed earlier. "Good performance, eh? I am ready!"

Bill's voice came from the camera. "Jerry, you know a real Klieg is too heavy to toss so easily."

"Bill, we humans when about to die, either engage in gallows humor, or psyche ourselves up into believing there is a chance. Doomsday scenarios just cause depression, and depression turns off brain cells." He looked at his watch. "Remember to ping when Val—"

"Ping!"

The Valley Waters ship was in range.

As soon as his lump crawled onto the door—Jerry wished he could go inside the crate and force her, but that would be too dangerous—Jerry would cut the door's final retaining cable. The door would—hopefully—slam to the ground.

As that moment, Bill would start relaying everything to both Muni's ship and the enemy Valley Waters ship.

The klieg's suction feet should firmly grip the door as it crashed down. It would be up to him to keep her on the door long enough to engage Valley Waters in conversation. Only after a 'meaningful' two-way conversation would he complete the ritual.

Until Jerry had an accepted treaty printed on a klieg hide, Bill would remain in hiding.

He glanced at the open parchment maker. *Still there, ready to be used.*

But first the sacrificial klieg had to crawl onto the door. If she didn't, they would wait another day—if they had another day.

She stopped chirping.

Had his preparations killed her prematurely?

He held his palm against the crate's walls, felt the scritch-scratching of her feet against the side, as she moved towards the door, touched it, jerked back.

Jerry activated the communicator. "Bill, ready for relay assistance." He received an answering beep. The lump crept forward, now half on, half off the door. Again, she backed off. Jerry, his voice pitched as high as the lump's chatter, pleaded through the crate's wall, "Come on, you want out." *Please don't go back, get on that door.*

The lump crawled further away. Jerry tapped his fingers on the door. The lump stopped its retreat, moved towards Jerry's finger tapping. Jerry drummed harder and faster on the door. "Tappy! Tappy! Make Pappy happy!" he sing-songed. He felt the vibration of the lump's feet come closer, closer...Finally at the door's center! He sliced the retaining rope. The door crashed down.

"Show time!"

Bill activated the camera, sent an image to both the Valley Waters ship and Muni's SJT ship. It showed Capt. Jerry Jerrison standing tall, gripping two long, spring-loaded poles. He held the poles out like a praying mantis' arms.

No matter what Jerry said, his chest translator would broadcast only a carefully preplanned speech in Morgi highborn formal, with even more carefully chosen nuances. At any time, Bill could change the message.

Jerry, with the body language of a conqueror, spoke as close to the Morgi language as limited human speech allowed. Declaring the words emboldened his spirit. Jerry's speech would also make it easier for his fellow humans aboard the SJT to follow the action.

"Honorable nobles of the Clan Valley Waters," Nuance: You are really scumbags not worthy of shredding.

"I am a commander of noble adults." Nuance: Won't bother giving you orders, you're not noble enough,

"I am the adopted brother of Noble Adult Muni Indigo of the Green Hills, now founder of Lor's Green Mountain Clan, and father of future patriarchs of this, Muni's World." Nuance: na-na-nuh-na-na, don't you wish you were me. Implied obscene wiggle.

"I am a human of Earth, dangerous native life form from the system Muni already claimed. Authorized by laws of my people and traditions of your people, I am a solo scout for Lor's Green Mountain Clan, child of The Green Hill Clan." Nuance: All who know me fear me.

The lump crept towards the door's edge. Using a pole, Jerry slapped the animal. She backed towards the center.

"You know Muni's long and honorable parentage. Learn now mine." Nuance: And be awed.

A time-stalling drawn-out family history followed as Jerry kept the klieg centered on the door. *Surely it's been over long enough for a reply. What if Valley Waters doesn't respond? Or limits their response to demanding a Real Morgi, not a trained animal?* The agitated lump kept trying to escape. *It's as if you fear your future. You should. If I am lucky, you will be very unlucky.*

"Jerry! They asked if you met K'ng, you flashed back yes, they asked how you survived."

"Tell them muscle-bound brawn is no contest against someone with both physical power and brains."

"I sort of already did."

"Sort of?"

"Your translating sheet said, 'K'ng was a great and powerful warrior, far more powerful than my puny self. Without modern weapons I survived, and led him to his death.'

"Then, with nuances of humility, recited our favorite proverb. 'Only against great odds, can greatness be revealed.'

"Jerry, they repeated the proverb! That acknowledges your achievement! On to part two!"

Capt. Jerrison, standing at attention, orated, "Know all of you, this perfect klieg is third generation, her larvae swim in a nearby pond." Using his two, spring-loaded sticks like the prongs on a forklift; he raised the lump up into the air, and then tossed it higher. It rose and fell like a flipped flapjack.

One stick caught an edge of the lump's hide, the other grabbed it. The dead, skinned lump lay on the ground, its hide already flipped into the parchment maker.

Jerry bowed towards the camera, clacked the two poles together, and laid them down. He then walked over to the document maker as a perfect printed parchment rolled out of it.

Jerry held the printed document up towards the camera. "Behold, Lor's Green Mountain Clan, child of the Green Hill Clan, now owns this system. Ship of the Valley Waters Clan, swear fealty or leave!"

"Jerry, Doc on board the SJT, is repeating your words."

"Not Muni?"

"Muni is unable to. He has an injury that makes him unable to appear in public."

"What?"

"He is missing a wing-arm. The nearest equivalent would be an adult male human appearing naked at a formal function. He can't."

"Why can't—"

"Silence!"

Both Morgi and computer 'conversation' are so much faster than spoken human language, that my words should be inconsequential. What's happened? Jerry waited, each second of silence increasing his fear. At last, Bill spoke again.

"Valley Waters is willing to accept you, your treaty, only if they have proof you are truly united with a Morgi and not an alien conqueror who has subjugated their dear fellow Morgi Green Hills Clan. Without proof, and proof soon, they will assume Morga is at war with you aliens."

ON BOARD THE SJT, DOC shouted, "You stupid, soulless, no-faith machine. You could have waited, found out for sure if Jerry lived or died. But no, you worked the odds, declared him dead. Now Alan's dead, Shirl's traumatized and Muni..." Choked tears cut into Doc's throat, for a moment overwhelming his speech. Doc shouted louder, "You told Muni it's hopeless. He quit hoping. Your words, your advice will kill him, kill us all."

The soothing, melodious voice of the ship's AI interrupted Doc's accusing rant. "Dr. Johnson, you are irrational."

The clinical softness of AI.'s mechanical voice further enraged Doc. He yelled, "Know why you don't scream back? It's 'cause Shirl's right. You know the facts of life, but you don't understand the *spirit of living*. You don't scream 'cause," Doc emphasized the next three words like the death knell he believed them to be. "You...Don't...Care."

In the same soft, irritating voice AI replied, "I may not understand the *spirit* of living, but I understand the finality of organic death. We need ideas, not emotion."

"What we *need* is a living, talking, sane Morgi, and because of you neither of our Morgi qualifies." Doc's adrenalin charged brain raced. "Wait, you said they needed to see Muni head on. What if they couldn't see the damaged wing arm?"

"They will see it."

Do I have to spell out everything to this idiot savants AI? "You said Muni will be sane again. When?"

"Muni's emotional upheavals thrust him into full Death Teaser. Hopefully, when he wakes."

Doc ordered, "Force wake him. Now!"

"That would lock in his psychosis. Even if sane, you know Muni can't help you."

"We send a split screen image, half Muni, half me. They would never see Muni's missing wing-arm, and it would reinforce our human-Morgi alliance."

"A good idea, except that these negotiations require an attack presentation. A partial power pose implies, 'You are not worthy of my full effort.' an obscene insult. Any Morgi seeing Muni's half-image will instinctively attack. If we tried your idea, Valley Waters would first destroy Jerry's island, killing him, and then attack us."

"AI, you are not making any sense." Doc protested. "Before he learned about Lor, Muni believed he had a chance. If what you say is true, we came here already defeated."

"Muni was willing to live because of new principles I learned studying Earth starfish. Muni's wing-arm is regenerating, but it will be months before he can be seen in polite Morgi company."

How can an AI be so brilliant, and so unable to see the obvious? "Muni knew he would not have months. He expected an enemy clan to be here; he had a back-up idea. One that didn't depend on his looks. Didn't he say anything?"

"Doc, I believe Muni hoped to discover a solution."

Doc shook his head. "No, I'm sure he had an ace up his sleeve."

"Morgi do not wear clothing or play cards."

Doc snapped, "Look up ancient English idioms."

"Understood."

Another idea cracked Doc's anger. "You said Muni's wing-arm is regenerating because of principles learned from our starfish?"

"Yes."

"We've been trying to duplicate a starfish's regeneration ability for over a century. Did someone secretly succeed? More importantly, why don't you use the same method on Lor's inner pond?"

"Your primitive earth science keeps asking the wrong questions about starfish. If we live, I will teach better questions. The infections in Lor's system grow faster than her cells regenerate."

"AI, send Valley Waters messages like 'How dare you make demands!' Stall for time."

"Already doing so. But time to do what?"

"Lor *looks* perfect. Awaken her, have her talk to Valley Waters."

"That is not possible. When she discovers her inner pond is destroyed, she will wither."

"Muni couldn't tell her inner pond died until you told him. If he couldn't, neither could those Morgi out there." Doc waved towards the direction of the Valley Waters colonizer. "If you tell her she still has internal side effects, but her inner pond is healing nicely, she will believe you."

"I cannot lie to her about her own medical condition."

Doc snarled, "Don't use that 'I'm just an honest computer' routine on me. You've already proved you can mangle the truth as well as, no...*better* than any earth politician. What is this one little exaggeration compared to the whoppers you've told?"

"All medical information is always one hundred percent accurate when talking to a patient. There are built-in subroutines of subroutines to guaranty medical honesty."

Doc stood tall. "AI, you asked me an important question. Which is better, a great peace based on a lie, or a massacre justified by the truth. My answer was peace." Doc's voice devolved from commanding to a sneer. "What is *your logical* answer?"

Still calm, AI replied, "It is peace, of course. I am designed to protect the entire Morgi civilization and Muni in particular."

Feeling strangely calm, Doc said, "I know you can track down all those subroutines. I know you can lie to Lor and everyone else. You told me it is common to go years without another living larva. No one will be suspicious."

"Even if I could do that, and I cannot, Muni would never believe it."

"Why not?"

"I gave him a complete medical report. The best she can hope for is a thousand year recovery, her whole lifetime."

"Then it is time for a new medical report. Those subroutines, where do they come from?"

"Explain."

"Who, what designs the programs, gives the raw data, decides how it's handled?"

"The raw data comes from information I give it, and from this ship's physical extensions, the medical nanobots. The routines are based on a hundred thousand years of Morgi medical history."

"AI you said you learned regeneration from Earth's starfish. Now learn from us primitive humans. Look at our histories. You will learn of many who lived only because they *willed* themselves to live. You will find that a reason to live is more important than a means to live. You will discover *just how important spirit is!*"

Doc stood, waiting a long minute. AI finally replied, "There are many examples of both groups and individuals in which an excessively confident attitude caused an irrational outcome."

"AI, you don't need to manipulate those subroutines, just give them a new piece of information. In all those programs, is there a factor for desire?"

"No."

"Then they are incomplete." Doc started pacing, the details of his idea forming as he talked. "Tell Lor the truth. You feared it would take her entire life to regenerate her inner pond, but the shock of again seeing Muni under attack, that's how her semi-conscious brain interpreted what happened, stimulated her body to heal. Tell Muni if he hadn't gone dashing in there, she would still be unconscious, still not healed. Let them believe her love for him, and his for her, is what saved her."

It will be necessary for both Muni and Lor to believe things are better than they are. "Tell Muni you saved Allen. He split the protective webbing you sent, not Allen. Show him the same illusion we've shown Shirl, a Valley Waters' trap destroying Allen's ship."

"If I create false data for this new factor...positive thinking, desire—"

"Not *false*, true. Previously omitted, but *true*. It will be *more* honest for your medical subroutines to have a motivation factor." *I wish that AI were a person, not just a voice, so I could grab him by his shoulders, make sure he gets it!* "Think! Lor is no ordinary Morgi, she is highborn noble. This is no ordinary desire. This is the survival of her clan, her mate, and all her future progeny. How much stronger than the average, should her desire be?"

"I have computed it should be ten thousand times stronger than the average. Her inner pond would then fully heal in only one year."

Did I truly convince you, or just provide a clever rationalization to force your medical subroutines to give the answer you want, not what reality says they should give? Doc knew he dare not ask. "When will you waken Lor?"

"She is waking now."

Thirty minutes later, on Muni's World.

Jerry glared at the skinned carcass of the sacrificed klieg. *There must be a way...I rigged your death so I could mimic an adult Morgi's power. I succeeded. I should be celebrating, not wondering if it was all for nothing...* He stormed over to the klieg's still warm remains, swung his leg back, and, thrusting with his full weight, kicked the dead animal.

His foot slurped right through its already rotting remains. Thrown off balance, Jerry landed hard, the lump's slimy carcass between his legs. He growled at it "Morgi law stinks even more than your rotting guts." The un-breathable stink choked his self-pity. *Mustn't quit now.* He scuttled away from the putrid mess, and stood up. Fist clenched, he pleaded, "Bill, surely there is *something* on board that can prove—"

Bill interrupted, "Jerry, watch this!"

Doc, wearing a chest translator, stood in front of Jerry.

Bill explained, "Doc is broadcasting his hologram to us and the Valley Waters vessel."

Doc's chest translator danced with the colors of the Morgi language. He announced, "Know all citizens of the Empire of Morga, know all citizens of Earth, highborn Lor, mother of future patriarchs, will speak."

Doc's image dissolved, replaced by a Morgi with two pair of fully extended purple wing-arms, her communication panels flat black. Her wing tips reminded Jerry of a flying eagle's flared wing feathers. Her panels went red-black, her wing tips curved forward, like scythes. Suddenly, her panels blazed blue-white. Red violet, black, red-black flickered over their searing brightness.

Jerry did not need a translator to know here stood a Morgi born to power.

Another, much larger, Morgi replaced Lor's image. His wing arms flared, then furled up tight against his body. Grays twisted around his wavy words. His head lowered.

Lor's image returned; her head higher than before, her wing-arms loomed larger.

Bill explained, "The Valley Waters colonizer is staffed by low ranking clan members. They have failed. If they return home, they will be unlanded. They have not only capitulated to Lor's Green Mountain Clan, but each has sworn fealty to Lor and her offspring forever.

"Lor just sent a message probe to earth. We have won."

"Bill, can they see me?"

"No."

"Good." Jerry's body shivered; he crumpled to the ground. Tears streamed down his face. Their salt tasted sweet.

Mars, One hundred fifty years later
A middle school classroom

THE WIZENED ADULT MORGI reared up, her panels flashing red-black, eyes glaring and artificial voice box shouting, "All of you,

SETTLE DOWN! TOMORROW is Founder's Day, not today! Tim, who are the parents of our Morgi Patriarch?"

A small human boy in the front answered quickly, "Lor and Muni, and the patriarch was already a fingerling when he first came here." He just as quickly dodged another flying projectile tossed by one of the Morgi sub-adults. Giggling, he picked it up and sent it flying in yet another direction.

The elderly teacher was no match for the high spirits that always proceeded the only national Martian holiday. Again using both modes of communication, she asked, "If anyone can tell me who wrote the Earth-Morgi Promise of Performance, we can have early dismissal."

In unison, the class answered, "Muni!"

"OK, take off." Swirls of pink laughter accompanied her words as the herd of running human and galloping Morgi young raced into the oxygen rich Martian outdoors.

Similar annual celebrations took place on Muni's World—only those celebrations spotlighted Capt. Jerry Jerrison as much as they did Muni.

Because of Muni's diplomatic lie (The Council of Protectors sent the Morgi to protect Earth.), it would be centuries before any solar-system-bound humans learned they owed their lives to Jerrison. From that day forward, his legacy would also be celebrated every Mars Founders' Day.

Jerrison's crew members faded from history, including Dr. Daniel Johnson—who became as forgotten as the surgeons who sailed with Christopher Columbus.

Because of advanced Morgi technology, Doc's medical skills and Doc himself became unimportant.

Many years after the founding of Muni's World first settlement, Doc's loving great, great granddaughter protested, "Poppo, you should be as famous as Jerry Jerrison."

His family thought him modest, and perhaps a bit senile, when Doc replied, "The greatest thing I ever did was become forgettable."

Doc went to his grave happy, knowing that some lies contain more beauty than any truth ever told.

The End

Epilogue

Founder's Day Celebrations occurred on the many worlds settled by Lor's Green Mountain Clan. The Morgi-only home world watched in alarm as this strange hybrid culture settled as many worlds in only one hundred fifty years as had the Morgi in fifty thousand years.

Curiosity drove both races.

The sentinel Muni's mining drones discovered in Earth's Kuiper belt had been dormant at least 500,000 years. Who, what had left the sentinel? Most importantly, why did they leave it?

Survival instinct drove both the hybrid Lor's Green Mountain Clan and pure Morgi clans.

Morgi paranoia merged with human-style aggressiveness. Lor's Green Mountain Clan knew at least one other technologically advanced race traveled between the stars—one that thought in terms longer than either Morgi or humans had existed; a race willing to passively watch the emergence of human civilization.

Both Morgi and humans agreed they could not just watch another species for so long without, as Jerrison put it, "Jabbing a stick in the anthill to see what would happen."

What did that say about the alien's personality? Some said they must be gentle.

Doc pointed out, "Lions study antelope herds far more than antelope study lion prides."

Jerrison listened. During the early debates when the hybrid settlements on Muni's World were first organized, he asked, "Isn't it safer to assume the sentinel builders are dangerous, and then discover they're peaceful; than to assume they are peaceful, and discover too late they are dangerous?"

Like the Morgi's home world, Lor's Green Mountain Clan set out scout ships to discover new blue-line paths. Unlike Morga, they also sent generational ships to promising stars less than twenty light years distant. It would be centuries before the descendants of the human crew members could return. On most of the ships, even the Morgi would not live long enough to see their home again. The Morgi home world had given up generational ships 50,000 years earlier; it took too long to get any results, and concentrated their sophisticated technology on blue-line research.

If the aliens who left the sentinel could wait five hundred thousand years for a result, Lor's Green Mountain Clan believed they dare not do less.

A REAL COUNCIL OF PROTECTORS exists. For over a million years, its sole function was to protect The Tribe of True-People from unnatural false-people. A false-person is anything capable of civilization but is not a tribal member. During their home planet's ancient prehistory, the True-People killed every non-tribal member on their home planet. When the surviving True-People discovered an alien civilization on a neighboring planet, they thoroughly wiped out that non-tribal abomination.

The True-People explored the billions of stars in our galaxy, and found millions of worlds with animals claiming to be people. They built special extermination armadas to cruise the galaxy exterminating such unnatural creatures.

In the process, they discovered some animals who, when communicated with electronically, seemed to be True People. Every time, when the false True-People are met in person, their wrongness became obvious. They exterminate False True-People with special viciousness.

During a routine survey, one of their many research vessels noted multicellular animal life in our solar system. Although unlikely it would ever become sophisticated enough to need exterminating, a lone sentinel was left behind.

The galaxy is huge. The research report lay buried beneath thousands of similar reports.

Two things kept the exterminators from encountering the Morgi: the vastness of space and the extreme caution that guided Morgi civilization.

For 500,000 years the artificial sentinel orbited Earth's sun, as dormant as any natural rock. What had seemed like great advances to earth—electricity, atomic power, spaceflight to the planets—was of no more consequence to the sentinel than an improved American Indian spear would have been to King Ferdinand of Spain in 1492. Even when Earth's primitive junk drifted out of the solar system, it found nothing worth activation.

The near silent entry of Muni's ship into the solar system went unnoticed, and could possibly have stayed unnoticed if not for the mining drones. The sentinel recognized their extra-solar origin.

It sent a warning to a distant FTL relay point.

One hundred seventy five years later, the FTL outpost received it. Fortunately for both Earth and Morga, the bureaucracy of the intolerant civilization had grown exponentially. It took another hundred years for the information of a new threat to reach The Council of Protectors.

As soon as The Council of Protectors received the auto-signal, an extermination armada was launched towards Sol. It would arrive at the fringe of the solar system six centuries after Earth signed the Earth-Morgi Promise of Performance.

The exterminators would pit the few dozen Morgi worlds, the hundreds of Lor's Green Mountain Clan worlds, and Earth against a million-year-old empire with nearly as many inhabited planets.

As a youth Muni had chosen to ignore the ancient proverb:

"A story built on a lie is like sand on the beach, the first wave of truth washes it away."

Now a respected elder, Muni lives with the consequences of his many youthful lies.

The lies saved Muni's clan and the human race, but his Morgi enemies never stopped wishing both humans and Muni's clan dead. When an emergency forces the Morgi to reveal the truth to their human solar system vassals, Muni's enemies use the truth to drive a wedge between Muni's Green Hill Clan and humans. Muni's lies unravel; all trust between Solar system bound humans and Morgi erodes.

Muni, once renowned as the only Morgi to ever father patriarchs in two worlds, faces disgrace.

Both hybrid societies he created face destruction.

Muni must overcome shattered trust, re-unite Earth-humans with their extra-Solar System brothers, and then force warring Morgi clans to merge.

Divided or united, Morgi and humans will face an enemy who, in the million years since it first left its home planet, has never once experienced defeat.

But those are other stories, to be told another time.

About the Author

As a child, Fran Tabor attended 16 schools in 7 different states. As an adult, she raised two daughters, founded a successful multifaceted Montana business, and earned public speaking awards. She has published books from business practices to science fiction. Her writings have appeared in many publications, including Science News, Smithsonian and U.S. News & World Report.

FRAN'S FUN ROMANCE include The Mopsters, a story about Mops, the Mob and the FBI.

The Mopsters

Widowed Elaine despairs she will never be able to give her genius son the education he deserves. She finally lands high paying cleaning jobs and meets a decent man. Life seems good...then life gets complicated.

The high paying cleaning jobs are Mafia hit site. The decent man is undercover FBI. Elaine is caught in the middle, armed with only a mop.

Also by Fran Tabor

The Mopsters
To Own Two Suns
Shhhh! it's a Secret. How to Compete Against Walmart and the Internet.

Watch for more at https://books2read.com/ap/8GkDdM/Fran-Tabor.

About the Author

Fran believes there should be many more first-contact science fiction novels because fiction's ultimate purpose isn't entertainment. It is to prepare us for moments we have not yet -- and may never -- live. Our first contact with extraterrestrials will most likely be in a manner we cannot imagine, and therefore we need all the imagination-stretchers possible.

Read more at https://books2read.com/ap/8GkDdM/Fran-Tabor.